He lives life
He'll put h
A bold,

HER KIND
OF MAN

Three of your favourite authors bring
you three dazzling romances

We're proud to present

MILLS & BOON SPOTLIGHT™

A chance to buy collections of bestselling novels by favourite authors every month – they're back by popular demand!

December 2009

Her Kind of Man

Featuring

Navy Husband by *New York Times* bestselling author Debbie Macomber
A Man Apart by *New York Times* bestselling author Joan Hohl
Second-Chance Hero by *USA Today* bestselling author Justine Davis

Wanted: Father for Her Baby

Featuring

Keeping Baby Secret by Beverly Barton
Five Brothers and a Baby by Peggy Moreland
Expecting Brand's Baby by Emilie Rose

HER KIND
OF MAN

DEBBIE MACOMBER
JOAN HOHL
JUSTINE DAVIS

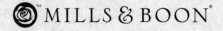
MILLS & BOON®

HER KIND OF MAN © Harlequin Books S.A. 2009.

First published in Great Britain 2009
Harlequin Mills & Boon Limited,
Eton House, 18-24 Paradise Road, Richmond, Surrey TW9 1SR

The publisher acknowledges the copyright holders of the individual works, which have already been published in the UK in single, separate volumes, as follows:

Navy Husband © Debbie Macomber 2005
A Man Apart © Joan Hohl 2005
Second-Chance Hero © Justine Davis Smith 2005

ISBN: 978 0 263 87168 5

64-1209

Printed and bound in Spain
by Litografia Rosés S.A., Barcelona

NAVY HUSBAND

BY
DEBBIE MACOMBER

Dear Friends,

Here it is – the very last book of my Navy series. A lot has changed since I wrote those first five books in the late 1980s and early nineties. There have been huge technological advances that affect our everyday lives – and life in the Navy, too.

Even after all these years, I'll never forget my first sight of an aircraft carrier when the *Nimitz* sailed into Sinclair Inlet that day in 1988. I still feel the excitement and joy experienced by the crowd of people waiting to see their loved ones. But I felt more than joy that day – I also felt pride and respect. All of those emotions led me to bring my hand to my heart and join in the singing of "God Bless America."

As you've probably worked out by now, I live in a Navy town. The Bremerton shipyard is directly across Sinclair Inlet from Port Orchard. Many of my neighbours are active or retired military families and a number of the women who attend my local autographings are Navy wives. (I've even met a few Navy husbands!) I'm proud to be part of this community, proud to support the military and their families. We are the land of the free because of the brave and I don't ever want to forget that.

I hope you enjoy *Navy Husband*. In case you're interested, the Navy tradition in my writing continues in the Cedar Cove series published by MIRA Books. (The next one, *44 Cranberry Point*, is available in February 2010.) This fictionalised town is based on Port Orchard and has lots of references to the Navy and the shipyard.

Thank you for reading my books. Now sit back, put your feet up and enjoy *Navy Husband*.

Warmest regards,

Debbie Macomber

PS I love hearing from readers. You can reach me through my website, www.debbiemacomber.com (write your comments in the guest book) or write to me at PO Box 1458, Port Orchard, WA 98366, USA.

Debbie Macomber hails from the state of Washington. As a busy wife and mother of four, she strives to keep her family happy and healthy. As a prolific author of dozens of romance novels, she strives to keep her readers happy with each new book she writes.

To Geri Krotow, Navy wife, with appreciation
for all her assistance. Dream big dreams, my friend.

Chapter One

"This is a joke—right?" Shana Berrie said uncertainly as she talked to her older sister, Ali, on the phone. Ali was the sensible one in the family. She—unlike Shana—wouldn't have dreamed of packing up her entire life, buying a pizza and ice-cream parlor and starting over in a new city. Oh, no, only someone completely and utterly in need of a change—correction, a *drastic* change—would do something like that.

"I'm sorry, Shana, but you did agree to this parenting plan."

Her sister was a Navy nurse stationed in San Diego, and several years ago, when she'd asked Shana to look after her niece if necessary, Shana had immediately said yes. It had seemed an unlikely prospect at the time, but that was before her sister became a widow.

"I did, didn't I?" she muttered lamely as she stepped

around a cardboard box. Her rental house was cluttered with the makings of her new life and the remnants of her old.

"It isn't like I have any choice in the matter," Ali pointed out.

"I know." Pushing her thick, chestnut-colored hair away from her forehead, Shana leaned against the kitchen wall and slowly expelled her breath, hoping that would calm her pounding heart. "I said yes back then because you asked me to, but I don't know anything about kids."

"Jazmine's great," Ali assured her.

"I know, but—but…" she stammered. Shana wasn't sure how to explain. "The thing is, I'm at a turning point in my own life and I'm probably not the best person for Jazmine." Surely there was a relative on her brother-in-law's side. Someone else, *anyone* else would be better than Shana, who was starting a new career after suffering a major romantic breakup. At the moment, her life still felt disorganized. Chaotic. Add a recently bereaved nine-year-old to the mix, and she didn't know what might happen.

"This isn't a choose-your-time type of situation," Ali said. "I'm counting on you, and so is Jazmine."

Shana nibbled on her lower lip, trapped between her doubts and her obligation to her widowed sister. "I'll do it, of course, but I was just wondering if there was someone else…."

"There isn't," Ali said abruptly.

"Then it's me." Shana spoke with as much enthusiasm as she could muster, although she suspected it must sound pretty hollow. Shana hadn't had much experience as an aunt, but she was going to get her chance to learn.

She was about to become her niece's primary caregiver while her sister went out to sea on an aircraft carrier for a six-month deployment.

Shana truly hadn't expected this. When Ali filled out the "worldwide availability" form—with Shana's name—she'd explained it was so the Navy had documentation proving Jazmine would have someone to take care of her at all times, ensuring that Ali was combat-ready. It had seemed quite routine, more of a formality than a possibility—and of course, Peter was alive then.

Ali had been in the Navy for twelve years and had never pulled sea duty before now. She'd traveled around the world with her husband, a Navy pilot, and their daughter. Then, two years ago, Peter had been killed in a training accident and everything changed.

Things had changed in Shana's life, too, although not in the same unalterable and tragic way. Brad—Shana purposely put a halt to her thoughts. Brad was in the past. They were finished. Done. Kaput. She'd told her friends that she was so over him she had to force herself to remember his name. Who was he, again? *That* was how over him she was. Over. Over and out.

"I don't have much time," Ali was saying. "The *Woodrow Wilson*'s scheduled to leave soon. I'll fly Jazmine up this weekend but I won't be able to stay more than overnight."

Shana swallowed a protest. For reasons of national security, Shana realized her sister couldn't say any more about her schedule. But this weekend? She still had to finish unpacking. Furthermore, she'd only just started training with the former owners of her restaurant. Then it occurred to Shana that she might not be the only one upset about Ali's sudden deployment. She could only guess at her niece's reaction. "What does Jazmine have to say about all this?"

Ali's hesitation told Shana everything she needed to know. "Oh, great," she muttered under her breath. She remembered her own childhood and what her mother had termed her "attitude problem." Shana had plenty of that, all right, and most of it was bad. Dealing with Jazmine's moods would be payback, she supposed, for everything her poor mother had endured.

"To be honest, Jazmine isn't too excited about the move."

Who could blame her? The little girl barely knew Shana. The kid, a true child of the military, had lived on Whidbey Island in Washington State, then Italy and, following the accident that claimed her father's life, had been shuffled to San Diego, California. They'd just settled into their Navy housing, and now they were about to leave that. In her nine years Jazmine had been moved from country to country, lost her father, and now her mother was shipping out for six long months. If that wasn't enough, the poor kid was being foisted on Shana. No wonder she wasn't thrilled.

"We'll be fine," Shana murmured, doing her best to sound positive. She didn't know who she was kidding. Certainly not her sister—and not herself, either. This was going to be another in a long line of recent disasters, or life-changing events, as she preferred to call them.

"So it's true you and Brad split up?" Ali asked with a degree of delicacy. She'd obviously been warned against bringing up his name.

"Brad?" Shana repeated as if she had no idea who her sister was talking about. "Oh, you mean Brad Moore.

Yes, it's over. We were finished quite a while ago, but either he forgot to tell me or I just wasn't paying attention."

"I'm so sorry," Ali said.

The last thing Shana wanted was Ali's sympathy. "Don't worry, I've rebounded. Everything's great. My life is fabulous, or it will be in short order. I've got everything under control." Shana said all of this without taking a breath. If she said it often enough, she might actually start to believe it.

"When Mom told me that you'd decided to leave Portland and move to Seattle, I thought it was job-related at first. You never said a word." She paused. "Did you move all those plants, too? You must have about a thousand."

Shana laughed. "Hardly. But yes, I did. Moving was…a spontaneous decision." That was putting it mildly. One weekend Shana had driven to Seattle to get away and to consider her relationship with Brad. She'd finally realized that it wasn't going anywhere. For five years they'd been talking marriage. Wrong. *She'd* been talking marriage. Brad had managed to string her along with just enough interest to placate her. And she'd let him until…

Unexpectedly, Shana had stumbled on Brad having lunch with a business associate. This so-called associate just happened to be a willowy blonde with a figure that would stop a freight train. It was a business lunch, he'd claimed later, when Shana confronted him.

Yeah, sure—monkey business. Shana could be dense at times but she wasn't blind, and she recognized this so-called associate as someone Brad had once introduced as Sylvia, an old flame. Apparently those embers were still very much alive and growing hotter by the minute, because as Shana watched, they'd exchanged a lengthy kiss in the parking lot and drove off together. She was embarrassed to admit she'd followed them. It didn't take her long to see where they were headed. Brad's town house—and she didn't think they were there to discuss contracts or fire codes.

Even when confronted, Brad insisted his lunch date was a client. Any resemblance his associate had to Sylvia was purely coincidental. The more he defended himself, the more defensive he got, complaining that Shana was acting like a jealous shrew. He'd been outraged that she'd question his faithfulness when *she* was the one so often away, working as a sales rep for a large pharmaceutical company. He'd been so convincing that—just for a moment—she'd wondered if she might've been wrong. Only when she mentioned that she'd followed them to his town house did Brad show any hint of guilt or regret.

He'd glanced away then, and the righteous indignation had been replaced by a look of such sadness she had to resist the urge to comfort him. He was sorry, he'd said, so sorry. It had been a fling; it meant nothing. He couldn't lose her. Shana was his life, the woman he intended to marry, the mother of his unborn children.

For a few days, he'd actually swayed her. Needing to sort out her feelings, Shana had driven to Seattle the next weekend. After five years with Brad she felt she knew him, but it now seemed quite clear that she didn't. He wanted her back, he told her over and over. He was willing to do whatever it took to reconcile, to make this up to her. He suggested counseling, agreed to therapy, anything but losing her.

That weekend, Shana had engaged in some painful

self-examination. She desperately wanted to believe the afternoon rendezvous with Sylvia was a onetime thing, but her head told her it wasn't and that they'd been involved for months—or more.

It was while she sat in Lincoln Park in West Seattle, analyzing the last five years, that she concluded there was no going back. Her trust had been destroyed. She couldn't build a life with Brad after this. In truth, their relationship had dead-ended three years ago. Maybe sooner; she could no longer tell. What Shana did recognize was that she'd been so caught up in loving Brad that she'd refused to see the signs.

"I was feeling pretty miserable," Shana admitted to her sister. Wretched was a more accurate description, but she didn't want to sound melodramatic. "I sat in that park in West Seattle, thinking."

"In West Seattle? How'd you get there?"

Shana sighed loudly. "I took a wrong turn when I was trying to find the freeway."

Ali laughed. "I should have guessed."

"I ended up on this bridge and there wasn't anyplace to turn around, so I followed the road, which led to a wonderful waterfront park."

"The ice-cream parlor's in the park?"

"No, it's across the street. You know me and maple-nut ice cream. It's the ultimate comfort food." She tried to make a joke of it, but at the time she'd felt there wasn't enough maple-nut ice cream in the world to see her through this misery.

"Brad drove you to maple nut?"

Shana snickered at Ali's exaggerated horror. After her decision to break off the relationship, she'd grown angry. Okay, furious. She wanted out of this relation-

ship, completely out, and living in the same city made
that difficult.

"Actually, West Seattle is a charming little community.
The ice-cream parlor had a For Sale sign in the window
and I got to talking to the owners. They're an older couple, sweet as can be and planning to retire. As I sat there,
I thought it must be a nice place to work. How could anyone be unhappy surrounded by ice cream and pizza?"

"So you *bought* it? Shana, for heaven's sake, what do
you know about running any kind of restaurant?"

"Not much," she said, "but I've worked in sales and
with people all these years. I was ready for a break, and
this seemed practically fated."

"But how could you afford to buy an established
business?"

Shana had an answer for that, too. "I had a chunk of
cash in savings." The money had originally been set
aside for her wedding. Saving a hundred dollars a month
and investing it carefully, she'd managed to double her
money. Just then, she couldn't think of a better way to
spend it. Buying this business was impulsive and irrational but despite everything, it felt…right.

That Sunday in the park she'd admitted there would
be no wedding, no honeymoon with Brad. Shana drew
in her breath. She refused to think about it anymore.
She'd entered a new phase of her life.

"It's a cute place. You'll like it," she murmured. She
had lots of ideas for fixing it up, making it *hers*. The Olsens had promised to help transfer ownership as seam-
lessly as possible.

"You rented a house?"

"That very same Sunday." Once she'd made her decision, Shana had been on a mission and there was no

stopping her. As luck would have it, there was a house two streets over that had just been vacated. The owner had recently painted it and installed new carpeting. Shana had taken one look around the 1950s-style bungalow with its small front porch and brick fireplace and declared it perfect. She'd given the rental agent a check immediately. Then she drove home, wrote a letter resigning her job—and phoned Brad. That conversation had been short, sweet and utterly satisfying.

"Making a move like this couldn't have been easy," Ali commiserated.

"You wouldn't believe how easy it was," Shana said gleefully. "I suppose you're curious about what Brad had to say." She was dying to tell her.

"Well…"

"I called him," Shana said without waiting for Ali to respond, "and naturally he wanted to know where I'd been all weekend."

"You told him?"

Shana grinned. "I couldn't get a word in edgewise. He was pretty upset. He told me how worried he was, and how he'd spent the entire weekend calling me. He was afraid of what I might've done. As if I'd do something lethal over *him*," she scoffed. Shana suspected that his concern was all for show, but none of that mattered now. "When he cooled down, I calmly explained that I'd gone for a drive."

"A three-day drive," Ali inserted.

"Right. Well, he got huffy, saying the least I could've done was let him know I'd made plans." What came next was the best part. "So I told him I'd made plans for the rest of my life and they didn't include him."

Ali giggled and it sounded exactly the way it had

when they were girls, sharing a bedroom. "What did he say then?"

"I don't know. I hung up and started packing stuff in my apartment."

"Didn't he try to phone you back?"

"Not for the first couple of days. He e-mailed me on the third day and I immediately put a block on his name." That must have infuriated him—not that Shana cared. Well, she did, a little. Okay, more than a little. Unfortunately she didn't have the satisfaction of knowing what his reaction had been. In the past, she'd always been the one who patched any rift. That was her problem; she couldn't stand conflict, so she'd done all the compromising and conciliating. Over the course of their relationship, Brad had come to expect her to make the first move. Well, no longer. She was finished. Brad Moore was history.

Instead of kicking herself for taking so long to see the light, she was moving ahead, starting over…and, to be on the safe side, giving up on men and relationships. At twenty-eight, she'd had her fill. Men weren't worth the effort and the grief.

"I never was that fond of Brad," Ali confessed.

"You might've said something." Shana realized her tone was a little annoyed. In the five years she'd dated Brad, there'd certainly been opportunities for Ali to share her opinion.

"How could I? We just met once, and you seemed so keen on him."

"If you'd stayed in one place longer, we might've gotten together more often."

Ali's sigh drifted over the phone. "That's what happens when you're in the Navy. They own your life. Now honestly, are you all right?"

Shana paused to consider the question. A second later, she gave Ali her answer. "Honestly? I feel great, and that's the truth. Yes, this breakup hurt, but mostly I was angry with myself for not waking up sooner. I feel *fabulous*. It's as if I've been released from a spell. I've got a whole new attitude toward men."

Her sister didn't say anything for a moment. "You might *think* you're fine, but there's a chance you're not totally over Brad."

"What do you mean?"

Again her sister hesitated. "I remember what it was like after Peter died. The shock and grief were over-whelming at first. I walked around in a fog for weeks."

"This is different," Shana insisted. "It's less…important."

"It is and it isn't," Ali fired right back.

"But you feel better now, don't you?"

"Yes. One day, out of the blue, I discovered I could smile again. I could function. I had to. My daughter needed me. My patients needed me. I'll always love Peter, though." Her voice wavered but eventually re-gained strength.

"I'll always love Peter, too," Shana said, swallowing hard. "He was one of a kind." Her brother-in-law had been a loving husband and father, and her heart ached for her sister even now. The situation with Brad didn't compare.

"I'll give you my flight information for this week-end," Ali said, changing the subject.

Shana had nearly forgotten that she was about to be-come a substitute mother. "Oh, yeah. Let me find a pen." Scrabbling through her purse, she dug one up and found a crumpled receipt she'd stuffed in there. Good—she could write on the back.

She was looking forward to some time with her sister. They saw each other so rarely, thanks to Ali's career. This upcoming visit would be a brief one, but Shana hadn't seen Ali—and Jazmine—since the funeral.

"You and Jazmine will do just fine," Ali said warmly. "Jazmine's a great kid, but be warned. She's nine going on sixteen."

"In what way?"

"Because she's an only child, she's rather…precocious. For instance, she's reading at ninth-grade level. And the music she likes is sort of—well, you'll see."

"Thanks for warning me."

"I'm sure this'll be easy for you."

Shana had her doubts. "If I remember correctly, that was what you told me when I asked if I could fly off the top bunk."

"What did I know? I was only six," Ali reminded her. "You've never forgiven me for that, have you?"

"I still remember how much it hurt to have the wind knocked out of me." It felt the same way now. Despite the assurances she so freely handed out, Shana was still struggling to recover her equilibrium—to reinvent her life on new terms. No Brad, no steady paycheck, no familiar Portland neighborhood. Now, her niece was about to complicate the situation. The next six months should be very interesting, she thought. Very interesting indeed.

She vaguely recalled an old Chinese saying, something about living in interesting times. Unfortunately, she also recalled that it was intended as a curse, not a blessing.

Chapter Two

Alison Karas couldn't help being concerned about leaving her nine-year-old daughter with her sister, Shana. This wasn't a good time in Jazmine's life, nor was it particularly opportune for Shana. Her sister *sounded* strong and confident, but Ali suspected otherwise. Despite Shana's reassurances, she'd been badly shaken by her breakup with Brad, even though she'd initiated it. Jazmine hadn't taken the news of this deployment well, and was reluctant to leave her newfound friends behind and move to Seattle.

But Ali really had no other option. Ideally, Jazmine would go to either set of grandparents, but in this case that wouldn't work. After the sudden loss of her father ten years earlier, her mother hadn't done well. She'd never recovered emotionally and was incapable of dealing with the demands of a young girl. Peter had been an only child and his parents had divorced when he was young. Both had gone on to other marriages and other children. Neither set of paternal grandparents had shown any great interest in Jazmine.

Jazmine wandered into Ali's room just then and flopped down on the bed with all the enthusiasm of a slug.

"Are you packed?" Ali asked, her own suitcase open on the opposite end of the bed.

"No," her daughter muttered. "This whole move is crap."

"Jazmine, watch your mouth!" Ali refused to get into an argument with a nine-year-old. The truth was, she'd rather not ship out, either, but for Jazmine's sake she put on a good front. This was the most difficult aspect of her life in the Navy. She was a widow and a mother, but she was also a Navy nurse, and her responsibilities in that regard were unavoidable. That was made abundantly clear the day she accepted her commission. When the Navy called, she answered. In fact, she wouldn't have minded six months at sea except for her daughter.

"Uncle Adam lives in the Seattle area," Ali reminded her. She'd been saving that tidbit, hoping the news would make her daughter feel more positive about this most recent upheaval in their lives.

"He's in Everett," Jazmine said, her voice apathetic.

"I understand that's only thirty or forty minutes from Seattle."

"It is?"

Her daughter revealed her first spark of interest since they'd learned of the transfer. "Does he know we're coming?" She sat upright, eager now.

"Not yet." Busy as she'd been, Ali hadn't told Adam

Kennedy—her husband's best friend and Jazz's godfather—that Jazmine would soon be living in Seattle.

"Then we *have* to tell him!"

"We will, all in due course," Ali assured her.

"Do it now." Her daughter leaped off the bed, sprinted into the living room and came back with the portable phone.

"I don't have his number." Ali hadn't been thinking clearly; their phone directory had already been packed away and she simply didn't have time to search for it.

"I do." Once more her daughter made a mad dash out of the bedroom, returning a moment later. Breathless, Jazmine handed Ali a tidy slip of paper.

Ali unfolded it curiously and saw a phone number written by an adult hand.

"Uncle Adam sent it to me," Jazmine explained. "He told me I could call him whenever I needed to talk. He said it didn't matter what time of day or night I phoned, so call him, Mom. This is *important.*"

Ali resisted the urge to find out if her daughter had taken advantage of Adam's offer before now and decided she probably had. For Jazmine, it was as if the sun rose and set on Peter's friend. Lieutenant Commander Adam Kennedy had been a support to both of them since the accident that had abruptly taken Peter out of their lives.

It sounded so cut and dried to say a computer had malfunctioned aboard Peter's F/A-18. He hadn't had a chance to recover before the jet slammed into the ground. He'd died instantly, his life snuffed out in mere seconds. That was two years ago now, two very long years, and every day since, Peter had been with her. Her first thought was always of him and his image was the last one her mind released before she went to sleep at night. He was part of her. She saw him in Jazmine's smile, in the three little lines that formed between the girl's eyebrows when she frowned. Peter had done that, too. And their eyes were the exact same shade of brownish green.

As an SMO, or senior medical officer, Ali was familiar with death. What she didn't know was how to deal with the aftermath of it. She still struggled and, as a result, she understood her sister's pain. Yes, Shana's breakup with Brad was different, and of a lesser magnitude, but it was a loss. In ending her relationship with him, Shana was also giving up a dream, one she'd held and cherished for five years. She was adjusting to a new version of her life and her future. Shana had flippantly dismissed any doubts or regrets about the breakup. Those would come later, like a sneak attack—probably when Shana least expected it. They had with Ali.

"Mom," Jazmine cried, exasperated. "Dial!"

"Oh, sorry," Ali murmured, punching out the number. An answering machine came on almost immediately.

"He isn't there?" Jazmine asked, studying her. She didn't hide her disappointment. It was doom and gloom all over again as she threw herself backward onto the bed, arms spread-eagled.

Ali left a message and asked him to get in touch.

"When do you think he'll call?" Jazmine demanded impatiently.

"I don't know, but I'll make sure we get a chance to see him if it's possible."

"Of *course* it's possible," Jazmine argued. "He'll want to see me. And you, too."

Ali shrugged. "He might not be back by the time I need to fly out, but you'll see him, don't worry."

Jazmine wouldn't look at her. Instead she stared morosely at the ceiling, as if she didn't have a friend in the world. The kid had moved any number of times and had always been a good sport about it, until now. Ali didn't blame her for being upset, but there wasn't anything she could do to change her orders.

"You'll love living with your aunt Shana," Alison said, trying a new tactic. "Did I tell you she has an ice-cream parlor? How much fun is that?"

Jazmine wasn't impressed. "I don't really know her."

"This will be your opportunity to bond."

Jazmine sighed. "I don't want to bond with her."

"You will eventually," Ali said with forced brightness. Jazmine wasn't fooled.

"I'm not glue, you know."

Alison held back a smile. "We both need to make the best of this, Jazz. I don't want to leave you any more than you want me to go."

Her daughter scrambled to a sitting position. As her shoulders slumped, she nodded. "I know."

"Your aunt Shana loves you."

"Yippee, skippy."

Alison tried again. "The ice-cream parlor is directly across the street from the park."

"Yippee."

"Jazmine!"

"I know, I know."

Ali wrapped one arm around the girl's shoulders. "The months will fly by. You'll see."

Jazmine shook her head. "No, they won't," she said adamantly, "and I have to change schools again. I hate that."

Changing schools, especially this late in the year,

would be difficult. In a few weeks, depending on the Seattle schedule, classes would be dismissed for the summer. Ali kissed the top of Jazmine's head and closed her eyes. She had the distinct feeling her daughter was right. The next six months wouldn't fly, they'd crawl. For all three of them…

Shana wanted children, someday, when the time was right. But she'd assumed she'd take on the role of motherhood the way everyone else did. She'd start with an infant and sort of grow into it—ease into being a parent gradually, learning as she went. Instead, she was about to get a crash course. She wondered if there were manuals to help with this kind of situation.

Pacing her living room, she paused long enough to check out the spare bedroom one last time. She'd added some welcoming touches for Jazmine's benefit and hoped the stuffed teddy bear would appeal to her niece. Girls of any age liked stuffed animals, didn't they? The bedspread, a fetching shade of pink with big white daisies, was new, as was the matching pink throw rug. She just hoped Jazmine would recognize that she was trying to make this work.

She wanted Jazmine to know she was willing to make an effort if the girl would meet her halfway. Still, Shana didn't have a good feeling about it.

Her suspicions proved correct. When Ali arrived, it was immediately apparent that Jazmine wanted nothing to do with her aunt Shana. The nine-year-old was dressed in faded green fatigues and a camouflage army-green T-shirt. She sat on the sofa with a sullen look that discouraged conversation. Her long dark hair fell across her face. When she wasn't glaring at Shana, she stared at the carpet as if inspecting it for loose fibers.

"I can't tell you how good it is to see you," Ali told Shana, turning to her daughter, obviously expecting Jazmine to echo the sentiment. The girl didn't.

Shana moved into the kitchen, hoping for a private word with her sister. They hadn't always been close. All through high school, they'd competed with each other. Ali had been the more academic of the two, while Shana had excelled in sports. From their father, a family physician, they'd both inherited a love of science and medicine. He'd died suddenly of a heart attack when Shana was twenty.

Within months, their lives were turned upside down. Their mother fell to pieces but by that time, Ali was in the Navy. Luckily, Shana was able to stay close to home and look after their mom, handle the legal paperwork and deal with the insurance, retirement funds and other responsibilities. Shana had attended college classes part-time and kept the household going. At twenty-two, she was hired by one of the up-and-coming pharmaceutical companies as a sales rep. The job suited her. Having spent a good part of her life around medical professionals, she was comfortable in that atmosphere. She was friendly and personable, well-liked by clients and colleagues. Within a few years, she'd risen to top sales representative in her division. The company had been sorry to see her go and had offered an impressive bonus to persuade her to stay. But Shana was ready for a change, in more ways than one.

The last time the sisters had been together was at Peter's funeral. Shortly afterward, Ali had returned to Italy. Although she could have taken an assignment back in the States, Ali chose to finish her tour in Europe. As much as possible, she'd told Shana, she wanted Jazmine to remain in a familiar environment. A few months ago, she'd been transferred to San Diego, but no one had expected her to be stationed aboard the *Woodrow Wilson,* the newest and largest of the Navy's aircraft carriers. According to her sister, this was a once-in-a-career assignment. Maybe, but in Shana's opinion, the Navy had a lousy sense of timing.

"Jazmine doesn't seem happy about being here," Shana commented when they were out of earshot. She understood how the girl felt. The poor kid had enough turmoil in her life without having her mother disappear for six months.

"She'll be fine." Ali cast an anxious glance toward the living room as Shana took three sodas from the refrigerator.

"Sure she will," Shana agreed, "but will I?"

Ali bit her lower lip and looked guilty. "There isn't anyone else."

"I know. These next six months will give Jazmine and me a chance to know each other," Shana announced, stepping into the living room and offering Jazmine a soda. "Isn't that right?"

The girl stared at the can as if it held nerve gas. "I don't want to live with you."

Well, surprise, surprise. Shana would never have guessed that.

"Jazmine!"

"No," Shana said, stopping her sister from chastising the girl. "We should be honest with one another." She put down Jazmine's drink and sat on the opposite end of the sofa, dangling her own pop can in both hands.

"This is going to be an experience for me, too. I haven't been around kids your age all that much."

"I can tell." Jazmine frowned at the open door to her bedroom. "I hate pink."

Shana had been afraid of that. "We can take it back and exchange it for something you like."

"Where'd you get it? Barbies R Us?"

Shana laughed; the kid was witty. "Close, but we can check out the Army surplus store if you prefer."

This comment warranted a half smile from Jazmine.

"We'll manage," Shana said with what she hoped sounded like confidence. "I realize I've got a lot to learn."

"No kidding."

"Jazmine," Ali snapped in frustration, "the least you can do is try. Give your aunt credit for making an effort. You can do the same."

"I am trying," the girl snapped in return. "A pink bedroom and a teddy bear? Oh, puleeeze! She's treating me like I'm in kindergarten instead of fourth grade."

Shana had barely started this new venture and already she'd failed miserably. "We can exchange the bear, too," she suggested. "Army surplus again?"

Her second attempt at being accommodating was less appreciated than the first. This time Jazmine didn't even crack a smile.

Ali sat in the space between Shana and Jazmine and threw her arms over their shoulders. "If I've learned anything in the last few years, it's that women have to stick together. I can't be with you, Jazz. That's all there is to it. I'm sorry, I wish things were different, but they aren't. If you want, at the end of this deployment, I'll resign my commission."

Jazmine's head rose abruptly. "You'd leave the Navy?"

Ali nodded. This was as much a surprise to Shana as it was to her niece. From all indications, Ali loved military life and had fit into it with comfort and ease.

"Now that your dad's gone, my life isn't the same anymore," Ali continued. "I'm your mother and you're far more important to me than any career, Navy or not. I won't leave you again, Jazmine, and that's a promise."

At those words the girl burst into tears. Embarrassed, she hid her face in both hands, her shoulders shaking as Ali hugged her.

Ali seemed to be trying not to weep, but Shana had no such compunction. Tears slipped down her cheeks.

It would be so good to have her sister back again. If she had any say in the matter, Ali would move to Seattle so the two of them could be closer.

"If you get out of the Navy, does that mean you'll marry Uncle Adam?" Jazmine asked with the excitement of a kid who's just learned she's about to receive the best gift of her life.

"Who's Uncle Adam?" Did this mean her sister had managed to find *two* husbands while Shana had yet to find one? Ah, the old competitive urge was back in full swing.

"He was one of my dad's best friends," Jazmine supplied with more enthusiasm than she'd shown since she'd arrived. "He's cute and funny and I think Mom should marry him."

Raising one brow, Shana turned to her sister for an explanation. Ali had never mentioned anyone named Adam.

"Uncle Adam is stationed in Everett. That's close to here, right?" Jazmine demanded, looking to Shana for the answer.

"It's a bit of a drive." She wasn't entirely sure, never

having made the trip north of Seattle herself. "Less than an hour, I'd guess."

"Uncle Adam will want to visit once he learns I'm here."

"I'm sure he will," Ali murmured, pressing her daughter's head against her shoulder.

"You like this guy?" Shana asked her. Ali was decidedly closemouthed about him, which implied that she had some feelings for this friend of Peter's.

"Of course Mom likes him," Jazmine said when her mother didn't respond. "So do I. He's totally *fabulous*."

Ali met Shana's gaze and shrugged.

"Another pilot?" Shana murmured.

She shook her head. "He's a Supply Officer. You'll like him," her sister was quick to say, as if this man might interest her romantically. No way. Shana had sworn off men and she was serious about that.

"He said I can talk to him anytime I want," Jazmine went on. "I can phone him, can't I?"

"Of course you can." Shana was more curious than ever about this man her sister didn't want to discuss.

Shana turned to gaze at Ali, silently pleading for more information. Her sister ignored her, which was infuriating. Clearly, Adam had already won over her niece; he must be the kind of guy who shopped at the army surplus store.

Chapter Three

First thing Monday morning, Shana drove Jazmine to Lewis and Clark Elementary School to enroll her. Shana had to admit her stomach was in knots. The school yard was jammed with kids, and a string of vehicles queued in front, taking turns dropping off students. Big yellow school buses belched out diesel fumes as they lumbered toward the parking lot behind the building.

Shana was fortunate to find an empty parking space. She accompanied Jazmine into the building, although the girl walked ahead of her—just far enough to suggest the two of them weren't together.

The noise level inside the school reminded her of a rock concert and Shana felt the beginnings of a headache. Or maybe it was caused by all those students gathered in one place, staring at Jazmine and her.

The school bell rang and like magic, the halls emptied. Within seconds everyone disappeared behind various doors and silence descended. Ah, the power of a bell. It was as if she were Moses, and the Red Sea had parted so she could find her way to the Promised Land, or in this case, The Office.

Wordlessly Shana and Jazmine followed the signs to the principal's domain. Jazmine was outwardly calm. She gave no sign of being ill at ease. Unlike Shana, who was on the verge of chewing off every fingernail she owned.

"This is no big deal," Jazmine assured her, shifting the backpack she carried. It was the size one might take on a trek through the Himalayas. "I've done this plenty of times."

"I don't feel good just leaving you here." They'd had all of one day together and while it was uncomfortable for them both, it hadn't been nearly as bad as Shana had feared. It hadn't been good, either.

When they took Ali to the airport, Shana had been the one in tears. Mother and daughter had hugged for an extra-long moment and then Ali was gone. It was Shana who did all the talking on the drive home. As soon as they were back at the rental house, Jazmine disappeared inside her bedroom and didn't open the door for hours.

Dinner had been a series of attempts on Shana's part to start a conversation, but her questions were met with either a grunt or a one-word reply. Shana got the message. After the first ten minutes, she said nothing. And *nothing* was what Jazmine seemed to appreciate most. They maintained an awkward silence and at the end of the meal, Jazmine delivered her plate to the kitchen, rinsed it off, stuck it in the dishwasher and returned to her room. The door closed and Shana hadn't seen her again until this morning. Apparently kids this age treasured their privacy. Point taken. Lesson learned.

"This must be it," Shana said, pointing at the door marked *Office*.

Jazmine murmured something unintelligible, shrugging off the backpack and letting the straps slip down her arms. Shana couldn't imagine what she had in that monstrosity, but apparently it was as valuable to the child as Shana's purse was to her.

"I was thinking you might want to wait a bit, you know," Shana suggested, stammering, unable to identify her misgivings. "Not do this right away, I mean." The students she saw in the hallway didn't look particularly friendly. Jazmine was only nine, for heaven's sake, and her mother was headed out to sea for half a year. Maybe she should homeschool her. Shana considered that option for all of half a second. First, it wouldn't be home school; it would be ice-cream parlor school. The authorities would love that. And second, Shana was completely unqualified to teach her anything.

"I'll be all right," Jazmine said just loudly enough for Shana to hear.

Maybe so, but Shana wasn't completely convinced *she* would be. This guardianship thing was even harder than it sounded. The thought of leaving her niece here actually made her feel ill.

Jazmine's eyes narrowed accusingly. "I'm not a kid, you know."

So nine-year-olds weren't kids anymore? Could've fooled Shana, but rather than argue, she let the comment slide.

Enrolling Jazmine turned out to be surprisingly easy. After Shana completed a couple of forms and handed over a copy of her guardianship papers, it was done. Jazmine was led out of the office and into a classroom. Shana watched her go, forcing herself not to follow like a much-loved golden retriever.

"It's your first time as a guardian?" the school secretary asked.

Shana nodded. "Jazmine's been through a lot." She resisted the urge to mention Peter's death and the fact that Ali was out at sea. Instinctively she realized that the less anyone knew about these things, the better for Jazmine.

"She'll fit right in," the secretary assured her.

"I hope so." But Shana wasn't sure that was true. There were only a few weeks left of the school year. Just when Jazmine had managed to adjust, it would be time for summer break. And what would Shana do with her then? It was a question she couldn't answer. Not yet, anyway.

With reluctance she walked back to her parked car and drove to Olsen's Ice Cream and Pizza Parlor. She'd thought about changing the name, but the restaurant had been called this for the last thirty years. A new name might actually be a disadvantage, so she'd decided to keep everything the same for now.

Shana's day went smoothly after her visit to the school. She was on her own now, her training with the Olsens finished. They insisted the secret to their pizza was the tomato sauce, made from their special recipe. That recipe had been kept secret for over thirty years. Only when the final papers had been signed was Shana allowed to have the recipe, which to her untrained eye looked fairly unspectacular. She was almost sure her mother used to make something similar for spaghetti and had gotten the recipe out of a "Dear Abby" column years ago.

There was a huge mixing machine and, following the Olsens' example, she went into the shop each morning to mix up a batch of dough and let it rise. Once the dough had risen, it was put in the refrigerator, awaiting the day's pizza orders. The restaurant opened at eleven and did a brisk lunch trade. How much or how little dough to make was complete guesswork. Shana's biggest fear was that she'd run short. As a consequence she usually mixed too much. But she was learning.

At three o'clock, Shana found herself watching for the school bus. Jazmine was to be dropped off in front of the ice-cream parlor. From noon on, she'd constantly checked the time, wondering and worrying about her niece. The elementary students she'd seen looked like a rough crowd—okay, maybe not the first- and second-graders, but the ones in the fifth and sixth grades, who were giants compared to Jazmine. Shana just hoped the girl could hold her own.

Business was constant—people waiting to catch ferries, high-school students, retired folk, tourists. Shana planned to hire a part-time employee soon. Another idea she had was to introduce soup to the menu. She'd already experimented with a number of mixes, both liquid and dry, and hadn't found anything that impressed her. Shana was leaning toward making her own from scratch but her experience in cooking large batches was limited.

A bus rolled into view and Shana instantly went on alert. Sure enough, Jazmine stepped off, wearing a frown, and marched inside. Without a word to Shana, she slid into a booth.

"Well," Shana said, unable to disguise her anxiety, "how was it?"

Jazmine shrugged.

"Oh." Her niece wasn't exactly forthcoming with details. Thinking fast, Shana asked the questions her mother had bombarded her with every day after school. "What did you learn? Anything interesting?"

Jazmine shook her head.

"Did you make any new friends?"

Jazmine scowled up at her. "No."

That was said emphatically enough for Shana to surmise that things hadn't gone well. "I see." Glancing over her shoulder, Shana sighed. "Are you hungry? I could make you a pizza."

"No, thanks."

The bell above the door rang and a customer entered, moving directly to the ice-cream case. Shana slipped behind the counter and waited patiently until the woman had made her selection. As she scooped chocolate chip–mint ice cream into a waffle cone, she realized something was different about Jazmine. Not until her customer left did she figure out what it was.

"Jazz," she said, startled, "where's your backpack?"

Her niece didn't answer.

"Did you forget it at school? We could run by to pick it up if you want." Not until the parlor closed at six, but she didn't mention that. During the summer it wouldn't be until eight o'clock; she didn't mention that, either.

Jazmine scowled even more ferociously.

Shana hadn't known how much fury a nine-year-old girl's eyes could convey. Her niece's anger seemed to be focused solely on Shana. The unfairness of it struck her, but any attempt at conversation was instantly blocked.

It was obvious that someone had taken the backpack from Jazmine. No wonder the girl wasn't in a happy frame of mind.

Feeling wretched and helpless, Shana slid into the booth across from her niece. She didn't say anything for several minutes, then gently squeezed Jazmine's hand. "I am so sorry."

Jazmine shrugged as if it was no big thing, but it was and Shana felt at a loss. Without her niece's knowing, she'd speak to the principal in the morning and see what could be done. She guessed it'd happened on the bus or off school grounds.

"Can I use your phone?" Jazmine asked.

"Of course."

Jazmine's eyes fleetingly met hers as she pulled a piece of paper from her hip pocket. "It's long distance."

"You're not calling Paris, are you?"

The question evoked an almost-smile. "No."

"Sure, go ahead." Shana gestured toward the phone on the back wall in the kitchen.

Jazmine thanked her with a faint smile. This counted as profuse appreciation and Shana was nearly over-whelmed by gratitude. Despite their shaky beginning she was starting to reach this kid.

"I'm phoning my uncle Adam," Jazmine announced. "He'll know what to do."

This uncle Adam seemed to have all the answers. She hadn't even met him and already she didn't like him. No one could be that perfect.

On Monday afternoon, Adam Kennedy opened the door to his apartment near Everett Naval Station, glad to be home. He'd just been released from the naval hospital, where he'd recently undergone rotator cuff surgery. His shoulder throbbed and he felt so light-headed he had to brace his hand against the wall in order to steady himself. He'd be fine in a couple of days, but at the moment he was still shaky.

The apartment was dark with the drapes pulled, but he didn't have the energy to walk across the room and open them.

It wouldn't be like this if he had a wife, who'd be able to look after him while he felt so weak. This wasn't the first time that thought had occurred to Adam. He'd never intended to be a thirty-two-year-old bachelor.

Adam sank into his favorite chair and winced at the pain that shot down his arm. Leaning his head back against the cushion, he closed his eyes and envisioned what his life would be like if he was married. A wife would be fussing over him now, acting concerned and looking for ways to make him comfortable. Granted, if comfort was all he wanted, he could pay for it. A wife— well, having a wife meant companionship and sharing things. Like a bed… It also involved that frightening word, *love*.

If he was married now, she'd be asking how he felt and bringing him tea and *caring* about him. The fantasy filled his mind and he found himself smiling. What he needed was the *right* woman. His track record in that department left a great deal to be desired.

He'd started out fine. When he graduated from college he'd been engaged, but while he was in Officer Candidate School, Melanie had a sudden change of heart. Actually, she still wanted to get married, just not to him. The tearful scene in which she confessed that she'd fallen in love with someone else wasn't a memory he wanted to reminisce over, especially now. Suffice it to say, his ego had taken a major beating. In the long run, though, Melanie wasn't that great a loss. If she had a roving eye this early in their relationship, it didn't bode well for the lengthy separations a Navy career would demand of their marriage.

The thing was, Adam wanted children. One of his proudest moments was when Peter had asked him to be Jazmine's godfather. He took his duties seriously and loved that little girl, and he'd felt especially protective of her since his friend's death. He hadn't heard from her in a while and wondered how she was doing after the recent move to San Diego. He'd have to get in touch with her soon.

Adam had envied Peter his marriage. He'd never seen two people more in love with each other or better suited. They were about as perfect a match as possible. Adam suspected that fact had been a detriment to him in his own quest for a relationship. He kept looking for a woman as well suited to him as Ali had been to his friend. If such a woman existed, Adam hadn't found her, and he'd about given up. It wasn't Ali he wanted, but a woman who was his equal in all the ways Ali had been Peter's. A woman with brains and courage and heart. At this stage he'd take two out of three. Ali had brought out the best in Peter; she'd made a good man better.

A sense of sadness came over him as he thought about Peter. Adam had a couple of younger brothers, Sam and Doug, and the three of them were close, but Peter and Adam had been even closer. They'd met in OCS, Officer Candidate School, kept in contact afterward and later were stationed together in Italy. During weekend holidays, Peter and Ali had him over for countless dinners. The three of them had sat on their balcony in the Italian countryside drinking wine and talking well into the night. Those were some of the happiest memories of his life.

Then Peter had been killed. Adam had been a witness to the accident that claimed his best friend's life. He still had nightmares about it and experienced the same rush of horror, anger, frustration he'd felt at the time. He'd gone with the Casualty Assistance Counseling Officer to tell Ali that her husband was dead. In his heart, he'd promised Peter that he'd look out for both Ali and Jazz but the Navy hadn't made it easy.

Ali was currently stationed at the hospital in San Diego and he was in Everett. He phoned at least once a month to check up on them and Jazmine called him every now and then when she needed to talk. He always enjoyed their conversations. Peter would be proud of both the women in his life, he mused. Jazmine was a great kid and Ali was a wonderful mother.

Adam noticed the blinking light on his answering machine. He knew there were more messages than he had the patience or endurance to deal with just yet. He'd leave it until morning when he had a fresh supply of energy.

He sighed. He wasn't used to feeling like this—despondent and weary. Coming home to an empty apartment underlined a truth he didn't want to acknowledge. Lieutenant Commander Adam Kennedy was lonely.

He stared blankly across the room, half toying with the notion of a romantic relationship with Ali. It didn't take him more than a second to realize it wouldn't work. He loved Ali—like a sister. Try as he might, he couldn't seem to view her as a marriage prospect. She was his best friend's widow, a woman he admired, a woman he thought of as family.

Yet…he wanted what she'd had, what she and Peter had shared, and the deep contentment their marriage had brought them.

By morning, he would've forgotten all these yearnings, he told himself. He'd lived alone so long now that he should certainly be accustomed to his own company. When he was at sea, it was a different story, since he was constantly surrounded by others. As a Supply Officer he was normally stationed aboard the *Benjamin Franklin*. Unfortunately the *Franklin* was currently headed toward the Persian Gulf. Until his shoulder healed, he'd be twiddling his thumbs behind some desk and hating it.

After a while Adam felt better. His head had stopped spinning and the ache in his shoulder wasn't quite as intense. It would be easy to close his eyes and sleep but if he slept now, he'd spend the whole night staring at the ceiling.

A wife.

It was something to consider. Maybe he should resume his efforts to meet someone, with marriage in mind. The time was right. His parents wanted more grandchildren and he was certainly willing to do his part. According to Ali, he was an excellent candidate for a husband and father. She'd tried any number of times to fix him up, but nothing had ever come of her matchmaking efforts.

A wife.

He relaxed and smiled. He was ready. All he needed now was the woman.

Chapter Four

Lieutenant Commander Alison Karas had been assigned as senior medical officer aboard the *USS Woodrow Wilson.* As much as she wanted to be with Jazmine and as difficult as it had been to leave her daughter with Shana, Ali was determined to fulfill her duty to the Navy. During her twelve-year career, she'd never been stationed aboard a ship. Before Jazmine was born, she'd done everything in her limited power to get such an assignment, but it hadn't happened.

So far, she'd served in a number of military hospitals. And now, when she least wanted sea duty, that was exactly what she got. Still, she loved the Navy with the same intensity her husband had.

Her quarters were shared with another woman officer. There hadn't been time to exchange more than a brief greeting before they'd each begun their respective assignments. The crew was preparing to set out to sea. Within a couple of days, the jets would fly in from Naval air stations all over the country. It was standard procedure for the F-14s to link up with the aircraft carrier.

Unlikely though it was, she hoped for an opportunity to watch, since the pilots' precision and skill were so impressive. Pilots were a special breed, as she well knew. Peter had wanted to fly jets from the time he was in grade school, according to his mother.

She smiled sadly at the thought of her husband. The pain of his loss remained sharp and—as always—Ali hoped he hadn't suffered. There must have been a moment of sheer terror when he realized he wouldn't be able to recover. She tried not to think of that.

Trite as it sounded, she'd learned that life does go on. It hadn't seemed possible in the beginning, when she'd been blinded by her grief. She was surprised to discover that everything continued as it had before. Classes were held in Jazmine's school; the radio still played silly love songs. People drove their cars and ate meals and bickered with each other. Ali hadn't been able to understand how life as she'd once known it could go on as though nothing had changed.

Jazmine was in good hands. Shana would look after her well. Ali needed to reassure herself of that several times a day. Leaving her daughter had been traumatic, but for Jazmine's sake, Ali had tried not to let her emotions show. Before she returned to San Diego, they'd talked, and Ali had a heart-to-heart with Shana, too.

She was still a little worried about Shana, but once they'd had a chance to really discuss the situation, Ali accepted that this impulsive change in her sister's life was probably the best thing she'd done in years. Shana needed a fresh start. The ice-cream parlor was charming and would undoubtedly be a big success. Jazmine had a bit of an attitude, but that wouldn't last long. And it helped that Adam was close by. The biggest disappointment of her stay was that they hadn't been able to reach him. Once he checked his messages, she knew he'd get in touch with Jazmine.

Ali found her daughter's suggestion that she marry Adam downright amusing. Ali thought the world of her husband's best friend, but there was no romantic spark on either side. What was particularly interesting was the fact that Jazmine seemed ready to discuss bringing another man into their lives.

Despite that, Ali had no intention of remarrying. She hadn't mentioned that to either her sister or Jazmine because it sounded too melodramatic. And both of them would argue with her. But a man like Peter only came around once in a lifetime, and she wasn't pressing her luck. If, by chance, she were to consider remarrying, she was determined not to fall in love with a Navy man. She'd already had one Navy husband and she wasn't going to try for two.

Ali had never removed her wedding band. After all these years, that ring represented perhaps the most significant part of her life. And although shipboard romances were strictly prohibited, it was a form of emotional protection, too. As far as her shipmates knew, she was married and that was the impression she wanted to give.

After spending her shift in the sick bay checking supplies, Ali went to the wardroom, where the officers dined. Two other women officers were in the room but their table was full and they seemed engrossed in conversation. Sitting alone at a corner table, she felt self-conscious, although she rather enjoyed watching the men and women as they chatted. In a few weeks, she'd probably be sitting with one of those groups. Life aboard a carrier was new to her, but eventually it would become familiar and even comfortable.

Just as she was finishing her dinner, the group that included the other women was joined by Commander Dillon. Ali read his name tag as he walked past her table. He acknowledged her with a stiff nod, which she returned. From the reception he received, it was clear that he was well-liked and respected by his fellow officers. She had no idea what his duty assignment might be.

Without being obvious—at least she hoped she wasn't—she studied Dillon. He was tall and lean with dark hair graying at the temples, which led her to believe he must be in his early to midforties. His most striking feature was his intense blue eyes. To her chagrin, she found herself looking at his ring finger and noticed it was bare. Not that it meant anything. Wedding rings were dangerous aboard ship, although she chose to wear hers. More than once Ali had seen fingers severed as a result of a wedding band caught in machinery.

As soon as she'd finished her coffee, Ali went back to her work space at the clinic and logged on to the Internet to write Shana and Jazmine a short note. Her sister and daughter would be anxious to hear from her after her first full day at sea.

Sent: May 19
From: Alison.Karas@woodrowwilson.navy.mil
To: Shana@mindsprung.com
Subject: Hello!

Dear Shana and Jazmine,

Just checking in to see how things are going with you two. It's a little crazy around here and I'm still finding my sea legs. Not to worry, though.

Hey, Jazz, I was thinking you should help your aunt come up with ideas for ice-cream sundaes. Remember how we invented our own versions last summer? Hot fudge, marshmallow topping and crushed graham crackers? You called it the Give Me More Sundae. Not bad.

Shana, be sure to look over Jazz's homework, especially the math. Okay, okay, I'll stop worrying. Send me an e-mail now and then, okay? I'm waiting with bated breath to hear how you two are surviving.

Love ya.
Ali (That's Mom to you, Jazz!)

It wasn't much of a message, but Ali was tired and ready to turn in for the night. As she started back to her quarters, she met Commander Dillon in the long narrow passageway. She nodded and stepped aside in order to allow him to pass.

He paused as he read her badge. "Karas?"

"Yes, sir."

"At ease." He glanced down at her left hand. "Your husband is Navy?"

"Yes, sir." She looked self-consciously at her wedding ring. "He—" She'd begun to explain that she was a widow, then stopped abruptly. Rather than make eye contact, she stared into the bulkhead.

"This is your first time aboard the *Woodrow Wilson?*" The question was casual, conversational in tone.

She nodded again. "This is my first time on any ship. I'm wondering how long it's going to take before I get used to it." She laughed as she said this, because being on an aircraft carrier was so much like being in a building. Every now and then, Ali had to remind herself that she was actually aboard a ship.

Commander Dillon's eyes narrowed slightly as he smiled. "You'll be fine."

"I know I will. Thank you, sir."

That very moment, an alarm rang for a fire drill. All sailors were to report immediately to their assigned stations. A sailor rushed past Ali and jolted her. In an effort to get out of his way, she tripped and fell hard against Commander Dillon, startling them both. The commander stumbled backward but caught himself. Instinctively he reached out and grabbed her shoulders, catching her before she lost her balance and toppled sideways. Stunned, they immediately grew still.

"I'm sorry," she mumbled, shocked at the instant physical reaction she'd experienced at his touch. It had been an innocent enough situation and meant nothing. Yet it told Ali a truth she'd forgotten. She was a woman. And, almost against her will, was attracted to a man other than Peter.

He muttered something under his breath, but she didn't hear what he said and frankly she was grateful. Without another word, they hurried in opposite directions.

Ali's face burned with mortification, but not because she'd nearly fallen into Commander Dillon. When her breasts grazed him and he'd reached out to catch her, he could have pulled her to him and kissed her and she wouldn't have made a single protest. Her face burned, and she knew she was in serious trouble. No, it was just the close proximity to all these men. At least that was what Ali told herself. It wasn't the commander; it could've been any man, but even as that thought went through her mind, she knew it was a lie. She worried that the commander might somehow know what she'd been feeling. That mortified her even more.

The scene replayed itself in her head during the fire drill and afterward, when she retired to her quarters. Once she was alone, Ali found a pen and paper. It was one thing to send Jazmine an e-mail but a letter was a tangible object that her daughter could touch and hold and keep. She knew Jazmine would find comfort in reading a note Ali had actually written.

When Ali had first started dating Peter, they'd exchanged long letters during each separation. She treasured those letters and savored them all, even more so now that he was gone.

On the night of their wedding anniversary last year, while Jazmine was at a slumber party, Ali had unearthed a stack and reread each one. She quickly surrendered to self-pity, but she had every reason in the world to feel sorry for herself, she decided, and didn't hold back. That night, spent alone in her bedroom, grieving, weeping and angry, had been an epiphany for her. It was as if something inside her—a wall of pretense and stoicism—had broken wide-open, and her pain had gushed forth. She believed it was at that point that she'd begun to heal.

Oh, she'd cried before then, but this time, on the day that would have been her twelfth wedding anniversary, she'd wept as if it was the end of the world.

By midnight she'd fallen asleep on top of the bed with Peter's letters surrounding her. Thankfully Jazmine hadn't been witness to this emotional breakdown. Her daughter had known the significance of the date, however, and had given her mother a handmade anniversary card the following afternoon. Ali would always love that sweet card. After she'd read it, they'd hugged each other for a long time. Jazmine had revealed sensitivity and compassion, and Ali realized she'd done her daughter a grave disservice.

All those months after Peter's death, Ali had tried to shield Jazmine from her own pain. She'd encouraged the child to grieve, helped her deal with the loss of her father as much as possible. Yet in protecting Jazmine, Ali hadn't allowed her daughter to see that she was suffering. She hadn't allowed Jazmine to comfort her, which would have brought comfort to Jazmine, too.

Later that same day, after dinner, Ali had shared a few of Peter's letters with Jazmine. It was the first time they'd really talked about him since his death. Before then, each seemed afraid to say more than a few words for fear of upsetting the other. Ali learned how much Jazmine needed to talk about Peter. The girl delighted in each tidbit, each detail her mother supplied. Ali answered countless questions about their first meeting, their courtship and their wedding day. Jazmine must've heard the story of their first date a dozen times and never seemed to tire of it.

Once Ali's reserve was down, not a night passed without Jazmine's asking about Peter. As a young child, her daughter had loved bedtime stories and listening to Ali read. At nine she suddenly wanted her mother to put her to bed again. It was so out of character for her gutsy, sassy daughter that it'd taken Ali a couple of nights to figure out what Jazmine really wanted, and that was to talk about her father.

In retrospect Ali recognized that those months of closeness had helped prepare Jazmine for this long separation. Ali didn't think she could have left her with Shana otherwise.

Shana. An involuntary smile flashed across her face as she leaned back in the desk chair. These next six months would either make or break her strong-willed younger sister. She'd taken on a lot all at once. Buying this restaurant on impulse was so unlike her. Shana preferred to have things planned out, down to the smallest detail. Not only that, this new venture was a real switch for her after her sales position.

If there was anything to be grateful for in Shana's sudden move to Seattle, it was the fact that Brad Moore was out of her life. Ali had only met him once, during a brief visit home, but he'd struck her as sleazy, and she hadn't been surprised to hear about his duplicity. Ali wondered how he'd managed to deceive her sister all this time, but whatever charms he possessed had worked about four and a half years longer than they should have. She supposed that, like most people, Shana had only seen what she'd wanted to see.

Before she returned to San Diego, Ali and Shana were able to spend a few hours together. Jazmine was asleep and the two sisters sat on the bed in Shana's room talking.

She'd seen how hurt Shana was by Brad's un-faithfulness. In an effort to comfort her sister, Ali had suggested Shana try to meet someone else as quickly as possible.

Her sister hadn't taken kindly to the suggestion. In fact, she hadn't been shy about sharing her feelings with regard to the male of the species. Shana claimed she was finished with men.

"You're overreacting," Ali had told her.

"And you're being ridiculous." Sitting with her knees drawn, Shana shook her head. "The absolute last thing I want to do now is get involved again. I was 'involved' for the last five years and all I got out of that relation-ship, besides a lot of pain, is two crystal champagne glasses Brad bought me. He said we'd use them at our wedding." Not that he'd actually given her an engage-ment ring or set the date. "Those glasses are still in the box. If he'd thought of it, he probably would've asked for them back."

"You feel that way about men now, but you won't always."

Shana frowned. "You're one to talk. I don't see you looking for a new relationship."

"Okay, fine, neither of us is interested in men."

"Permanently," Shana insisted.

Ali had laughed then and said, "Speak for yourself."

Funny, as she reviewed that conversation, Commander Dillon came to mind. It was unlikely that she'd see him on a regular basis; with a crew of five thousand on this ship, their paths wouldn't cross often. Ali wasn't entirely sure why, but she felt that was probably a good thing.

Chapter Five

The next few days were intense for Shana. She insisted on driving Jazmine to school, and every morning she joined the long line of parents dropping off their kids at the grade school. If Jazmine appreciated her efforts to build a rapport between them, she gave no indication of it. The most animation she'd witnessed in the girl had been after Monday's lengthy telephone conversation with her uncle Adam.

Shana, her aunt, a blood relative, was simply Shana, but Adam Kennedy, family friend, was *Uncle* Adam. The *uncle* part was uttered with near-reverence.

Okay, so she was jealous. Shana admitted it. While she struggled to gain ground with her niece, Jazmine droned on about this interloper.

Tuesday afternoon, the school bus again let Jazmine off in front of the ice-cream parlor. Her niece had dragged herself into the shop, as though it demanded all her energy just to open the door. Then she'd slipped onto one of the barstools and lain her head on her folded arms.

Wednesday afternoon, Shana watched the school bus approach and the doors glide open. Sure enough, Jazmine was there, but this time she leaped off the bus and hurried toward the restaurant.

Shana stopped and stared. No, it couldn't be. But it was. Jazmine had her backpack. From the size and apparent weight of it, nothing seemed to be missing, either.

The instant Jazmine stepped inside, Shana blurted out, "You've got your backpack." It probably would've been better to keep her mouth shut and let Jazmine tell her, but she'd been too shocked.

"I know." Jazmine dumped her backpack on the floor and hopped onto the barstool with a Bugs Bunny bounce, planting her elbows on the counter. "Can I have some ice cream?"

Taken aback, Shana blinked. "Who are you and what have you done with my niece?"

"Very funny."

Shana laughed and reached for the ice-cream scoop. "Cone or dish?"

"Dish. Make it two scoops. Bubblegum and strawberry." She paused, her face momentarily serious. "Oh—and thank you."

"You're welcome." Bending over the freezer, Shana rolled the hard ice cream into a generous ball. "Well," she said when she couldn't stand it any longer. "The least you can do is tell me what happened."

"With what?" Jazmine asked, then giggled like the

nine-year-old she was. "I don't know if you noticed or not, but I was pretty upset Monday afternoon."

"Really," Shana said, playing dumb.

"Two girls cornered me in the playground. One of them distracted me, and the other ran off with my backpack."

Shana clenched her jaw, trying to hide her anger. As Jazmine's legal guardian, she wanted these girls' names and addresses. She'd personally see to it that they were marched into the principal's office and reprimanded. On second thought, their parents should be summoned to the school for a confrontation with the authorities. Perhaps it would be best to bring in the police, as well.

"How'd you get it back?" Shana had given up scooping ice cream.

Looking more than a little pleased with herself, Jazmine straightened her shoulders and grinned. "Uncle Adam told me I should talk to them."

Wasn't *that* brilliant. Had she been asked, Shana would've told Jazmine the same thing.

"He said I should tell them it was really unfortunate, but it didn't seem like we could be friends and I was hoping to get to know them." This was uttered in the softest, sweetest tones Shana had ever heard from the girl.

"They fell for it?"

Jazmine's eyes widened. "I meant it. At first I thought they were losers but they're actually pretty cool. I think they just wanted to see what I carried around with me."

Frankly Shana was curious herself.

"Once they looked inside, they were willing to give it back."

"You're not missing anything?"

Jazmine shook her head.

"Great." Muttering under her breath, Shana dipped the scoop into the blue bubblegum-flavored ice cream. The bell above the door rang, but intent on her task, Shana didn't raise her head.

"I'll have some of that myself," a male voice said.

"Uncle Adam!" Jazmine shrieked. Her niece whirled around so fast she nearly fell off the stool.

Hearing his name was all the incentive Shana needed to glance up. She did just in time to watch Jazmine throw her arms around a man dressed casually in slacks and a shirt. From the top of his military haircut to the bottom of his feet, this man was Navy, with or without his uniform. His arm was in a sling and he grimaced when Jazmine grabbed hold of him but didn't discourage her hug. From the near-hysterical happiness the girl displayed, a passing stranger might think Shana had been holding Jazmine hostage.

"You must be Ali's sister," he said, smiling broadly at Shana.

She forced a smile in return. She'd been prepared to dislike him on sight. In fact, she'd never even met him and was already jealous of the relationship he had with Jazmine. Now he was standing right in front of her—and she found her tongue stuck to the roof of her mouth. He seemed to be waiting for her to reply.

"Yes, hi," she said and dropped the metal scoop into the water container, sloshing liquid over the edges. Wiping her wet hand on her white apron, she managed another slight smile. "Yes, I'm Ali's sister."

On closer inspection, she saw that he was tall and apparently very fit. Some might find his looks appealing, but Shana decided she didn't. Brad was just as tall and equally fit—from spending hours in a gym every week, no doubt admiring himself in all the mirrors. Adam's hair was a deep chestnut shade, similar to her own. No. Not chestnut, she decided next, nothing that distinguished. His was plain brown. He might've been considered handsome if not for those small, beady eyes. Well, they weren't exactly *small,* more average, she supposed, trying to be as objective as she could. He hugged Jazmine and looked at Shana and—no.

But he did. He looked at Shana and *winked.* The man had the audacity to flirt with her. It was outrageous. This was the very man Jazmine wanted her mother to marry. The man whose praises she'd sung for two full days until Shana thought she'd scream if she heard his name one more time.

"I'm Adam Kennedy." He extended his free right hand.

She offered her left hand because it was dry and nodded politely. "You mean *Uncle* Adam." She hoped he caught the sarcastic inflection in her voice.

He grinned as if he knew how much that irritated her. Okay, now she had to admit it. When he smiled he wasn't ordinary-looking at all. In fact, some women— not her, but others who were less jaded—might even be attracted to him. That she could even entertain the remote possibility of finding a man attractive was upsetting. Wasn't it only a few days ago that she'd declared to her sister that she was completely and utterly off men? And now here she was, feeling all shaky inside and acting like a girl closer to Jazmine's age than her own. This was pathetic.

In an attempt to cover her reaction, Shana handed Jazmine the bowl of ice cream with its two heaping scoops.

"Uncle Adam wants one, too," Jazmine said excitedly, and then turned to him. "What happened to your arm?" she asked, her eyes wide with concern. "Did you break it?"

"Nothing as dramatic as that," he said, elevating the arm, which was tucked protectively in a sling. "I had a problem with my shoulder, but that's been taken care of now."

Jazmine didn't seem convinced. "You're going to be all right, aren't you?"

"I'll be fine before you know it."

"Good," Jazmine said; she seemed reassured now. Taking Adam by the hand, she led him across the restaurant to a booth.

Shana could hear Jazmine whispering up a storm, but hard as she strained, she couldn't hear what was being said. Working as fast as her arm muscles would allow, she hurriedly dished up a second bowl of ice cream. When she'd bought this business, no one had mentioned how hard ice cream could be. She was developing some impressive biceps.

She smiled as she carried the second dish over to their booth and hoped he enjoyed the bright teal-blue bubble-gum ice cream. After she'd set it down in front of him, she waited. She wasn't sure why she was lingering.

Jazmine beamed with joy. Seeing her niece this happy about anything made Shana feel a pang of regret. Doing her best to swallow her pride, she continued to stand there, unable to think of a thing to say.

Her niece glanced up as if noticing her for the first time. "I was telling Uncle Adam about my backpack. He's the one who said those other girls just wanted to be friends. I didn't believe him, but he was right."

"Yes, he was." Shana might have been able to fade into the background then if Adam hadn't chosen that moment to turn and smile at her. Ignoring him would be easy if only he'd stop smiling, dammit.

"The girls gave it back?" Adam's gaze returned to Jazmine.

Her niece nodded. "Madison asked me to sit next to her at lunch today and I did."

Adam reached across the table and the two exchanged a high five. "That's great!"

"Can I get you anything else?" Shana asked, feeling like a third wheel. These two apparently had a lot to discuss, and no one needed to tell her she was in the way. Besides, she had a business to run. Several customers had come in; at the moment they were studying the list of ice-cream flavors but she'd have to attend to them soon.

"Nothing, thanks." He dipped his plastic spoon into the ice cream. Then, without giving her any warning, he looked at Shana again and their eyes met. Shana felt the breath freeze in her lungs. He seemed to really *see* her, and something about her seemed to catch him unawares. His brow wrinkled as though he was sure he knew her from somewhere else, but couldn't place her.

"How long can you stay?" her niece asked.

Adam turned his attention back to Jazmine.

Shana waited, curious to know the answer herself.

"Just a couple of hours."

"Two hours!" Jazmine didn't bother to hide her disappointment.

"I've got to get back to base for a meeting."

"Right," Shana said, diving into the conversation. "He has to go back to Everett. We wouldn't want to detain him, now would we?" She didn't mean to sound so pleased about sending him on his way, but she wanted him out of there. Shana disliked how he made her feel—as if…as if she was on the brink of some important personal discovery. Like she'd told her sister, she was off men. For good. Okay, for a year. It would take that long to get Brad out of her system, she figured. Now, all of a sudden, there was this man, this uncle Adam, whose smiles made her feel hot, then cold. That wasn't a good sensation for her to be having. It contradicted everything she'd been saying—and it made her uncomfortable.

"I'll stop by again soon," Adam promised, looking directly at her as he said it.

"I want to know what happened to your arm," Jazmine insisted.

"Surgery."

"Does Mom know?"

Adam shook his head. "She's got enough on her plate without worrying about me."

"You've talked to her?" Shana demanded. She forgot that she was pretending not to listen to their conversation. Catherine, the woman who worked part-time, arrived then and immediately began taking orders while Shana handled the cash register.

Adam shifted toward her. "She e-mailed me."

"Oh." Embarrassed, Shana glanced away. "Of course."

"I wish the base were closer," Jazmine muttered.

"Everett isn't that far and with light duty, I'll have more time to spend with you."

"Exactly how soon do you have to leave this afternoon?" Jazmine pressed. "Couldn't you please, please have your meeting tomorrow?"

This kid wasn't easily put off, Shana thought. While she was more than ready to usher Adam Kennedy out the door, her niece was practically begging him to stay.

"It's not really up to me. I've got to go soon, but I'll visit as often as I can."

"He's busy, I'm sure," Shana said before his words sank into her consciousness. *He'd be back...often.* In other words, she'd better get used to having him around, and judging by that smirk, he intended to smile at her some more. Oh, great.

"As often as you can?" Jazz repeated. "What does that mean?"

"I'll make sure I'm here at least once a week to check up on my favorite girl."

Instead of shouting with happiness, Jazmine hung her head. "*Only* once a week?"

Once a week? That often? Shana's reaction was just the opposite. As far as she was concerned, weekly visits were far too frequent.

Ali's little sister seemed oversensitive, Adam observed with some amusement as Shana returned to the ice-cream counter. That wasn't the only thing he'd noticed, either. She was beautiful with classic features, dark hair and eyes and a face he found utterly appealing. Ali was a beautiful woman, too, but in a completely different way. Although both had dark brown hair and eyes, the resemblance stopped there. Shana was the taller of the two and model-thin, whereas Ali had more flesh on her. If he were ever to say that out loud, she'd no doubt be insulted, but it was the truth. Ali wasn't overweight by any means, just rounded in all the right places. In his opinion, the little sister could stand to gain a few pounds. He wasn't sure why he was concentrating on the physical, because his reaction to Shana was much more complex than that. He was attracted to her. Period. He liked what he saw and he liked what he didn't see—what he sensed about her. Attraction was indefinable, more about the sum of a person than his or her parts. People called it chemistry, sparks, magic, all sorts of vague things. But whatever you called it, the attraction was obviously there.

Something else was obvious. *She* felt it, too. And she didn't want to. In fact, she seemed determined to make sure he knew that. He didn't go around ravishing young women, willing or unwilling, but he definitely got a kick out of her reaction to him. He couldn't keep from grinning as he headed into the heavy freeway traffic on I-5 North.

On second thought, *he* might be overreacting. Perhaps it was all those musings about his lack of female companionship following his release from the hospital. Pain could do that to a man. Maybe he was wrong about Shana's interest in him; maybe he'd simply been projecting his own attraction and— Damn, this was getting much too complicated.

That same evening, when Adam logged on to the Internet, he discovered two messages from Ali. In the first, she was eager to know if he'd made contact with Jazmine; in the other, she asked if he'd be able to give her sister a break now and then. He immediately e-mailed back that he'd seen Jazz and everything seemed to be fine with her and Shana. He also said he'd visit as often as he could. Several questions regarding Shana went through his mind, but he didn't ask them, not wanting Ali to get the wrong impression. He also feared she'd relay his interest to her sister—and he just wasn't ready for that.

An hour later, his phone rang. It was Jazmine, who spoke in a whisper.

"Where are you?" he asked.

"In the closet." She was still whispering.

"What's the problem?" So Jazmine wanted to talk to him without her aunt listening in. Interesting.

"I hate it here and—oh, Uncle Adam, it's just so good to see someone I know."

Adam wished he could be there to wrap his arm around the girl's thin shoulders. "It'll get better." He didn't mean to sound trite, but he couldn't come up with anything else to say. "Didn't you tell me you'd made friends with those two girls who took your backpack?"

"Yeah, I guess, but it isn't like California. Seattle isn't like anyplace I've been. I miss my mom and...I just don't like it here."

"I feel that way whenever I've got a new duty assignment," he said, wanting to comfort her and not knowing how. "I'm in a new work environment myself and to be honest I'd much rather be in Hawaii. It's the perfect duty station. But you do get used to wherever you are, Jazz...."

"I just want to be with my mom," Jazmine said, sounding small and sad. "I wouldn't care where it was."

"Are you getting along with your aunt?"

Jazmine hesitated. "She tries, and I appreciate everything she does, I really do, but she doesn't know that much about kids." As if she felt bad about criticizing her aunt, the girl added, "It's not as bad as it was on Monday, but..."

Adam wanted to continue asking questions about Shana, but he preferred not to be obvious about it. "She seems nice."

"She is, but she's got issues, you know."

It was difficult for Adam not to laugh outright at Jazmine's solemn tone. "What kind of issues?" he asked gravely.

Jazmine snickered. "Where would you like me to start? She has this old boyfriend that she dumped or he dumped her—I don't know which—but she won't even say his name. I heard her talking to Mom, and every time she got close to mentioning his name, she called him that-man-I-used-to-date. Is that ridiculous or what?"

Adam murmured a noncommittal reply.

"That's not all. Shana used to have a regular job, a really good one for a drug company. Mom said she made fabulous money, but she quit after she broke up with this guy. Then she bought the ice-cream parlor. She doesn't know a thing about ice cream or pizza or anything else."

Still, Adam had to admire her entrepreneurial spirit. "She seems to be doing all right."

"That's only because she phones the former owners ten times a day, and I'm not exaggerating. She finally figured out she can't do everything on her own and she hired a lady to come in during the afternoons to help her. I'm only nine-going-on-ten, and *I* figured that out before she did." Jazmine stopped abruptly, as if something had just occurred to her. "You're not *attracted* to her or anything, are you?"

Adam relaxed in his chair and crossed his ankles. "Well…I think she's kinda cute."

"No, no, no!" Jazmine said, more loudly this time. "I was afraid this would happen. This is terrible!"

Adam loved the theatrics. "What is?"

"Shana," Jazmine cried as if it should all be perfectly logical. "What about *Mom?* If you're going to fall in love with anyone, make it my mom. She needs you, and you'd be a great stepdad."

"Jazmine," he said, the amusement suddenly gone. "I think the world of your mother. She's a wonderful woman, and I love her dearly, but—"

He had no idea how to put this without upsetting her. "Your mother and I, well…"

"You love her like a sister," Jazmine finished for him. She sounded resigned and not particularly surprised.

Adam almost wished he *could* fall in love with Ali. Perhaps if he'd met her before Peter did, things would've been different. But he hadn't, and now it was impossible to think of Ali in any other way.

"That's pretty astute of you," he said.

"What's astute?"

"Smart."

Jazmine sighed heavily. "Not really. I said something about you to Mom, and what she said is she loves you like a brother."

So it was a mutual feeling, which was a relief. "Did your mother tell you she was ready for another relationship?" he asked.

"I think she is," Jazmine replied after a thoughtful moment. "But I don't know if *she* knows it." She hesitated, and he could almost see her frown of concentration. "Mom's been different the last few months." She seemed to be analyzing the situation as she spoke. "She's less sad," Jazmine went on. "We talk about Dad a lot, and Mom laughs now and she's willing to do things and go places again. I guess someone mentioned that to the Navy, because they decided to give her sea duty."

"I'm grateful your mother's feeling better about life. When the time's right, she'll meet someone special enough to be your stepdad."

"But it won't be you."

Adam heard the sadness in her voice and regretted it. "It won't be me," he said quietly.

"You *are* attracted to Shana though, right?"

"Maybe." That was all he'd admit. He found himself wondering about the man Shana had recently dumped or been dumped by.

"So this guy she used to go out with—"

"They were *engaged,* I think, but she won't talk about it." There was a pause. "She didn't get a ring, though."

Engaged? Even an unofficial engagement suggested this had been a serious and probably long-term relationship. Which could explain why Shana had seemed so skittish.

"Are you gonna ask her out, Uncle Adam?"

Adam wasn't prepared to make that much of a commitment, not yet, anyway. "Uh, we'll see."

"I think she'd say yes," Jazmine said brightly. "Don't you?"

"I don't know. Some women seem to need a man in their lives, but…" His voice trailed off; he wasn't sure how to complete that thought.

Jazmine muttered a comment he couldn't hear.

"Pardon?" he said.

"Just remember, she's got issues—lots and lots of issues."

Adam managed to stifle a chuckle. "I'll do my best to keep that in mind. Listen, Jazz, do you feel okay now?"

"Yeah... I guess I should come out before Shana finds me in here. Oh!"

That small cry was followed by some muffled words, but he caught the drift of what was happening. Shana had just discovered where Jazmine had taken the phone.

Chapter Six

"You don't like him, do you?" Jazmine asked the next day as they drove home from the restaurant. She sat next to Shana with her arms defiantly crossed.

Shana knew better than to pretend she didn't understand that her niece was referring to Lieutenant Commander Adam Kennedy. "I think your uncle Adam is…nice." The word was lame and the hesitation was long, which gave Jazmine cause to look at Shana intently. But really, what else could she say? Her unexpected attraction to this man had completely overwhelmed her. She could only hope it passed quickly. How could she be devastated by her breakup with Brad and at the same time, experience all the symptoms of extreme attraction toward another man? A man she'd met for about five minutes and been determined to dislike on sight.

"He's really cute, too." Jazmine seemed to feel obliged to remind her of this.

As if Shana needed a reminder.

"He is, isn't he?" Jazmine challenged.

"All right, he's cute." The words nearly stuck in her throat, but with no small effort, Shana managed to get them out. She didn't know why Jazmine was so insistent. The girl seemed to think she had a point to prove, and she wasn't letting up until she got Shana to confess she was interested in Adam Kennedy. She wasn't, of course. Okay, she was, but that was as far as it went. In other words, if he asked her out, which he wouldn't, she'd refuse. Well, she might consider it briefly, but the answer would still be no.

Jazmine was suspiciously quiet for several minutes and then gave a soft laugh. "I bet you're hot on him."

"What?" Shana nearly swallowed her tongue. The last thing she needed was Jazmine telling Adam this. "No way," she denied vehemently. She could only pray that wasn't what Jazz had said to Adam in the closet.

One glance told her Jazmine didn't buy her denial. She shouldn't have bothered to lie.

"You're saying that because of your old boyfriend, aren't you?"

"Absolutely not," Shana protested. She stepped hard on the brake at a stop sign she'd almost missed, jerking them both forward. Thank goodness for seat belts. Glaring at her niece, she asked, "Who told you that?"

Jazmine blinked wide eyes at Shana. "I overheard my mom talking to you. I wasn't listening in on your conversation, either, if that's what you're thinking. I tried to find out from Mom, but all she'd tell me was that your heart was broken, and that's why you moved to Seattle."

Shana was too tired to argue and too emotionally drained to be upset with her sister. If Ali had told Jazmine about Brad, then it was because she felt Jazmine needed to know. "I'm completely over Brad. I'm so over him it's hard to remember why I even got involved with him." The words had begun to sound like a worn-out litany.

"Brad," Jazmine said, and seemed satisfied now that she knew his name.

Shana struggled to hide her reaction. Even the mention of Brad's name irritated her. She might have worked the last twelve hours straight, and on her feet at that, but she had enough energy left to maintain her outrage toward Brad. Still, she would've preferred never to talk about him—or hear about him—ever again.

"You still have a heart, though," Jazmine pressed. "Right?"

"Of course I have a heart." Shana didn't know where this was leading and she didn't care, as long as it didn't end up on the subject of Adam Kennedy.

"That's why you're so hot on my uncle Adam." Darn.

"I am *not* hot on your *uncle* Adam."

"Are too."

"Am not."

"Are too."

"Jazmine!"

Her niece laughed and despite her irritation, Shana smiled. This was not a conversation she wanted to have, but she'd walked right into it and was determined to extricate herself as gracefully as possible. "Don't get me wrong," she said in conciliatory tones. "I think he's a very nice man, but I don't want to get involved with anyone at the moment. Understand?"

Jazmine bit her lower lip, as if she wanted to argue, but apparently changed her mind. "For how long?"

Shana decided to nip this question in the bud. "Forever."

"That long?" Jazmine threw her a crushed look. "You don't want children? That means I'll never have cousins!"

"Okay, months and months, then." At this point Shana was ready to agree to just about anything.

"Months," Jazmine repeated. She seemed to accept that—or at any rate ventured no further argument.

Shana parked in front of her house, grateful to be home. "You know what? I don't want to cook. Do you have any suggestions?"

"I can open a can of chili," Jazmine said. "I'm not very hungry."

Shana wasn't all that hungry, either. "Sounds like a perfectly good dinner to me."

"Let me do it, okay?"

"Thanks, Jazz." Shana had no intention of turning down this generous offer. "Fabulous." Then considering her role as guardian, she felt obliged to ask, "Do you have any homework?"

"A little."

Now came the dilemma. A really good substitute mother would tell Jazmine to forget dinner; Shana would rustle up a decent meal while the kid did her schoolwork. A woman of character would insist on opening that can of chili herself. But not one with tired feet and the start of a throbbing headache, brought on by all this talk about Adam Kennedy.

Once inside the house, Shana left the front door open to create a cooling breeze. She lay back on the sofa and elevated her feet. It was little wonder the Olsens had been ready to sell their restaurant. This was hard work. For part of each day, Shana had her face buried in three-gallon containers of ice cream. Her nose felt like she was suffering from permanent frostbite.

Jazmine immediately went into the kitchen and started shuffling pans, clanking one against the other. "Do you need any help?" Shana felt she had to ask, but the question was halfhearted, to say the least.

"No, thanks."

"This is really very sweet of you."

Jazmine grumbled a reply and Shana realized she'd failed again. A kid like Jazmine, who wore ankle-high tennis shoes to school, didn't take kindly to the word *sweet.* Sooner or later, Shana would need to develop a more appropriate vocabulary. Later, she decided.

A good ten minutes passed and if not for the sounds coming from the kitchen, Shana would be napping by now. Her head rested against the cushion, her feet were propped up and all was well. For the first time since she'd arrived, Jazmine was talking freely with her. She wasn't sure whether she should credit Adam Kennedy with this improvement or not. She'd rather think she was making strides in her relationship with her niece due to her own efforts.

"Uncle Adam says you need a man in your life."

Her peace shattered, and Shana's eyes sprang open. She sat up, swung around and dropped her feet to the floor. "*What* did you just say?"

Jazmine appeared in the doorway between the kitchen and the living room, wearing a chagrined expression. "I…Uncle Adam said you're the kind of woman who needs a man in her life."

That did it. She'd utterly humiliated herself in front

of him, and he thought…he *assumed* she was making some kind of play for him. This was the worst possible scenario.

"Shana?" Jazmine whispered. "You look mad."

She wondered if the smoke coming out of her ears was any indication. "That's ludicrous!"

"I'm pretty sure he meant it as a compliment."

Shana doubted it, but gave her niece credit for some fast backtracking.

"He thinks you're beautiful."

He did? Although it shouldn't have mattered, his comment gave Shana pause. "He said that?"

Jazmine hesitated. "Well, not exactly."

Okay, then. "Listen, it's not a good idea for us to talk about your uncle Adam right now." When she saw him next, she'd have plenty to say, though.

"You don't want to talk about him?"

"Nope." The kid was catching on fast.

"You don't want to talk about Brad, either."

Right again. "You could say men aren't my favorite topic at the moment."

"I guess not," Jazmine said pensively. "I won't mention either of them if that's what you want."

"I want." Her serenity gone, Shana gave up the idea of resting and joined Jazmine in the kitchen. Her niece's backpack was propped against the kitchen chair; she seemed to keep it close at all times.

Despite her intentions to the contrary, Shana gave the sexy lieutenant commander plenty of thought. What she had to do was keep her distance. She would be polite and accommodating if he wanted to spend time with Jazmine, but other than that, she'd be cool and remote. Never again would she allow him the opportunity to suggest that she needed a man—least of all him.

Jazmine stirred the chili with her back to Shana. "I probably shouldn't have said anything."

"Don't worry about it." Shana was eager to drop the subject.

"You're not mad, are you?"

"Not anymore," Shana assured her.

"You look mad."

"I'm not," she said.

"Are too."

"Am not."

"Are too."

"Am not."

They both broke out laughing. Obviously Jazz remembered that this childish interchange had amused her earlier, and she wasn't above repeating it.

Shana had to admit it felt good to laugh with her niece; it was almost like having her sister there. Jazmine was a petite version of Ali and after she'd lowered her guard, they got along well.

Shana wondered if she should clarify her position in case Adam asked Jazmine about her again or made some other ridiculous statement. No, she decided. She'd enlighten him herself.

"You know you're not getting any younger," Jazmine said out of the blue.

Once Shana got over her shock, she had to acknowledge that the kid was ruthless in achieving her goals. She went directly for the jugular. But Shana kept her response light. "After a day like this one, that's certainly true."

On Saturday morning, Jazmine agreed to come down

to the ice-cream parlor with her. In fact, Shana had no choice but to bring her. Catherine, her employee, wouldn't be in until that afternoon.

At this point Catherine was only part-time, but with the summer traffic, business was picking up and she'd need a second part-time employee. As the season progressed and the parlor was open later in the evening, she'd add more staff. The Olsens had told her that her biggest expense would be the staff payroll and warned her not to hire more people than she needed. Shana had taken their words to heart, doing as much as she could herself.

"Can I bring my Rollerblades?" Jazmine asked, standing in the doorway of her bedroom.

"Sure." Shana hated the thought of Jazmine hanging around the restaurant all day with nothing to do. Since Lincoln Park was directly across the street, there'd be plenty of paved sidewalks for her to skate. It would be a good opportunity to meet other girls her age, too.

By noon the parlor was crowded. Shana worked the pizza side and Catherine, a grandmotherly woman in her early sixties, dealt with the ice-cream orders. Catherine had been recommended by the Olsens and was great with kids. Shana had already learned a lot from her.

A young red-haired man with two children about three and five came in and ordered a vegetarian pizza and sodas. While Shana assembled the pizza, she watched the man with his kids, admiring the way he entertained them with inventive games.

Jazmine rolled into the parlor, stopped to take off her skates and before long was deep in conversation with the father and his two kids. Shana couldn't hear what was being said, but she saw the man glance in her direction and nod.

A couple of minutes later, Jazmine joined Shana in the kitchen, which was open to the main part of the restaurant.

"Hi," Shana said, sliding the hot pizza from the oven onto the metal pan. As she sliced it, the scent of the tomato sauce and cheese and oregano wafted toward her.

"He's single."

"Who?" Shana asked distractedly as she set the pizza on the counter. "Do you want to take this out to the guy with the kids?" she asked.

"Can I?" Jazmine beamed at being asked to help out.

Her niece carefully carried the pizza to the table and brought extra napkins. She chatted with the man and his children for a few more minutes, then hurried back to Shana, who was busy preparing additional pizzas. "He asked me to introduce you."

"What?"

Jazmine's eyes widened with impatience. "I was telling you earlier. He's divorced and he wants to meet you."

"Who? The guy over there with the kids?"

"Do you see any other guy in here?"

The restaurant had any number of patrons at the moment, but the young father was the only man—and the only customer looking in her direction. He saluted her with a pizza slice.

Flustered, Shana whirled around and glared at Jazmine. "Exactly what did you say to him?"

"Me? I didn't say anything—well, I did mention that you broke up with Brad, but that was only because he asked. He said he's been in here before."

Shana didn't remember him.

"I told him that my uncle Adam said you're the kind of woman who needs a man in your life."

Shana's heart stopped. "You didn't!"

"No." Jazmine hooted with laughter. "But I thought it would get a rise out of you."

The kid seemed to think she was being funny, but Shana wasn't laughing.

"Are you interested? Because if you are, let's go say hello to him. If you're not, it's no big deal."

Shana needed to think about this. "Promise me you didn't tell him I'm single."

"I did, and I said you were looking for a husband," Jazmine said gleefully. "You don't mind, do you?"

Shana felt the blood drain out of her face. Slowly turning her head, she saw the father still watching her. She jerked around again and noticed that Jazmine was grinning from ear to ear.

"Gotcha," she said and doubled over laughing.

Shana was glad someone found her embarrassment amusing.

Chapter Seven

Jazmine had her nose pressed against the living room window early on Sunday afternoon, waiting for her *uncle* Adam. He'd phoned the previous Monday, promising to take her out for the day. He'd mentioned the Museum of Glass in Tacoma, where there was a large Dale Chihuly exhibit.

Shana was almost as eager to see the lieutenant commander as her niece was, but for distinctly different reasons. She had a thing or two she wanted to say; he didn't know it yet, but the lieutenant commander was about to get an earful. How *dare* he suggest she needed a man! Every time she thought about it, her irritation grew—until she realized she couldn't keep quiet for even one more day.

At twelve-forty-seven precisely, Jazmine dashed away from the window and announced, "He's here!"

"Good." Shana resisted the urge to race outside and

confront him then and there. She'd need to bide her time. She'd waited this long—ten whole days. What was another five minutes?

Jazmine held the screen door open, swinging it wide in welcome. "You aren't late or *anything*," she boasted so eagerly it was endearing.

"Hiya, kiddo," Adam greeted Jazmine and gave her a big hug. "It's good to see you."

"You, too! It didn't seem like Sunday would ever get here."

Shana stepped forward, saying, "Hello, Adam," in cool, level tones.

He grinned boyishly and for an instant Shana faltered. But no, she wasn't about to let him dazzle her with one of his smiles. Not this time. Her defenses were up. As far as she was concerned, he had some serious explaining to do. Still, she had to admit this guy was gorgeous. Well, *gorgeous* might be a slight exaggeration, but with those broad shoulders and the way his T-shirt fit snugly across his chest, she couldn't very well ignore the obvious. His arm was out of the sling now.

"You'd better grab a sweater," Shana suggested and Jazmine instantly flew out of the room, eager to comply so they could leave.

This was the minute Shana had been waiting for. "It's time you and I had a little talk," she said, crossing her arms.

"Sure," he said with another of those easy grins.

Again she faltered, nearly swayed by his smile, but the effect didn't last. "I want you to know I didn't appreciate the comment you made about me being—and I quote—'the kind of woman who needs a man.'"

To his credit, his gaze didn't waver. "Jazmine told you that, did she?"

So it was true. "As a matter of fact, Jazmine has re-peated it any number of times."

"I see." He glanced toward the bedroom door; Jaz-mine hadn't come out yet.

Shana sincerely hoped she'd embarrassed him. He deserved it. "I don't know where you get off making comments like that but I have a few things to say to you."

"Go right ahead." He gestured as though granting her permission to speak. That must be how it was in the mil-itary, she thought. These officers seemed to think they could say and do whatever they pleased—*and* they got to boss other people around. Well, Shana wasn't mili-tary and she felt no restraint in speaking her mind. And she refused to call this guy by his title. He wasn't *her* commander.

"Are you married, *Mr.* Kennedy?" She already knew the answer and didn't give him an opportunity to re-spond. "I believe not. Does being single make you feel in any way incomplete?" Again he wasn't allowed to an-swer. "I thought not. This might come as a shock to you, but I am perfectly content with my life as it is. In other words, I don't need a man and your insinuating that I do is an insult."

"Shana—"

"I'm not finished yet." She held up her hand, cutting him off because she was just getting started. Before he left, she expected a full apology from Adam Kennedy.

"By all means continue," he said, his pose relaxed.

His attitude annoyed her. He acted as though he was indulging her, which Shana found condescending. "Since you're single you must want a woman in your life." She gave him the once-over. "In fact, you look like a man who *needs* a woman."

To her horror, Adam simply laughed.

"I was trying to make a point here," Shana said in as dignified a tone as she could manage.

"I know," he said and made an attempt to stifle his humor.

That only served to irritate her further. "Never mind. I can see my opinion is of little interest to you."

Suddenly they both turned to see Jazmine, who stood rooted in the bedroom doorway, a sweatshirt draped over her arm. "I should've kept my mouth shut, right?" she murmured apologetically. "I'm afraid Aunt Shana might've taken what you said the wrong way."

"So I gathered." He looked down, but Shana saw that the corners of his mouth quivered.

"Shana's right, you know," Jazmine stated for Adam's benefit, as she moved toward them. "You do need someone special in your life."

Adam's smile disappeared.

Aha! She wondered how he'd feel being on the other side.

"Jazmine took your comments to heart," Shana primly informed him. "She tried to match me up with a divorced father of two."

Adam's gaze shot to Jazmine.

"Well… It didn't work out—but I'd be a good matchmaker."

As far as Shana could tell, Jazmine was completely serious. *That* had to stop. She certainly didn't need her niece dragging eligible bachelors into the pizza kitchen every chance she got.

"He might've been interested, too," Jazmine added. "He seemed really nice."

"I don't need anyone's help, thank you very much," Shana insisted.

"Hold on," Adam said, glancing from one to the other. He motioned at Jazmine. "Go back to the beginning because I think I missed something."

"I found out he was single and I told him my aunt was, too, but that was all I did. She wouldn't let me introduce her."

"This is entirely your fault." Shana felt it was important that Adam understand it was his comment that had begun this whole awkward situation.

"You're finished with Brad," Jazmine reminded her. She turned to Adam and added, "He's the guy previously known as the-man-I-used-to-date. Sort of like Prince. That's what Mom said, anyway."

Adam burst out laughing.

"There is a point to this, isn't there?" Shana asked her niece.

Jazmine nodded and threw one fist in the air. "Get out there, Aunt Shana! Live a little."

Adam laughed even more.

"You think this is funny, don't you?" Shana muttered. He wouldn't find it nearly as funny when Jazmine was busy selling his attractions to single women in the museum.

"I'm sorry." But he didn't look it. For her niece's sake, she resisted rolling her eyes.

"I think it's time we cleared up this misunderstanding," he said and gestured toward the sofa. "Why don't we all sit down for a moment?"

Shana didn't take a seat until Adam and Jazmine had already made themselves comfortable on the sofa.

To her chagrin, Adam smiled patiently as if explaining the situation to a child. "I'm afraid Jazmine read more into my comment than I intended," he began. "What I said was that *some* women seem to need a man in their lives. I wasn't talking about you. Although, of course, any man in his right mind would be attracted to you. You're a beautiful woman."

"Oh." It would be convenient if Shana could magically disappear about now, but that was not to be. "I see. Well, in that case, I won't hold you up any longer." She sprang to her feet, eager to get them both out the door before she dissolved into a puddle at his feet. "I—that's a very nice thing to say…" She stared at her watch.

Adam took the hint and stood, and Jazmine rose with him. "Is there any special time you want her back this evening?" he asked.

"No…anytime is fine," she said, then quickly reconsidered. "On second thought, Jazmine has school tomorrow so she shouldn't be out too late."

"I'll have her here by seven."

"Thank you." Shana waited by the door as they left, her heart going a little crazy as she tried to regain her composure.

"Bye, Aunt Shana."

"Bye."

She closed the door. She'd hoped to put the mighty naval officer in his place and all she'd managed to do was amuse him. Depressed, Shana sank into the closest chair and hid her face in her hands—until she realized something. For the first time since Jazmine had arrived, she'd called her Aunt Shana. Twice.

Apparently her status had been sufficiently elevated that the nine-year-old was no longer ashamed to be related to her. That, at least, was progress.

* * *

Adam waited until they'd almost reached Tacoma before he mentioned the scene at Shana's. Jazmine had barely said a word from the moment they'd left. Now and then she glanced in his direction, as if she was afraid he was upset, but really he had no one to blame but himself. He did know women who were lost without a relationship, although he didn't think Shana was like that. Intentionally or not, Jazz had misunderstood his remark and used it for her own purposes.

"You really did it this time," he murmured.

"Are you mad?"

"No, but your aunt was."

"I know, but don't you be mad, okay?"

"I shouldn't have said anything. You and I should not have been discussing male-female relationships."

"Did you mean what you said about my aunt being beautiful and all that?"

"Yes." This was only the second time he'd seen Shana; again, he'd come away wanting to know her better. He might have ruined any chance of that, but he hoped not. When he'd started out from Everett, he'd considered inviting Shana to join them. But it hadn't taken him long to decide that today probably wasn't opportune.

"What I told your aunt is the truth. She is a beautiful woman," he said casually as he headed south on the interstate.

"She likes you."

Adam chuckled.

"No, I'm serious. She's got the hots for you. I can tell."

"I don't think so." Back to reality. Shana might be attracted to him, but she'd never admit that now.

"I know so!"

"Jazmine, listen…"

"Okay, but can I say what I want to first?"

Apparently she was taking lessons from her aunt Shana. "Fine."

"I was thinking about what you said—about not feeling sparks with Mom. But I thought you might with Aunt Shana."

"Jazmine, you're far too interested in matters that are none of your concern. How do you know about this stuff, anyway? MTV?"

She groaned. "Why do adults always say things like that?"

"Because they're true."

"All I want is for you to marry her and be happy."

"Uh…"

"Has the cat got your tongue?" Jazmine teased. "Adults say that, too. No, really, I *am* serious. If you married my aunt Shana, everything would be perfect. She needs a husband and you need a wife."

"I don't need a wife," he argued. "And it's none of—"

"But you'd like to be married one day, wouldn't you?" she broke in.

"Yes," he said reluctantly. He'd had the very same thought just recently, but he'd credited that to feeling sorry for himself after the surgery. Granted, Shana was attractive but he didn't need a nine-year-old playing matchmaker. Although… He smiled involuntarily. Shana appealed to him, and he was more and more inclined to pursue the relationship. On his own schedule and in his own way.

"I can help," Jazmine offered.

"It would be best if you left this between your aunt and me. Agreed?"

After a moment, Jazmine nodded. "Agreed."

"Good, now let's have a wonderful day, all right?"

Jazmine turned a smile of pure joy on him. "All right."

A surprise awaited him when they arrived at the Museum of Glass. The Dale Chihuly exhibit was in the Tacoma Art Museum and Union Station, not in the nearby Museum of Glass. Jazmine and Adam took the guided walking tour of his permanent display and were awestruck by the Bridge of Glass. The five-hundred-foot pedestrian bridge linked the Tacoma waterfront to Pacific Avenue.

Originally Adam had gotten information about Chihuly over the Internet when he was researching a destination for today's outing. Chihuly was known for his massive glass installations, but the man's talent was even more impressive than Adam had realized. Both he and Jazmine loved his vibrant use of color and unique style. Following the walking tour, they stopped at the Museum of Glass. Adam was in for a surprise there, too. The museum was huge: it contained thirteen thousand square feet of open exhibition space. Jazmine was enthralled by the Hot Shop Amphitheater, which was the building's most striking feature. Cone-shaped, it leaned at a seventeen-degree angle, and was ninety feet high and a hundred feet wide. The theater included a glass studio where a team of artists blew and cast glass. Afterward, Adam and Jazmine ate sandwiches in the museum café and visited the gift shop. When Adam had suggested this, it had seemed like an entertaining thing to do, but he'd quickly become caught up in the excitement and drama of watching the artists work.

By the end of the afternoon, he needed a break, and

sat with a cup of coffee while Jazmine leafed through a book he'd bought her.

Before they left, Jazmine bought a postcard of the Dale Chihuly glass flowers displayed on the ceiling of a Las Vegas casino to send her mother.

"Are you ready to go back to your aunt's?" he asked, sipping his coffee.

"I guess," Jazmine said. "But only if you are."

Adam recognized a trap when he saw one. If he appeared too eager, little Jazmine might suspect he wanted to see Shana again. He did, but he sure wasn't going to admit it, especially to her.

Chapter Eight

For Shana, having an entire Sunday to herself was sheer luxury. Catherine was working at the restaurant and this was the first day she'd taken off since she'd purchased the business. Shana intended to take full advantage of this gift of time.

Working as many hours as she did, she'd been putting off a number of tasks and spent two hours doing paperwork. The Olsens had trained her well in every aspect of owning a restaurant, but they'd failed to warn her how much paperwork was involved. Getting everything organized wasn't difficult but it was time-consuming. After working all day and handling the closing in the evening, she was exhausted, and making sense of anything more than the remote control was beyond her.

Once the paperwork was up-to-date, she polished her toenails, and between three loads of wash, she luxuriated in a new mystery she'd been trying to read for weeks. She'd been reading at night in fits and starts, but couldn't manage more than fifteen or twenty minutes at a time. The author was one of her favorites but to Shana's surprise her mind kept wandering away from the page. She supposed it was because she felt guilty about all the things she should be doing.

When she wasn't fretting over that, her thoughts were on Jazmine and Adam. She knew they were going to the Museum of Glass, but that couldn't possibly take all afternoon. Well, maybe it could; she didn't know.

Finally Shana gave up and shut the book. This was Adam Kennedy's fault. Even when he was nowhere in sight, he wouldn't leave her alone.

When she could stand it no longer, Shana logged on to the computer and left her sister a message.

Sent: Sunday, June 12
From: Shana@mindsprung.com
To: Alison.Karas@woodrowwilson.navy.mil
Subject: Adam Kennedy: Friend or Foe?

Dear Ali,

Just checking in to let you know that despite our rocky start, everything's going well with Jazz and me. She's a great kid.

The upcoming week is the last of the school year. I'm thrilled at how quickly Jazmine has adjusted and how fast she's made friends. I guess she's had lots of practice. She's a tremendous help at the ice-cream and pizza parlor and insists on taking pizzas to the customers' tables, which I appreciate.

The other reason I'm writing is that I've got a question about Peter's friend, Adam Kennedy. I must have met him at Peter's funeral, but if so I don't remember. Jazmine seems to think you're romantically interested in him. Are you? You've never mentioned him before—at least not that I can recall. Before you make anything of this inquiry, I want it understood that I find him arrogant and egotistical. Jazmine, however, thinks the guy walks on water. They're off this afternoon to explore some glass museum. I'd be grateful if you'd tell me what you know about him. For instance, has he ever been married? If not, why? I don't want to give you the wrong impression or anything—I *do* find him arrogant. But he sort of interests me, too. Fill in the blanks for me, would you?

Love,
Shana

At six Shana tossed a salad for dinner. The house seemed terribly quiet, and she turned on the television for company. That wasn't like her. In all her years of living alone, she'd never once felt this lonely. At first she wondered if it was due to the breakup with Brad, but all she felt when she thought about him was regret for all that wasted time—and anger. She was just plain glad he was out of her life. In fact, she rarely thought of him at all and that surprised her.

Jazmine had been with her for only a few weeks, and already Shana couldn't imagine life without her. She missed Jazmine's energy—blaring her music or talking on the phone, or plying Shana with questions about all sorts of things. The difference between the unhappy nine-year-old who'd arrived on her doorstep and the girl she was now—well, it seemed nothing short of astonishing. She'd become extroverted, interested and...interfering.

A little after seven, Jazmine burst into the house. "I'm back!" she shouted.

Before Shana could issue a word of welcome, Jazmine regaled her with details of how they'd spent their day. She talked about the walking tour and chattered excitedly about watching the artists work in the Museum of Glass. She'd fed the seagulls along the waterfront on Rustin Way and then Adam had taken her for a quick visit to the zoo at Point Defiance Park. Shana could hardly believe the girl could talk so fast and breathe at the same time.

"I guess you had a completely rotten time?" Shana asked, teasing her. Shana realized as she spoke that the lieutenant commander was nowhere in sight. "Where's Adam?"

"We were kind of late and he had to get back." Jazmine's smile widened. "Did you *want* him to come inside?"

"Not really. I just thought he might like to...visit for a few minutes." Actually, after the way she'd torn into him on his arrival, she didn't blame him for avoiding her.

"We should probably have a little talk," Shana said, slipping an arm around Jazmine's shoulders.

Her niece stiffened. "I have a feeling this is the same little talk Uncle Adam and I had, only now it's going to be the Aunt Shana version."

Her interest was instantly piqued. "Really? And what did Adam have to say?"

Jazmine gave a long-suffering sigh. "That it would be a good idea if I left the two of you alone."

"He's right." Shana was grateful Adam had taken it upon himself to explain this. Jazmine would accept it more readily coming from him.

"He also said I'm concerning myself with matters that aren't any of my business."

"Exactly." Obviously Adam had been very forthright during his version of the "little talk."

"I promised him I wouldn't try matching you up with other men."

"I'd appreciate that," Shana said solemnly.

Jazmine sighed again. "I wouldn't like it if you went around talking to boys about me."

That was exactly how Shana had planned to approach the subject herself. "Did Adam make that comparison?"

Her niece nodded. "He said it on the drive back."

"He's smarter than he looks," Shana muttered. Then, because she felt her niece should know this, she added, "A man and a woman can be friends without being romantically involved, Jazmine. It's called a platonic relationship."

The phone rang then, and without waiting for a second ring, Jazmine leaped like a gazelle into the other room. She ripped the receiver off the wall. "Hello," she said urgently. "No, she's here, you have the right number." Jazmine held out the phone. "It's for you."

Shana started to ask who it was, but didn't. Taking the receiver, she raised it to her ear. "This is Shana."

"Shana. I can't tell you how wonderful it is to hear the sound of your voice."

For the first time in her life, Shana's knees felt as if they were about to buckle. It was Brad.

"Hello, Brad," she said evenly, amazed at her ability to respond without emotion. The man had guts; she'd say that for him. "How'd you find me?" she asked coolly.

"It wasn't easy. It's taken me weeks."

She supposed she should be complimented that he'd made the effort, but she wasn't. "I don't mean to be rude, but there was a reason I kept my number unlisted."

"The least you can do is listen to what I have to say," he told her.

"Everything's been said."

"But Shana—"

"There's nothing more to say," she insisted.

"At least give me your address. I can't believe you're living in Washington. Did you get a transfer?"

"That's nothing to do with you."

Jazmine was watching her carefully, eyes wide and quizzical as if she was hoping to memorize each word so she could repeat it.

"I would prefer if you didn't phone me again." Shana was prepared to cut him off, but he stopped her, obviously guessing her intentions.

"Don't hang up," he pleaded. "Please, Shana, just hear me out."

"It won't do any good." She'd gone ramrod-straight, her resistance up. She didn't even find this difficult, although she had to admit she was mildly curious as to why he'd sought her out.

"I don't care. I need to get this off my chest. Just promise me you'll listen."

She didn't want to encourage him with a response.

He continued despite that. "You told me you were leaving Portland, but I didn't believe you. Shana, I miss you. I need you. Nothing is the same without you. I feel so empty. You have no idea how awful it's been for me."

That was their problem in a nutshell. The entire relationship had revolved around Brad Moore and his needs. *He* missed her, *he* needed her. She was convenient, loyal and endlessly patient. Well, no more.

She rolled her eyes and made a circular motion with her hand as though to hurry him along.

Jazmine planted her hand over her mouth to smother her giggles.

"Are you listening?" he asked, finishing up a five-minute soliloquy about how much he missed all their special times. Translation: all the "special" times when she'd been there to see to his comfort. He recounted the little ways she'd indulged him—the meals she'd cooked according to his likes and dislikes, the movies she'd watched because he'd chosen them, the Christmas shopping she'd done for him… Not once did he say any of the things that might have changed her mind, including the fact that he loved her.

So far, everything he'd said reaffirmed her belief that she'd made the right decision. It would always be about Brad and what he needed from her and how important she was to his comfort. Apparently Sylvia wasn't nearly as accommodating as Shana.

Finally she couldn't take it any longer.

"Are you finished yet?" she asked and yawned rudely to signal her boredom.

Her question was followed by a short silence. "You've changed, Shana."

"Yes," she told him in a curt voice. "Yes, I have."

"I can't believe you don't love me anymore."

Shana noticed he hadn't even bothered to ask about the girl who'd answered the phone.

Brad seemed shocked that she wasn't ready to race back into his arms just because he'd made an effort to find her. A short while ago, she'd been grateful for each little crumb he'd tossed her way. Those days were over. Oh, this felt good. *She* felt good.

"What's happened to my sweet Shana?" he asked. "This isn't like you."

"I woke up," she informed him, "and I didn't respect the woman I'd become. It was time to clean house. Out with the old and in with the new."

The line went silent as he absorbed this. "You're dating someone else, aren't you?"

The temptation to let him believe that was strong, and she might have given in to it, if not for Jazmine. With her niece listening to every word, Shana felt honor-bound to tell the truth.

"It's just like you to think that, but no, I'm not seeing anyone else." She bit back the words to tell him she could if she wanted to. Well, there was that single father who might've been interested—and Adam Kennedy.

His relief was instantaneous. "You'll always love me...."

"No," she said firmly. "I won't. I don't. Not anymore. For your sake and mine, please don't call me again."

He started to argue, but Shana wasn't willing to listen. She should've hung up the phone long before, but some perverse satisfaction had kept her on the line.

As she replaced the receiver, she looked over at Jazmine. Her niece gave a loud triumphant shout. "Way to go, Aunt Shana!"

They exchanged high fives. Shana felt exuberant and then guilty for not experiencing even the slightest disappointment. She was actually grateful Brad had phoned because this conversation had provided complete and final proof that she'd reclaimed her own life.

"Can I tell Uncle Adam about this?" Jazmine asked happily.

"Adam?" Her suspicions immediately rose to the surface. "Whatever for?"

"Because," Jazmine replied as if it should be obvious. "He should know that you really are over Brad. The door's open, isn't it? I mean, you're cured."

Shana liked the analogy. "I am cured, but let's just keep this between us for now, okay?"

Jazmine frowned. "If you say so," she said without enthusiasm.

The kid was certainly eager to get her and Adam together. Presumably she'd abandoned her earlier hopes for Adam and her mother. "I want your promise that you won't talk to Adam about any part of my conversation with Brad."

Muttering under her breath, Jazmine shook her head. Halfway to her room, she turned back. "Uncle Adam wanted me to tell you he'll be by next Saturday. That's all right, isn't it?"

"Of course it is." Not until later did Shana realize how dejected she was at the thought of waiting almost a week before she saw Adam Kennedy again.

Chapter Nine

Ali read Shana's e-mail a second time and smiled. This was exactly what she'd hoped—but didn't dare believe—would happen. Although her sister was skirting the issue, she was interested in Adam; her e-mail confirmed it. Adam had definitely gotten Shana's attention.

It took half an hour for Ali to answer her sister. She worked hard on the wording for fear she'd say too much or not enough. Adam was a lot like Peter in the ways that really mattered. He was loyal, compassionate, with a strong work ethic and an endearing sense of humor. Through the years, Peter had encouraged him to settle down and get married. Personally Ali didn't understand why Adam hadn't. Aside from the important stuff, he was good-looking. As far as she knew he dated, but obviously hadn't found the one woman with whom he wanted to spend the rest of his life. Could Shana be that woman? Far be it from her to suggest such a thing. Much better if a relationship developed without her meddling. From the sounds of it, they were getting all the romantic assistance they needed—or didn't need—from Jazmine.

Once she'd finished her e-mail, Ali prepared for her shift. It'd taken some adjustment, but she'd become accustomed to life aboard the aircraft carrier. Routine helped pass the days, and being able to stay in touch with her daughter through the Internet eased her mind about Jazmine.

The hours went by quickly as she responded to small medical emergencies.

She was almost finished with her shift when Commander Frank Dillon entered the sick bay. His complexion was sickly pale, and his forehead was beaded with sweat. When he saw that Ali was the duty nurse, he attempted a weak smile but she noticed that his jaw was clenched and he was clearly in pain.

Ali remembered him from her first day in the wardroom. Since then, she hadn't seen him at all but thought about him often, reliving those few seconds when he'd reached out to steady her in the passageway. Just seconds—it couldn't have been more than that. She didn't know why she'd read anything into such a minor incident. Still, she'd fantasized about him an embarrassing number of times in the weeks since. No one had to remind her of the professional issues involved in fraternization aboard ship.

"Commander Dillon," Ali said, coming forward to assist him. He held his hand pressed against his side. "What happened?"

"Something's wrong," he muttered. He looked as if he was close to passing out. "I need a doctor."

Ali led him into an examination room, and learned that he'd had a stomachache for the last couple of days. It'd had grown steadily worse and now the pain had become intolerable. She alerted Captain Robert Coleman, the physician on duty, who examined the commander.

Ali suspected it was his appendix, and apparently Dr. Coleman did, too. Following the examination, he ordered X-rays. Ali accompanied Commander Dillon while the X-rays were taken. The commander didn't utter a word, although she knew every touch, no matter how gentle, brought him pain.

One look at the film confirmed her fears. Time was critical; judging by the amount of pain he was suffering, his appendix could rupture any minute. Dr. Coleman scheduled emergency surgery, which he planned to perform immediately.

Ali helped prep the commander, explaining what was happening and why. She hooked up the IV and taped the needle in place. After checking the fluid bag, she glanced down and discovered him watching her. She smiled shyly, unaccustomed to such intent scrutiny.

Frank closed his eyes and drew in a deep breath.

Ali squeezed his hand. "Don't worry, we'll have you back to your command as good as new," she promised.

He was silent until just before he was rolled into the surgical bay. He gripped Ali's hand unexpectedly and with surprising strength. Half rising from the gurney, he said, "It's bad. Listen, if I don't make it…if there are complications…"

"You're going to live to tell about this, Commander,"

she assured him. She gave his hand another squeeze and urged him back down. Their eyes met and she did her best to let him know that the medical staff would take good care of him and all would be well.

The commander dragged in another deep breath. "I don't mean to sound fatalistic, but I don't have any family. My wife left me years ago—no kids. My brother died a few years back and I've never updated my will."

"I'm sorry about your brother," she told him softly.

His hand clutched hers. "Money to charity. Decide for me. Promise you'll decide for me."

"I will, but, Commander…"

He wasn't listening anymore, she realized. The pain was too intense.

"I'm going into surgery with you," she whispered. "If God decides it's your time, He'll have to argue with me first." Although she was certain he was past hearing anything, she thought she detected a faint smile.

As the surgery progressed, Ali wanted to chastise the commander for waiting so long to seek medical attention. He had risked his life because of—what? Pride? Ignoring the pain hadn't made it go away. An infected appendix was not going to heal itself.

The surgery was routine until they found that, exactly as she'd suspected, the appendix had burst. Extra time and care was needed to ensure that the infection was completely eradicated before it could spread to the entire abdominal area. Peritonitis could be fatal. Having a ruptured appendix wasn't as life-threatening as in years past, but it was serious enough.

After the surgery, Commander Dillon's incision was closed and he was taken into Recovery. Lieutenant Rowland was sent in to replace Ali, whose shift had ended.

"I'll stay with him a bit longer," she told Rowland. Sitting at the commander's bedside, she took his blood pressure every twenty minutes until he woke from the anesthesia several hours later.

He moved his head instinctively toward Ali, who sat by his side.

She smiled and touched his brow. "God didn't put up much of an argument. It seems that neither heaven nor hell was interested in collecting your soul, Commander."

"You sure about that?" he whispered weakly. "I thought this pain meant I was in hell."

"How are you feeling now?"

"Like someone hacked me open with a saw blade."

"I'll give you something for the pain." She stood and reached for his chart to make a notation. "Rest now. Your body's had quite a time of it." That was an understatement, but she felt better knowing he was awake. His vital signs confirmed that he was out of immediate danger.

Ali sat with the commander for another hour and then reluctantly turned her patient over to Rowland.

"Do you know the commander?" the lieutenant asked as she left the recovery area.

"I met him our first day out."

Rowland seemed surprised that she'd stayed with him. It surprised Ali, too. She was busy these days and got as little as four or five hours' sleep a night, but hadn't been able to make herself leave. One thing was certain: this man had her attention. Just as Adam had Shana's…

Frank Dillon was lost in a dark, lonely world. Every so often he heard a soft, feminine voice and it confused him. He couldn't figure out where he was. Then he remembered the pain, the surgery, the nurse—that soft voice was the nurse talking to him. The one who haunted his dreams. He prayed it was her and in the same breath pleaded for God to send her away. Her touch was light, and on the rare occasions when he found the strength to open his eyes, she was standing by his side.

She smelled good. Not of flowers or perfume, but a distinct womanly scent. Clean and subtle and…just nice. It lured him unlike anything else he'd ever experienced. He wasn't a man accustomed to the ways of women. He'd lived his life in the Navy and for the Navy, and he'd learned the hard way that he wasn't meant to be a Navy husband.

He'd married at twenty-five and Laura had left him two years later. That had been nearly twenty years ago. His wife had walked out when she realized no amount of crying, pleading or cajoling would persuade him to resign his commission. She knew before they were married that he'd made the Navy his career, the same as his father and grandfather had. Nothing was more important to Frank than duty and honor. Not his marriage, not Laura, not one damn thing. She hadn't been able to reconcile herself to that and he doubted any woman ever could. Other commitments took second place to military life. He'd accepted that, and dedicated himself to his career. Not once in all those years had he regretted his decision. Until now—and now he would willingly have sold his soul to keep this woman at his side. He needed her, wanted her and he didn't care what it cost him.

Some of his fellow officers had been against letting women serve at sea. Frank hadn't been one of them. Now he wasn't so sure his peers had been wrong. Senior Medical Officer Alison Karas had taken up far more of his thoughts than warranted. He'd decided from their first, chance encounter to stay away from her; he wasn't risking his career for a shipboard romance. Avoiding her was easy enough to accomplish with five thousand sailors aboard the *USS Woodrow Wilson*. It was just his luck that she was the one on duty. Luck or fate? He wasn't sure he'd like the answer.

A cool hand touched his brow, followed by Alison's quiet voice. Unable to make out the words, Frank thought it might have been a prayer. Apparently he was worse off than he'd known, although she seemed to think she had some influence with the Man Upstairs. Her constancy touched him. No one had ever done anything like that before—not for him.

The darkness didn't bother him anymore. He was at peace, even though a vague memory, something about Alison, hovered just out of reach. She was with him. He planned to tell her how much her presence meant to him.

If he lived through this.

The next morning, the *USS Woodrow Wilson* was hit by a raging storm. The massive ship had turned into the typhoon, and there was nothing to do but ride it out. Thankfully, Ali had never been prone to seasickness, but a number of men were sent to sick bay. She had her hands full the first day of the storm, but things had settled down by the second. During a quiet moment, she went in to check on Commander Dillon. He was sitting up in bed, still pale and not in the best of moods.

"What the hell is going on topside?" he demanded the moment he saw her.

"We're in the midst of a typhoon, Commander."

He tossed aside his sheet and seemed ready to climb out of bed. "Get me out of here."

"No." She prevented him from moving farther.

From the way his eyes widened, Ali could tell that it wasn't often anyone stood up to the high and mighty commander. "I'm the navigator and I'm needed topside," he argued, his face reddening.

"This might come as a shock, Commander Dillon, but the Navy stayed afloat without you for more than two hundred years. They'll manage to survive for another day or so. Now stay in bed, otherwise I'll have you restrained."

His blue eyes flared. "You wouldn't."

Although her heart was pounding, Ali didn't dare let her nervousness show. "I don't think that's something you'd like to find out. Your orders are to stay in bed until Captain Coleman says otherwise. Do I make myself clear?"

His gaze challenged hers, but then, apparently reaching a decision, he nodded. Although he wasn't happy about it, he would abide by what he knew was best.

Ali was grateful. Under normal circumstances, the commander wasn't a man to cross; she'd figured that out quickly enough. And if his scowl was any indication, he was on the mend. He'd been in bad shape the first few days, but his improvement was steady. To show him how much she appreciated his cooperation, she patted his arm.

He stiffened as if he found her touch offensive and Ali quickly backed away. While he was under anesthesia, she'd touched him many times. In an effort to comfort him, she'd stroked his brow and talked to him in soothing tones. She'd frequently taken his pulse and blood pressure and let her hand linger on his arm, hoping he'd sense her encouragement and concern. Perhaps she'd grown too familiar, too personal.

"I apologize," he muttered gruffly.

Embarrassed, Ali retreated an additional step. "No, the fault is mine—I'm sorry." By all rights, she should turn and leave. The clinic was busy. Sailors were waiting. She should get while the getting was good, as her grandmother used to say.

"You were with me in Recovery until I regained consciousness, weren't you?" he whispered.

She nodded, afraid they were taking a dangerous risk by acknowledging this attraction. Not since Peter's death had Ali allowed herself to feel anything for another man. In fact, she'd been certain she never would and now…now she wasn't sure what to think.

"Any particular reason you stayed with me all those hours?" he asked.

Ali didn't know what to tell him. Honesty might be the best policy, but there were times the truth was better avoided. This appeared to be one of those times.

"Your appendix had ruptured, Commander. In such cases, there's a significant chance of complications. It was easier for me just to remain on duty than explain the situation to my shift replacement." Ali used her best professional voice, making it as devoid of emotion as she could.

He seemed to accept her explanation and answered with an abrupt nod.

"Is there anything else I can do for you?" she asked, moving away from his bedside.

"Not a thing," he replied in clipped tones, and Ali knew he was referring to a whole lot more than his medical situation.

Chapter Ten

As promised, Adam Kennedy was at the restaurant by ten on Saturday morning. Shana had anticipated this moment—no, dreaded it—all week. She might've been able to push the lieutenant commander from her mind if it weren't for Jazmine, who found every excuse in the world to bring up his name. They could be discussing the migration habits of Canada geese, and Jazmine would somehow link the topic with her uncle Adam. It didn't matter *what* they discussed, Adam Kennedy became part of the conversation.

Shana didn't resent the fact that her niece called Adam her uncle anymore. It seemed natural for her to do so. What didn't seem natural—or fair—was the way he'd infiltrated her thoughts. And, in all honesty, that wasn't just due to Jazmine.

"Good morning," Adam said as he marched into the

restaurant with a crisp military gait that said he was ready for action. He wore black jeans and a casual denim shirt with the sleeves rolled up.

"Hi." Her voice faltered a little. This was one attractive man, a fact she was trying hard to ignore. Nonetheless, her hands trembled as she reached for a paper towel and wiped them clean. "Jazmine brought her Rollerblades." Thankfully it was early enough that the ice-cream parlor didn't have any customers yet.

"I saw. She put on a show for me in the parking lot."

"Oh." Now *that* was an intelligent response and Shana resisted the urge to kick herself. She intensely disliked the way Adam made her feel like an awkward teenager. Until recently, she'd considered herself a competent professional, a woman who could cope with any social situation, and it irked her no end that this man could agitate her like this. "Where are you two headed today?" she asked conversationally, hoping to hide her complete lack of a brain.

Adam sauntered up to the cash register, apparently in no hurry to leave. "I haven't decided yet. I thought I'd get some suggestions from Miss Jazz."

"Good idea." Before she sent him off with Jazmine, perhaps she should enlighten him about her niece's continuing efforts to match up the two of them. "Do you have a few minutes before you go?"

"Sure." He slid onto one of the stools.

Rubbing her palms against her apron, Shana took a moment to clear her thoughts. "I don't know if you've noticed," she began, "but Jazmine seems to be working hard at, uh, getting the two of us together." She paused. "This is in spite of your...little talk."

Adam leaned forward. "I got the hint in our last

phone conversation, when she started mentioning your name in practically every sentence."

"She does that to you, too?" Interesting. And, she supposed, predictable. "You're a frequent topic of conversation yourself."

He chuckled. "She's been e-mailing me updates on you."

"Updates on *what?*"

"I haven't paid a lot of attention."

She was unexpectedly miffed by that but decided his indifference was probably for the best.

"By the way, how's Brad?"

Shana nearly bit her tongue in an effort to hide her reaction. "I thought you said you weren't paying attention," she said. "Brad isn't important."

"Really? That's curious because—"

"I have something to discuss," she said, cutting him off before they both got sidetracked by the unpleasant subject of Brad.

"Have at it," Adam said, gesturing toward her.

"First, since we're both aware that Jazmine's busy playing matchmaker, it seems the best defense is to be honest with each other." She half expected an argument.

"I agree."

He seemed utterly relaxed; in contrast, Shana's nerves were as tight as an overwound guitar string.

"Okay," she said, taking a deep breath. "I think you're wonderful with Jazmine and…and mildly attractive." The man already had an overblown ego and she wasn't about to give him any encouragement.

"Really?" He perked up at that.

"Yes," she admitted reluctantly, "and there are probably a few other positive traits I could add."

He checked his watch. "I have time."

She ignored him. "But without going into why I feel a relationship between us wouldn't work—"

"Aren't you being a little hasty?" he asked without allowing her to finish.

"No," she insisted. "Besides, I'm not interested." She wondered if a big red neon light spelling *liar* was flashing over her head. She *was* interested, but she suspected this whole attraction thing was just the result of being on the rebound. She needed to take it slow, ease into another relationship. Letting Adam Kennedy sweep her off her feet was definitely a bad idea.

He stared at her blankly. "Interested in what?"

"You. I don't mean to be blunt or rude, but I felt I should be clear about that."

"No problem." He shrugged, his expression unchanged.

"I didn't mean to offend you."

"You didn't," he assured her and he certainly didn't look put off by her confession.

"It's just that this isn't the right time for me to get involved," she rushed to add, confused now and more than a little embarrassed. She wished she'd thought this through more carefully. "I've only had the business a short while, and all my energy and resources are tied up in it."

"Of course. That makes perfect sense."

"This has nothing to do with you personally." She was only digging herself in deeper now but couldn't seem to stop.

"Shana, it's not a problem. Don't worry, okay? If anything, it's a relief."

"It is?" she blurted out.

"We should keep each other informed," he murmured. "Just like you suggested. Jazmine is a sweet kid, but we both need to be aware of her game plan."

"Exactly." She felt guilty about the things she'd said. "I hope I didn't offend you—sometimes my tongue goes faster than my brain."

"Not at all," he told her patiently.

"Good." It was probably ridiculous to be so worried about a nine-year-old's scheme and even more ridiculous to mention it to Adam. Thankfully he'd taken everything with a sense of humor.

"Uncle Adam!" Jazmine skated into the parlor and at one glance from Shana, sat down and removed her skates. "Are you done yet? Can we leave now?"

"In a minute."

"Great!" Jazmine looked about as happy as Shana could remember seeing her. "School's out for the year." She slipped on her tennis shoes without bothering to tie them.

Shana's cheeks still burned with embarrassment and she was eager to see Adam and Jazmine leave. "You guys have a great time," she mumbled. "Bye."

Adam slid off the stool and with Jazmine at his side, they ambled out. After the door closed, Shana felt oddly depressed, although she couldn't name the precise reason. She didn't want to analyze it, either.

Business was slow for a Saturday, but experience told Shana it would pick up around lunchtime. She had two part-time employees now in addition to Catherine, the retired woman the Olsens had recommended, who was Shana's most valuable employee. She moved easily between the ice-cream section and the pizza parlor, and she was fully capable of taking over if Shana wanted time off, which was reassuring. This was the one buffer

Shana felt she needed now that she was Jazmine's guardian.

Around eleven, the young father Jazmine had talked to a few weeks earlier stepped into the restaurant. He was without his kids today. He strolled up to the pizza counter; from there he could see Shana in the kitchen, where she was busy stirring a vat of soup. She'd discovered a brand of concentrated soups that tasted as good as homemade and was pleased with the results.

"Hi," he said casually, leaning against the counter.

"Can I help you?" Shana pretended not to remember him, which was the exact opposite of the way she treated her other customers. She worked hard at remembering people's names and creating a warm and welcoming atmosphere. She knew his, too—Tim—but refused to acknowledge it.

"I was wondering if you'd be interested in dinner and a movie."

His invitation took her completely off guard. "I—I beg your pardon?"

"I...well, actually, I was asking you out on a date." His voice was a monotone now, as if she'd deflated his ego, and Shana instantly felt bad.

"I'm flattered, but—"

"Your niece mentioned that you're single, and well, so am I and I was wondering, you know, if you'd like to go out sometime."

Shana wasn't sure what to say. She hesitated, and then decided she could only be honest. "Thank you. I'm flattered that you'd ask, but I just don't have time to date right now." She motioned around her. "This is a new venture for me and I...have to be here."

He frowned. "Is there any particular reason you don't want to go out with me?"

A couple of dozen quickly presented themselves but Shana couldn't manage to get out a single one. "You seem very nice, but—"

"It's the kids, isn't it?"

"No, not at all," she hurried to assure him. "It's like I told you—the timing is wrong." That was the excuse she'd used with Adam; it was also the truth. She'd untangled herself from one relationship and wasn't ready to get involved in another.

"You mean I should've waited until you were finished for the day?"

"No…"

He wiped his face. "You'll have to excuse me. I'm new at this. My wife, I mean ex-wife, and I met in high school and well, it just didn't work out. I don't blame her. We were both too young, but Heather's the only woman I've ever dated and—I don't know what the hell I'm doing." He looked completely crestfallen by the time he'd finished.

Shana felt even worse. "Under other circumstances, I'd be happy to—" She stopped, afraid she'd just make matters worse if she continued. "Would you like a cup of coffee?"

He nodded and sat down on the stool. "That would be great, thanks."

"It's Tim, right?"

He smiled dejectedly. "I'm surprised you remember."

He'd be shocked at everything she did recall about the last time he'd been in the ice-cream parlor—even if she preferred not to.

Shana made them each an espresso, double shot. If he didn't need it she did. When she set the tiny cups on the counter, Tim reached for his wallet. Raising her hand, she said, "It's on the house."

"Thanks."

She waved off his gratitude. For reasons she didn't want to examine too closely, she felt guiltier than ever for rejecting him.

"Can you tell me what I did wrong?" he asked after the first tentative sip.

"It isn't you," she said earnestly. "It really is because of the timing. My new business and looking after my niece and everything."

Over the next three hours, she heard the story of Tim's ten-year marriage and every detail of his divorce. The only time he paused was when she was bombarded with questions from customers or staff, or if the capable Catherine needed her assistance.

She also learned practically the entire story of Tim's life. He seemed to need a willing ear and she provided it, between serving ice cream in three dozen different flavors.

"You know, Tim, it seems to me you're still in love with your wife," she commented while he was on his third espresso.

His eyes flared and he adamantly shook his head. "No way."

"Sorry, but that's how I see it."

"You're wrong."

"Could be, but it's obvious you're crazy about your kids."

He had no argument with that. "They're fabulous."

"So—what else can I do for you?" she asked when he showed no sign of leaving anytime within the foreseeable future.

"You could always go to dinner with me," he suggested.

Shana laughed, knowing she'd be in for a repeat of his disagreement with the divorce attorney. She gave him an A for effort, though. "I thought we already went over that."

"Are you sure you mean no?" he asked again.

"If the lady says no, that's what she means," Adam Kennedy said from the doorway leading into the restaurant. He glared at Tim as if he wanted to teach him a lesson. His tone was friendly enough, but his demeanor wasn't. Shana sighed in exasperation. She was all too aware of the interest Catherine and the others were taking in this little scene. Tim was harmless, his self-esteem in shreds following his divorce, and he was counting on Shana to boost his confidence.

"Thank you very much, Adam," she said tightly, fighting the temptation to say a great deal more, "but the lady can answer for herself."

To her surprise Jazmine laughed outright. "Hello, Mr. Gilmore, remember me?"

Tim looked as if he didn't know what to say. He got off the stool. "I guess it's time to go."

"Sounds like a good idea to me," Adam murmured.

"Adam," Shana chastised, but his gaze didn't waver from Tim's face.

As soon as the other man was out the door, Shana whirled on Adam. "That was completely unnecessary and uncalled for," she said, trying to keep her voice down in deference to her staff and customers.

Adam looked away. "Perhaps, but I wanted to be sure he got the message."

"And what exactly is the message?" Shana demanded.

Adam grinned as if the answer should be obvious.

"Hands off," Jazmine supplied. "You're already spoken for."

* * *

With her shift over, Ali went to check on Commander Dillon one last time and discovered he was asleep. His face was turned toward her and in slumber his features had relaxed. He looked younger than she'd first assumed.

As she stood there, Ali hesitated, resisting the urge to move closer. She longed to place her hand on his arm, to touch him and feel the warmth of his skin. A chill ran down her spine as she remembered he didn't want her anywhere near him. That had been made abundantly clear during her last visit.

She wished she had someone she could talk to about the way she felt. This wasn't something she could discuss with the other women on board. She could be putting her career in jeopardy. Any hint of a romantic entanglement, and she could be in more trouble than she wanted to consider.

Before she left, Ali logged on to her computer.

Sent: June 20
From: Alison.Karas@woodrowwilson.navy.mil
To: Shana@mindsprung.com
Subject: Hello!

Dear Shana,

Just wanted to see how you're doing this week. I think of you and Jazmine every day. I'm doing well myself. We had an emergency appendectomy this week—Commander Dillon. I might have mentioned him before. Before he went under, he seemed to think he might not make it, and asked if I'd look after his affairs. I told him I would, but thankfully that wasn't necessary. He's recuperating nicely now. I think he's

Ali hesitated, remembering the intense look in Frank's eyes as he confessed he had no family. What a lonely life he must lead. Divorced and his brother dead. It didn't sound as if his parents were still living, either. He'd wanted her to dispose of his earthly goods by giving whatever he had to charity. Ali told herself he didn't have time to ask anyone else; she'd been handy, so he'd reached out to her. Still, she sensed that he trusted her. They were basically strangers but he felt he could speak to her and that she would follow through with whatever he'd requested. Had it been necessary, she would have.

After a moment's hesitation, Shana returned to her e-mail. She deleted the last three words and began a new paragraph.

Jazmine mentioned that Adam was stopping by on Saturday. How did that go? I know you think my daughter's trying to match the two of you up and I agree she has no business doing that. But the truth is, I don't think it's such a bad idea.

Adam is a good man and while you might have a dozen excuses not to recognize what a find he is, look again. This is your big sister talking here. I mean it: take a close look at this guy. Adam is easy on the eyes (nice but not essential), he's intelligent and hard-working and wonderful with kids.

I just hope keeping Jazmine for the next six months will convince you that you want children of your own.

I can tell how close the two of you are getting just from the e-mails. It's almost enough to make me jealous!

Your e-mails mean the world to me. Keep them coming.

Love,
Ali

It didn't take long for Ali to get a response. She wasn't sure if it was because of the time difference or if she happened to catch her sister at the computer.

Sent: June 21
From: Shana@mindsprung.com
To: Alison.Karas@woodrowwilson.navy.mil
Subject: Commander, you say?

Dear Ali,

No, you didn't mention anyone named Commander Dillon. What gives? Is he all right? I assume he must be. But the fact that you're saying anything at all tells me you're interested in him. This is a development worth watching. I know, I know, all shipboard romances are strictly taboo. But tell me more!

I'm afraid I made an idiot of myself in front of Adam this morning. Trust me, any romantic interest he might have felt toward me is deader than roadkill. I'm such a fool.

All right, all right, I'll tell you what I did, but you've got to promise not to mention it again. I decided he should be aware of Jazmine's little scheme. That seems only fair, don't you think?

In retrospect, I still feel it needed to be said but maybe I didn't handle it in the best possible way. When I assured him I wasn't interested in him, I came off sounding like…I don't know what. I keep saying it, but this isn't the right time for me to get involved. It really isn't, not with just starting this business.

And guess what? Another guy, who was recently divorced, came in later this afternoon and asked me out. I turned him down using the same excuse and felt terrible. (By the way, it's thanks to the little matchmaker that he knew I was single.)

Oh, and did I mention Brad phoned? Let me tell you that was a short conversation. If I needed confirmation that I did the right thing in breaking up with him, our conversation was it.

Hearing from you is wonderful. Both Jazmine and I miss you terribly. I never realized how much effort went into being a parent. Don't get me wrong, Jazz is one fabulous kid and I'm crazy about her, but I didn't have any idea how much my life would change when she came to live with me.

You're right, Ali, I'm absolutely certain now that I want to be a mother one day. That's a bit intimidating, though. With everything that's happened in the last few months, I've pushed all thoughts of another relationship out of my mind. I still think I need to wait a while. Is that a biological clock I hear ticking? Not to worry, I have plenty of time. Lots of women have children when they're in their mid or even late thirties these days.

Nevertheless, I need a while to clear my head. Adam's attractive, for sure, and I might be interested in Tim if he wasn't so hung up on his ex-wife. (Tim's the divorced father I mentioned earlier.)

Write back soon and tell me more about this commander guy. He sounds like one of those mucky-muck officers. Is that good or bad?

Love ya,
Shana

Ali read the e-mail through twice and discovered she was smiling when she finished. She wasn't going to give up on Shana and Adam just yet.

Chapter Eleven

"It's summer," Jazmine announced the first Monday after the end of school. "Uncle Adam's got three days off. We should all do something special to celebrate."

Shana hated to discourage Jazmine's enthusiasm, but she couldn't leave her restaurant on a whim. "Do something?" she repeated. "Like what?"

That was all the invitation Jazmine needed. She hopped onto the barstool and rested her arms on the counter. "When my dad was stationed in Italy, he took me to Florence right after school was out. We had so much fun, and I saw Michelangelo's David. It's really cool, you know?"

"We have some interesting museums in the area," Shana suggested, but her heart wasn't in it. Given her druthers, of which she had few, she would opt to visit Victoria, British Columbia. She'd heard it was a lovely city and very English in style.

Jazmine sighed and shook her head. "I've been to dozens of museums, but that feels too much like a school outing. This should be *special.*"

"What about an amusement park?" Perhaps on Sunday Shana could stuff herself into a swimsuit, make Jazmine promise not to take her picture, and they could head for the local water park.

Again Jazmine was less than excited. "I suppose, but I'm looking for something that's not so...ordinary. Everyone goes to parks. This is a celebration. I survived a new school, made friends and Aunt Shana's still speaking to me." She giggled as she said this, and Shana laughed, too.

"We had a bit of a rough start," Shana acknowledged.

"It took me a while to adjust," Jazmine admitted in turn. "Uncle Adam helped me."

"With what, exactly?" She recalled the backpack advice, and the fact that he'd apparently told her to stop matchmaking—hadn't he?—but she didn't know what else he'd said.

"Never mind." Jazmine slid off the barstool. "That's an idea—I'll call Uncle Adam."

"To do what?" Shana asked, but her question went unanswered as Jazmine hurried toward the phone.

"You should take a day just for the two of you," Catherine suggested, apparently listening in on their conversation. "You've been here nearly every day for weeks."

"New business-owners don't take days off," Shana said. It was true that she'd spent every day at the restaurant, although she'd taken brief breaks and nearly one whole Sunday the week before. She'd felt like a new woman afterward. The thought of one entire twenty-four hour period when she didn't have her hands in pizza dough or her face in a three-gallon container of ice cream sounded heavenly. Getting away was just the respite she needed.

"It isn't for you as much as your niece," Catherine continued. "Kind of a reward for doing so well."

Shana knew she was right. Against the odds, Jazmine had succeeded in adapting to a new school and a new home, and she'd made friends.

A few minutes later, Jazmine set the phone aside and raced over to Shana. "Uncle Adam suggested visiting Victoria, B.C.," she said breathlessly. "I've never been there and he said it's a wonderful day trip."

"That does sound nice," Shana said wistfully. She was astonished at the way Adam's suggestion reflected her own earlier musings about Victoria. It was almost eerie.

"He wants to talk to you," Jazmine said. She ran to get the portable phone and handed it to Shana.

Shana walked into the back room, nervously tucking a strand of hair behind her ear. She'd moussed it into submission that morning, but whole sections were already attempting a breakout.

"Hello," she said and hoped her voice didn't betray her feelings. She thought about this man far too often and had an intense love-hate relationship with him that he knew nothing about. She was attracted to him and yet she didn't want to be. The fact that he—

"Shana?" Adam said, cutting into her thoughts.

"I'm here," she said primly.

"That's a great idea of Jazmine's. You can come, can't you?"

"To Victoria, you mean? Ah…"

"We'll make it a day trip. I'm off until Thursday. I'll pick you and Jazmine up, then we'll take the Fauntleroy ferry over to the Kitsap Peninsula, drive to Port Angeles and take another ferry across the Strait to Victoria."

"I...I'm—" Shana hesitated when she saw Jazmine staring at her with pleading eyes. She'd folded her hands as if in prayer, and Shana's resolve weakened. "I'll need to check with Catherine before I take a whole day." Shana instantly felt guilty; she'd invested her life savings in this business and she shouldn't be running off for a day of fun. She should be at work.

"Ask her," Adam urged.

Shana turned away from the phone and came face-to-face with Catherine, who had her hands on her hips. "Go. I'll manage just fine. It's only one day, for Pete's sake."

"But..."

"Aunt Shana," Jazmine said pulling on her arm. "Just do it. We'll have a blast."

Shana wasn't nearly as sure. That night, long after Jazmine was in bed and she herself should have been, she e-mailed her sister.

Sent: June 24
From: Shana@mindsprung.com
To: Alison.Karas@woodrowwilson.navy.mil
Subject: Jazmine, Adam Kennedy and me

Dear Alison,

As you probably already know, I'm going off on a day trip to Victoria, British Columbia, with Jazz and Adam. Basically I got talked into it, and I'll give you three guesses whose fault that is. Your daughter could talk circles around Larry King. Mark my words, that kid will have her own talk show one day.

Yes, Adam Kennedy will be there, too. I don't mind having him around anymore. I put up a good fight, let him know I wasn't interested in a relationship and even made a point of telling him about Jazz playing matchmaker. He listened politely and agreed with everything I had to say. The least he could've done was argue—just kidding! Without even trying, he's worn down my defenses. I have to admit I've enjoyed the time I've spent with him. Twice now, after he's visited Jazz, he's stayed for a cup of coffee and we've talked. There hasn't been a hint of romance, although, yes—I'm attracted. I definitely feel we have some chemistry, but I'm too preoccupied (and too scared!) to do anything about it.

Okay, I've bared my soul. It's your turn. What's up with you and this Commander Dillon? I know you, Ali. You wouldn't have mentioned him at all if you didn't care, so I repeat—what's up?

It's almost eleven and I should be in bed. Adam's arriving very early. I offered to drive over to his place, but he said it was no trouble coming to get us.

Write soon. Jazmine and I both look forward to your e-mails.

Love,
Shana

* * *

Less than twelve hours later, Shana was on a mid-morning ferry that had left Port Angeles for Vancouver Island. An excited Jazmine jogged up and down the outside deck while Adam and Shana drank cups of coffee inside. They were seated on wooden benches, across from each other.

"I can't believe I'm doing this," she muttered. The alarm had rung at four that morning and they were on the road by five.

"Did you see the Olympic Mountains?" Jazmine dashed inside shouting—as if they could possibly have missed them. "I learned in class that some of those mountains have never been climbed or explored."

This was news to Shana, but she wasn't much of an expert on Washington State history or geography.

"Do either of you know about Point Roberts?" Adam asked when Jazmine threw herself down on the bench, sitting next to Adam and across from Shana.

Both Shana and Jazmine shook their heads. "Never heard of it," Shana said.

"It's a little piece of the United States that is geographically part of Canada."

"What?" Jazmine frowned. "I don't get it."

"The United States and Canada are separated by the 49th parallel at Washington and British Columbia. There's a small point of land that drops below it. That's Point Roberts. Maybe we can go there sometime."

"So it's in Canada but not really?"

"Take a look at a map and you'll see what I mean."

While Jazmine walked over to examine the wall at the other end of the ferry, where a map of Washington was posted, Shana sipped her coffee and smiled at Adam. "She idolizes you, you know."

Adam shifted on the hard bench and crossed his arms. "As it happens, I think the world of her, too."

It was confession time for Shana, although what she had to say was probably no secret to Adam. "I was jealous of that in the beginning."

Adam's gaze held hers. "And now?"

"Now…" She hesitated. "I appreciate the fact that she has you. She needs a strong male figure in her life, especially with her dad gone."

"She's come to love you, too, Shana. And it's all happened in remarkably little time. That says a lot for you, I think. You've been patient with her and you've managed to find just the right approach."

His praise brought a sheen of tears to her eyes. Embarrassed and wanting to hide the effect of his words, Shana quickly blinked them away.

"Listen," Adam said, lowering his voice. "There's something I should probably tell you. There's a rumor floating around that several of us could be transferred to Hawaii. I've wanted to go back for quite a while— ever since I left, really. I just wish the timing was better. I should also tell you it could be soon."

"No," Shana cried, unable to hold back the automatic protest.

Everyone in the immediate vicinity seemed to stop and look in their direction.

Adam leaned forward and reached for her hand. "Dare I hope that response is for you as well as Jazmine?"

Shana ignored the question. "I guess I should congratulate you, then—since this is an assignment you want."

"What about you, Shana?" he pressed. "Will you miss me?"

He wasn't going to drop this as easily as she'd hoped. "Of…course." The lump in her throat was growing as she dealt with the coming disappointment—her own and Jazmine's. This would devastate her niece.

"I'll miss you and Jazmine, too." Adam's eyes held hers, and he brushed his thumb over her hand. "I've enjoyed our visits. Especially those talks over coffee."

As the old expression had it, hope sprang eternal. "It's not a for-sure decision, right? I mean, there's a possibility you won't be going."

"I wouldn't count on it."

"Oh, well," she said, doing her best to seem non-chalant about this unexpected turn of events. He'd probably known for some time and was only now free to mention it. "I guess that answers that." She tried to speak lightly, concealing her sense of loss.

He grinned sheepishly. "I have to admit that Jazmine's matchmaking plans didn't upset me nearly as much as they did you."

Her responding smile felt a little shaky, which was exactly how she felt herself. During the last few weeks, she'd come to like and trust Adam, and just when she was feeling comfortable with him, he made this announcement.

Adam switched seats so that he was sitting next to her. "I probably shouldn't have said anything about Hawaii yet, but I wanted you to know as soon as possible, so we can prepare Jazmine."

"No—you did the right thing." Until she'd learned that he might leave, Shana hadn't realized how much she'd come to rely on Adam. She and Jazmine would be on their own for the next four and a half months, and just then that felt like an eternity.

"Hey, guys," Jazmine said, running toward them. She flopped down on the wooden seat. "I found Point Roberts on the map! It's really cool, isn't it?"

"Really cool," Adam agreed solemnly.

Shana didn't know how a whole day could pass so quickly. Victoria was everything she'd heard and read. Although she'd never been to England, she imagined it must be like this. They explored the harbor, rode a horse-drawn carriage through the downtown area, had high tea at the Empress Hotel and toured some quaint little shops. In one of them, Shana couldn't resist buying a made-in-England teapot covered in delicate little roses, while Adam got each of them a sweatshirt with maple leaves dancing across the front.

"I loved the carriage ride best," Jazmine told them on the ferry ride back to Port Angeles. "I wish we had time to visit Butchart Gardens." She waved a brochure she'd picked up. "The pictures of the flowers are so beautiful. I always wanted a garden...." She leaned her head against Shana and closed her eyes. Within moments she was asleep.

Shana carefully eased the girl off her shoulder and gently laid Jazmine's head down on the seat. Lifting the girl's legs, she set them on the bench, then covered Jazmine with her jacket. Her niece looked angelic, and Shana's heart swelled with love for this child. She felt protective and proud. Jazmine had taught her so many lessons about love.

Adam slid over so Shana could sit with him across

from Jazmine. The day had been wonderful but, like Jazmine, she was tired. When Adam placed his arm around her, she gave in to the urge to rest her head against his shoulder. It was an invitation to intimacy, she realized, and she relaxed, comfortable and suddenly happy. "Thank you for such a special day," she whispered as he twined their fingers together.

His hold on her tightened momentarily.

Shana turned her head to look up at him—and that was when it happened. She read the intention in his eyes and knew he wanted to kiss her. At first, she wondered if what she saw was a reflection of her own desire, but instinct told her he felt the same thing. For the briefest of moments, she had a choice—she could either pull away or let him kiss her. Without rational thought, she closed her eyes, lifted her mouth to his and accepted his kiss. As soon as their lips met, Shana knew she'd made the right decision. She felt his kiss all the way to her toes.

His lips glided over hers in a slow, sensual exploration that had her nerves quivering. Luckily she was seated; otherwise she was sure her knees would have given out on her. Then his hands were in her hair, his fingers splayed as he positioned his mouth over hers. When he finally eased away, she needed a moment to regain her composure.

"Wow," Adam whispered.

"You can say that again," Shana said, still caught up in the feelings his touch had aroused.

Adam slowly expelled his breath. "Okay, now what?" His eyes burned into hers, as if seeking answers to questions she had yet to form.

"Now…" Shana hesitated. "Now we know."

"Do you want to play this by ear?"

She pressed her forehead against his chest. "I'm not sure I've had enough piano lessons."

Adam grinned and kissed the top of her head. "Don't worry, I'm in no rush. We'll take this one step at a time."

"First piano lessons, and now we're out on the dance floor. Can't you just hold me for a few minutes and leave it at that?"

"For now."

For now, that was enough. As far as anything else was concerned, she'd have to see what her heart told her.

Chapter Twelve

Ali read her daughter's e-mail a second time and smiled.

Sent: June 26
From: Jazmine@mindsprung.com
To: Alison.Karas@woodrowwilson.navy.mil
Subject: Guess what I saw

Hi Mom,

I had a great day and my favorite things were the carriage (our horse was named Silver) and having tea in a fancy hotel and watching Uncle Adam try to fit his finger in the handle of a little china cup. On the ferry home Uncle Adam and Aunt Shana sat next to each other and I was mostly asleep. They got real quiet

and so I peeked and guess what? THEY WERE KISS-
ING. Didn't I tell you they were falling in love? I knew
because Uncle Adam comes by almost every day he
has off now.

It gets even better. On the drive home, Aunt Shana had
her head on his shoulder and then she didn't when I
pretended to wake up. They were whispering a lot,
too. I tried not to listen, but I couldn't help it. They were
talking about Hawaii and I think it might be where they
want to spend their honeymoon. Is this cool, or what?

Love ya,
Jazz

Ali leaned back in her desk chair, feeling satisfied
and more than a little cheered. Her daughter was full of
news about the romance between Adam and Shana, and
gladly accepted credit for it. She seemed convinced that
Shana and Adam were just days away from an engagement—or maybe an elopement. That certainly wasn't
the impression Shana gave her, but she could see real
change in her sister's attitude toward Adam.

In their last conversation, before Alison flew out of
Seattle, Shana had told her she'd completely sworn off
men. Apparently she'd reconsidered. This time, however, Shana had found herself a winner. Adam was as
different from Brad as snow was from sun, and Ali
hoped her sister realized it.

Her first indication of the possible romance had been
the e-mail Shana had sent full of questions about Adam.
Several more had followed the original; all had thinly

veiled inquiries about him. Shana had become more open and honest, admitting she felt an attraction even if she hadn't decided what to do about it. Despite that, Alison saw the evidence of a growing relationship with every e-mail.

Glancing at her watch, she turned off her computer. It was time to relieve Rowland in medical. As she checked her schedule, her gaze fell on her wedding band and she paused. Should she switch it to her right hand—or remove it entirely? She wanted to pass it on to Jazmine one day. Slipping the ring off her finger, she held it in the palm of her hand, weighing her options. No, she wasn't ready to give it up yet. She placed it on her right hand, instead.

The very fact that she'd questioned wearing her wedding band was a sign. She would always love Peter but her life with him was over. She supposed her uncertainty about the ring had something to do with Commander Dillon, too. She didn't want him to believe she was married, but it might be safest if he did.... Still, moving the ring that represented her love for Peter to her right hand was a compromise.

As far as she could tell, this feeling of hers for Frank Dillon was completely one-sided. If he'd noticed her lately, he hadn't given the tiniest hint. He couldn't. One thing she knew about Commander Dillon was that he lived and breathed for the Navy. He wouldn't go against regulations if his life depended on it, and Alison wouldn't want him to. But it made for an uncomfortable situation as they pretended there was nothing between them. Perhaps there wasn't. She couldn't be sure, but in her heart she felt there was.

Commander Dillon was still recuperating in sick bay. He hated it, longed to get back to work and he was undeniably a pain in the butt. Her colleagues made their feelings known on a daily basis, but Alison simply didn't acknowledge his bad moods. As a result, the cantankerous commander didn't know what to think of her, and that was just fine with Ali.

While others avoided him, she saw as much of him as her busy schedule would allow, which was never longer than a few minutes at a time. Her feelings for him grew more intense with each day.

When she stepped into the infirmary, Lieutenant Rowland handed her his notes. "You're welcome to the beast," he muttered under his breath. "He's been in a hell of a mood all day. Doc says he'll have him out this week, but I don't think that's near soon enough to suit the commander."

That went without saying. When he'd first arrived at the infirmary Frank Dillon had been in agony, which meant his attitude was docile—at least compared to his current frame of mind. After reading Rowland's notations, Alison pulled back the curtain surrounding him. The commander sat up in bed, arms folded across his chest. He scowled when he saw her.

"You've become a rather disagreeable patient, Commander."

"I want out of here," he barked.

"That's no reason to yell. I believe you've made your wishes quite clear."

He narrowed his gaze.

"As it happens, Commander, you aren't the one making the decisions. You can huff and puff all you want, but it isn't going to do you a bit of good." She reached for his wrist and found his pulse elevated. Little wonder, seeing how agitated he was.

"How much longer is this going to take?" he demanded gruffly.

As the lieutenant had reported, their patient was in a foul mood. Having her around hadn't eased his temper, either. "I understand you'll be released this week," she said as she lowered the bed so that he was flat on his back. She needed to examine his incision. By now he knew the procedure as well as she did.

Ali carefully peeled back the bandage to check for any sign of infection. With the tips of her fingers she gently tested the area while the commander stared impatiently at the ceiling.

"This is healing nicely," she assured him.

"Then let me get back to work."

"It isn't my decision."

He sounded as if he was grinding his teeth in frustration. "I can't stand wasting time like this," he growled.

"Can I help in some way?" she asked, thinking she could find him a book or a deck of cards.

"Yes," he shouted, "you can get me out of here!"

"You know I can't do that," she said reasonably. "Only a physician can discharge you."

"I've got to do something before I go stir-crazy." He grimaced with pain as he attempted to sit up.

"Commander, you're not helping matters."

He glared at her as though she was personally responsible for this torture. "Just go. Get out of my sight. I don't want you around anymore, understand?"

She hesitated. "I'm responsible for your care."

"Get someone else."

"Commander," she tried again, but he cut her off.

"Get out!" He pointed at her. "And that's an order."

Alison swallowed down the hurt as she walked out of his cubicle. His words, harsh and vindictive, rang in her ears during the rest of her shift. He didn't want her anywhere near him and he wasn't afraid to say so. Her stomach twisted in a knot, and she felt like a fool for having made assumptions about mutual feelings that obviously didn't exist. Not on his part, anyway.

She didn't blame Frank for wanting to be back on duty, but he'd taken all his resentment and anger out on her. That wasn't fair, and it added to the hurt Alison felt.

Silently she watched as the corpsman delivered his dinner tray. Dillon glanced at her, then turned away, as if he found the sight of her repugnant.

Thirty minutes later, when she walked past, she noticed that he'd barely touched his meal. She considered reminding him that he'd need his strength, but he wouldn't want to hear it. And she wasn't willing to risk another tongue-lashing.

Twice more during the course of her shift, Ali resisted the urge to check on him. Frank had been very explicit about the fact that he didn't want her company.

When she'd finished, she returned to her quarters and curled up on her bed. After her shift she usually wrote Jazmine and her sister, but not tonight. Instead she reviewed the conversation with Frank.

She told herself it was silly to have her feelings hurt by his rudeness, that he didn't mean it, but she couldn't help taking it personally. Earlier she'd always shrugged off his abrasive manner, and she couldn't understand why today was so different. Probably because she'd let her attraction to him get out of hand.

Ali wouldn't be surprised if he was released the next

morning, which was just as well. In a little more than four months, she reminded herself, she'd be home with her daughter and soon after that she'd be a civilian. This was an unsettling thought because Ali loved the Navy, but her resignation was necessary. Jazmine needed her, and Alison had given the Navy all she had to give, including her husband.

As she'd suspected, Commander Dillon was released the following morning. Alison hated that his last words to her had been spoken in anger, but she tried to forget it. She wished him good health, but he was out of her life now, and it was unlikely they'd see each other again. Perhaps in another time or place they might have made a relationship work. But not here and not now.

Of more interest was the romance developing between her sister and Adam Kennedy, and as soon as she could, Alison logged on to the computer to check her e-mail. She could count on hearing from Jazmine at least once a day.

To her delight, there was an e-mail from Adam, too, but as she read it, her pleasure quickly evaporated. Adam feared that now his shoulder had healed, he was about to be transferred. He'd told Shana, but didn't have the heart to mention it to Jazmine until he got his papers. Almost in passing, he added how much he'd enjoyed getting to know Shana.

This was dreadful! Jazmine would be devastated if Adam was transferred out of the area, and she wasn't the only one. Shana was going to be just as disappointed.

With a heavy heart she read her daughter's chatty e-mail next.

Sent: June 30
From: Jazmine@mindsprung.com
To: Alison.Karas@woodrowwilson.navy.mil
Subject: Update—sort of

Hi Mom,

Aunt Shana said we could plant a garden! She said
we could grow vegetables and flowers. I don't want
to plant green beans because then I might have to
eat them. Zucchini would be all right, though. Will
you give Aunt Shana your recipe for baked zucchini?
Tell her to add more cheese than what the recipe
calls for, okay? You had a good recipe for green peppers, too, didn't you? I could even eat those raw, but
I like them better stuffed.

I think a garden will be lots of fun, don't you? Uncle
Adam said he'd help. Isn't that great?

See you soon.

Love,
Jazmine

Alison didn't know where Shana would find time to
start a garden. As it was, her sister worked from dawn
to dusk, but the plans for this latest project showed her
how hard Shana was trying with Jazmine. Somehow, the
two of them had managed to talk Adam into helping.
How much he could do was questionable, since he

couldn't risk damaging his shoulder again, but he seemed a willing participant.

The last e-mail came from onboard ship. Not until she opened it did she see that it was from Commander Dillon. Ali stared at his name for a moment before she read his message. Five words said it all. *Thank you for your excellent care. Commander Frank Dillon.*

"No," she whispered. "Thank *you,* Commander." She had much to be grateful for. Because even if this was as far as it went, Frank had shown her that her heart was still alive.

Sheer weakness had prompted him to send Alison Karas that e-mail, Frank thought as he returned to his stateroom at the end of his shift. Frank was not a weak man, and he was irritated with himself for more reasons than he wanted to count.

He knew he wasn't a good patient. He just couldn't tolerate lying around in bed all day. He wanted to be back on the job, doing what he enjoyed most, contributing his skills where they were needed. If his appendix was going to give out on him, he would've preferred it to happen while they were in port.

The worst part of his ordeal wasn't his ruptured appendix and the subsequent surgery. That he'd come through with only minor difficulties. But he wasn't sure he would survive Lieutenant Commander Karas. After all these years on his own, without female companionship, committed to the Navy, he was finally attracted to a woman. *Strongly* attracted. She invaded his dreams and haunted his waking moments. Every day for damn near a week she'd been at his bedside.

He didn't like it. Just when his mind had started to clear and his system was free of those drugs they'd given him, he saw something he hadn't noticed earlier. *Her wedding ring.* It shook him.

That first time they met, Alison Karas hadn't denied being married and she'd worn a wedding ring—on her left hand. He stared at the computer screen. *Married.* He'd forgotten about it until this week. Then, when he'd remembered—and realized he was fantasizing about a married woman—he'd lost it. Even worse, she'd moved the ring to her right hand. What did *that* say about her?

He'd been impatient to get back to his duties before, but after he saw that wedding band, he was downright desperate to escape the infirmary. *There's no fool like an old fool*, as they said.

His anger had turned on Alison and he wanted her as far away from him as possible. Later he regretted that outburst. She'd done nothing to deserve his tongue-lashing. But he found it difficult to be civil, and all because he'd realized there was no hope of any kind of relationship, let alone a permanent one.

He could accept that, but he wasn't a man who enjoyed temptation and this woman definitely fit that description. Still, he felt compelled to apologize for his rudeness. Seeing her again was out of the question, so he'd decided to send an e-mail. He wrote a dozen versions before he settled on the brief and simple message, then hit Send before he could change his mind.

For better or worse, she had it now, and that was the

end of it. He made his way to the first deck and lifting his head he scanned the horizon. All that stretched before him was ocean—a huge blue expanse of emptiness. He saw his life like that and it bothered him.

Until now, it never had.

Chapter Thirteen

Adam was charmed by Jazmine's excitement about their little garden. He'd managed to find someone to turn over a small patch at the back of Shana's rental house. Then Jazmine and her aunt had planted neat rows of red-leaf lettuce, peas, green peppers and three varieties of tomato. Although they'd been warned by the man at the local nursery, they'd purchased a number of zucchini plants, too. Apparently it did exceptionally well in the Seattle area and supplied an abundant crop. Jazmine claimed her mother had fabulous recipes for zucchini. Baked zucchini and zucchini bread and something else.

"Around September if you see anyone buying zucchini in the grocery, you'll know that's a person without a friend," the nursery owner had joked as he hauled their plants out to the vehicle.

Once they were back at the house and the plants were in the freshly tilled soil, Adam watched Jazmine with amusement. Every five minutes, the girl was out in the garden checking on the plants' growth, making sure there were no slugs in the vicinity. God help them if they were. Just to be on the safe side, she carried a salt shaker.

The flower beds—well, they were another story. He'd lost track of all the seedlings Shana had purchased. Most of them he didn't even recognize. Pink ones and white ones, purple and yellow. They certainly made the yard look colorful. Pretty but... Women and flowers—he never could understand what they found so fascinating. For himself, he thought practical made more sense than pretty, although he hadn't shared that reaction with Shana.

True, he'd had a jade plant once but it died for lack of attention. Shana, predictably, had clusters of house plants—on windowsills and tables—but he couldn't begin to guess what types they were. Knowing Jazmine, he wouldn't have thought she'd be too interested in this kind of thing, either, but apparently he was wrong. The kid loved it as much as Shana did.

"Aunt Shana said she'd be home around eight," Jazmine informed him on Saturday at five. They'd spent a quiet afternoon together. While he watched a Mariners baseball game on television, Jazmine tended the garden. He'd found it relaxing, but he missed being with Shana. He would've stopped at the ice-cream parlor, but he knew that Saturdays, especially in summer, tended to be busy.

Jazmine had patiently watered the rows of newly planted seedlings, being careful not to oversaturate the soil. She'd examined every inch to check for weeds and had ruthlessly yanked up a number of small green plants; Adam suspected they were actually vegetables.

He glanced up from the post-game analysis and saw that Jazmine was standing in front of him. "We should make dinner," she announced. "A real, proper dinner."

"We?" he muttered. In case Jazmine hadn't noticed, he wasn't the domestic type. Besides he had to protect his shoulder. Every meal in the last few weeks had come out of a microwave or in a pizza box.

"We could do it," Jazmine insisted, as if putting together a three-course meal was no trouble at all.

"Really? I wouldn't mind getting takeout. Or maybe Shana could bring home a pizza. Wouldn't that be easier?"

Frowning, Jazmine shook her head. "She has pizza all the time. Besides, home cooking is better for you."

Adam wondered when she'd become such an expert. "You're sure the two of us can do this?"

"Of course."

Ah, the confidence of the young. Still, Adam had his doubts. "You should know I'm kitchen-challenged."

Jazmine giggled. "I cook a lot. I'll do it."

If Jazmine knew her way around the kitchen, then perhaps this wouldn't be so complicated. He could supervise from in front of the TV.

"You'll have to help, though."

He should've known she wouldn't let him off scot-free. "What do you want me to do?"

"The grocery store won't sell me wine, so you'll have to buy that."

His eyebrows shot up. "Wine?"

Jazmine nodded. "And flowers," she said in a tone that brooked no argument.

"Yes, ma'am. Any particular kind?" He resisted mentioning that there was a yard full of flowers outside, although they were mostly quite small.

"I want you to buy roses and we're going to need candles, too. Tall ones."

"You got it." He bit his tongue to keep from reminding her that it wouldn't be dark until ten. "Should I buy red or white wine?" he asked.

Jazmine stared at him blankly.

"Red generally goes with meat and white wine is served with chicken or fish."

"What goes with everything?"

"Champagne is good."

She grinned then, her decision made. "Buy champagne and make it a big bottle, okay?"

"Have you decided what you're cooking?" he asked.

"Of course I have," she told him scornfully.

"And that would be?"

She sighed, as though she was a master chef dealing with obtuse underlings. "I've decided to cook my specialty."

"Which is?"

"A surprise," she said without pause, using her hands to shoo him out the door. He watched her march into the kitchen. From the corner of his eye, Adam saw her pull several cookbooks off the shelf.

After he'd finished his errands, Adam decided to visit the ice-cream parlor, after all. It was just too hard to stay away. As he'd expected, Shana was doing a robust business. Catherine worked on the pizza side with a young assistant, while Shana and another part-time student served ice cream. They had at least a dozen customers waiting their turn. Adam took a seat and when Shana saw him, she blushed, fussed with her hair, then went back to helping her customers. Her self-conscious reaction pleased him. Ten minutes later, she had a chance to take a break.

After washing her hands, she joined him. "Hi," she said, offering him a shy smile.

He hadn't known there was a shy bone in her body until he'd kissed her. That kiss had been a revelation to him. Their feelings weren't simple or uncomplicated, although he hadn't deciphered the full extent of them yet. He did know their kiss had changed them. Changed their relationship.

He'd been attracted to her from the beginning and was sure she'd felt the same way about him. They'd skirted each other for weeks, both denying the attraction, and then all of a sudden, after that day in Victoria, it was there. Undeniable. Unmistakable. He no longer tried to hide his feelings and she didn't, either.

"Where's Jazmine?" she asked. "In the park?"

He shook his head. "At home, cooking dinner. Her specialty, she says. I don't suppose you have any clue what that might be?"

"You left her alone?" Shana's eyes widened with alarm. "In the kitchen with the stove on? Adam, she's only nine! Sometimes that's hard to remember, but she's still just a kid."

"She seemed perfectly fine," he said, suddenly deciding Shana was right. "She's the one who sent me to the store." He slid out of the booth. "I'll get back now."

Shana sighed, then stretched out one hand and stopped him. "It was good to see you," she said in a low voice.

He gave her hand a small squeeze. "You, too. Don't be late for dinner."

"I won't," she promised.

Once again Adam started toward the door, then paused and turned around. "What's her specialty?"

Shana grinned. "It's probably canned chili with grated cheese on top."

He dismissed that. "I think it might be more involved. Whatever it is requires a cookbook."

Shana's grin faded. "In that case, you'd better hurry."

"I'm on my way."

Shana smiled again, and it reminded him—as if he needed reminding—how attracted he was to her. And just when their relationship was beginning to show real promise, he'd be leaving the Seattle area.

She followed him to the front door. "Any word on that transfer?" she asked.

If he didn't know better, he'd think she'd been reading his mind. "Not yet." It wouldn't be long, though. Hawaii was a dream assignment. Who wouldn't want to be stationed there? With its endless miles of white sandy beaches and sunshine, Hawaii had always appealed to him. Yet Seattle, known for its frequent drizzle and gray skies, was of more interest now than the tropical paradise.

"Did you mention anything about the transfer to Jazmine?" she asked.

He shook his head. He couldn't make himself do it.

"Coward," she muttered.

Adam shrugged lightly. "Guilty as charged."

Shana glanced at her watch. "I'll be leaving in about an hour and a half."

"Okay, I'll let Martha Stewart know." Feeling the need to touch her, he reached for her hand. Even with the restaurant full of customers, they entwined their fingers, and it was a long moment before either of them moved. He felt the urge to take her in his arms and she must have felt the same impulse because she swayed toward him before shaking her head and dropping her hand.

"I should get back to work and you need to get back to Jazmine," she said, her voice little more than a whisper.

"Right."

"Bye." Shana gave him a small wave. Adam heard the reluctance in her voice, a reluctance he shared.

Jazmine met him at the front door, took his bags and banned him from the kitchen. "I can't be disturbed," she said grandly.

Adam turned the television on again and sat with one ankle balanced on his knee, aiming the remote. He couldn't find anything he wanted to watch. "Need any help in there?" he called out.

"No, thanks."

Five minutes later he repeated the offer.

This time Jazmine ignored him, but soon afterward, she asked, "Aunt Shana isn't going to be late, is she?"

"She'd phone," Adam said, and hoped she would.

At three minutes after eight, Shana walked into the house. "I'm home," she said unnecessarily.

Adam stood and Jazmine hurried eagerly out of the kitchen. "I hope you're hungry."

"Famished," she said.

As if on cue, Adam's stomach growled.

With a sweeping gesture of her arm, Jazmine invited them into the kitchen. The table was covered with a tablecloth twice the right size. The cloth brushed the floor, and Adam wondered if she'd used a floral printed sheet. The candles were stuck in empty Coke bottles—apparently she hadn't found real candle-holders—and were positioned on either side of the roses, which she'd arranged in a glass bowl. The effect was surprisingly artful. There were place settings, including wine goblets, in front of the three chairs.

"Jazmine!" Shana exclaimed, hugging her niece. "This is absolutely lovely."

The nine-year-old blushed at the praise and wiped her hands on her apron. "Uncle Adam helped."

"Not much," Adam protested.

"We can start now," she said with authority. "Please light the candles and pour the champagne. I'm having soda in my glass."

He bowed slightly. "At your service."

"Everyone, sit down," Jazmine ordered when he'd finished. She gestured toward the table. "I have an appetizer." Following that announcement, she brought out a bowl of dry Cheerios mixed with peanuts, raisins and pretzels.

"Excellent," Shana said, exchanging a look with Adam. They both struggled to maintain their composure.

"This is only the start," Jazmine promised, flitting about the kitchen like a parrot on the loose. "I made all our favorites—macaroni and cheese, Tater Tots and salad. Uncle Adam, there's no tomatoes in your salad and, Aunt Shana, no croutons on yours."

Shana's eyes met Adam's. "She's paying attention."

"I'll say."

"Plus macaroons for dessert," Jazmine added proudly.

"Macaroons?" Adam repeated.

Jazmine removed the bowl of Cheerios. "Yes, *chocolate* macaroons. Those are my favorites, so no complaining."

It was an odd meal, but Adam had no complaints and neither, apparently, did Shana.

"We'll do the dishes," he said when they'd eaten. The champagne had relaxed him and Shana, too, because they lingered over the last glass while Jazmine moved into the living room.

"This really was sweet of her," Shana whispered.

"Very sweet," Adam agreed. What happened next, he blamed on the champagne. Before he could question the wisdom of it, he leaned close to Shana, intending to kiss her.

She could've stopped him, but didn't. Instead she shut her eyes and leaned toward him, too. The kiss was every bit as good as their first one. No, it was better, Adam decided. In fact, her kisses could fast become addictive—a risk he'd just have to take. He brought his chair closer to Shana's and she gripped his shirt collar as they kissed again.

She pulled away sometime later and pressed her forehead against his. It took him a moment to find his focus. He savored having her close, enjoyed her scent and the way she felt. Jazmine might see them, but he didn't care as long as Shana didn't—and obviously she didn't.

"You two need help in there?" Jazmine called from the living room.

Like guilty teenagers, Shana and Adam broke apart. "We're fine," Shana answered.

Adam wasn't so sure that was true.

Sent: July 6
From: Jazmine@mindsprung.com
To: Alison.Karas@woodrowwilson.navy.mil
Subject: My plan is working

Dear Mom,

I cooked dinner all by myself! You know what I like best about Uncle Adam? He doesn't treat me like a kid. He spent Saturday afternoon with me because Aunt Shana was at the ice-cream parlor and when I told him I was going to cook dinner, he let me. He even went to the store and left me by myself. I don't need a babysitter anymore.

When he got back, he said Aunt Shana was upset with him for leaving me all alone, but nothing happened. I made macaroni and cheese in the microwave and baked Tater Tots and made a salad. It turned out really good, and guess what?

Uncle Adam and Aunt Shana kissed again, and they didn't even care that I could see them. I pretended I didn't, but I really did. They said they wanted to wash the dishes and it took them more than an hour. Miss you bunches and bunches.

Love,
Jazmine

Chapter Fourteen

If Ali had been at home instead of aboard the *USS Woodrow Wilson,* she would've turned to her favorite comfort food: cookie dough. It was that kind of day. Yes, she knew she shouldn't eat raw eggs. But when she reached this point—of being prepared to scarf down a bowl of unbaked cookies—salmonella seemed the least of her worries. Those ice-cream manufacturers knew what they were doing when they introduced cookie dough as a flavor. That, in her opinion, was the ultimate comfort food.

What had upset Ali, or rather *who,* was none other than Commander Frank Dillon. After managing fairly successfully to keep him out of her thoughts, he was back—not only in her thoughts, but unfortunately, in sick bay.

Earlier in the day he'd returned with a raging fever and an infection. Infection was the biggest risk with a ruptured appendix, and he hadn't been spared this complication. Ali was worried when she saw that his temperature was nearly 103 degrees. Furious, she'd asked why he hadn't come in earlier.

He'd refused to answer, but insisted that all he needed was a shot, and that once she'd given it to him, he could go back to his duties as navigator. When she told him Captain Coleman had ordered antibiotics via IV, he seemed to blame her personally. In his anger and frustration, he'd lashed out at her once again and questioned her competence.

As soon as he was hooked up to the antibiotics, and relatively free of pain, he slept for the remainder of her shift. Before leaving, she'd checked on him, taking his temperature, which had fallen to just over 100 degrees.

She felt both irritated and sad. Irritated that he'd delayed seeking medical attention. And sad because she suspected she might be the reason he'd stayed away. According to his own comments, he wanted nothing to do with her. She couldn't help wondering if that was because of her wedding ring—and yet how could it be? She'd removed it from her left hand.

Anytime he'd so much as glanced in her direction this afternoon, he'd scowled as if he couldn't bear to be in the same room. That was ridiculous. Ali hadn't done anything to deserve this wrath. After all, he was the one who'd sent her an e-mail thanking her for the excellent care. But from the way he regarded her now, anyone might think she'd attempted to amputate his leg while he wasn't looking. She tried not to dwell on the things he'd said to her, either today or during his first hospitalization, but she couldn't help that her feelings were hurt. She'd misread the situation and now he was back and not happy about it, either.

Frank didn't understand or recognize how serious this
infection was. With a fever that high, he must've been terribly sick. Damn, he should never have waited this long!

Sent: July 7
From: Alison.Karas@woodrowwilson.navy.mil
To: Shana@mindsprung.com
Subject: It's cookie time!!

Dear Shana,

I'm tired and I want to come home. I sound like a cry-
baby but I don't care. The day has been long and
awful, and if I was home right now I'd have the mixer
going, blending sugar and flour and eggs with oatmeal and raisins. Yup, it's one of those days.

How are things with Jazmine? I need some news to
cheer me up. Got anything wonderful to tell me?
How's Adam? Any news about the transfer?

Love,
Alison

It wasn't long before she received a reply.

Sent: July 9
From: Shana@mindsprung.com
To: Alison.Karas@woodrowwilson.navy.mil
Subject: Fireworks and all

Dear Alison,

My goodness, what's happening? I haven't heard you sound so down in ages. When you start talking about cookie dough, I know there's got to be a man involved. I figure this must have something to do with that commander you mentioned. I thought you said you wouldn't be seeing him again. But apparently you have and it didn't go well. Tell all!

Jazmine is fabulous, but the truth is, I had a miserable day myself. I worked from dawn to dusk, and financially it was my best business day ever, so I should be happy, right? I wasn't. I wanted to be with Jazmine and Adam, who were off at a community fair while I was stuck at the ice-cream parlor.

I can't even begin to tell you how much work is involved in owning a business like this. Catherine was the only employee willing to work this weekend and thankfully, her husband came in to lend a hand. I don't know what I would've done otherwise. I *really* hated not being with Adam and Jazmine. They must've known it, because they showed up to collect me the minute I closed for the night. I didn't have time to change my clothes or anything. Adam drove to a hilltop where we had a picnic, even though it was almost dark. Adam had bought deli sandwiches and salads. By the time we arrived home, it was after eleven. I'm afraid I was exhausted and not much fun. Sometimes I wonder if buying this business was the wisest choice, but it's too late to think about that now.

Write soon.

Love,
Shana

Alison read her sister's e-mail and tried to translate the message between the lines. Like Alison, Shana was tired. According to Jazmine, she worked long hours, starting early in the morning when she mixed the pizza dough and set it out to rise. She usually stayed until closing, which meant she often wasn't home until after nine. Thankfully her sister had had the wherewithal to hire Catherine, who'd quickly become indispensable. Her other employees, mostly high-school kids, didn't seem all that reliable, but at least she had them.

Adam was spending a lot of time with Jazmine, and Alison knew very well that her daughter wasn't the only draw. He and Shana were definitely getting along, and that thrilled her. But if Adam was transferred to Hawaii, that might be the end of their relationship. Still, Alison couldn't worry about that when she had troubles of her own.

Fortunately, she had Lieutenant Rowland to talk to. He was waiting for her when she reported for duty the next afternoon.

"How's the beast doing?" she asked in a stage whisper. Compared to the commander, their other patients were downright jovial.

Jordan's responding grimace answered her question. "Same. Bad-tempered as ever."

"Oh, great."

Rowland rolled his eyes. "He's certainly got a burr under his saddle—and I think I know why."

Alison did, too. "He hates being sick." No one enjoyed it, but the commander was worse than most. He resented every minute away from his duty station. What he didn't realize was that he wouldn't be released anytime soon. She wasn't going to be the one to tell him, either.

"His problem," Rowland said with an air of superiority, "appears to be you."

"Me?" she protested, flustered that Frank's ranting from the day before had obviously continued.

"He asked me to keep you away from him."

Alison's face burned with mortification. "What did you tell him?" she asked, her voice indignant despite her efforts.

Rowland's smile lacked humor. "That the United States Navy was fortunate to have you, and if he has a problem he should take it up with Captain Coleman."

"Thank you," she said, and swallowed a painful knot of gratitude.

"The mighty commander didn't have anything to say after that."

"Good." Her anger simmering just below the surface, Alison squared her shoulders. "I think it's time I faced the beast on my own."

Rowland's dark eyes flared. "I don't know if I'd advise that."

Alison was past accepting her friend's advice. If Frank Dillon had even a clue what she was thinking, she'd likely be up for court-martial.

Before common sense and what remained of her Navy career could stop her, she tore back the curtain to his cubicle and confronted the commander. Although he appeared to be sleeping, he must have heard her because his eyes fluttered open.

"I understand you requested not to be under my care."

He blinked, and Alison was shocked to see that he refused to look at her. "You heard right."

"That's fine with me, Commander. As far as I'm concerned, you're cantankerous and impatient and rude and…and *more.*"

Barely controlled anger showed in the tight set of his mouth. No one with any desire to advance in the Navy spoke to a senior officer the way Alison just had.

"What's the matter, Commander, no comment?" Feet braced apart, she gave him a defiant glare.

"It would be best if you left now," he muttered.

"I don't think so."

He frowned as if he'd rarely been challenged, but Alison was beyond caring.

"You don't like me, Commander, and that's perfectly okay, but I would prefer to keep personalities out of this. I am a professional and I pride myself on my work. Not only have you insulted me but you've—" Angry though she was, she couldn't complete the thought.

His eyes hardened, but he still wouldn't look at her.

Unable to bear another minute in his presence, she turned and walked away, feeling as though there was a huge hole in her stomach.

Chapter Fifteen

Shana was in much better spirits the following weekend. Her business continued to prosper, and she'd hired a new part-time employee, a teenage boy this time, named Charles. Not Charlie, but Charles. Hiring, training and dealing with employees had proved to be her biggest difficulty to date. This was an area where she had little experience and it seemed her lessons were all learned the hard way. She'd had to let the other two go and seemed to feel worse about it than either teenager. Charles was proving himself to be responsible and good-natured, and he and Catherine liked each other, quickly developing a bantering relationship. Shana couldn't even begin to imagine what she'd do without Catherine.

After several weeks of hanging around the ice-cream parlor, Jazmine's entrepreneurial talent suddenly kicked in, and her ideas weren't bad. The kid had real imagination when it came to inventing sundaes and candy treats. She took long strands of red and black licorice and—hands carefully gloved—braided them, decorating each end with colorful ribbons. Then she enclosed the entire creation in cellophane wrap. She hung them everywhere she found space, creating a festive atmosphere. The price was reasonable and the kids who came into the parlor were intrigued by them, so they sold quickly.

Jazmine's creativity had sparked Shana's, and she made up and displayed small bouquets using colorful lollipops and ribbons. The candy business contributed only a small portion to the total revenue but was gaining in popularity.

Working long hours had one advantage, Shana decided; she didn't have time to think about Adam's leaving. She was afraid it would be soon, and if she allowed herself to brood on it, she'd remember how much she enjoyed his company—and how much she was going to miss him.

Adam still hadn't mentioned the possibility of a transfer to Jazmine. Shana didn't feel it was her place to tell Jazz, unless Adam wanted her to, but he agreed the news should come from him. He'd promised he would last weekend, but then for one reason or another, he hadn't. Shana knew it would be hard to tell her and that he wanted to delay it until the transfer was official. She supposed it would be best to say nothing until he was sure. Her heart ached at the thought of Adam moving to Hawaii. Yes, it was a wonderful assignment and one he'd sought out, but Shana wanted him in Seattle, selfish though that was…

At the height of the lunch business, when the restaurant smelled of baking dough and tomato sauce, and it was all Shana could do to keep up with the pizza orders, the phone rang. Catherine bustled over to answer it and her gaze flew to Shana.

"It's for you," she said, holding out the receiver.

Shana finished slicing a sausage pizza still steaming hot from the oven. If it was Adam, she'd call back the minute she had time to breathe. "Who is it?" she asked.

"Adam, I think," Catherine told her.

She realized he might have news; if so, she wanted to know as soon as possible. "Ask him if it's important."

Catherine grabbed the phone and as Shana watched, the older woman nodded at her.

Her stomach tensed with anxiety. Shana could feel it coming even before he told her. Adam had received his transfer papers or whatever the Navy called them. That must be it; otherwise he would've phoned her tonight.

Wiping her hands on her apron, she asked Charles to fill in for her while she answered the phone. "Could you bring this pizza to table ten?"

"Sure."

Shana walked to the other side of the room and took the phone from Catherine. "Adam?"

"I'm sorry to bother you now."

She leaned against the wall, hardly able to breathe.

"Listen," he said, and she could hear the regret in his voice.

She could think of no reason to delay his news, so she said it before he had a chance. "You got the transfer to Hawaii."

"Yes, my orders hit the boards."

"They what?"

"They're official. And I have to fly out almost right away. The officer I'm replacing had an emergency."

There it was, what she'd dreaded most. "I see." Shana closed her eyes. Although she'd known this was coming, she still felt a sense of shock. The tightness in her chest was painful, and she bit her lower lip to keep from protesting aloud.

"I fly out in the morning."

"So soon?" She'd hoped they'd have some time to say their farewells. At least one more chance to talk and decide—not that there was really anything to decide. But it felt wrong for him to go like this, so quickly, without any opportunity for Jazmine or her to adjust.

"I'm sorry," he said.

"I know." She couldn't seem to say more than two words at a time. "Tonight?" she managed through her painfully dry throat.

Despite her lack of clarity or detail, he understood the question. "Unfortunately, I can't. There's too much to do."

"I know…"

"Is Jazmine there?"

Shana pressed her hand against her forehead. "No, she's at the park skating with her friends."

"You may need to tell her for me."

"No!" Shana's objection was immediate. "You *have* to do it."

"I'll phone if I can, but there are no guarantees. She's a Navy kid. She'll understand."

Until recently Shana hadn't had much to do with the Navy. All at once she found her entire life affected by it, and frankly she was starting to get annoyed.

"I'll be in touch, I promise," Adam assured her. "Leaving you and Jazmine like this isn't what I want, either."

His words didn't lessen the dejection she felt. She remembered, in an immediate and visceral way, the emotions she'd experienced when she saw Brad and Sylvia together, knowing exactly what they were doing. The sensation that she'd lost something vital had refused to go away. With Brad that was the signal she'd needed, because what they'd had wasn't real, not on his part, anyway. With Adam…with Adam all she felt was loss.

"I don't want you to go." She knew it was childish to say that.

"I'll be able to visit. About Jazz—I've got meetings this afternoon, and tonight I have to pack. I'll phone when I can. *If* I can."

Shana knew what he was asking. She sighed wearily. "I'll tell her."

"I'm sorry to put this on you, but if I don't reach her, you'll have to."

"I know."

"I meant what I said," he reiterated. "I'll visit as often as I can."

While Adam might have every intention of flying in to see them, it would be time-consuming and complicated. Shana recalled that the flight between Hawaii and Portland was a good five hours. She'd taken a brief vacation there with friends; it was the longest flight she'd ever taken. Yes, his intentions were good but that was all they were—intentions.

"I've got your e-mail address," he reminded her. "Yours and Jazmine's, and I'll stay in touch."

"You promise?" She hated the fact that she still sounded like a thwarted child, but she couldn't pretend this wasn't hard.

"Yes—I promise."

Shana had no choice but to comfort herself with his word. Doing her best to seem reconciled to what was happening, she straightened. "Have a safe flight, and don't worry about Jazmine. I'll explain everything to her."

"Thank you."

"No...Adam, thank you." Her voice cracked before she finished and she knew she had to get off the phone or she'd embarrass herself further. "I'm sorry, but I really need to get back to work now."

"I understand, but Shana, one last thing—about you and me. We have to talk. Soon, okay?"

She didn't answer. She couldn't. Replacing the receiver, she let her hand linger while she struggled to overcome her disappointment. With Adam stationed in Hawaii, she could forecast their future and she didn't need the aid of a crystal ball. For Jazmine's sake, he'd stay in touch. Later, when Alison returned and Jazmine went back to live with her mother, he and Shana would both make an effort. At least in the beginning. Then their time together would dwindle until they were forced to face the inevitable. It was how long-distance relationships usually ended.

Shana had seen it with friends. Couples would e-mail back and forth, and on special occasions they'd phone, just for the pleasure of hearing each other's voices. Adam could fly on military transports, so there might even be a weekend now and then when he'd be able to visit the mainland, but she suspected those opportunities would be few and far between. They'd both try, but in the end the obstacles would be too much.

Adam had been a brief season in her life. Instead of complaining, she should be grateful. The lieutenant commander had given her back her self-confidence; he'd made her feel beautiful and...cherished. When she'd met him, another relationship was the last thing on her mind. But Adam had proved there were still good men left in this world, and that not every man was like Brad.

"Are you okay?" Catherine asked, joining her. She rested a gentle hand on Shana's shoulder. "Was it bad news?"

"Everything's all right," she said, shaking her head in order to dispel the lethargic feeling that had stolen over her. "Or it will be soon," she amended.

The look Catherine threw her said she wasn't convinced, and of course the older woman's instincts were accurate. Heaviness settled over Shana's heart. She didn't know why her relationships with men always fell apart. In retrospect, though, she realized she'd carried the relationship with Brad. She'd trusted, believed and held on. She refused to do that with Adam. She wanted a relationship of equals or not at all—and she'd grown increasingly sure that this was it. Her future. Good grief, she was reading a lot into a couple of kisses! It was just that everything had felt so right—and now this.

An hour later, just when the pizza sales had started to diminish, Jazmine returned, her face red and sweaty from her trek around Lincoln Park on her Rollerblades.

"I sold three more of your licorice braids," Shana told her, trying to act normal.

Jazmine shrugged, but Shana could tell she was pleased. Shana had managed to pick up quite a bit of the girl's body language. It wasn't cool to show too much enthusiasm if there was the slightest possibility someone her own age would see it.

As long as Shana remembered that, she was fine. But when she forgot, problems developed. However, if Jazmine and Shana were alone, or if it was Jazz with Shana and Adam, a completely different set of behavioral rules applied.

"Would you like to make up a few more?" Shana asked.

"Maybe."

This meant she'd be happy to, but not if a friend came by and thought she'd willingly agreed to do anything with or for an adult.

"Good."

At closing time, Shana counted out the money from the cash register, while Jazmine sat in a booth curled up with a book. Every now and then, Shana felt the girl's eyes on her. Catherine and Charles were finishing the cleanup in the kitchen.

"Is there anything I should know about?" her niece asked as soon as they were alone. She laid her book on the tabletop, her elbows on either side of it, and stared at Shana.

Jazmine's intuition surprised her. Shana stopped in midcount and looked up. "Like what?"

Jazmine frowned. "I'm not sure, but I have the feeling you know something I don't. I hate that."

Shana wrapped elastics around the bills of various denominations, setting each stack aside. "I always did, too," she said. After tucking the cash in the deposit bag, she joined her niece, sliding into the booth across from her.

"So there *is* something wrong." Jazmine's eyes seemed to grow darker. "My mom's okay, isn't she?" Her anxiety was unconcealed, and Shana wanted to reassure her as quickly as possible.

"Oh, yes! No worries there."

"Then what's wrong?"

Her sigh of relief touched Shana's heart. "This has to do with your uncle Adam." How times changed. Only recently she'd begrudged Adam the term *uncle*. At first, the word had nearly gotten stuck in her throat, but now it fell easily from her lips.

Shana was going to miss him so much, but at the moment she was furious that he'd left the job of telling Jazmine up to her—even if she'd agreed to it. "What about Uncle Adam?" Jazmine's eyes seemed more frightened by the second. She scrambled out of the booth.

Shana stood, too, and placed her arm around Jazmine's thin shoulders, but her niece shook it off. In her need to comfort the girl, Shana had forgotten the rules.

"Just *tell* me," Jazmine insisted.

Shana decided her niece was right. She'd give Jazmine the news as clearly, honestly and straightforwardly as she could. "The Navy is reassigning him to Hawaii."

Jazmine spent a moment digesting the information. This was followed by a series of quickly fired questions. "When's he flying out? He is flying, isn't he? Does he get leave first? Because he should. What about the garden? He said he'd help and isn't there a whole lot more that needs to be done? Besides, he promised me he'd be here and…and now he's breaking his word." As if she'd said too much she covered her mouth with both hands.

Shana didn't know how to respond, where to start. "He phoned this afternoon to say his orders, uh, hit the boards and he had to leave first thing in the morning."

Jazmine's eyes flared. "Already?" She sounded shocked, disbelieving.

"I'm afraid so."

"When did he find out?"

"He just got the final word this afternoon."

"But he must've known *something* before now."

Shana nodded.

"He never said a word."

"I know." Shana could kick him for that, especially now that she was the one telling Jazmine.

Jazmine sat down again and glared at Shana suspiciously. "He told you before this afternoon, though, didn't he?"

Shana could probably talk her way out of this, but she didn't want to lie to her niece. "He did, or…well, he mentioned the possibility. But he dreaded telling you, so he put it off. Besides, he wasn't sure it would go through at all and certainly not this soon."

"So he made you tell me." Jazmine's anger was unmistakable, despite the softness of her voice.

Shana nodded. Adam would pay dearly for that, she suspected.

Jazmine considered this information for a couple of minutes, then casually tossed back her hair. Propping her chin on her palm, she sat very still. "How do you feel about this?"

"I'm fine with it." Shana managed to sound almost flippant. "But to be on the safe side, I'm bringing home a container of chocolate-mint ice cream."

Her niece gave her a confused look.

"I'm throwing myself a pity party," Shana explained. "You're invited."

"What are we going to do other than eat ice cream?"

"Watch old movies," Shana decided. The two of them could snuggle up together in front of the television, wearing their oldest pajamas.

"*Sleepless in Seattle* is one of my mom's favorites," her niece told her. Apparently the kid was familiar with this particular brand of mood therapy. Shana would have to ask Alison about it at the first opportunity. Perhaps tonight, when she e-mailed her sister.

"Do you have any others we could watch?" Jazmine asked. "I've seen *Sleepless* so often I can say all the lines."

"*The Bridges of Madison County*," she suggested, but sometimes that one made her angry, when what she really wanted was to weep copiously at a fictional character's tragic life. Pure catharsis, in other words.

"Mom said I was too young to see it," Jazmine muttered disgustedly, as though she no longer required parental guidance.

At times it was hard to remember that her niece was only nine. The kid was mature beyond her years. Alison was right about the movie, though. A story featuring infidelity hardly seemed appropriate for a child.

"For her pity parties, Mom likes popcorn best. The more butter the better," she said matter-of-factly. "We had several of them after Dad died. But Mom didn't call them pity parties."

"What did she call them?"

"Tea parties, but we only had them when we were feeling sad."

"Always with buttered popcorn?"

"It goes good with tea," Jazmine said. "I don't think she had a name for them at first. I woke up one night and saw her crying in front of the TV, and she said sad movies always made her cry. Then I asked her why she watched them."

Shana already knew the answer to that. "Because she needed a good cry."

Jazmine nodded again. "That's exactly what Mom said." The girl sighed heavily, then added in a small voice, "I don't want her to be sad."

"Me, neither, but it's part of life, Jazz. It's not good to be *too* sad or for too long, but being sad has its place. For one thing, sadness makes happiness that much more wonderful."

Jazmine looked at her thoughtfully, awareness dawning in her eyes.

"Now, it's been a while since I had an official pity party," Shana said briskly. "One is long overdue." She'd made a couple of weak attempts when she left Brad, but she'd been too angry with him to do it properly. If anything, their breakup had left her feeling strong and decisive. That high hadn't lasted, and she'd found it emotionally difficult to reconcile herself to the end of the relationship—but only for a short time. Thanks to Adam…

She thought that breaking off her engagement—or whatever it was—with Brad did call for a party, but a real party with banners and food, champagne and music and lots of people. She smiled as she considered how far she'd come.

"What's so funny?" Jazmine asked.

Shana instantly sobered. "Remember a few weeks ago, when you said I had issues?"

"Yeah."

"One of those issues was Brad."

Jazmine rolled her eyes. "Tell me about it!"

Shana laughed out loud. "I was just thinking I never really had a pity party over him."

Jazmine cocked her head quizzically. "Do women always throw these parties because of men?"

"Hmm."

Shana had never given the matter much thought. "Yes," she said firmly. "It's always about men."

"That's what I figured." Jazmine shook her head sadly, as if this reasoning was beyond her.

They loaded up with chocolate-mint ice cream, and whipped topping for good measure, and headed out the door. Shana had to make a quick stop at the bank, but they were home before the ice cream had a chance to melt.

Within ten minutes, they were both lying on their backs, dressed in old flannel pajamas, studying the ceiling.

"Remember when Brad phoned you a little while ago?" Jazmine asked.

"Yup." Shana didn't want to dwell on Brad. She wanted to think about Adam and how much they were going to miss him. Brad paled in comparison to Adam Kennedy.

"Why did he call?"

Shana rolled onto her stomach and raised her head. "He realized the error of his ways."

Jazmine rolled over, too. "Are you going to take him back?"

Shana didn't even need to think about it. "No."

Jazmine solemnly agreed. "He had his turn."

Boy, did he!

"Uncle Adam is next in line."

It occurred to Shana to explain that pity parties were usually wakes for relationships. This wake was for Adam and her. Shana was cutting her losses now, doing her best to accept the likely end of their brief romance and move forward.

"What if Brad came to Seattle?" Jazmine asked excitedly, as if that were a distinct possibility. "What would you do then?"

Shana flopped onto her back again. "Nothing."

"Not a thing?"

"Not a single, solitary thing."

"What if he offered you an engagement ring?"

Shana grinned. "First, I'd faint from the shock of it, and then I'd…I'd ask to see his ID. Make sure this was really Brad."

"Would you cry?"

"I doubt it."

"But you'd turn him down, right?"

"Wait a minute." Shana pulled herself into a sitting position. "Is there any particular reason for all these questions about Brad?"

Jazmine sighed loudly. "I wanted to be sure you're really, really over that rat."

"Rat?"

"That's what Mom called him."

Shana smothered a giggle. "Hey, I thought we were throwing this party because of your uncle Adam," she said. It hadn't escaped her notice how cleverly Jazmine had changed the subject.

"We are."

"So, why bring up Brad?"

Her question was met with silence, and then Jazmine ventured, "Remember how you knew Uncle Adam might be stationed in Hawaii and you didn't tell me?"

"Yes, but what's that got to do with—" She hesitated and drew in her breath. "Is there something *you* aren't telling *me?*" she demanded, aware that she was repeating Jazmine's earlier question.

Her niece sighed dramatically. "Promise you won't be mad."

"Jazmine!"

"Okay, okay. Brad phoned again. I answered and I told him you're seeing someone else now."

"You didn't!"

Jazmine giggled. "I did, and you don't want to know what he said about that, either."

Chapter Sixteen

"What do you mean Brad phoned?" Shana demanded. "When? And why?" Not that she cared. Okay, she did, but only a little. He'd talked to her once, a few weeks ago, and she'd been polite and stiff and frankly had never expected to hear from him again. At one time, she'd dreamed about a big wedding with lots of bridesmaids all dressed in lovely pastel dresses of pink and yellow. Her sister and three of her best friends would've looked like a neat row of huge after-dinner mints. At least she'd spared them that.

"He called last week and I answered the phone," Jazmine muttered. "We…talked. For a while."

That sounded ominous. Shana could only imagine what Brad had to say to her niece—and vice versa.

"He told me he wants you back."

"Of course he does," Shana muttered. *That* made

sense. Now that she was out of his life, he missed everything she'd done for him.

"When he asked how your social life was these days—that's exactly what he said—I told him about Uncle Adam and he wasn't very happy," Jazmine continued.

"No," Shana agreed. "He probably wasn't." Just like Brad to pump a nine-year-old for information.

"I shouldn't have said anything," Jazmine muttered, "but I wanted Brad to know he lost out on the opportunity of a lifetime."

That was a typically grandiose Jazmine remark, and Shana smiled. Still, it was gratifying to know Brad missed her, even if it was for the wrong reasons. He must've been shocked to learn she'd met someone else.

"I hope you aren't mad."

"No, but…it isn't a good idea to be giving out personal information over the phone."

"I know, but he kept asking me about your social life and if you were seeing anyone, and it felt good to tell him you were and that Uncle Adam is a lieutenant commander in the United States Navy." This was said with a good deal of pride.

Shana bet that caused ol' Brad to sit up and take notice.

"I wish my mom was here," Jazmine confessed suddenly. "I'm worried about her."

Shana wrapped her arm around Jazmine's shoulders and drew her close. "She seems to be in good spirits." Or she had been until recently.

"She sounds happy when she e-mails me," Jazmine said. "But sometimes I wonder if she's telling the truth."

The kid certainly had her mother pegged.

Jazmine leaned against Shana. "This has been good,"

she said decisively. "It's even better than a tea party. Except we didn't watch a movie or eat our ice cream—but we can do that now. How about…the first Harry Potter movie? I've got the DVD."

"Sure."

"I'm going to miss Uncle Adam," Jazmine told her sadly. "It won't be the same without him."

Shana could only agree.

Jazmine was asleep an hour later. She lay curled up on the sofa with an afghan covering her. Shana turned off the television set and logged on to the computer.

Sent: July 15
From: Shana@mindsprung.com
To: Alison.Karas@woodrowwilson.navy.mil
Subject: My love/hate relationship with men!

Dear Ali,

I hope you realize what a terrific kid you have. Jazmine and I have just spent the last two hours sharing secrets (plus eating ice cream and watching a Harry Potter movie).

Adam got his orders for Hawaii and didn't even have time to say goodbye. Even worse, I got stuck telling Jazmine.

Trust me, I wasn't too happy with him. I would've let him know how I felt about that, but I was in shock. Do transfers always happen this fast in the Navy? Never mind, he already explained that they don't.

Getting back to Jazmine. She took the news about Adam fairly well. I wasn't sure what I expected and I know she's upset, but as Adam said, she's a Navy kid. She did ask if I knew in advance, and I had to confess that I did. Once I admitted I'd been holding out on her, her own heavily guarded secret came out.

Are you ready for this? Our Jazmine had a conversation with Brad! Apparently he phoned and she informed him I was seeing someone else. I wish she hadn't…. Well, to be honest, that's not entirely true. He told Jazmine that he misses me. Interesting, don't you think? Not to worry, I'd never go back to him.

Once we'd both confessed our secrets, we talked about you and discovered we're both concerned. Jazz is afraid you're hiding your feelings from her— and Alison, I have to tell you that your daughter has good instincts. I didn't say anything, but I know you've been down lately. You refuse to answer my questions about Commander Dillon, and my guess is this involves him. I know, I know, you've already said it a dozen times—there's nothing between you. Technically I'm sure that's true, but…there's more to the situation, isn't there?

What you say or don't say to Jazz is up to you, but she sees through you far too easily, so don't try to pull the wool over her eyes. Jazmine would rather deal with the truth than worry about what's troubling you.

Oh, one last thing. The kid has graduated from tea parties to ice cream. You can thank me for that.

Keep in touch.

Love,
Shana

The following evening, when Shana arrived home from work exhausted, cranky and hungry for something other than pizza or canned chili, the phone rang. With unwarranted optimism, she opened the refrigerator and searched for inspiration—something easy and fast that would pass for healthy. Or sort of healthy. The wilted green pepper, leftover Chinese fried rice and half can of clam chowder weren't appealing.

The phone was still ringing and Shana looked around to see where Jazmine had disappeared. Normally she didn't need to worry about answering the phone because her niece leaped on it like a hungry cat on a cornered mouse.

"I'll get it," she called out when she saw that the bathroom door was closed. Grabbing the phone, Shana cradled it against her shoulder and turned to the cupboard in a second attempt to find a supper solution.

"Hello." The cupboard, stacked with canned foods, offered little in the way of ideas.

"Shana."

"Adam?" In her excitement she nearly dropped the phone. She'd hoped she'd hear from him, but hadn't dared believe. He missed her, he said; he'd been thinking about her. Instantly her heart went on alert. She was afraid to put too much weight on a single phone call and yet so pleased it was all she could do not to leap up and down.

"How's my girl?" he asked in a low, sexy voice.

Shana sighed and leaned against the wall. "I'm doing great." Especially now that she'd heard from him.

"I was asking about Jazmine," he teased.

Shana laughed. "She's great, too. I want you to know we had a pity party over you."

"A what?"

"Never mind—it's a girl thing." She felt so buoyant, so happy, she couldn't prevent a giggle from slipping out.

Adam went directly to the reason for his call. "I got an e-mail from Jazmine and it started me thinking."

"You received an e-mail from her already?"

"Actually she sent this before I flew out. Can I ask you something?"

"Sure."

"Jazz said that Brad phoned you recently."

"Jealous?" she asked lightly, dismissing the question because he had no reason for concern. It would be manipulative to play one man against another, and she refused to do it.

"A little," he admitted with obvious reluctance. "I need to know if you're serious about Brad."

"You're phoning me all the way from Hawaii because you're afraid of a little competition?" she asked. "Adam, you should know better than that."

"Competition doesn't frighten me, but I have to know where I stand with you."

"I can't believe you're talking about Brad," she said, letting her bewilderment show in her voice.

Adam held his ground. "According to Jazmine, you

have what she calls *issues* and one of those issues is Brad, and I figured—"

"Brad," she interrupted, "is out of my life."

"Apparently no one bothered to tell him that. I know of two times he's contacted you. Are there others?"

Shana was completely dumbfounded now. "You men are all alike," she snapped. "You're so…so territorial. Why are we even having this conversation?" She lifted the hair from her forehead and pressed her hand there as if to contain her outrage—or her growing headache. Unfortunately it didn't work. She could think of only one reason Brad had revealed any new interest, and that was because he believed she'd become involved with another man. He considered Shana "his." Now Adam was doing the very same thing.

"Are you upset with me?" he had the audacity to ask.

"You must be joking." If she had to tell him, then there was something lacking in her communication skills. "Yes, Adam, I am upset. You don't seem to care about *me*. Your big concern is that I might be tempted to go back to Brad."

They both took a moment to let the sparks die down. Shana was afraid to say anything more, afraid the conversation would deteriorate further and they'd reach a point of no return.

The bathroom door opened then and Jazmine stepped out, hair wrapped in a towel.

"Here," Shana said, shoving the telephone receiver toward her. "It's your uncle Adam. Talk to him."

"Shana, we aren't finished yet," she heard him yell.

"Oh, yes, we are," she said loud and clear. She just couldn't resist.

Jazmine tentatively accepted the phone, but the conversation was short. Angry, and uncertain how to cope with her anger, Shana paced across the kitchen floor to the window and stood there, staring out at the garden.

Jazmine turned to her after she'd hung up the phone. "Should I get out the ice cream?"

Shana managed to smile. "You know, that doesn't sound like a bad idea."

Chapter Seventeen

Commander Frank Dillon figured he had to be the biggest jerk alive, but in his own defense, his behavior toward SMO Karas was motivated strictly by self-preservation.

A week after he'd gone back to sick bay, he was released. Unfortunately, it wasn't soon enough. Every second he spent in close proximity to Alison was pure agony. More times than he wanted to admit, he had to remind himself that she was married. Married with a capital *M*. All he had to do was glance at the ring to remember she was off-limits. Granted, she'd switched it to her right hand, but that act of deception actually bothered him more.

He'd fallen for her, and fallen hard. Whenever he saw her, his heart did a free fall—like a paratrooper diving from a plane—until he saw that damned ring. Then he knew it was time to pull the rip cord and put an end to his ridiculous fascination with the woman.

This sort of thing didn't happen. Not to him. He was particularly confused by the fact that although Alison wore a wedding band, she'd sent him some pretty clear signals—signals that said she was interested and available. While he was undeniably tempted, Frank felt sickened by her lack of respect for her husband and her vows. He wanted nothing more to do with her.

Back on the bridge at the end of his shift, Frank knew the crew had been eagerly waiting for the *USS Woodrow Wilson* to make its port call in Guam. Shore leave had been granted.

During his years in the Navy, Frank had sailed all over the world, and his favorite destination was the South Pacific. He'd read many accounts of the action here during World War II, as well as histories of the explorers.

"You headed ashore?" Commander Howden asked, joining Frank on the bridge.

Frank, still feeling the effects of his surgery, had decided against leaving the carrier. There would be ample opportunity on other voyages. "Not this time."

"A few of us are talking about golf and dinner. Why don't you come along?"

"Thanks, I'll give it some thought." Frank wouldn't willingly admit it, but he felt too weak. A round of golf would probably do him in.

Howden started to walk away, then unexpectedly turned back. "I met the senior medical officer the other day—Alison Karas," he said casually.

Frank stiffened at the sound of her name.

"She's a good woman. I knew her husband."

Frank's jaw tightened at his use of the past tense. "Knew?"

Hal nodded. "He was killed a couple of years ago in a training accident. He'd been aboard the *USS Abraham Lincoln*. You heard about it," he said.

"Yes—but I didn't make the connection." Frank spoke quietly.

"No reason you should, I suppose," Howden continued. "I just realized it myself."

Frank felt angry with himself for the false assumptions he'd made. Alison was a widow and all along, all this time, he'd believed she was married and unfaithful. He hated everything he'd been thinking about her, hated the way he'd magnified her supposed transgressions in his mind. He knew why he'd done it—because he was afraid of what might happen.

As soon as possible, Frank went down to sick bay. He needed—no, wanted—to apologize. He couldn't explain his behavior, but he could let Alison know he regretted what he'd said and done. Perhaps the best course of action was to leave things as they were, but he was unwilling to do that.

He found Lieutenant Rowland on duty in sick bay. Not an enviable task when the majority of his shipmates were touring paradise. The lieutenant snapped to attention when Frank came in.

"Can I help you, Commander?"

Frank returned the salute. "At ease. I'm looking for Ali. Do you know where I might find her?"

"Ali?" The young officer couldn't hide his surprise. "I'm sorry, sir, she's gone ashore."

Frank had guessed as much. "Did she happen to mention where she was going?"

"No, sir, but I suspect she's headed toward the Farmer's Market. A few of the other women officers mentioned they were planning to check it out."

"Thank you," Frank said as he spun around. His energy had been waning, but adrenaline pumped through him now as he hurried off the ship. Fortunately, he was familiar with the island and grabbed the first taxi he saw, paying the driver handsomely.

The streets swarmed with sailors, tourists and locals. The carnival-like atmosphere was everywhere. Music played, chickens squawked and locals hawked their wares, eager to separate the sailors from their hard-earned dollars. The market was so crowded it was nearly impassable.

In this mass of humanity, Frank wondered if locating Alison was a lost cause. That didn't discourage him, but he knew his odds weren't good.

What he should do, Frank decided after a fruitless hour, was think like a woman. The problem with that was he didn't *know* how a woman thought. If he did, his marriage might've lasted longer than two years.

Marriage. The word shot through his brain. Even if he located Ali, he wasn't sure exactly what he'd say to her, or how she'd react. He'd apologize, that much he knew. He must've been intolerable the entire time he was in sick bay, and he admired the way she'd confronted him, admired her professionalism. It wasn't easy to admit he'd been a colossal jerk; if for no other reason, Frank owed her an apology. Then, with his conscience clear, he'd walk away and that would be the end of it.

Suddenly he saw her. She was with a group of female officers, examining a bolt of silk. A flower lei was draped around her neck and the sun shone on her gleaming dark hair. Gazing at her, Frank stood stock-still as the human traffic moved around him.

He watched Ali run her palm over the red silk and ask the proprietor one question and then another. Frank couldn't hear the man's response, but apparently she didn't like it because she promptly shook her head and left without further haggling.

She hadn't seen Frank, since she was moving straight toward him. He remained frozen, waiting for her to notice that he was there. The two women with her recognized him first. One of them, another lieutenant commander, tilted her head toward Alison and he saw Alison's eyes swing in his direction. Almost immediately she looked away, an expression of discomfort on her face.

"Lieutenant Commander Karas," he said crisply, stepping up to her. Perhaps she'd think he was on official business. "I need a moment of your time."

She blinked as if gathering her composure.

He scowled at her companions and they quickly took the hint.

"We'll meet up with you later," one friend stated, setting off.

The other lingered a moment, obviously concerned about leaving Ali in the company of the ogre patient. But at Ali's nod, she rejoined the first woman.

"How can I help you, Commander?" Ali asked. Her shoulders were back as if she expected another ugly confrontation.

Frank wasn't good at apologizing. It wasn't something he'd had much practice at. He began to speak, and then paused to clear his throat before he could get out even one short sentence. "I want to apologize for last week."

Her eyes flared briefly, but she didn't respond.

"I have no excuse for my rude and arrogant behavior," he went on, repeating the very words she'd used to describe him. He despised humiliation in any form, but in this instance he deserved it.

"Apology accepted, Commander. No one likes being sick and helpless."

"That's true," he agreed, willing to accept her explanation.

His remark was followed by silence. Frank usually didn't have problems expressing his views, but just then, standing in a crowded market in the middle of a South Pacific island—standing there with Ali—he couldn't think of a single intelligent thing to say.

"I appreciate everything you did to make my stay as comfortable as possible," he muttered.

"You're welcome," she said abruptly. She seemed eager to leave.

Frank didn't blame her.

"Is there anything else?" she prodded when he didn't resume the conversation.

"No," he said without inflection, but he wanted to scream that there *was*. He just didn't know how to say it. Had they been anyplace else, he might have found the courage to let her know he admired her.

Without another word, she turned and walked toward her friends who stood at a booth, ignoring the proprietor and focusing their attention on him and Ali. Both women seemed to have plenty of opinions, because their heads were close together and they talked rapidly. Frank hated being the object of their scrutiny, but there was no help for it. He'd done what he could; now he had to leave things as they were.

"Lieutenant Commander Karas," he called out sharply, stopping her.

Alison glanced over her shoulder.

"I heard—I'm sorry about your husband."

For the briefest of moments, in the second or two it took her to blink, Alison's eyes went liquid with grief. She quickly regained control of her emotions. "Thank you, Commander. Like you, Peter dedicated his life to the Navy."

He nodded and felt properly put in his place.

That said, Ali joined her friends. The three of them left and were swallowed up by the crowd.

If searching for Ali was out of character, what he did next was even more so. He returned to the silk merchant and purchased the entire bolt of fabric Alison had so recently examined. The hell if he knew what to do with fifteen yards of red silk.

Chapter Eighteen

"I'd like to talk to you when you've got a free moment," Catherine said as soon as Shana showed up for work Monday morning.

Dread instantly filled her. It was said bad news came in threes. Adam had left for Hawaii, Brad wanted her back—or so he'd claimed—and now she feared the worst calamity of all. Her most valued employee was about to quit. Shana could deal with just about anything except that.

"N-now is convenient," she managed to stutter. It wasn't, but she'd have an ulcer if she put this off.

Catherine joined her in the kitchen but kept an eye on the ice-cream counter in case a customer came in.

"You aren't going to quit, are you?" Shana asked point-blank. Catherine had quickly become her friend and confidante. "Because if you do, I'm throwing in the towel right now."

Catherine brushed aside her concern with a wave of her hand. "Of course I'm not quitting. I love my job."

Relief washed over her, and Shana reached out to hug the other woman. "I'm so grateful… I don't think I could take much more."

"That's one of the reasons I thought we should talk," Catherine said. "I don't mean to put my nose where it doesn't belong, but like I said when you interviewed me, I worked in the school cafeteria for almost fifteen years. We were a close-knit group and were able to discuss everything with one another."

"I want you to feel free to do the same here," Shana assured her.

A smile relaxed the older woman's features, and Shana could see that she'd been worried. "Okay. I have a couple of ideas I'd like to try out, so we can take ice-cream requests in a more orderly fashion," Catherine said, "but I understand this is your business and I won't take offense if you don't think they'll work."

"Anything you can suggest would be appreciated," Shana told her. "You're my most important asset, and I want you to know that."

"I wrote everything out for you to read at your leisure," Catherine said, handing her an envelope.

Shana tucked it inside her apron pocket. "Please feel free to share any ideas you have with me," she said. "I'm interested in all your suggestions."

Catherine positively beamed at the praise. "Now, I don't want you to get the notion that I'm taking over the shop or being dictatorial," she said.

That notion was laughable. "I'd never have survived the last couple of weekends without you and your husband."

DEBBIE MACOMBER189

Catherine's eyes brightened at the mention of her
husband. "Louis had the time of his life."

They'd been wonderful with the customers and reminded Shana of the Olsens, who'd owned the shop for
all those years. Catherine and Louis were so natural
with children and treated everyone like family. Shana
envied their ability, and knew this kind of friendliness
was a big reason her customers returned over and over
again. She'd been fortunate to hire Catherine, and Louis
was a bonus…and a darling.

"You know who to call if you want another day off."
Catherine smiled. "In fact, Louis said if you're ever
looking to sell, we'd like the right of first refusal, but I
told him you'd just bought the business and it wasn't
likely you'd be interested in selling."

"No, but I'll certainly keep that in mind." Shana had
invested her entire financial future in this shop. So far,
she was meeting payroll and keeping her head above
water, but this was her busy season. The Olsens had
warned her that the winter months could be a fiscal
challenge. Shana hoped to find ways to stay afloat when
the weather was dreary. Ice-cream sales would decrease
in winter, but she hoped the pizza part of the business
would continue to flourish. Thankfully, Lincoln Park
was much-used year round.

"Also," Catherine added, sounding hesitant. "I know
this isn't any of my concern, but it seems to me you
haven't been yourself the last few days."

So it was that obvious.

"Is there a problem?" the other woman asked gently,
in the same way Ali might have done had she been
there. Trading e-mails was better than nothing but they
weren't a substitute for face-to-face communication.

Shana slumped against the wall and automatically shook her head. For three nights straight, she hadn't slept more than a couple of hours. When she did manage to drift off, she dreamed of Adam and then woke tired and depressed.

"Man troubles?" Catherine asked. "You don't need to tell me, not unless you want. But sometimes just talking things out with someone else can help."

Shana nodded, reflecting that the school district had lost a wonderful employee. In Shana's opinion, Catherine was much too young to retire.

"It's just that, well…this is complicated." Shana wasn't sure how to explain without going into more detail than necessary.

"Does this have to do with Brad or Adam?" Catherine prompted.

Shana's mouth fell open. "How do you know about Brad?" Her eyes narrowed and she answered her own question. It could only be her niece. "Jazmine."

Catherine nodded, folding her hands. She looked about as guilty as a woman can. "Jazmine and I are friends, and the truth of it is, she confided in me because she's worried about you."

"She is, is she?" Shana couldn't wait to ask Jazmine about this.

"Jazmine is a dear girl and she meant well," Catherine said immediately.

"Who else has she told?" Shana demanded. Apparently her heart-to-heart with her niece hadn't been as effective as she'd hoped. Jazmine seemed intent on spreading Shana's problems throughout the entire neighborhood.

"I don't think she's mentioned it to anyone else,"

Catherine was quick to reassure her. "Certainly not Charles. I can't be positive, of course, but…" Her voice trailed off.

"Of course," Shana echoed. Jazmine was a handful. Spending her days at the park with friends or in the ice-cream parlor with Shana wasn't the ideal situation, but it was the best that could be done for now. Unless Shana looked into some kind of summer camp for her…

"The only reason Jazmine said anything was because I asked her if she knew what was bothering you. So if any-one's to blame, it's me," Catherine insisted, her face red-dening. "I apologize, Shana."

"Don't worry about it." But Shana decided she'd still ask Jazmine later.

"Is there anything I can do to help?" Catherine of-fered. "Like I said, I'm a good listener."

After several sleepless nights, Shana could use some advice. "All right," she agreed with a deep sigh. "My life's a bit of a mess at the moment," she said, then pro-ceeded to tell Catherine about her five-year relationship with Brad and how it had ended. She described how he'd been an important part of her life, and then he was gone; just after that, Jazmine had arrived and on the heels of her niece Adam Kennedy showed up.

Catherine nodded often during the course of their lengthy one-sided discussion.

"Are you in love with Adam?" she asked when Shana had finished.

"Yes. *No.* How can I be?" She paused. "Good grief, I'm the last person who'd know."

"You love Brad, though?" Catherine continued.

"No." This came without the slightest hesitation. "Al-though I loved him at one time. At least, I believed I did."

"I don't think breaking off a relationship is ever as easy as we want it to be," Catherine said thoughtfully. "We invest our hopes and dreams in a particular relationship, and when that doesn't work out, we sometimes have difficulty admitting it."

"That's true." Shana nodded, remembering the years she'd devoted to Brad with such hope for a future together.

"I wonder if what you really want is for Brad to recognize how much he wronged you."

Shana grinned. That was so true, it was almost painful.

"It gives women a sense of vindication," Catherine pronounced solemnly, "when a man realizes the error of his ways."

Shana nodded again. She wished she'd talked to her friend weeks ago; Catherine saw everything with such clarity and insight.

"Are you tempted to take him back?"

"Not at all…" She let the rest fade.

"You're sure?"

"Yes, but…" The thought had only occurred to her now. "Until I talk to him…" Even as she said the words, Shana knew that a telephone conversation wouldn't be enough. She needed to see Brad, talk to him in person, which she hadn't really done, not after that one dramatic scene when she'd confronted him with what she knew about Sylvia. Then she'd gone to Seattle to think. She'd phoned him, but hadn't spoken to him in person. Shana had never honestly explained her dissatisfaction with the relationship—aside from the Sylvia issue—nor had she made clear that reconciliation was out of the question. Her severing of the relationship wasn't a ploy to get him back. And it wasn't something she'd done on a whim.

Shana looked at Catherine.

"Actually," Catherine said, "I think talking to Brad is a good idea."

"I do, too." Shana removed her apron and carelessly tossed it over the back of a chair. "Can you take over for me?"

"Now?" Catherine asked, seemingly surprised at how quickly Shana was acting.

"Please. I'll take Jazmine to Portland with me."

"I'll need to call Louis, but I'm pretty sure he hasn't got anything planned for the next few days. Let me find out." She walked over to the phone, and after just a minute's discussion, replaced the receiver. "He said he'd be delighted."

"Good." Her decision made, her resolve strong, Shana went outside to collect Jazmine.

"One question," Catherine said, stopping her on her way out the door. "What do you want me to say if Adam phones?"

That wasn't likely to happen, but she certainly didn't want her friend to divulge that she'd gone off to see Brad. "Our last conversation ended kind of badly, so I doubt—"

"You said that earlier," Catherine broke in, "but I bet he'll be phoning soon. He probably regrets how things went as much as you do."

Shana did regret it and although she hadn't said so, Catherine had intuitively known. "Tell him I'm visiting an old friend out of town." It would be the truth, because she planned to call Gwen Jackson as soon as she got home. As she spoke, Shana absently watched a delivery truck pull into the parking space in front of the restaurant.

The bell above the door jangled cheerfully, and

Catherine hurried out of the kitchen. Shana followed her, sorry their conversation had been interrupted.

All she saw was a large FedEx box.

"Shana Berrie?" the delivery man asked.

Catherine gestured toward Shana.

"I'm Shana," she responded, trying to remember if she'd recently ordered anything that would come by overnight courier. She couldn't think of a thing.

Jazmine trailed the delivery man inside. "What's that?" she asked excitedly.

"I don't know yet." Shana signed the clipboard and yanked the tab at the end of the box. The sender's name was that of a floral company in… It started with a *W* but a large smudge obscured the rest of the word.

"It's probably from Brad," Jazmine muttered disdainfully. "I told you he wants you back."

"No way," Shana said, shaking her head. Anything he had to send her wouldn't come in a box. She'd been waiting for a small jewelry box from him long enough to guarantee that.

When the carton was open, two orchid leis slid onto the counter. Waikiki—that was it. Hawaii. Well, that was one puzzle solved. Catherine gave an immediate gasp of wonder at their delicate beauty.

"Uncle Adam," Jazmine burst out in a squeal of unrestrained delight.

"Is there a card?" Catherine asked.

Shana searched the inside of the box and found it. *"To my two favorite girls. I miss you. Adam."*

Jazmine draped one of the leis over her shoulders, beaming with joy.

Shana wasn't nearly as pleased. "That was a cowardly thing to do," she declared. Just leave it to a man to let flowers do his talking for him. Well, she'd deal with Adam later, but at the moment she had another man on her mind, and that was Brad Moore.

Chapter Nineteen

Shana felt as if she was on a mission now. What Catherine had said was so true—it was as difficult to let go of the expectations created by a relationship as the relationship itself. She needed to complete the process of disconnecting herself from Brad.

The minute she arrived home, Shana instructed Jazmine to pack an overnight bag.

"Where are we going?" Jazmine asked, catching Shana's enthusiasm. The lei still hung around her neck. Shana wore hers, too. She appreciated Adam's gesture, but not as much as she would have if he'd e-mailed or phoned her first. She didn't *want* to think about him now, and yet it was impossible not to. The orchids wafted a lovely scent, reminding her of Adam and their shared kisses.

"To Portland."

"Portland?" Jazmine moaned. "Why are we going *there?*"

Shana already had her suitcase out of her closet and open on top of her bed. She didn't need much—her pajamas, a set of clothes and clean underwear. Her toiletries and makeup. That was it.

"Aunt Shana…"

She whirled around, almost forgetting Jazmine was in the room. "I'm sorry. You asked me why we're going to Portland." The girl deserved the truth. "I need to talk to Brad."

"Brad!" Her niece spit out the name as if she had a bug in her mouth. "Why?" she cried with such a shocked look that Shana nearly laughed. "You're wearing Uncle Adam's lei and you want to visit *Brad?*"

"I need to talk to him."

"But why?"

"It's important," was all Shana could tell her.

"You're not going back to him, are you?" Jazmine's eyes pleaded with hers.

"No. Now pack an overnight bag. I want to head out as soon as we can." Shana had no intention of being away from the business for more than twenty-four hours. She'd already called Gwen and left a message, asking if she could put them up for the night. If not, they'd get a hotel room—a reasonably priced one. The trip would be an adventure, and Shana would make an effort to see that Jazmine had fun. If there was time, they'd stop at Jensen Beach to shop and play tourist. Her niece would enjoy that.

Jazmine hesitated in the doorway. "You're sure about this?"

"Very sure." This was a conversation she should've had with Brad when she left him.

"Are you still in love with Brad?" Jazmine asked urgently, staring up at her.

"No. I told you that."

Jazmine frowned, apparently not entirely convinced. "Do you always do stuff like this?"

"You mean act on impulse?" Shana clarified. She didn't think she did, but she realized she was only beginning to know herself. Buying the ice-cream parlor had been the first impulsive thing she'd done in years. Now this. Perhaps it came from a new sense of having control over her own life.

"Are you packed?" Shana asked, knowing very well that she wasn't.

"Not yet." Her niece dawdled for another few minutes. "I don't think I can leave," she said with a shrug. "My garden needs watering, and Uncle Adam said it's important to give the plants a drink every morning and every night." A smile raised the edges of her mouth. "He said I should sing to them, but nothing too fast or with a strong beat."

Shana smiled, too. "I think they can go without water for a day. You can make it up to them later and give them an extra drink and sing a few lullabies."

Jazmine still hesitated, then finally appeared to reach a decision. She went into her own bedroom.

It seemed to take her niece forever to assemble what she needed. When she reappeared, she was dragging her backpack behind her as if it weighed fifty pounds. "We can go now," she said with an undisguised lack of enthusiasm.

"Good." Shana stood by the car, waiting impatiently. She wondered if Jazmine had transferred the entire contents of her dresser into her backpack, but decided against asking.

"Everything locked up?" Shana had checked the back door and the windows.

Jazmine nodded, climbed into the car while Shana heaved her backpack into the trunk, and fastened her seat belt. Then she sighed heavily.

Shana walked around to the driver's side. "Think of this as an adventure," she said in a breezy voice.

Jazmine's chin drooped to her chest. "Are you going to tell Uncle Adam what you did?"

Involuntarily Shana fingered the lei. "I don't know. Maybe."

"What if Brad gets you to move back to Portland?"

"That won't happen," Shana promised, hiding a smile.

"I just don't understand why it's so important for you to see him again," Jazmine whined. "You said it was over. You said you didn't want to have anything to do with him again. You said—"

"I know what I said." Shana cut her off, started the car and pulled away from the curb.

Jazmine was quiet for the first few minutes. "Where will we stay the night?" she asked.

"At a friend's place."

"What friend?"

"Gwen. You haven't met her."

"Does she have kids?"

"No," Shana murmured as she merged onto the West Seattle freeway and toward Interstate 5.

"Do I get to come along when you talk to Brad?"

Shana hadn't actually considered that, but the answer wasn't difficult. "Probably not."

Jazmine's shoulders slumped forward. "That's what I figured."

"Jazz, this *isn't* what you think. I'm going to see Brad to tell him something…." Only now were her thoughts catching up with her actions.

"What?" Jazmine asked, looking at her for the first time since she got into the car.

"To tell him I made the right decision when I left Portland."

"You mean you're not *sure?*" Her niece seemed about to burst into tears.

"No. Why are you so worried?"

Jazmine stared out the passenger window as if the concrete freeway interchanges were the most fascinating scenery in the world. "Brad phoned, and I told you and then…then you and Uncle Adam had an argument, and now you're driving to Portland. I'm not stupid, you know. I can connect the dots."

"Well, you're looking at the wrong picture." Shana could understand why Jazmine had reached those conclusions but they weren't correct. "You don't need to be concerned, Jazz. I promise."

"I want you to marry Uncle Adam. Don't you want to?"

"Let me deal with one man at a time, okay?" At the moment Adam was the last person she wanted to think about. "Once I talk to Brad, you and I can discuss your uncle Adam."

"Oh, sure," Jazmine muttered. "You don't have to explain anything to *me.* I'm just a kid," she said sarcastically.

Shana sighed. Jazmine really ought to enroll in a drama class because she clearly had talent. In fact, maybe they could find one when they got back….

"Did you mention this to Mom?" Jazmine asked after a precious few moments of silence.

Shana kept her eyes on the road. "There wasn't time to e-mail her."

"Does your friend have a computer I can use?"

"I'm sure she does."

"I'll let Mom know where we are and what you're doing." Jazmine announced this with a great deal of satisfaction.

"Fine." Shana just bet the nine-year-old would delight in letting her mother know they were in Portland. Smiling, she wondered how Jazmine would embellish the tale.

"What if he isn't there?"

Uh-oh. "You mean Brad?" Not once had Shana stopped to consider that. "I…I don't know." This wasn't a situation in which she'd be comfortable leaving behind her newly printed business card. If Brad learned she'd come by his office, or even his condo, he'd assume the wrong thing.

"He has to be there," she said aloud. "He just has to."

Adam checked his watch and calculated the time in Seattle. Three-thirty. The leis should have arrived by now, according to the delivery schedule. He imagined Shana's surprise and pleasure at opening the box and discovering the leis. The orchids were supposed to pave the way for part two of his reconciliation plan—a phone call.

He wasn't sure how it had happened, but somehow his previous conversation with Shana had gone in completely the wrong direction. He certainly hadn't intended to become embroiled in an argument. He couldn't even figure out what kind of mistake he'd made. Whatever it was, he sincerely hoped she was over it by now.

Adam had talked to one of his friends about Shana's reaction. John, another lieutenant commander, had said his wife always started an argument before he left. Apparently it was common among Navy wives. For whatever reason, women found it easier to send their men off to sea if they were upset with them about something. Adam didn't understand it, but John claimed their disagreement was simply Shana's way of letting him know she was in love with him.

That had taken Adam by surprise. *Shana loved him?* Shana loved him! He chose to believe it because he so badly wanted to. He wasn't much of a romantic, but the thought of Shana waiting for him back in Seattle made him happy in a way he'd never experienced before.

He hurried home to make the call in privacy. When he didn't think he could bear to wait another minute, he reached for the telephone and punched out the number for the ice-cream parlor. Leaning back on his sofa, feet stretched out on the coffee table, he listened to the ringing of the phone.

"Olsen's Ice Cream and Pizza Parlor."

The man's voice shook Adam. "Who's this?"

"Who's this?" the male voice echoed.

Adam dropped his stocking feet to the floor and leaned forward far enough to prop his elbows on his knees. "Is Shana there?"

"No. Who's calling, please?"

"Lieutenant Commander Adam Kennedy."

"Oh, hello." The voice instantly became friendly. "This is Louis, Catherine's husband. I'd better let you talk to her. Hold on."

"Should I call back later?"

"No, no, it's fine. Here's Cath."

A couple of seconds later, Shana's number-one employee was on the line. "Adam, hello." She sounded slightly breathless. "What can I do for you?"

"I actually called to talk to Shana."

She paused a telltale moment. "I'm sorry, but you missed her. Shana took Jazmine on a...short vacation."

Adam's disappointment was keen. "Did the leis arrive?" Those had cost him a pretty penny, and he hoped they weren't sitting in a box wilting before Shana even had a chance to see them.

"Oh, yes, and she was...pleased. Jazmine, too."

"Did she mention where she was going?" Perhaps he should try reaching her on her cell. He'd just assumed she'd be at the restaurant.

"Yes, yes, she did," Catherine said. She seemed distracted; either Adam had phoned at a bad time or she was reluctant to tell him exactly where Shana had gone.

"I'll try her cell," he murmured.

"You could do that, of course," Catherine agreed politely. "But...but she might be out of reach."

"Why? Did they drive into the mountains?"

"Uh, no."

Her hesitation made him suspicious. "The ocean?"

"No, ah—listen, I need to go.... There are customers waiting."

"Catherine," Adam said softly. She was hiding something, and he wanted to know what.

"I'll tell Shana you phoned."

"You said Jazmine's with her?"

"Of course she is," Catherine answered sharply.

"What's going on there?" Adam demanded. "Where's Shana?"

Catherine sighed deeply. "I told her. The minute she

said she was leaving, I told Shana you'd phone. Sure
enough, here I am, having to tell you."

"Tell me what?"

"Shana's in Portland, visiting a friend. Gwen—a female friend." She spoke with finality, as though she
hoped that was the end of his questions.

"Portland?" A chill raced down Adam's arms, one
that had nothing to do with the tropical breeze coming
through the sliding glass door. "I don't suppose this has
anything to do with Brad?"

"You'll have to ask her that." Catherine sighed again.
"I refuse to incriminate myself—or her."

Adam snorted. "I see."

Dammit, he did see—and he wasn't enjoying the
view.

Chapter Twenty

Shana's stomach tensed with anxiety. What had been a brilliant idea that morning seemed utterly ridiculous now. She waited inside the lobby of Brad's office building, pacing back and forth, trying to put words to the mangled feelings inside her head. She was *not* looking for a reconciliation. But Catherine's insight had made her aware that she'd abandoned her previous life without really settling matters with Brad. There were things that had to be said…except now, all she could think about was Adam.

Thankfully Jazmine was safely ensconced at Gwen's. Her friend was a nurse who worked the night shift; she was up and about when Shana and Jazmine arrived on her front porch. As soon as she heard the reason for Shana's visit, she'd sent her off with a pep talk. Gwen's encouragement had carried Shana all the way to downtown Portland.

However, Shana's resolve had quickly waned when she stepped inside the luxurious lobby. All of a sudden, her tongue felt glued to the roof of her mouth, and when someone casually walked past and greeted her, her returning "good afternoon" came out sounding like "goonoon."

Mortified, Shana hurried into the ladies' room and locked herself inside a stall. She hadn't even bothered to change clothes. Filled with purpose, she'd driven to Portland in shorts and a T-shirt with a smudge of chocolate ice cream on the hem. She was about to have one of the most important conversations of her life, and she resembled someone trying out for clown school.

Sitting on the toilet seat, Shana buried her face in her hands. What was she thinking? She was astonished at her own audacity and horrified at this latest example of impulsive behavior.

Her goal, when she left Seattle in a heated frenzy, had been to make Brad Moore realize what he'd lost—and whose fault that was. She was going to end the relationship properly, definitively, for her own sake, and ultimately for his, too. After coming this far, she refused to turn back. She'd simply buy something appropriate. There was time.

That decision made, Shana walked into an ultra-expensive boutique in the lobby. Either the sales clerk took pity on her or she was afraid Shana was about to shoplift a mannequin, because she immediately shot out from behind the cash register.

"Can I help you?"

"Can you ever." Shana threw herself on the mercy of a complete stranger. "I need an outfit that'll make a man rue the day he—"

"Say no more." The clerk raised her hand. "I have just the dress." She looked Shana up and down. "Size four?"

Maybe ten years ago. "Six," she muttered.

"Four. This dress is expensive enough to be a four."

Shana laughed. She didn't care how much it cost; her ego was at stake.

Once she stood in front of the mirror, Shana barely recognized the woman staring back at her. The knee-length floral dress was simple yet elegant, fanning out at her waist in pleats that emphasized her hips and long legs.

"Wow," she whispered, impressed. She didn't even glance at the price tag. It was better not to know.

The clerk nodded approvingly. "Perfect."

Shana twisted around to take a gander at the back and decided that view was even sexier. She hoped Brad took a good, long look when she walked away.

Not wanting to show up clutching a bag with her shorts and T-shirt inside—that kind of contradicted the classy image—she ditched her old clothes.

The only unfortunate part of the new outfit was the matching shoes. The one pair left was a full size too small for Shana, but the slinky sandals were gorgeous. With a minimum of regret, she purchased them anyway. By the time she walked out of the boutique, her little toe on each shoe had squeezed between the narrow straps and escaped. She'd be fine as long as Brad didn't look at her feet.

Shana was still testing her ability to walk when the elevator opened and Brad Moore entered the lobby. Swallowing her breath, Shana nearly choked when Brad saw her. He stopped abruptly, his shock unmistakable.

"Shana," he cried. He held out his arms to her, surprise replaced by delight. "You look fabulous."

"Yes, I do." Now wasn't the time for modesty, especially in light of what she'd paid for this outfit.

She tilted her head to one side and allowed him to kiss her cheek.

"What are you doing here?"

No need to beat around the bush. "I came to see you."

"Great." He didn't bother to hide his enthusiasm. "Shall we have a drink somewhere and talk?"

"That would be fine." She played it cool, refusing to let him see how flustered she was.

Taking her by the elbow, Brad led the way out of the high-rise office tower. Shana struggled to keep up with him, the too-tight shoes pinching her feet unmercifully. Her little toes hung over the edge of the shoes and she prayed no one would notice. Thankfully there was a hotel bar across the street.

Brad led her to a small table, ordered them each a glass of merlot and grinned at her as if she were a delectable dessert.

The cocktail waitress brought their wine and Brad sent a flirtatious glance in her direction.

Once he'd finished paying for their drinks, he smiled at her confidently. "You got my message?"

"You mean the one you weren't willing to say to me yourself?"

He had the good grace to look embarrassed. "I would have if you'd been home. Who is that kid, anyway?"

Shana was surprised Jazmine hadn't enlightened him. "My niece. You remember my sister, Alison, don't you? Jazmine is her daughter."

"I met your sister once, right?" Brad raised both eyebrows. "The kid's got attitude."

He hadn't seen anything yet.

"How've you been?" he asked, but before she could respond he added, "I've missed you."

This was where—according to his script—she was supposed to tell him how lonely she'd been without him and how much she regretted the things she'd said and done.

He waited, and when she didn't immediately offer the desired response, he frowned. "I'm glad you're here. We have a lot to discuss."

"I came because—"

Brad reached for her hand, stopping her. "You don't need to say it. We both made mistakes and we're both sorry. Let's leave it at that."

"You think I made a mistake?"

"That's why you're here, isn't it?"

She took her first sip of wine and let its smoothness flow over her tongue. "I came because when I walked out on you, I was angry and hurt."

"I know…"

"I don't feel either of those things anymore. I wanted to look you in the eye, see what I used to find so attractive." She sighed. Whatever it was had long vanished. "I really just came, Brad, to clear the air once and for all, and to do it properly."

Brad's expression changed and he stared at her. "You are coming back to Portland, aren't you?"

She loved this city and missed her job. The ice-cream parlor demanded constant attention and supervision. The hours were long and the financial compensation small. As a pharmaceutical salesperson, she'd been able to leave work at the end of the day and not give her job another thought. Having a business of her own was a completely different proposition. The ice-cream and pizza parlor had seemed like an escape from an unhappy situation, but for the first time, she wondered if she'd made the right decision.

"Shana?" Brad asked, breaking into her musings.

"Portland? I don't know," she admitted honestly.

"You love me, don't you?" He asked the question but she could tell he wasn't as sure of himself as he'd been earlier.

Seeing the crack in his confidence weakened her resolve. "That's just it," Shana said. "I loved you so completely and I was so sure you loved me."

"I do love you," Brad insisted. "I know you were upset and you had every right to be. I was a fool, but I swear to you it'll never happen again. I regretted it immediately. I was sick that I lost you because of Sylvia."

Shana didn't trust him enough to believe his promises.

He seemed to be debating how much of the truth to reveal. "We went out two or three times, but that's beside the point. It didn't take me long to realize I'd made the biggest mistake of my life. It's *you* I love, Shana. It's you I want to be with."

The complete absence of the word *marriage* didn't escape her. In other words, they'd resume their relationship exactly where they'd left off. His script again—but not hers.

Brad must have seen the strength and determination in her eyes. "You mean it, don't you?" he asked morosely. "This really is goodbye."

"Yes."

"But you loved me at one time. I can't believe you don't now."

A sad smile formed but she refused to answer him.

His own smile returned. "You do love me. You wouldn't be here now if you didn't still have feelings for me."

Brad's gaze pleaded with her as he clasped her hand in both of his. "You do love me," he said again.

She remained silent, and all at once he seemed to realize she wasn't changing her mind. That was when he said the one thing that, a few months ago, might have swayed her.

"I want to marry you."

Even that didn't elicit a response.

"I'm sincere, Shana. I couldn't be any more serious. You set the date and the time."

Rather than drag this out, she told him the truth. "I met someone else."

Brad frowned. "Is this the guy your niece mentioned?"

"Yes."

"Certainly didn't take you long, did it?" he asked, sitting back. "So the real reason you're here is to rub my face in it."

"No." Until this moment she hadn't planned to say anything about Adam.

"I thought you were in love with *me*. Pretty fickle, aren't you?"

She smiled, knowing she'd asked for that. "I *was* in love with you, but that's over." She paused. "It's funny, you know."

"I'm not laughing."

She shook her head. "I didn't think it was possible to feel like this about a man on such short acquaintance. Adam's good to me and to my niece…. He's a family friend. That's how we met."

"Bully for you."

"Don't, Brad." She hadn't expected to be this honest with him but it seemed important. She had no intention of being vindictive or mean-spirited. She might not love him anymore, but she didn't begrudge him happiness.

"And what does Adam do?" Brad asked, his words

hard and clipped. "Oh, yes, I remember now. He's some big deal in the Navy." He lifted his brows dismissively. "So. Can you tell me exactly why you're here?"

Shana sipped her wine. "I came here this morning, convinced I had to see you. I already told you why. I felt—and still feel—that I had to end this relationship properly."

Brad closed his eyes for a moment. "Okay. Consider it ended."

"Thank you," she said graciously. "I even went so far as to buy this dress at a price so outrageous I'll be making payments for the next six months." She glanced down at her feet and tried to remember what size shoe her sister wore and hoped it was a seven.

"So this outfit was for my benefit?"

Shana nodded. "I wanted you to be sorry you lost me."

His eyes grew gentle. "I was sorry before you got here. I've been sorry for months."

Despite her mood, she smiled. "That's probably the sweetest thing you've ever said to me."

"So you didn't come here to make me feel bad about you and Popeye?"

Shana inhaled softly. She knew exactly why she'd found it necessary to drive to Portland. "No, I didn't," she said softly. "I came to say goodbye."

Chapter Twenty-One

Adam Kennedy wasn't having a good day. In fact, the entire week was down the septic tank, and he blamed Shana Berrie for that. If she was trying to make him jealous, it was damned well working.

"That's what women do to you," his friend John told him. They sat across from each other at Navy Headquarters for the Pacific Fleet. "They mess with your mind and they make irrational demands. Take my wife, for example. Angie got upset with me because there was a cockroach in the house, as if it's my duty as her husband to rid the place of bugs. Can you believe it? She's afraid of a stupid bug, and if I don't deal with it, I might as well not go home tonight."

Barely hearing his friend's rant, Adam scowled. Shana certainly hadn't wasted any time giving up on him. As far as she was concerned, it seemed to be out of sight, out of mind. Well, fine, great, whatever. If she wanted to race back to lover boy, then that was perfectly fine by him.

The hell it was, Adam decided quickly. He hadn't slept well; his appetite was gone and he had a sick feeling that refused to go away. He didn't know how everything had fallen apart so quickly. In his view they'd *had* a promising relationship, with emphasis on the past tense.

The phone rang and Adam left it for John. What he needed was a bout of hard exercise, but with his shoulder golf was still out of the question and swimming would be just as painful. He could always jog, he supposed, but it wasn't something he enjoyed.

John answered the phone, and Adam watched as his gaze shot across the room. He put the caller on hold. "It's for you. A woman. Says her name is Shana." He gave Adam a significant look, both eyebrows raised.

It took Adam a moment to assimilate that. His pulse accelerated and then immediately slowed. The call was most likely a courtesy to let him know she was going back to lover boy in Portland.

With that in mind, Adam reached for the telephone receiver. He responded in a crisp military tone, keeping his voice devoid of emotion.

"Adam, hello," Shana said, her own voice friendly.

Adam nearly weakened, but he realized she was probably warming him up before she dropped the news. She'd led him on, he mused darkly, and now she was going to make a fool of him.

"I wanted to thank you for the leis. Jazmine and I were thrilled. It was so generous of you."

Adam kept silent, bracing himself.

After an awkward moment, during which he said nothing, Shana said, "I feel badly about the way our last conversation went."

"Forget it," Adam said in the same emotionless tone. He wanted her to think it hardly mattered to him. He should've taken the hint then. Shana was trouble and he'd best get out of this unpredictable relationship. But even as the thought went through his mind, he didn't believe it.

"I blame myself," Shana added, "for picking a fight with you. I was just reacting to your leaving, I guess." She hesitated. "We had so little time, and I knew I was going to miss you so much. Jazmine, too, of course."

John had explained that this was the same reaction he got from his wife, but Adam couldn't really accept that. Why would Shana care whether he was stationed in Hawaii if she was going back to the guy in Portland?

She seemed to realize he wasn't responding. "Are you upset about something?" she asked tentatively.

"Should I be?" He answered her question with one of his own.

"I don't think so." Her voice gained conviction, but gone was the sweet joy he'd heard in her earlier. Now she sounded wary.

"I understand you were out of town," he said, broaching the subject that was foremost on his mind.

His announcement was followed by stark silence. "You know about that?"

"I do. So if you're planning to tell me what I think you are, I'd appreciate if you'd just say it and be done with it."

"Say *what?*"

"You want out," he said flippantly. "So let's just call it quits."

"You're willing to end this without another word?" She seemed shocked—and annoyed.

"I'm not the one who drove down to visit an old lover. You never did say how things went between you and Bernie."

"It's Brad," she corrected. "And you're right, I didn't."

He waited, unwilling to cut off the conversation and at the same time reluctant to continue trading barbs.

"Isn't this all a little silly?" Shana asked.

"When did you decide to go?"

"In the morning. It was a spur-of-the-moment idea. Jazmine and I spent the night with an old friend—an old female friend," she added. "I saw Brad and we talked."

"About what?" He didn't mean to ask and wanted to withdraw the question the moment it left his mouth.

She paused, taking a moment before she answered. "I don't remember if I told you I moved to Seattle in kind of a rush."

"You might've said something like that." He tried to play it cool, but the truth was, he hung on every word.

"So I needed to see Brad."

"I'm sure you did," he muttered, unable to disguise his sarcasm.

His comment generated a lengthy silence. "We had a chance to talk and to say certain things that needed to be said," she finally told him.

She didn't enlighten him as to what those things might be. "So you're back in Seattle?"

"Yes. I have to go now. The only reason I phoned," she said, "is to thank you for the leis. Jazmine and I love them. Now I should get back to work."

Adam had to bite his tongue to keep from pleading

with her to stay on the phone a bit longer. He wished they could start the entire conversation over.

"How's Jazmine?" he asked, using the question as a delaying tactic.

"Fabulous…wonderful. Thank you again for the orchids."

And with that, the line was disconnected. He waited a few seconds while the buzz sounded in his ear. Adam replaced the receiver and glared at the phone as he replayed the conversation. He knew he'd made a number of tactical errors, and that was because his ego had gotten in the way.

"So, how'd it go?" John asked conversationally.

"Not good."

"Sorry to hear that. I told you—women mess with your mind. You should've figured that out by now."

John was right; he should have.

The tension in Adam's stomach didn't diminish all day. At the end of his watch, he returned to his quarters to find the message light on his phone blinking. It was too much to hope that Shana had called him a second time. Holding his breath, he pressed the message button.

Jazmine's voice greeted him. "Uncle Adam, what's with you? You've really blown it now. Call me at the house when you get home. I'll make sure I answer."

Adam reached for the phone. Here he was, conspiring with a nine-year-old. *That* was a sign of desperation.

Chapter Twenty-Two

Ali was quite entertained by the tone of Shana's e-mails in the last week. Her sister was not in a good mood. She'd only brought up Adam's name once, but Ali was well aware that the lieutenant commander was the sole source of Shana's irritation.

Thankfully, Jazmine had been able to fill Ali in. Apparently Adam and Shana had some form of falling-out. Shana had driven to Portland to say a final goodbye to Brad, and Adam was out of sorts about it. From what Jazmine said, they were currently ignoring each other.

Ali didn't usually meddle in other people's romances. She hadn't said anything when Shana was involved with Brad, and she wouldn't interfere now. At least she didn't *think* she would. But those two were perfect together, and it would be a shame if this relationship died because they were too stubborn to admit they were attracted to each other. Although Ali suspected that their feelings had gone way beyond attraction…

Preoccupied, she walked toward the wardroom. She generally ate with the other officers at six every evening, but tonight she was later than usual. Life at sea had grown monotonous, and the days seemed to run into each other without any real break to distinguish one from the next. When she entered the room, there were a few officers at various tables, but she noticed only one.

Commander Frank Dillon.

Ali hadn't seen or talked to him since they'd met in the Farmer's Market in Guam. Just seeing him again gave her pause. She'd thought about their brief conversation that very afternoon; even now she wasn't sure what to make of it. Her friends, too, were full of questions she hadn't been able to answer. Ali filled her tray and started for a table.

"Good evening, Commander," she said, greeting him.

"Ali." He didn't look any too pleased to see her, if his scowl was any indication.

She sat down several tables away, but facing him. It would be utterly rude to present him with her back. "I do hope you've sufficiently recovered." Ali knew she sounded stilted but couldn't help it. She avoided eye contact by reaching for the salt shaker.

"I have, thank you. And you?"

His question caught her unawares. "I haven't been ill, Commander."

"Yes, of course." He stood as if he couldn't leave fast enough and disappeared with such speed, it made her head swim. Clearly she was the last person he wanted to see. Only this time, Ali didn't take offense.

She'd come to the conclusion that she flustered

Commander Dillon, which was a heady sensation. She recalled how gruff and rude he'd been in sick bay and, thanks to their brief conversation on Guam, she finally understood the reason. He'd thought she was married.

The next evening, Alison purposely delayed her meal and arrived at the same time as the night before. Sure enough Frank was there, sitting at the same table, lingering over coffee. He looked up and smiled uncertainly when he saw her.

"Good evening, Commander." She greeted him the same way she had the previous night. After getting her meal, she chose a seat one table closer.

"Lieutenant Commander." His eyes held hers, and he didn't immediately leap up and run away.

"I have a question for you," she said and again reached for the salt shaker. It was a convenient excuse to avert her gaze. She feared he might read her intense interest in him, which seemed to compound after each meeting.

He straightened. "Fire away."

"Do I frighten you?"

He raised one eyebrow. "Truthfully? You terrify me."

"Any particular reason?"

He expelled his breath. "As a matter of fact, there are several. Most of them would get me court-martialed if I mentioned them."

"I see." She didn't really, but she was definitely curious.

"Does that amuse you?" he asked, his face deadpan.

"Commander, are you flirting with me?"

This question seemed to take him aback, and he frowned. "I can assure you I wouldn't know how. Is that what you think I'm doing?"

She shook her head. "I'm not sure, but I do have another question for you."

"All right. I just hope it isn't as difficult as the first." A hint of a smile touched his eyes.

Alison dipped her fork into the creamy mashed potatoes. "I wonder, do you know anything about a bolt of red silk that was delivered to the ship in my name?"

"Red silk?" He shrugged. "I'm afraid I can't help you there."

"That isn't an answer to my question, Commander."

He glanced at his watch, and as if he'd suddenly realized he was late for an important meeting, abruptly stood. He grabbed his coffee cup and took one last swallow before he excused himself and hurried away.

Alison hadn't known what to think when the silk had appeared in her quarters. She was able to track down the petty officer who delivered it, and learned that the man from the market had brought it to the docks. He'd left instructions that it should be taken directly to her. Alison had badly wanted that silk, but the price was more than she'd been willing to pay.

Just before she drifted off to sleep the night before, she'd remembered haggling with the silk merchant just before she'd run into Frank. He must have purchased it for her. It was the only thing that made sense—and yet it didn't. But judging by the way he'd reacted to her questions this evening, she had to wonder.

The following night when Alison arrived at the wardroom, Frank wasn't there. Her heart sank with disappointment. She really didn't have much of an appetite and ate very little of her meal. She'd almost decided against coffee but it was her habit to end her dinner with a cup.

Just when she was ready to leave, uninterested in the

remains of her cooling coffee, Frank rushed in, looking harried.

"Good evening, Commander," Alison said, smiling her welcome. Hiding her pleasure at seeing him had become impossible.

He poured himself a cup of coffee and joined her. This was progress. They'd begun by sitting several tables apart and had drawn closer with each encounter.

He was silent for a few minutes, concentrating on his coffee, methodically adding sugar and cream, then stirring. "You have children?" he asked unexpectedly.

"A nine-year-old daughter."

He nodded.

"Jazmine is living with my sister in Seattle right now."

He nodded again. "Is this the first time you've been apart for so much time?"

"Yes." Then, feeling it was only fair that she be completely honest, Alison said, "This will be my last duty assignment."

"You're leaving the Navy?" He made it sound like an incomprehensible decision.

"My husband loved the Navy the way you do. He couldn't imagine civilian life."

"Can you?" he asked.

"No. But it's something I have to do." The Navy had shaped her life, but now she had to put Jazmine's welfare first. She was proud of how well her daughter had adjusted to a new environment, but a child needed roots and stability. Alison felt obliged to provide that, especially since she'd become, however unwillingly, a single parent.

"Where will you settle?" Frank asked.

"I haven't decided yet. I'm considering Seattle. Jazmine seems to like it there, and it's where my sister lives."

"Is she married?"

"Single," Ali explained. "But she's romantically in- volved with someone."

Frank stared down into his coffee, cupped between his outstretched hands. "I don't know much about ro- mance." He took a swig of coffee. "I'm pretty much a failure in that department."

"You're divorced, aren't you?" She recalled that he'd told her this.

"A long time now."

Alison studied him as he sipped his coffee. "Given up, have you?"

He raised his head, his gaze burning into hers. "Until recently I had." His shoulders rose as if he was taking in a deep breath. "It's not appropriate to ask now, but I was wondering…I was thinking that in a few months, when you've…resigned your commission, you might consider going to dinner with me. It wouldn't mean anything. I mean, there'd be no obligation on either part, and if you're not ready—"

"Commander," Alison said, breaking into his soliloquy. This was the most he'd ever said to her at one time. "Yes."

"Yes?" He eyed her quizzically.

"I'd be honored to have dinner with you."

He seemed tentative, unbelieving, and Ali smiled.

"More than honored," she added softly and reached for her own coffee. She needed a sip to ease the dryness in her mouth and throat.

"It won't be for several months," he warned.

"I'm well aware of that, Commander."

He sighed and looked away. "Don't take this personally, but it's not a good idea for us to continue meeting here."

Disappointment hit her hard. "Why not?" Their meetings were completely innocent. This was the third night in a row, and not once had they even touched.

"Lieutenant Commander," Frank said, his voice barely above a whisper. "You tempt me and while I'm a disciplined man, I don't think I can hold back my feelings for you indefinitely. Give me a date and a time I can meet you in Seattle and I'll be there."

Alison met his eyes and smiled. "January twenty-seventh. One o'clock in the afternoon. At the bronze pig in Pike Place Market."

She'd chosen the date a bit recklessly, perhaps, but that was Peter's birthday, which made it easy to remember. And she was very sure Peter would approve....

Chapter Twenty-Three

"Aren't you going to call Uncle Adam?" Jazmine was pestering Shana for about the hundredth time that week.

"Why should I?" Shana muttered, scooping ice cream from the bottom of the caramel pecan container and packing what remained into a quart-size one. This was her life these days. For at least two hours every day, she risked frostbite with her face in the freezer.

"You know," she said, righting herself and holding up the ice-cream scoop for emphasis, "when I moved to Seattle, I decided I was finished with men. I didn't need a man in my life then and I don't need one now. I'm better off without them."

Jazmine sat on the other side of the counter, her chin propped in her hands. Shana noticed that she was frowning.

"We don't need boys?"

"We don't," Shana reiterated.

"At all?"

"Well, technically we do, but only for reproductive purposes." This was definitely an area she didn't want to get into with a nine-year-old.

"But aren't they kind of fun to have around?"

She realized she was tainting her niece's mind because of her own negative experiences. That had to stop. Besides, Adam had potential—or he did when he wasn't overtaken by jealousy. The thing was, he had absolutely nothing to be jealous about. It was almost as if he *wanted* to be upset with her. Fine, then, she'd just let him.

"Men have their uses," Shana replied guardedly.

"I thought you liked Uncle Adam."

"I do…I did…I do." While Shana was still annoyed with Adam, she missed him, too. That was the point. She didn't want to think about him, but she couldn't help it—which annoyed her even more.

"You should call him," Jazmine suggested again.

Shana refused to do that. "I phoned last time. It's his turn."

"Oh." Her niece sounded distressed.

"What's wrong?" Shana asked, unsure what had brought the woebegone expression to Jazmine's face.

Jazmine sighed deeply. "I was just hoping you liked Uncle Adam the same way he likes you."

Now Shana was the one frowning. "I do like him. It's just that two people don't always see eye-to-eye." This was difficult enough to explain to an adult, let alone a child. "Sometimes it's best to simply leave things alone."

"It is?" Jazmine squinted as though confused. "Is that how you felt about Brad?"

Shana thought for a moment, then nodded. "Yes, in the beginning. When I first broke up with him."

"But you went to see him again 'cause you didn't like the way it ended, right?"

"Right. I regretted the fact that I'd run off in a fit of righteous indignation. It was over, and I wanted him to know that in a civilized manner."

"You aren't being impulsive now? About not phoning Uncle Adam?"

Coming out from behind the counter, Shana slid onto the stool next to her niece. Sighing expressively, she said, "You're pretty smart for a kid."

Jazmine flashed her a bright smile. "How come?"

"You just are." Her niece had told her what she needed to hear. She'd refused to phone Adam strictly out of pride. Their last conversation had been painful. She'd been lighthearted and hopeful when she called him, but his gruff responses had short-circuited her joy. He hadn't phoned her since and she hadn't phoned him, either. They were behaving like children.

"That's what I don't understand," Jazmine murmured, returning to her original pose, chin cupped in her hands, elbows splayed. "You went to talk to Brad, but you won't go see Uncle Adam."

"He's in Hawaii." It wasn't like he was a three-hour drive down the interstate. "It isn't that easy to get to Hawaii."

"Don't they have ninety-nine-dollar flights there?"

"I doubt it." More than likely it would be five hundred dollars. Shana sat up. Then again, going to see him in Hawaii might help clear up this misunderstanding—

resolve this stalemate—and she wanted that. She believed he did, too. One of them had to make the first move and it might as well be her.

Shana was shocked at herself. She was actually considering this. She'd spent all that money on the dress she'd worn to see Brad, and now she was about to spend more. She supposed she could always wear her new dress when—if—she went to see Adam. Why not?

"You could check the computer," Jazmine said confidently. "There are advertisements on TV all the time about airfare deals over the Internet."

"You think I should?"

Jazmine nodded eagerly. "If you find a cheap ticket to Hawaii, you should go."

"I can't close the restaurant."

"You don't need to close it. Catherine ran it when we went to Portland," Jazmine reminded her. "And that was just to see Brad."

She opened her mouth to claim that seeing Brad was different. Well…it was and it wasn't. She'd been willing to make arrangements and a few sacrifices in order to talk to him. And she cared about Adam a hundred times more than she did Brad.

"Remember Tim, the single dad who wanted to go out with you?" Jazmine asked.

"Yes. Why?"

"I saw him in the park. He's back with his wife and he said it was because of you."

"Me?"

"Yup—he said you were the one who told him he was still in love with her. He knew you were right but the hardest part was telling Heather—that's her name. He's really glad he did, though."

"I'm glad, too. But why are you—"

Before Shana could finish the question, Jazmine blurted out her reply. "Because the hardest part is you telling Uncle Adam how you feel—so do it!"

"I will." Shana closed her eyes. She wanted this relationship with Adam to work. All the years she'd been with Brad, friends and co-workers had said he didn't deserve her, and she'd refused to listen. Now the people she loved and respected most were telling her that Adam was a dream come true—and once again she hadn't been listening. But that was about to change.

"It all depends on whether Louis and Catherine can work while we're away," Shana murmured, biting her bottom lip.

"They can," Jazmine said immediately. "They love it here. And if you marry Uncle Adam, they want to buy the business." She leaned close and whispered conspiratorially, "I heard them talking about it."

Now that the idea had taken root, Shana was convinced it was the right thing to do. She knew that if she sat down with Adam for five minutes, they'd get past the false impressions and false pride. She wanted him in her life; it was that simple.

"We're going to Hawaii?" Jazmine asked, her look expectant.

Shana smiled and slowly nodded. Yes, they were going to Hawaii. Adam might think this relationship was over, but she wasn't willing to lose out on her best chance for happiness yet. If everything went as she prayed it would, she just might end up with a Navy husband.

Adam's bad mood hadn't improved in a week. A dozen times, probably more, he'd lifted the receiver to call

Shana. This estrangement was his fault. But for reasons he didn't want to examine, he'd been reluctant to phone.

Okay, it was time to own up to the truth. He'd been waiting for her to break down and phone *him*. After more than a week, he might as well accept that it wasn't going to happen.

"You feeling better?" John asked when Adam arrived at the office Friday morning.

"I don't know." He shook his head. "What do you think are my chances of hitching a transport to Seattle this weekend?"

John perked up. "You're going to see her?"

Adam nodded. As best as he could figure, this was the only way he and Shana would ever make any progress. He was ready to take responsibility for his part in this fiasco and admit he'd overreacted. After all, she'd said it was over between her and this Bernie character.

From today, from this moment forward, he chose to believe her. His next task was to tell her he'd been wrong. He didn't like apologizing, but having Shana in his life was worth a few minutes of humiliation.

"This *is* good news," John said, grinning broadly. "Finally."

Adam leaned back in his chair. He'd get to Seattle one way or another, even if it meant paying for a commercial flight.

"Are you going to let her know you're coming?" John asked.

"No."

"So you're going to surprise her?"

"I believe I will," he said, already deep in thought.

He pictured the reunion: Shana would be at the ice-cream parlor with a dozen kids all placing their orders at once. She was great with kids, great with Jazmine, patient and generous.

She'd be scooping ice cream for all those kids, and then she'd look up and there he'd be, standing in the doorway. He'd wear his uniform. Women were said to like a man in uniform, and Adam decided he needed all the help he could get.

He returned to his imagined scenario. Naturally Shana would be astonished to see him; she might even drop the ice-cream scoop. Their eyes would meet, and everything else in the room would fade as she came around the counter and walked into his embrace. Adam's arms suddenly ached with the need to hold her. Until this very minute, he hadn't realized just how badly he wanted Shana in his life. He'd felt the need to link his life with a woman's earlier that summer, and that need had grown stronger, more irresistible, ever since he'd met Shana.

"You really think surprising her is such a great idea?" John asked skeptically.

"Of course it is," Adam said. Why wouldn't it be?

Chapter Twenty-Four

"I am so bummed," Jazmine muttered, sitting in front of the computer after e-mailing her mother.

Shana was disappointed, too, but she tried not to let it show. She'd spent half her day on the Internet, searching for last-minute bargain tickets to Honolulu. Apparently there was no such thing. It didn't matter what she could or would have been willing to pay. There simply weren't any seats available for the next few days. The best rates were for the following week.

"Waiting a week won't be so bad," Shana assured her niece.

"We should let Uncle Adam know we're coming."

That meant Shana would have to pick up the phone and call him, which was something she hadn't managed to do in more than two weeks. Jazmine was right, though. It probably wasn't fair just to land on his doorstep and expect everything to fall neatly into place.

The doorbell rang and Jazmine was out of the computer chair and racing to the front door. Shana walked briskly behind her, uncomfortable with the girl flinging open the door without first checking to see who was there.

Her worries were for nothing. Jazmine stood on the tips of her toes, peering through the tiny peephole. She stared for the longest moment, then her shoulders sagged and she backed away. "It's for you," she said in a disappointed voice.

Shana moved in front of her niece and opened the door. She was in no mood to deal with a salesman or a nuisance call. When she found Adam Kennedy standing on the other side, she was stunned into speechlessness.

"Adam?" His name was a mere wisp of sound. He looked good, no, better than good. *Great*. He was a thousand times more compelling than she remembered, and her heart felt in danger of bursting right then and there. If their disagreement had given him a minute's concern, his face didn't reveal it. He seemed rested and relaxed.

He smiled, and Shana's knees started to shake. It shouldn't be like this, the rational part of her mind inserted. She shouldn't be this happy to see him or this excited. But she was.

"Can I come in?"

"Sure." Jazmine was the one who answered. The nine-year-old slipped around Shana and held open the screen door. Judging by the broad smile on the girl's face, anyone might think she was ushering in Santa Claus.

Shana frowned. "You knew about this?" she asked her niece.

Jazmine shook her head, denying any knowledge. "But I fooled you, didn't I? You didn't guess it was Adam." Then she grinned at the man in question. "We were coming to see you, only we couldn't get a flight for this weekend. We have tickets for next week."

"You were flying to Hawaii to see me?" Adam's eyes probed Shana's.

She nodded, and found the shock of seeing him in the room with her nearly overwhelming. Placing her hand on her chest, she felt her heart hammer against her palm. Even with the evidence standing right in front of her, she had a hard time taking it in.

Reaching for Adam's hand, Jazmine led him into the living room. "You can sit if you want."

Adam chose the sofa.

"You, too, Aunt Shana," Jazmine said, orchestrating events as though she were moving figures on a chessboard. She took Shana's hand next and led her to the overstuffed chair.

"Okay," Jazmine said, standing in the middle of the room between them. "You two need to talk. I can go to my room or I can stay and supervise."

Shana's gaze didn't waver from Adam's. "Your room," she murmured, hardly able to catch her breath.

"Your room," Adam echoed.

"Really?" Jazmine's frustration echoed in her voice.

"Go." Shana pointed down the hall, although her eyes were still on Adam. She was afraid that if she glanced away he might disappear.

Jazmine started to walk in the direction of her bedroom. "I'm leaving my door open, and if I hear any yelling, I'm coming right back. Okay?"

Adam's mouth quivered with the beginnings of a smile. "Okay."

After Jazmine left, there was a moment of awkward silence—and then they both started to speak at once.

"I'm so sorry…."

"I'm an idiot…" Adam held up his hand and gestured for her to go first.

Shana moved to the edge of the cushion, clasping her hands together. "Oh, Adam, I'm so *sorry*. I wanted to call you, I really did. I thought about it so many times."

"I was afraid of losing you."

"That won't happen," she told him. "Don't you know how I feel about you?"

When he didn't reply, she said, "I wasn't planning to fall in love again, but—"

"You love me?" he interrupted.

Shana hadn't meant to declare her feelings so soon, and certainly not like this. The way she'd envisioned the scene, it would be a romantic moment over dinner and champagne, not in the middle of her small rental house, with her niece standing in the bedroom doorway listening to every word.

"She does," Jazmine answered for Shana. "She's been impossible ever since you went to Hawaii."

"Jazmine," Shana warned.

"Sorry," the girl muttered.

"Maybe it'd be best if you closed your door," Adam suggested.

Jazmine stamped her foot and shouted "Okay," but when Shana's gaze shot down the hallway, she noticed that her niece's bedroom door was only halfway shut.

"You were saying?" Adam said and motioned for her to continue.

"I forget where I was."

"I believe you'd just declared your undying love for me. I'd like to hear more."

"I'm sure you would," she said, smiling despite their interruptions, "but I was thinking it would be good to hear how you feel, too."

"You will, I promise," Adam assured her, "but I'd appreciate if you finished your thoughts first. You were saying you hadn't planned to fall in love…"

Shana lowered her eyes. It was difficult to think clearly when she was looking at Adam. The effect he had on her was that powerful. "I think sometimes love finds you when you least expect it. As you might've guessed, my opinion of the opposite sex was somewhere in the basement when I came to Seattle. And then Jazmine arrived. At first I envied the easy relationship you two shared. And my sister couldn't stop singing your praises."

"You weren't in the mood to hear anything positive about a man. Any man."

"Exactly," Shana concurred. "But you were so patient with Jazmine and…you were patient with me, too."

"I was attracted to you from the moment we met."

"Really?"

"You knocked my socks off." They both grinned at that. Then his expression grew serious again. "Having this surgery wasn't a pleasant experience." He pressed his hand gently to his shoulder. "I was in pain, and my life felt empty, and all of a sudden you were on the scene. I felt as soon as we met that I could love you."

"You did?" Her voice lifted with joy.

"And I do love you. I recognized that I had to give you time. Coming out of a long-term relationship, you were bound to need an adjustment period. I understood that. But I don't think you have any idea how badly I wanted to be with you."

"You love me," she repeated, hardly hearing anything else he'd said. "You love me!"

"I know you wanted to marry Bernie—"

"It's Brad, and no...not anymore."

"Good, because I'm hoping you'll marry me."

Jazmine's bedroom door flew open. "Aunt Shana, say yes. I beg of you, say yes!"

"Jazmine!" Shana and Adam shouted simultaneously.

"Okay, okay," the nine-year-old moaned and retreated back inside her bedroom.

Adam hesitated only briefly. "Well, what do you think?"

"You mean about us getting married?" Just saying the words produced an inner happiness that radiated from her heart to every single part of her. "Being your wife would make me the happiest woman alive."

Adam stood and she met him halfway. Seconds later, they were locked in each other's arms and his mouth was on hers. From the way he kissed her, she knew he'd been telling the truth. He loved her! After several deep kisses, Adam raised his head and framed her face with both hands. His eyes bored intently into hers.

"One question, and if my asking offends you, I apologize in advance. I need to know something."

"Anything."

His eyes flickered with uncertainty. "Why was it necessary to talk to Ber—Brad?"

Shana sighed and kissed his jaw. "I wanted to say goodbye to him properly."

"And you intended to see me next week."

She nodded, then caught the lobe of his ear between her teeth and gently bit down on the soft flesh. The shiver that went through him encouraged her to further exploration.

"What were you going to say to me?" he asked, his voice a husky whisper.

"Hmm…" she responded, her thoughts clouded with desire. "Hello, and that I'm crazy in love with you."

"Good answer." Adam directed his mouth back to hers, and soon they were deeply involved in another kiss.

The sound of a throat being cleared broke into Shana's consciousness several seconds later.

"Did you two forget something?" Jazmine asked, hands on her hips. "Like *me?*"

Shana buried her face in Adam's shoulder.

"Howdy, squirt," he managed in a voice Shana barely recognized as his.

"This is all very good, but we have a wedding to plan, you know."

"A wedding?" Shana lifted her head and murmured, "We have plenty of time to work on that."

"I don't think so," Jazmine insisted. "We'll be in Hawaii next week. We should do it then. Let's get this show on the road!"

"Next week?" Shana looked questioningly at Adam, not sure that arranging a wedding in such a short time was even possible.

"Would you be willing?" he asked, catching Jazmine's enthusiasm.

Shana nodded. "Of course, but only if Ali can be there. I want her at our wedding."

Adam brought her close. "I do, too."

Jazmine applauded loudly. "I know it isn't good manners to say I told you so," she announced with smug satisfaction, "but this time I can't help it."

"We'll let you," Adam said, his arms around Shana. "Because this time you're absolutely right."

Shana leaned against the man who would soon be her husband and sighed with contentment. She'd never known that being wrong could feel so right.

Chapter Twenty-Five

"Mom!" Jazmine slammed into the bathroom of Shana's old house in West Seattle, where Ali was preparing for work. They'd been living there for the last seven weeks, ever since her discharge from the Navy. Her life and that of her sister's had been a whirlwind for the past half year.

Once Shana and Adam had decided on marriage, their wedding had happened fast, but not quite as fast as originally planned. Fortunately—for the convenience of the guests—it had taken place in Seattle, not Hawaii. No sooner had Ali returned to San Diego in December than she boarded a plane to Washington for the wedding. From everything she heard, in phone calls and e-mails, Shana and Adam were blissfully happy and enjoying life in Honolulu.

At the end of her tour, Alison had left the *USS Wood-*

row Wilson and within a matter of weeks was released from her commitment to the Navy.

Because Shana had signed a lease on the rental house in Seattle, Ali was able to move there. Jazmine was back in the same school now and doing well. Ali liked Seattle and it was as good a place to settle as any.

The retired couple who'd purchased Shana's ice-cream and pizza parlor had been accommodating and helpful when Ali arrived in Seattle. They loved her daughter and she loved them, too.

"Mom," Jazmine repeated. "Do you remember what today is?"

As if anyone needed to remind her. "Yes, sweetheart, I remember."

"It's Dad's birthday—and it's the day you're meeting Commander Dillon." Apparently her daughter felt it was necessary to tell her, anyway. "What time?" she asked urgently.

"One o'clock in Pike Place Market." Alison had arranged a half day off before she'd been hired at West Seattle Hospital. Her hand shook as she brushed her hair. Frank and Alison talked nearly every day and sent e-mail messages when it wasn't possible to chat on the phone.

Because of Navy regulations, they'd controlled their growing attraction and their intense feelings for each other while they were aboard the carrier. But now that Alison had been officially discharged, they were free to explore those emotions, and to express them. Circumstances had made that challenging; Alison had moved to Seattle and Frank was stationed in San Diego with the *USS Woodrow Wilson*.

"He's going to ask you to marry him."

"Jazmine!" Overnight her daughter had turned into

a romance expert. Given the success of her matchmaking efforts with Shana and Adam, the girl was convinced she had an aptitude for this.

"Mom, Commander Dillon would be a fool not to marry you."

Frank and Jazmine routinely chatted via the Internet, too. Maybe her daughter knew something she didn't, but Alison doubted it.

"You're in love with him," Jazmine said with all the confidence of one who had insider information, "and he's crazy about you."

"Jazmine!"

"Yup, that's my name."

Alison put down her brush and inhaled a calming breath. "I'm very fond of Frank…. He's a wonderful man, but we barely know each other."

"I like him," her daughter said.

"I know and I like him, too."

"Like?" Jazmine scoffed and shook her head. "Who are you kidding? I don't understand adults. Every time I tell him he should marry you, Commander Dillon—"

"What?" Alison exploded, outraged that her daughter had this sort of conversation with Frank. Her face burned with mortification; she could only imagine what he must think.

"Don't go ballistic on me, Mom. You know Commander Dillon and I e-mail each other."

"Yes, but…"

"Okay, okay," Jazmine asserted, shaking her head as if she were losing her patience. "Here's the deal. You and Commander Dillon talk, and if you need me to sort anything out for you, just let me know. He's coming to dinner tonight, isn't he?"

"I invited him, but—"

"He'll be here." She kissed Alison on the cheek and added, "I've gotta go or I'll be late for the bus. Have a great day." With that Jazmine headed out of the bathroom. She grabbed her coat and backpack, and adjusted her hood against the January drizzle.

Alison followed her to the door and watched her daughter meet her friends and walk to the bus stop. Jazmine seemed utterly sure that this meeting with Frank would have a fairy-tale ending. Alison wished she shared her daughter's positive attitude. She was nervous and didn't mind admitting it.

In an effort to settle her nerves, Alison reached for the phone to call her sister. Remembering the time difference between the West Coast and Hawaii, she replaced it. Eight Seattle time was far too early to phone Shana and even if she reached her, Alison wouldn't know what to say.

By noon when she left the hospital and drove into downtown Seattle her stomach was in a state of chaos. Jazmine knew her far too well. Alison did love Frank. She had for months, and now they were finally meeting at the time and place they'd arranged last summer. Because she was no longer in the Navy, there were no official barriers between them. As for other kinds of obstacles… She didn't know.

After parking in a waterfront lot, Alison climbed the stairs up to Pike Place Market, coming in the back entrance. They'd agreed to meet at the figure of the bronze pig in front. Her heart pounded hard, but that had little to do with the flight of stairs she'd just climbed. A glance at her watch told her she was fifteen minutes early.

A part of her feared Frank wouldn't show. Shades of that old movie, *An Affair to Remember.*

It had started to rain and the sky was dark gray. This was an ominous sign as far as Alison was concerned. The fishmongers were busily arranging seafood on beds of crushed ice as tourists and shoppers crowded the aisles. With extra time on her hands, Alison could do a bit of shopping. But her nerves were stretched so tight she didn't think she was capable of doing anything more than standing next to the bronze pig.

To her surprise, Frank was already there, looking around anxiously. He seemed uncomfortable and unsure of himself, and almost immediately Ali's unease left her.

"Did you think I wouldn't come?" she asked softly, walking over to meet him.

From experience, Alison knew Frank wasn't a man who smiled often. But when he saw her, his face underwent a transformation and he broke into a wide grin.

Alison wasn't sure who moved first, but in the next moment, she was in his arms. They clung to each other for a long time. It would be completely out of character for him to kiss her in such a public place, and she accepted that.

"Have you had lunch?" he asked, as she reluctantly stepped out of his embrace.

"No, but there's a great chowder bar on the waterfront," she told him. As they held hands, she led him down the same path she'd recently taken from the parking area. She liked the feel of his hand in hers, and the way that simple action connected them.

They ordered fish and chips and ate outside under a large canopy on the wharf, protected from the elements. She felt too tense to be hungry. They talked very little.

"The ferry's coming in," Alison said and by unspoken agreement they walked to the end of the pier to watch it glide toward the dock.

Standing side by side, they gazed out over the choppy water of Puget Sound. After a few minutes, Frank placed an arm around her shoulders. Alison leaned against him, savoring this closeness to the man she loved.

Without warning, he turned her so that she faced him and then he kissed her. His mouth was gentle and she instinctively opened to him. Seconds later his hands were in her hair, bunching it as he slanted his lips over hers and his kiss grew more insistent.

With his arms around her, Frank rested his chin on her head. "I told myself I wouldn't do that," he said in a low voice. "Not here, not like this."

"I think I would've died if you hadn't," she whispered back.

"I'm no bargain, Alison."

"Stop."

"No, I mean it, but God help me, I love you and I know I'll love Jazmine, too."

Alison smiled softly. "She's eager to meet you in person."

His arms relaxed as he brushed his lips against her temple. "I have a week's leave, but then I have to head back to San Diego. It isn't much time to make an important decision, but I'm hoping that by the end of the week you'll know how you feel about me."

Alison didn't need any time; her decision was made.

"I know you loved Peter and that he's Jazmine's father," Frank continued.

"I'll always love Peter," Alison said.

"I want you to. He was your husband and he died serving his country. I respect him and I have no intention of replacing him in your life or Jazmine's."

"Frank, what are you saying?"

He inhaled harshly. "I was hoping, praying actually, that by the end of this week you might know your feelings well enough… What I mean is that I'd like you to be my wife."

"I don't need a week—"

"You do," he told her, "we both do." And he kissed her again with such abandon and joy that when he released her, Alison was convinced she'd rather be in his arms than breathe.

A week later, just before Frank was scheduled to return to San Diego, the three of them planned dinner together. While Alison flitted about the kitchen checking on their meal, Jazmine set the table.

Before they sat down to eat, Frank pulled two small boxes out of his pocket and ceremonially placed them on the table.

Alison was carrying a large green salad and nearly dropped the bowl when she saw the velvet cases.

Frank glanced at her with a mildly guilty look. "If you'd rather wait until after dinner, that's fine, but I know I'd enjoy the meal a lot more if I had your answer first."

"Do I get to choose between two rings?" she asked, wondering why he'd brought two boxes.

"No," he said. "There's a necklace in one of them for Jazmine."

Her daughter came out of the kitchen clutching three bottles of salad dressing. It didn't take her long to assess the situation. "The answer is yes," Jazmine stated matter-of-factly.

"Yes," Alison echoed, nodding vigorously.

Frank opened the first of the two velvet boxes and slipped the small single-pearl necklace around Jazmine's neck and fastened it. "I felt it was important that I make a promise to you, too," he said to Ali's daughter. "I wanted to assure you that I will love you. I plan to be a good stepfather and, most importantly, I vow to always love your mother."

Jazmine blinked back tears and so did Alison. "I'll wear it every day and I swear I'll never lose it." Frank hugged the child.

Then he opened the second box and took out a large solitaire diamond ring. While Alison tried not to weep, he slipped it onto her ring finger. He held her gaze, and in his eyes Alison saw his love and the promise he was making. "I love you," he whispered.

"I love you, too."

The doorbell chimed, and before Jazmine could race toward it, the door opened and Shana hurried into the house, Adam directly behind her. "We aren't too late, are we?" she asked, laughing and excited. "Frank's still here, isn't he?"

"Shana." Alison ran across the room to her sister and they threw their arms around each other.

Frank and Adam shook hands and introduced themselves.

"Actually, your timing's perfect," Alison told Shana, and with tears clouding her eyes, she thrust out her left hand so her sister could examine her engagement ring.

Shana squealed with joy and hugged Alison excitedly, then hugged her brother-in-law to be.

"How did you know?" Alison asked.

"We didn't," Adam answered. "We came because we have some exciting news of our own."

"We're pregnant," Shana burst out.

Now it was Alison's turn to shout with happiness.

"Can I babysit?" Jazmine asked. "I could spend the summers with you in Hawaii and—"

"We'll decide that later," Alison said, cutting her daughter off. "We were about to sit down for dinner. Join us," she insisted.

The two women immediately went into the kitchen. While Alison got out extra silverware, Shana took the dinner and salad plates from the cupboard, along with two extra water glasses. Jazmine promptly delivered them to the table.

Shana paused. "Less than a year ago who would've believed we'd both have Navy husbands?"

"Navy husbands," Alison repeated as her diamond flashed in the light. "It has a nice sound to it, doesn't it?"

"The nicest sound in the world," Shana agreed.

* * * * *

Don't miss 44 Cranberry Point, *part of*
Debbie Macomber's successful CEDAR COVE *series,*
available from MIRA Books *in February 2010.*

A MAN APART

BY
JOAN HOHL

Joan Hohl is the *New York Times* bestselling author of over forty books. She has received numerous awards for her work, including the Romance Writers of America's Golden Medallion award. In addition to contemporary romance, this prolific author also writes historical and time-travel romances. Joan lives in eastern Pennsylvania with her husband and family.

Melissa & Tara
Gee, it's good to be back home again.

One

Justin Grainger was a man apart—and he liked it that way. He was content with his life. Possessing a nearly uncanny affinity for horses, he was satisfied with his work of running his isolated horse ranch in Montana.

But Justin was not a hermit or even a true loner. He enjoyed the easy camaraderie shared with his ranch hands and his foreman, Ben Daniels. And though Justin had never again wanted a woman on the property, since his failed marriage five years before, he had accepted the presence of Ben's new young wife, Karla. She had been the former personal assistant to Justin's brother, Mitch, who managed the family-owned gambling casino in Deadwood, South Dakota.

Justin had other family members he occasionally visited. His parents, retired now in Sedona, Arizona, were both still healthy and socially active. His sister, Beth, as yet unmarried, was off doing her fashion thing in San Francisco. And his eldest brother, Adam, headed up various family businesses from their corporate offices in Casper, Wyoming.

Adam was married to a lovely woman named Sunny, whom Justin had set out to tolerate in the name of family unity and had quickly come to admire, respect and love almost as much as his own sister. Adam and Sunny had a baby daughter, Becky, whom Justin quite simply adored.

On occasion Justin even spent recreational time with an accommodating woman—no strings attached. And that suited him fine. He claimed that horses were much easier to deal with, less contentious and argumentative, thus easier to talk to and get along with.

Although, these days, after a long, hot work-filled summer, a busy autumn, and winter just settling in, Justin was a bit restless and didn't grumble

too much when he received an urgent and demanding phone call from Mitch the week before
Christmas.

"I need you to come to Deadwood," Mitch said,
in his usual straightforward way.

"Yeah? Why?" Justin replied, in his usual dry,
less-than-impressed manner.

"I'm getting married, and I want you to be my
best man," Mitch shot back. "That's why."

As an attention getter, his brother's explanation was a winner, Justin conceded…to himself.
He never had conceded much of anything—except
absolute loyalty and devotion—to any one of his
siblings.

"When did you lose it, Mitch?" he asked in soft
tones of commiseration.

"Lose what?" Mitch sounded slightly baffled.

Justin grinned. "Your mind, old son. You must
have lost it if you're going to take the marital
plunge."

"I haven't lost my mind…old son," Mitch retorted, a trace of amusement undermining his
rough voice. "Trite as it might sound, it's my heart
I've lost."

There was no way Justin could let his brother's
remark pass without comment. "No 'might' about

it," he drawled, enjoying himself. "That is trite. Sappy, too."

Mitch laughed. "I don't know what to tell you, bro," he said, suddenly dead serious. "I'm way deep in love with her."

Oh, yeah, Justin thought, hearing the heartfelt note in his brother's voice. Mitch was seriously serious. "It's Maggie Reynolds. Right?"

"Yes...of course."

Of course. Justin wasn't surprised, not really. A faint smile tugged at his lips. In fact, after all the rave reviews he'd heard from Mitch about Ms. Reynolds ever since she'd replaced Karla as his personal assistant, Justin should have been expecting the marriage announcement.

"Well?"

Mitch's impatient voice sliced across Justin's thoughts. "Well what?" he asked.

Mitch sighed loudly, and Justin managed to contain a burst of laughter.

"Will you be best man at my wedding?"

"Might as well," Justin drawled. "Why change the status quo now...as I always was the best man, anyway."

"In your dreams, maybe," Mitch said amiably going along with the old joke. "Because you're never gonna live long enough to see that day while you're awake."

"Ha! Don't bet the casino on it."

"As if..." Mitch made a snorting sound; he never gambled on anything, never mind the family owned casino. "You know damn well I never..."

"Yeah, yeah. I do know, so spare me the drill. When do you want me in Deadwood?"

"We've set the date for the first Saturday in the new year. But you could come for Christmas," Mitch suggested, cautiously hopeful.

"I don't think so." Justin slanted a wry look at the tall, glittery tree placed in front of the wide living room window. The tree—along with other assorted holiday decorations—was a concession to Ben's new bride. "You know I'm not—"

"Into Christmas," Mitch finished for him. "Yes, I know." He heaved a tired-sounding sigh. "This Christmas it'll be five years since Angie took off with that sales rep. Don't you think it's time to put it behind you, Justin, find a nice, decent woman and—"

"Back off, Mitch," he growled in warning, closing his mind to the memory of that bitter winter. "The only woman I'll be looking to find won't be either too nice or too decent, just ready and willing."

"Tsk, tsk," Mitch said, clicking his tongue in disapproval. "I do hope that if you're thinking of looking while you're here in Deadwood, you'll be discreet about it."

"Don't want me to shock the sensibilities of the future missus, hmm?" Justine taunted.

"My future missus and Ben's missus and Adam's missus," Mitch taunted right back. "Not to mention the sensibilities of our mother and sister."

"Ouch." Justin laughed. "Okay. I'll be extra discreet…even circumspect."

Mitch chuckled. "Whatever."

"By the way, is Karla going to be matron of honor?"

"Well…yes, but there'll be two of them."

"Two what?"

"Well, two attendants," Mitch said. "Maggie's best friend will be coming from Philadelphia via Nebraska to be Maggie's *maid* of honor."

"Philadelphia via Nebraska?"

"She lives in Philadelphia," Mitch explained. "That's where Maggie's from, you know."

"Yeah, I know, but…where does Nebraska come in?"

"Hannah's originally from Nebraska, and she'll be visiting her family before coming on to Deadwood."

"Hannah, huh?" Justin had an immediate image of an old-fashioned female to fit the old-fashioned name—prim, proper, virginal and probably plain.

"Yeah, Hannah Deturk."

Add *prudish* to the list.

"And you'd better be nice to her," Mitch warned.

"Of course I'll be nice to her. Why the hell wouldn't I be nice to her?" Justin said, genuinely hurt by his brother's warning, by the idea that Mitch felt it necessary to issue the warning.

"Well…" Mitch's tone was now conciliatory. "You've never made a secret about how you feel about women, and I just don't want anything to upset Maggie."

"You sound as smitten as Ben," he said. "You really do have it bad, don't you?"

"I love her, Justin, more than my own life," Mitch admitted in a quiet, but rock-solid tone.

"I hear you, and I promise I'll behave." He knew he'd never felt like that about a woman, not even his ex-wife, Angie, and was certain he never would.

Hell, he never wanted to experience that kind of intense emotion for any woman, Justin thought minutes later, frowning as he cradled the receiver. That path only led to pain.

First Ben and Karla, now Mitch and Maggie, he mused, staring into space, and all within one year.

Hmm. While Justin wasn't fanciful, he did wonder if there was some type of aphrodisiac in Deadwood's water, or maybe it was the atmosphere in the casino, some sort of love and marriage spell.

The day after Christmas, Justin set off for Deadwood, convinced he was impervious to anything like a spell or potion. He'd learned his lesson.

Hannah Deturk had not been exactly thrilled to be leaving Philadelphia at the end of the third week of December, of all times of the year, for the upper Midwest. South Dakota via Nebraska. To Hannah Deadwood, South Dakota was the back of beyond and, if possible, even more remote than the area of Nebraska where she had been born and raised.

After graduating college and relocating, first to Chicago, which was too windy, then to New York City, which was too big, and finally settling into

Philadelphia, Hannah had vowed that other than brief visits home to visit her folks, she would never go back to that desolate part of the country. She certainly wouldn't travel there in the winter months of November, December, January, February and March, and she even considered October, April and May pretty chancy.

Only a request by her parents or, as was the case, the marriage of her dearest friend, Maggie, could induce Hannah to take the three hard-earned vacation weeks she had allotted herself and spend them in Deadwood, South Dakota, of all places.

She didn't even gamble, for goodness sake, had never even visited the casinos in Atlantic City, a mere hour or so drive down the Atlantic City expressway from Philly.

And yet when Maggie had called her to tell her she was getting married in January and asked Hannah to be her maid of honor, Hannah hadn't so much as entertained a thought of refusing.

So, a few days into the new year, after spending Christmas with her family in Nebraska, Hannah found herself on the road, steering a leased four-wheel-drive vehicle through a blessedly light fall of snow, heading for Deadwood.

It was dark, and the snowfall heavier when

Hannah finally arrived in the town made legendary by its historical reputation of being wide-open and the larger-than-life characters of Wild Bill Hickok and Calamity Jane.

Those days were long-gone, as were the infamous pair. Other than having legal gambling casinos, Deadwood looked to Hannah much like any other small upper Midwest town.

She missed Philadelphia, where it would be evening rush hour and the traffic would be horrific. She even missed that.

Then again…perhaps not.

Smiling wryly, Hannah peered through the windshield to look for the turnoff Maggie had indicated in her directions. A few minutes later she brought the vehicle to a careful stop in front of a large Victorian house that had been converted into apartments.

No wonder Maggie had fallen in love with the house, Hannah thought, stepping out of the Jeep to stare through the swirling snow at the old mansion that had once been the Grainger family home. It was an imposing sight, and conjured images of a bygone era of grace and style.

"Hannah!"

Hannah blinked back into the present at the excited sound of Maggie's voice calling her name. Her coatless friend was dashing down the veranda steps toward her.

"Maggie!" Hannah flung out her arms to embrace her friend. "Are you nutty, or what?" she asked, laughing, as she stepped back to gaze into her friend's glowing face. "It's snowing and freezing out here."

"Yes, I'm nutty." Maggie laughed with her. "So nutty and crazy in love, I don't feel the cold."

"Got your love to keep you warm, do you?" Hannah dryly teased.

"Yes…yes." Despite her heartfelt assertion, Maggie shivered. "I can't wait for you to meet him."

"I'm looking forward to it," Hannah said, grasping Maggie's arm to lead her toward the house. "But meanwhile let's get inside, where I hope it's warm."

"Well, of course it's warm." Maggie flashed a grin. "Even up in my nest on the third floor."

Releasing her hold on Maggie's arm, Hannah turned back to the car. "You go on ahead, I'll just grab my bags and be with you in a minute."

"Did you bring your dress for the wedding?" Maggie called from the shelter of the veranda.

"Of course I did," Hannah yelled back over the

open trunk lid, shivering as the sting of wind-driven snow bit into her face. "Now go into the house."

A half hour later, her bags unpacked, the special dress she had frantically shopped for before leaving Philly hanging on a padded hanger to de-wrinkle, Hannah sat curled on the cushioned seat in the bay window alcove in Maggie's warm "nest," her hands cradling a steaming cup of marshmallow-topped hot chocolate.

She took a careful sip, and winced. "Mmm...delicious. But very hot. I scorched my tongue."

Maggie laughed. "It's supposed to be hot." Her eyes danced with amusement. "That's why it's called *hot* chocolate."

Hannah's pained expression smoothed into a gentle smile. It was so good to hear her friend laugh again, see the glow of happiness in Maggie's face that had replaced the bitter hurt of betrayal of the previous summer.

"You really are in love this time," Hannah said, taking another careful sip. "Aren't you?"

"Yes...though I wouldn't have believed it possible mere months ago...I really am in love." Maggie heaved a contented sigh. Her eyes took on a dreamy look. "Mitch is so wonderful, so, so..."

"Everything Todd was not?" Hannah interjected, her normally husky voice lightened by expectation.

"Todd who?" Maggie asked with assumed innocence.

Hannah grinned, finally convinced her friend was back on track at last. "Oh, you know, Todd what's-his-name, the jerk you were engaged to marry. The same jerk who eloped with his boss's daughter."

Maggie grimaced. "Oh, *that* jerk. Yes, Mitch is everything Todd was not." Her lips formed a soft smile. "And a whole heck of a lot more."

"Good." Allowing herself to fully relax, Hannah settled more comfortably into the corner of the alcove. Smiling, she studied her friend's radiant face. "You really are genuinely in love this time," she murmured in tones of wonder. "Aren't you?"

Maggie laughed. "Didn't I just answer that question moments ago? Yes, Hannah, I am deeply, genuinely, madly, desperately, deliriously…"

"Okay, okay," Hannah broke in, holding up her hands and laughing. "I believe you."

"About time." Maggie laughed with her. "More hot chocolate? A cookie?"

"No, thank you." Hannah shook her head. "I still

have some chocolate—" she grimaced "—and I've already had too many cookies. They're delicious."

"Karla baked them."

Hannah frowned. "Karla?" Then, remembering, she said, "Oh, the woman whose job you took over, the one who's going to stand as matron of honor."

"Mmm." Maggie nodded. "She loves to cook, and baked these for Christmas. She brought some with her for us."

"That was thoughtful of her." Hannah smiled. "So, she's here already, too. I'm eager to meet her."

"Yes, she's here in Deadwood. Karla and her husband, Ben, and the baby." Maggie laughed. "Matter of fact, the whole gang's here."

"Gang?" Hannah lifted one perfectly arched brow.

"Yes, Mitch's family," Maggie explained. "They arrived in dribbles and drips over the past two days…"

"Dribbles and drips," Hannah interrupted, laughing. "Your Pennsylvania Dutch country origins are showing."

"Whatever." Maggie shrugged. "Anyway, they're here. Mitch's parents, two brothers, one alone, one with his family, and his sister. You'll meet them Friday evening at the rehearsal, and get to know them a little at dinner afterward."

"Dinner?" Hannah swept the room with a skeptical glance. "Where?"

"Mitch made arrangements for dinner at the Bullock Hotel."

"Oh." Naturally, Hannah hadn't a clue where the Bullock Hotel might be located, but it didn't matter. "And is that when I'll meet your Mitch?" Now, that did matter, a lot. She had witnessed the hurt and humiliation inflicted on Maggie by her former fiancé. Hannah had never been able to bring herself to trust or like the too-smooth Todd. Subsequently, to her dismay, her suspicions about him had proved correct.

"No." Maggie shook her head. "You'll meet Mitch tonight. He's going to stop by later. Though he's eager to meet you—I've told him so much about you—he wanted to give us some time alone together, to catch up." Her eyes softened. "He's so considerate."

Hmm, I'll be the judge of that, Hannah mused. But it sure sounded like Maggie did have it bad. "How does it really feel? Being in love, I mean?"

"All the things I mentioned before…and perhaps a little scary, too."

"Scary?" Hannah was at once alert, her protective instincts quivering. Was this Mitch Grainger a bully? She couldn't imagine her independent friend falling for a man who would intimidate her, but then again, Maggie had been about to marry that deceitful jerk Todd.

"Well, maybe not exactly scary," Maggie said, after giving it some thought. "It's all so new and sudden, and almost too exciting, too thrilling. You know how love is."

Whoa, Hannah thought, serious stuff here…. Too exciting? Too thrilling? Now she really couldn't wait to meet the man. "Actually, no," she admitted, wryly. "I don't know."

Maggie blinked in astonishment. "You're kidding."

"No, I'm not."

"You've never been in love? What about that guy you dated in college?"

"Oh, I thought I was in love," Hannah said. "Turned out it was a combination of chemistry and itchy hormones, commonly called lust." Her tone was dry, her smile self derisive.

"But…since then…?" Maggie persisted.

"Nope." Hannah swallowed the last of the chocolate; it had gone as cold as her love life…or lack of same. "There were a couple of infatuations, some sexual activity, but not much. There was one brief and I thought promising relationship I never told you about. But it really never got off square one, so to speak." She shrugged. "Nothing even remotely resembling what you've described."

"Oh, too bad. All this time we've known each other, and I never knew, never even guessed… you've always been so closemouthed about your personal life."

Hannah laughed. "That's because I didn't have one, at least nothing that warranted discussion."

"I never imagined…" Maggie sighed, then brightened. "Oh, I can't wait for you to fall in love someday, experience this excitingly scary champagne-bubbly feeling."

"I'm not sure I want to." Hannah slowly moved her head back and forth.

"Not want to?" Maggie exclaimed, surprised. "But…why not?"

"Because…" Hannah hesitated, carefully choosing her words so as not to offend her friend by voicing doubt. "I don't think I want to expose myself to that degree."

"Expose yourself?" Maggie frowned in confusion. "I don't get your point. Expose yourself to what?"

"That sort of emotional vulnerability," she said.

Maggie's amusement showed with her easy laughter. "You're wacko...you know that? Don't you realize that if I'm emotionally vulnerable, stands to reason Mitch is, too?"

"I suppose so," Hannah murmured. But is he? She kept the question and her doubts to herself. She had always considered herself a pretty good judge of character, and she had been right about Todd.

Wait and see, she told herself, lifting an eyebrow in question when Maggie, suddenly frowning, nibbled on her lower lip in consternation.

"Is something wrong?"

Maggie lifted her shoulders in an indecisive shrug. "Not really...it's just..."

"Just?" Hannah prompted.

Maggie sighed. "Well, I think maybe I should give you a heads-up on the best man, Mitch's brother, Justin."

"A heads-up?" Hannah grinned. "Why, is he some kind of ogre or monster?"

Maggie grinned back. "No, of course not. It's just...well...he's different, a little rough around the edges, not nearly as polished as Mitch or their oldest brother, Adam."

"Like, crude?" Hannah raised an eyebrow.

"No, no." Maggie shook her head. "Just a little

brusque. I understand he is something of a loner, thinks women are good for one thing only."

"I don't think I need ask what the one thing might be," Hannah drawled. A thought occurred that brought a glint of anger into her eyes. "Was this 'loner' brusque and perhaps a little rude to you?"

"Heavens no!" Maggie exclaimed on a laugh. "Actually, he was quite civil, really very nice."

"Then, how do you know that he—"

Maggie interrupted. "Because Mitch gave me a heads-up." She laughed. "He told me I should tell him at once if Justin said one word out of line." Her laugh turned to a giggle. "Mitch said if he did, he'd mop the casino floor with him. Which, after I met him, I thought was hilarious."

Thoroughly confused, Hannah was about to demand a fuller explanation when Maggie glanced at the clock, pushed her chair away from the table and stood.

"I think I'd better get dinner started," Maggie said. "I don't know about you, but I'm getting hungry. And I told Mitch we'd have coffee and dessert with him."

"Okay. I'll help," Hannah said, stretching as she stood.

"But…you're my guest," Maggie protested. "The first one I've had in this apartment."

"Guest, shmest," Hannah retorted. "I'm not a guest, I'm a friend...your best friend. Right?"

"Right." Maggie gave a vigorous nod, then qualified, "After Mitch, of course."

Oh, brother, Hannah thought. "Oh, of course," she agreed with a smile, skirting around the table. "What's on the menu?"

"Pasta."

Hannah rolled her eyes. "What else?" Being Maggie's second-best friend, she was well aware of her passion for past dishes. "What kind?"

"Penne with snow peas, baby carrots, walnuts and a light oil-balsamic-vinegar sauce."

"Yummy." Hannah's mouth watered. "And dessert?"

"A surprise." Maggie's eyes gleamed.

"Oh, come on," Hannah groused, grinning.

Maggie shook her head. "All I'll tell you is that Karla showed me how to make it." Her eyes now sparkled with a teasing light. "And it's a delight," she finished on a suspicious-sounding giggle.

After their fabulous meal, Hannah leaned back in her chair. "That was wonderful," she said, sighing with repletion.

"Thanks." Maggie arched an eyebrow as she rose to start clearing the table. "How's the career progressing?"

"Right on schedule. I figure by the time I'm eighty or ninety, I'll be the best damn consultant in the entire marketing industry," Hannah drawled, rising to help clean up.

Maggie shot a frown at her. "No, seriously, how is it going for you?"

"Very well, actually," Hannah answered, helping Maggie to fill the dishwasher. "I gave myself a raise by raising my fee in November. Not one of my clients objected. My end-of-year earnings have put me into a higher income tax bracket, and I don't even mind."

"That's great," Maggie exclaimed, rewarding her with a hug. "Congratulations."

"Thank you," Hannah said simply, going on to candidly admit, "At the risk of sounding arrogant, I'm rather pleased with myself at the moment."

"And why not?" Maggie demanded, her hands planted on her slender hips. "You should be pleased and delighted. You've worked your butt off getting yourself established. I know. I was there. Just as you've always been there for me. Remember?"

Hannah smiled, recalling the day the previous June when she had walked into Maggie's apartment to witness her friend slashing the exquisitely beautiful, extremely expensive wedding dress to shreds. "Remember? How could I forget all the pain—and fun—we've shared?"

"Well, while you're here, let's just remember the fun, and say to hell with the pain. Deal?"

Hannah laughed. "Deal."

They shared a hug and, sliding an arm around each other's waists, strolled to the other side of the room to settle back down on the window seat behind the table, chattering away while they waited for Mitch.

With each passing moment, Maggie's face took on a becoming glow, her eyes shining with anticipation. And with each of those moments, Hannah felt her own anticipation rise, as she wondered what kind of man this Mitch Grainger must be. Not to mention his enigmatic brother.

Two

Having listened to Maggie rave, through several long-distance phone calls, about how handsome, exciting, wonderful and flat-out sexy her employer and fiancé was, Hannah was prepared for the visual impact of Mitch Grainger.

So, when he arrived at the apartment a half hour later, she was neither surprised nor disappointed. Mitch appeared to be everything Maggie claimed him to be and then some. His manner was polite. He was gentle and tender with Maggie, and the perfect gentleman toward Hannah.

She couldn't help but notice that every time Mitch looked at Maggie, his eyes gleamed with near adoration, joy and male sexual hunger. Strangely, that gleam of light gave Hannah an odd little twist in her chest.

Surely not envy of Maggie and the emotions the mere sight of her so obviously induced in Mitch?

Envy? Of her very best friend? The very idea was both confusing and shaming. Hannah might have examined her unusual feeling more closely if there had been just the three of them around the small table.

But Mitch had not come to the apartment alone.

While Hannah had been prepared for Maggie's fiancé she hadn't at all been prepared for the impact of Mitch's older brother, Justin.

And what an impact he made. Hannah felt the reverberations in every molecule of her being— felt it and resented it. In looks, the brothers were quite similar, but altogether different in attire.

Mitch was dressed in a navy-blue business suit, ice-blue shirt, a striped, pale-blue and grey tie and a long gray obviously cashmere coat, the walking picture of the conservative businessman. Justin, on the other hand, had removed a brown, well-worn Stetson and shrugged out of a deep-collared suede jacket. Beneath his coat he wore a blue chambray shirt tucked into faded low-slung jeans plastered to his slim hips and long legs to cover the tops of smart-looking boots.

Justin Grainger towered over Hannah's five foot ten by seven and a half inches. His raw-boned frame was rangy but muscular, a tower of powerful masculinity.

At once, Hannah understood how Maggie had found it hysterical when Mitch threatened to mop the casino floor with his brother if he said one word out of line. While Mitch appeared quite capable of wiping the floor with most men, she knew his brother wasn't one of them.

Justin Grainger had dark hair, streaked with silver at the temples, and a little long at the nape. His eyes were gray, cold as the North Atlantic in January, sharp as a bitter wind, yet aloof and remote. And every time he turned his cold, calculating, but somehow tinglingly sexy sharp-eyed gaze on Hannah, she felt a chilling thrill from the tingling top of her head to the curling tips of her toes.

Hannah's immediate assessment of the two brothers was that Mitch was forceful and dynamic, whereas Justin was a silent but simmering volcano of leashed sexuality, with the potential to erupt without warning all over any innocent, unsuspecting female to cross his path.

Fortunately, having survived that one unsuccessful and unsettling relationship two years before—a relationship in which she had been burned so badly she hadn't even confided in Maggie about the affair or aftereffects—Hannah was neither innocent nor unsuspecting. To be sure, she was suspicious as all get-out.

On Maggie's introduction, Hannah accepted Mitch's proffered hand first. It was warm, his grip polite. But she barely registered his greeting, since all she could hear was the sound of static electricity as she took Justin's extended hand. She not only heard it, she felt it zigzag from her palm to every particle of her body.

Hannah slid a quick glance toward Maggie and Mitch only to find that they had moved across the room to the hallway closet to put away the men's coats.

"Miss Deturk."

That's all he said. Her name. Not even her first name. His voice was low, disturbingly intimate. Hannah's hand felt seared. She hadn't realized his fingers were still firmly wrapped around hers. She turned her gaze back to his, her mouth going dry at the sight of tiny flames flickering in the depths of his cold gray eyes.

Feeling slightly disoriented, and resenting the sensation, she slid her hand free, murmuring, "Mr. Grainger."

"Justin."

"If you wish." She inclined her head, feeling like an awkward teenager, not having a clue she gave the impression of a haughty queen condescending to acknowledge one of her lowest subjects.

A smile shadowed his masculine, tempting lips. "May I call you Hannah?"

Oh, hell, she thought. His voice was even lower, more intimate, and too damn beguiling. Certain her brain had been rendered into nothing more than a small blob, Hannah could manage only to parrot herself.

"If you wish."

"Well, ready for dessert?" Maggie's bright voice dissolved the strange misty atmosphere seemingly surrounding her and Justin Grainger.

Thank heavens for small mercies, Hannah thought, turning away from him.

"Do you have coffee?" Mitch asked.

"Of course." Maggie crossed to the small kitchen area.

Grateful for a moment's respite from Justin's nearness, Hannah hurried after Maggie to help. She served the coffee, careful not to look directly at him. She thought she had herself under control when she again seated herself next to him at the table.

The moment she was settled, she knew she was wrong.

Beneath Justin Grainger's keen gaze, Hannah's enthusiasm waned for the coffee and the surprise dessert promised by Maggie.

"What is it?" Mitch asked, eyeing the dessert dish Maggie set before him, which appeared to contain a mixed-up blob of ingredients.

Maggie grinned. "Karla calls it Heavenly Hawaiian Surprise. It's got pineapple and cherries and pecans and marshmallow and sour cream, and trust me, it is heavenly."

"We shall see, or better yet taste," Mitch said, his teasing eyes alight with affection.

His brother beat him to it. Scooping up a spoonful of the mixture, he popped it in his mouth.

"Decadent," he pronounced. "Delicious."

Once again Justin's low, ultrasensual tones sent an unfamiliar, unwanted and unappreciated chill down Hannah's already quivering spine. At the same time, the spark in his eyes caused a strange melting heat deep inside her.

Hannah resented the sensation but, to her chagrin, she felt every bit as attracted to Justin as she was wary of him. All he had to do was look at her to make her, in a word, sizzle.

Dammit.

It had been some time since Hannah had warmed to a man and she had certainly never sizzled for one. But innate honesty compelled her to admit to herself that she did indeed sizzle for Justin.

And she didn't like it at all.

The conversation around the small table was general; for Hannah, desultory. Appearing for all the world comfortable and relaxed, inside she felt stiff, frozen solid.

Later that night, after the brothers had finally left, Hannah lay awake in the surprisingly comfortable roll-away bed Maggie had prepared for her. She examined the conflicting emotions Justin Grainger had so casually and seemingly effortlessly aroused inside her mind and body.

She felt empty, needy. It was almost frightening. How could it have happened? Hannah asked herself. She was hardly the type to become all squishy and nervy from the mere expression in a man's eyes and the low, sensual sound of his voice.

Certainly, Justin had not said or done anything out of line. He had been every bit as polite and respectful as had his brother Mitch.

Except for his eyes. Dear heavens, Justin Grainger's sharp and compelling eyes.

A shiver trickled through Hannah, and she drew the down comforter more closely around her. She knew it wasn't the coldness of the air but an inner, deeper chill that wouldn't be banished by burrowing under three down comforters.

Hannah decided that getting through the next days—the rehearsal, the dinner, the wedding and reception ought to prove more than a little interesting. In fact, she was afraid it would be an endurance test.

Was she up to the sort of sensual challenge those glinting, gray eyes promised?

Hannah believed she was. She was her own woman, which was why she had struck out on her own, preferring to work her tail off to establish herself rather than work for somebody else.

There was just one tiny flaw in all this—while Hannah *believed* she could handle the situation, return home unscathed by Justin Grainger, she wasn't absolutely certain.

And *that* was frightening.

* * *

"So what did you think of her?" Mitch asked as he and Justin settled into his car after leaving the large house.

Her? Justin hesitated. "Who?"

Mitch glanced over to give Justin an are-you-kidding? look. "Maggie, who else. You remember—the woman I'm going to be marrying in just a few days."

"Well, of course I remember," Justin retorted, feeling like an idiot and not liking the feeling. 'But if you'll recall, there were two women in the apartment," he said in his own defense. "Although I did notice you had eyes only for Maggie."

Tossing him a grin, Mitch flicked on the motor. "I do recall that there were two, smart-ass," he chided. "I also recall that you seemed to stare at Hannah a lot."

Justin shrugged in what he hoped was a care-free way. "Hey, she's an attractive woman."

"Yes, she is," Mitch agreed. "But, that doesn't answer my question. What did you think of Maggie, your future sister-in-law?"

"She is both beautiful and nice, as you well know," Justin answered, relieved to have the topic back on Maggie and off Hannah. "And she is most obviously head-over-heels in love with you. Although I can't imagine why."

"Because I'm sexy as hell?"

Justin gave him a droll look. "Since when?"

"Since I was fifteen," Mitch shot back, as he shot out of the parking lot at the rear of the house. "Of course," he qualified, "I was following your bad example."

"Hmm. Bad example, huh?" he drawled. "Personally, I never considered it bad to be sexy."

After returning to the hotel, Justin closed his room door behind him and leaned back against it. He inhaled deeply and released the breath on a soft "Whew."

Old fashioned? Prim? Proper? Virginal? And probably plain? Had he really held such a preconceived opinion of who Hannah would turn out to be?

"Hah." Shaking his head as though he had just taken a blow to the temple and was still groggy in the mind, Justin pushed away from the door muttering to himself.

"Hannah Deturk is the most cool, composed, beautiful, long-legged woman this ol' son's weary eyes ever landed on."

He chuckled. "And you, Justin Grainger are talking to yourself."

Well, at least he wasn't cursing, Justin consoled himself, releasing a half groan. He was surprised at his unexpected emotional, and physical, reaction to the blond goddess.

Sure, it had been a while since he'd been with a woman, but not nearly long enough to explain the immediate surge of lust he'd experienced at first glance. He'd felt like a teenager in the throes of a testosterone rush.

In that instant Justin decided he had to have Hannah Deturk, in every way possible. Either that or he just might expire from the mind-blowing need.

The tricky part was; how and when? Well, he knew exactly how, Justin mused, a smile twitching the corners of his mouth. But the trick was when. Time was limited.

There were only a few days to go until the wedding. As Maggie and Hannah hadn't seen each other for six months, they'd likely be spending most of those days—and nights—together, chattering away.

Poor Mitch was going to be sleeping alone from now until his wedding night. He'd probably be a bear until then, working overtime to conceal his feelings.

Then Justin realized something—Mitch wouldn't be the only man working to control strong urges.

Damnation.

He mulled over the problem of private time and place with Hannah as he sat on the edge of the bed and pulled off his best pair of boots. Standing to shuck out of his clothes, he folded them neatly before sliding them into the plastic laundry bag provided by the hotel. His mother had been a real stickler about neatness.

Naked as a newborn, he stretched his length between the chilled sheets, doused the bedside light and started up at the ceiling. Of course, he really couldn't see the ceiling, as the closed drapes shut out even the tiniest glimmer of moonlight and the room was as dark as pure nothingness.

It didn't matter to Justin, because he could still see a shimmering image of Hannah Deturk.

"Oh, hell," he muttered, his breathing growing shallow as his body grew hard. "Think, man. When are you going to have the chance to approach her?"

The days leading up to the big event were out. There was the rehearsal late in the afternoon the day before the wedding, to be followed by the rehearsal dinner. That night was out, as well. Justin knew full well his family would make a lengthy celebration of the dinner.

Naturally, the actual day of the wedding was out.

The day—or night—after the wedding? Justin mulled over the problem, allowing his body to cool down a few degrees. He was in no hurry to get back to the ranch, he could spare a few days for fun and games.

Not in a hotel room. Justin gave a sharp shake of his head against the pillow. Not with Hannah. He didn't want to delve into why it mattered. It never bothered him before where he spent time romping with a woman—a hotel room, motel room, her apartment, it made no difference to him. This time, if there were to be a time with Hannah, it did matter.

So then, if not the hotel, where?

He could probably have the use of Mitch's apartment, seeing as how he and Maggie were off the day after the wedding to one of those island resorts exclusively for couples.

No, that wouldn't do. Mitch's apartment was on the top floor of the casino, and there was no way

Justin would escort Hannah either through the front entrance of the casino or up the back stairs.

Without knowing how he knew, Justin felt Hannah was definitely not a back stairs kind of woman. Scratch Mitch's place. The same for Maggie's attic hide-away. He felt positive that Hannah would not for a second even consider her friend's home for what he had in mind.

Suddenly he was struck by a memory. There was an apartment two floors below Maggie's place. Karla had lived there before marrying Ben. It hadn't been rented since then. So they would have privacy for their baby, Ben and Karla were staying in it now. They were planning to leave the morning after the wedding, as well.

Perfect. All he had to do was inform his brother of his intention to stay in the apartment for a couple of days after the wedding. It would be empty. Besides, the house belonged to the family, and he was a member, wasn't he?

The best part was he had already laid the groundwork by telling Mitch he would be looking for female company while he was in town.

Suddenly Justin laughed aloud. Damned if he wasn't planning a seduction. Hell, he had never in his life made plans to actually seduce a woman.

He had simply homed in on a female who appealed to him, made his move and, if the woman was willing, let it all happen.

His laughter faded as fast as it had erupted. Of course, everything depended on when Hannah was planning to return to Philadelphia and, more important, if she would be willing to spend some mutually entertaining time with him.

Of course, Hannah hadn't appeared overwhelmed by his masculine appeal. Come to think of it, she had barely spoken or looked at him during dinner. But he had a feeling something shimmered between them from the moment he touched her hand. And damned if he wasn't going to give it his best shot.

"So, I understand our family's going to go off in separate directions right after the big day," said Justin who was seated at a small table in Mitch's office the following morning. He'd called his brother and invited himself for breakfast. They had finished their meal, and Justin sat back in his chair, sipping at a mug of steaming coffee.

"Far as I know, everybody's taking off about the

same time," Mitch replied from opposite Justin, his hands cradling a matching mug. "Aren't they?"

"I'm not." Justin took another sip. "Ben can take care of things at the ranch, so I think I'll lug my gear over to the apartment Ben and Karla are presently occupying and camp there for a couple days."

"Why?" Mitch raised his eyebrows.

Justin gave him a slow, suggestive grin. "I do recall telling you I'd be on the lookout for some female companionship, didn't I?"

Mitch grinned back. "You're incorrigible."

"Not at all," Justin denied. "I'm just hot to trot, is all. You don't mind if I use the place for a while?"

"Why should I mind?" Mitch shrugged. "The house belongs as much to you as it does to me." He gave Justin a wry look. "As long as you wait until everybody has left to track down a playmate."

"Everybody?" Before Mitch could respond, he went on, digging for information. "Just the family, or does that include other guests?"

"Other guests?" Mitch frowned. "What other guests? Since Maggie's parents decided not to fly in from Hawaii after we informed them we'd stop by on the way to our honeymoon, the only other guests are employees and a few local residents."

"And Hannah." Justin kept his voice free of inflection, other than a slight hint of disinterest.

"Oh, yeah, Hannah." Mitch pursed his lips. "Hmm…you know, I don't have a clue as to her plans. Maggie hasn't said a word. I'll have to ask her."

"Is it important?" Justin had to focus to retain his near-bored tone. "I mean, does Hannah come under your no-shock edict?"

Mitch pondered the question for a few seconds, then said, "I haven't given it a thought. Does it matter?"

"Only if it's going to cramp my style. Such as it is."

Mitch shook his head. "I wasn't aware that you had a style. I thought you just jumped the first woman that appealed to you."

"Only if she's willing."

Mitch raised his eyes, as if seeking help from above. "You are not to be believed." His lips twitched. "My very own brother, a philanderer, of all things."

"Hey," Justin objected. "I am not a philanderer. I'm a normal male, with a healthy sexual appetite. And do you have any idea how long it's been since I've appeased it?"

Mitch let rip a deep, rich laugh. "I don't think I want to know anything about your sex life, thank you."

"Sex life? Who the hell has a sex life?" Justin chuckled. "I talk to horses most of the time, and most of the time I don't mind. But, every now and again, a man needs a woman. And in my case, buddy, it's been months."

"Okay. Okay." Mitch held his hand up in surrender. "I give up. Have your R and R, but try not to lose the ranch at the tables downstairs."

Justin didn't bother to respond. Mitch knew damn well he wasn't stupid; he would set a limit, a fairly low one, and stick to it. He hid an inner smile. "If things break my way, I'll be too busy with more important—and a helluva lot more interesting—things than gambling."

Three

Friday arrived much too soon to suit Hannah. Although they talked almost nonstop, there hadn't been nearly enough time for her and Maggie to catch up with each other's lives. Not once had either one of them run out of things to say.

The rehearsal was scheduled for five in the small church just a few blocks from the big Victorian house. Dinner would be at the Bullock Hotel immediately following the rehearsal.

By four o'clock Maggie was a nervous wreck.

"All this over a rehearsal?" Hannah said, trying

hard to contain a laugh. "I can't wait until tomorrow. You'll probably be a basket case. Instead of walking in front of you, Karla and I might have to walk behind, in case you collapse on the way down the aisle."

"Not at all," Maggie said, giving a dainty but superior sniff. "Don't forget, I'll have Mitch's brother Adam to walk me down the aisle." She no sooner had the words out, when she burst out laughing. "And believe me, friend, Adam's big enough to handle delicate little ol' me."

"Shall we be off?" Hannah asked.

"I suppose we'd better," Maggie agreed.

Giggling like two teenagers, they clattered down the stairs and out of the building to Hannah's rented SUV.

The streets had been cleared of snow and the short jaunt to the church took only minutes. That parking lot, also cleared, already contained several vehicles.

"It looks like we're the last to arrive," Maggie said, her voice quavery with tension.

"Yes, it does," Hannah agreed, tossing her friend an exasperated look. "And will you calm down, for pity's sake? It is only the rehearsal."

"I know…but…"

"No buts." She pushed open the door. "Let's go and get this show on the road, so we can get to dinner." She grinned at Maggie, hoping to ease her nerves. "I'm starving."

The rehearsal went off without a hitch…for everyone except Hannah. She was fine at the beginning. Maggie introduced her to more of Mitch's family including his brother Adam. Hannah had immediately liked him.

Adam was just as tall and handsome as his brothers, a little older, but pleasant and charming. His eyes, unlike Justin's, were warm, friendly. So she was feeling good, relaxed, until she began leading the procession. The sight of Justin, standing beside Mitch at the end of the aisle, had the strangest effect on her.

In direct contrast to Mitch, who was wearing a dark suit, white shirt and striped tie, Justin was dressed in a soft brown pullover sweater, tan casual pants and the same black boots he'd worn at Maggie's that first night.

Hannah couldn't help but wonder if he were planning to wear the boots for the wedding. The errant thought flittered through her mind that at least the boots were shined.

But his footwear or clothes weren't the cause

of her weird reaction. It was his eyes, his laser-sharp eyes. After slowly raking the length of her body, they seemed to bore right through her, to her every thought, every emotion. And Hannah's range of emotions were running wild, shaking up every particle of her being.

She suddenly felt nervy, excited and vaguely frightened, chilled and hot all over, as if in anticipation of something earth-shattering about to happen.

Weird hardly described it.

It seemed to take forever for her to traverse the relatively short aisle, and yet she reached the end way too soon. And there he was, his piercing gray gaze glittering with a sometime-soon promise of that anticipated, dreaded, earth-shattering event. The heat causing the glitter left little doubt in her mind what he intended that event to be.

Hannah's breathing was labored, uneven. Relief rushed through her when she stepped to the side, out of his direct line of vision. Hannah rigidly avoided his eyes through the rest of the proceedings.

After that, everything went off without a hitch…until they arrived at the hotel.

Dinner itself was fine. The food served was ex-

cellent, Mitch's family friendly, easy to talk to…
that is, except Justin. He had waited until Hannah
was seated, then, deliberately, she felt certain,
seated himself directly opposite her. At once he
proceeded to renew sending his silent, visual messages to her. Hard as she tried—and she gave it her
best shot—Hannah couldn't misinterpret his intent.

She was not without experience in the nuances
of eye conduct and body language. He had plans,
for her and him together, those silent messages
promised. And, as she had suspected in the church,
every one of those plans were sexual in nature.

While Justin's hot-eyed gaze revealed his car-
nal thoughts to Hannah, his occasional and brief
comments were bland, almost banal.

Hannah didn't know whether to be amused or
run for her life.

She attempted to assure herself her feelings
were caused by revulsion, but she knew she was
lying. The truth, which she would fiercely deny if
questioned, was that her feelings stemmed from
excitement.

Hannah was fearful her feelings, the heat
steadily building inside, were clearly revealed on
her face, in her eyes. She hoped the picture she

presented to the company, even the most keen of observers, was that of cool, controlled composure.

Especially to Justin.

Justin could read Hannah like an open book. Far from being repelled by his stare of unconcealed desire, Hannah was receptive, her own needs and desires revealed in the depths of her so-cool eyes.

He couldn't wait to get her alone, feel her mouth yielding to his kiss, her naked body sliding against his, her long legs curling around his waist.

Stop it, Justin ordered his wayward thoughts. Damned if he wasn't getting hard, right there under the table. He drew a mental image of himself, trudging across the frozen tundra, chilled to the bone.

Moments later he was surprised by the strains of music from a group positioned in front of a small dance floor at the end of the private dining room. Leave it to Mitch to have arranged for dancing after dinner.

In a flash, Justin was on his feet, circling the table to Hannah. "I suppose we're expected to rehearse the wedding party reception dance, too," he said, holding out his hand in invitation.

"Ahh…" she responded, her voice laced with uncertainty and a strong hint of reluctance.

"That's right," Maggie said, laughing—bless her heart. "We want everything perfect."

Hannah sighed, but complied, placing her hand in his as she rose from her chair.

Justin's own heart was starting to speed up as he led Hannah to the dance floor. While he wouldn't be able to feel her satiny skin sliding against him, or her tempting mouth pressed to his, or the embrace of her slender legs, he was determined to feel the thrill of her supple body held close to his in the dance.

Not exactly the dance Justin would have preferred, but it would have to do…for now.

Fortunately, the group was playing his kind of music, a ballad, allowing for only slow dancing. At the edge of the dance floor, Justin drew Hannah to him, circling her waist with his arms, leaving her little choice but to circle his neck with her own. The sensation created by the feel of her tall body held closely against his was thrilling beyond anything he had ever felt while fully clothed.

Scratch that last thought, he corrected himself, drawing in a quick breath at the sensations sent skittering through him at the touch of her hand sliding from the back of his neck to the center of his chest. Though he knew her movement was intended to keep some distance between them, Justin was forced to suppress an involuntary shiver at the scorching feel of her palm against him, right through his shirt.

"What are you afraid of?" he asked, his voice pitched low for her ears only. "You don't like dancing?"

Hannah lifted her head to gaze at him, a wry curve on her maddeningly tempting lips. "Not particularly," she drawled. "And I don't need my suit pressed, thank you."

He laughed, refraining himself from telling her he intended to press a lot more than her clothes. He held himself in check for one reason; he had heard the slight breathy catch in her voice underlying her dry tones.

Deciding to play it cool, he made a half step back, feeling a chill, even from that tiny span between them.

"I'm glad you find me so amusing," she said, keeping her hand solidly pressed to his chest.

"Oh, I find you a lot more than amusing," he said, fighting an urge to be explicit, and a bigger urge to show her, right there on the dance floor.

But no, the room was full of people, most of whom were family members. If he gave in to the urge, Mitch and Adam would be all over him like a bad rash in no time. He'd hate like hell to have to deck the two of them in front of the family. The thought made him smile.

Hannah felt...bedazzled. Where the heck had that almost boyish, impish smile come from? she wondered, feeling an unfamiliar warmth around her heart. What in the world was Justin thinking about to cause that smile?

"You look pensive," he murmured, trying to move her closer to him, relenting when she resisted.

Having lowered his head, his breath tickled her ear, all the way to the base of her spinal cord. Two conflicting thoughts tangled together in her bemused mind—wanting this dance to end soon and hoping it would go on forever.

Throwing caution aside, she decided to be candid. "I was just wondering where that smile came from...and who it was for."

He laughed. Damn, Hannah wished he wouldn't do that. His laughter had an even more intense effect than his smile. It was low, infectious, relaxed, and scattered the warmth in her chest, setting off minisparklers throughout her body.

Now he grinned. She swallowed a groan.

"Actually, I was thinking about having to take down both of my brothers in front of everybody here."

Startled by his reply, Hannah stared at him. "But…why would you think of such a thing?"

His eyes gleamed with devilment. "In self-defense, of course. Why else?"

The music stopped. She made a move. He didn't. His hold was unbreakable. She swept a quick look around to see if anyone was watching them. There were three other couples on the floor: his parents, Mitch and Maggie, and Ben and Karla. The three couples were too absorbed in one another to pay any attention to her and Justin. Still, Hannah had just opened her mouth to protest, when the music started again. He moved, taking her with him, and they continued dancing.

Hannah sighed, heavily so he couldn't possibly miss it, but she had to ask, "Why on earth would you need to defend yourself from your brothers?"

"Because they'd jump me for sure," Justin responded patiently, as if the answer should be obvious.

Hannah didn't know whether to hit him or scream at him. She did neither. She sighed again and narrowed her eyes. "Okay, if you want to play games. Why would they jump you?"

"Because I want to play games," he explained, the gleam in the depth of his so cool eyes literally dancing.

"Justin…" Her voice held a gravelly, distinct note of warning.

"Okay. But don't say you didn't ask." He shrugged. "I figured if I acted on impulse, pulling you tightly against me and ravishing your mouth with mine, Mitch and Adam might think it was their duty to rescue you from the clutches of their womanizing brother." Laughter skirted on the edges of his serious tone. "And in that case, of course, I'd have little recourse but to sweep out this barn with them."

Sweep out this barn? Barn? Hannah sent a quick glance around the well-appointed dining room. But she didn't question his remark. Her attention had focused on one word. "Womanizing?"

Justin nodded solemnly, immediately ruining the effect of his somber expression with another one of those breath-stealing smiles.

She stopped moving so suddenly his big body crashed hard into hers, knocking the breath out of her. Reflexively he tightened his arms around her, steadying her while keeping them both upright, her body crushed to his.

"Nice," he murmured, his breath ruffling the tiny hairs at her temple…and her senses.

"You're a womanizer?" she blurted without thinking, her voice betraying her shock.

"No, sweetheart," he denied, his tone adamant, thrilling her with the casually stated endearment, his lips setting off a thrill as they skimmed a trial from her ear to the corner of her mouth.

"But, you said…" she began, stirring—not struggling—to put some small distance between them. Her puny efforts proved unsuccessful.

"I know what I said." His arms tightened even more. "Stay still. You feel so good." His mouth took a slow, erotic journey over her surprised, parted lips. "You taste so good. I could make a feast of you."

Because she suddenly craved a deeper taste of him, she felt a faint curl of panic. Afraid of the strange sensations churning inside her, Hannah turned and pulled her head back, away from his tantalizing mouth.

"You've got the wrong woman," she said, somehow managing to infuse a thread of strength into her breathy voice.

"No." Justin shook his head, but loosened his hold, allowing her to move back a half step. "I've got the right woman." His smile and eyes were soft, almost tender. "Hannah, I am not a womanizer."

She frowned. "Then why did you say you were?"

"Because my brothers tease me about my lifestyle every time we're together." He grinned. "Matter of fact, Mitch called me a philanderer just the other day." He heaved a deep sigh. "It was unkind of him. I was crushed."

"Right," Hannah drawled, raising an eyebrow in disbelief. "I know it's none of my business, but..." she hesitated. It most certainly was her business: Justin Grainger had definite and obvious designs on her.

"But?" he prompted, a dark brow mirroring hers.

"What is your lifestyle...exactly."

"Pretty damn boring," he said, releasing her when the music stopped. "I ranch, and I don't go to town, any town or city, too often."

"Have you ever been married?" she asked.

"I was. I've been divorced now for almost five year," he said, his voice hard and flat. "And no,

I don't want to talk about it. I want to forget about it."

Feeling rebuffed, Hannah's spine stiffened. "I don't recall asking you to talk about it…or to dance in the first place as far as that goes. Now, if you'll excuse me?" She didn't wait for an answer but strode away, head held high.

A little while later—though it seemed like hours to Hannah—the party began to break up. At last, she thought, rising and scooping up her handbag. After not having exchanged one word with Justin since returning to the table, she not only didn't say good-night, she avoided eye contact with him.

Feeling a need to escape the room, and Justin, she found Maggie, who was lingering over saying her farewells to the others, and murmured her intention of getting the car.

Hannah saw the snow flurries a moment before she reached the hotel exit. Fortunately, only a fine coating of white covered the parking lot. She didn't notice the thin layer of black ice beneath the snow as she stepped outside.

She took only three steps before she felt the heel of her right boot begin to slip. Hannah tried to regain her balance, but knew for certain she was going down.

"Son of a…" she began, her arms flailing.

"Whoa," Justin said from right behind her, his strong hands grasping her upper arms to catch her, ease her upright. "Is that any way for a lady to talk?" His hands moved, swinging her around to face him.

"I wasn't feeling much like a lady at that moment," Hannah said, still catching her breath from the near tumble, and not the nearness of the man, she assured herself.

"I can understand your reaction. That was a close one." Though it would seem impossible, his voice contained both concern and amusement. "Good thing I was only a few steps behind you."

"Thank you," Hannah said, a bit shakily, forcing herself to look directly into his eyes.

"You're welcome." His smile was a tormenting tease, his eyes held that gleam again.

He was close, too close. She could smell the clean, spicy, masculine scent of him, feel the warmth of him through her winter coat. "Were you following me?" She attempted a step back; he drew her closer.

"Yes." His lips brushed her ear, his warm breath tickling the interior.

A thrill shimmered the length of her spine; Hannah told herself it was the chill in the air, the feel of the cold fluffy snowflakes kissing her cheeks. "Why were you following me? What do you want from me?" Stupid question, as if she didn't already know the answer. Nevertheless, when it came, so blunt, so determined, she was shocked...and a lot more than thrilled. She felt allover warm and excited.

"Long, hot nights on smooth, cool sheets."

Four

At last the wedding day arrived. The candlelight ceremony was scheduled for six, with the reception following immediately at the hotel.

To Hannah's amazement, after the nervous fits Maggie had suffered the day before, her friend had been calm and remained so throughout the day.

Although she revealed not the slightest hint of it, Hannah felt like the basket case she had expected Maggie to be. Of course, her inner jitters had nothing whatever to do with her encounter with Justin in the parking lot, she kept telling herself.

Yeah. Right.

So stunned had she been by Justin's blatant suggestion—suggestion, heck, it was an outright declaration of intent—Hannah retained only a vague memory of him, chuckling softly as he walked her to her car. And, darn it, how had he been so surefooted, when he'd been wearing heeled boots, too?

"Time to dress," Maggie happily announced, ending Hannah's brooding introspection.

At last. At last. Hannah smiled, nodding her agreement. She was of two minds about the coming hours; relieved at finally getting it over with, and filled with conflicting amounts of trepidation and anticipation, more of the latter than the former.

Calling herself all kinds of a ditz didn't do a thing to calm down her seesawing emotions.

One thing was for certain. Hannah was determined there would be no slipping on black ice. At her advice, both she and Maggie wore low-heeled winter boots and carried their fancy wedding shoes in shoe bags. At least they didn't have any concerns about holding up their dresses out of the slushy mess, as both garments were cocktail length. Maggie's dress was a simple and elegant, long-sleeved white velvet, with a nipped-in waist and full skirt. She looked both innocent and gorgeous.

Hannah's dress was as simple and elegant—a sheath with three-quarter-length sleeves and a modest neckline.

They arrived at the church with five minutes to spare until show time. Apparently everyone else, including the groom, was already in place. Karla and Adam were waiting in the small foyer. Adam took their coats, and Karla handed them their bouquets. Maggie's was made of white orchids. Hannah's bouquet was the same as Karla's, a mix of dark-red rosebuds with lacy ferns and delicate white baby's breath.

Now Hannah knew why Maggie had insisted she hunt down a dress in forest green. Hers was only a shade darker than Karla's.

Music from the organ filled the church.

Flashing Maggie an encouraging smile, Karla stepped out, heading down the aisle. Offering her own smile to the bride, while drawing a calming breath for herself, Hannah followed two steps behind Karla.

And there he was, standing beside Mitch, looking devastating in a white shirt, somber tie and dark suit that was fitted perfectly to his wide-shouldered, narrow-waisted, long-legged body.

As she drew nearer, Hannah lowered her gaze, fully expecting to find black slant-heeled boots. Surprise, surprise. Justin was actually shod in classic black men's dress shoes.

When she raised her eyes, her gaze collided with his smoldering stare.

Good grief! The man was a menace. Hannah felt hot. She felt cold. She felt exhilarated. She felt exhausted. In short, she felt like a woman fiercely physically attracted to a man. A man who didn't so much as attempt to hide his intention from her.

Unaware of the ceremony going on about her, she automatically received Maggie's bouquet.

Her heart pounding, her pulse racing, finding it increasingly difficult to think straight, Hannah almost completely missed the exchange of vows.

"With this ring, I thee wed."

The firm, clear sound of Mitch's voice broke through Hannah's mental fog. She blinked, and just caught the movement of Justin handing Mitch a plain gold ring.

Her cue. Releasing a soft sigh of relief for coming to her senses in time, Hannah slipped a larger matching gold band from her thumb, just as Maggie repeated the vow.

Moments later Mitch kissed Maggie, to the applause of the guests, and it was over. They were married.

Hopefully, till death did them part, Hannah thought, frowning as she saw Justin take Adam's place in line, leaving his older brother to escort Karla.

What was the devil up to now? Steeling herself, she took Justin's arm to follow the newlyweds down the aisle to the church foyer.

"Your place or mine?" Justin murmured, his eyes glittering with a positively wicked gleam of amusement.

He knew. Damn the man, he knew exactly how she was feeling, *what* she was feeling, as if the word *ready* had magically appeared branded on her forehead in capital letters.

"I don't have a place here," Hannah muttered, riveting her gaze on the back of Maggie's head. "My place is hundreds of miles from here, in Pennsylvania."

He chuckled.

Hannah cringed, covering it with a tight smile as she hugged first Maggie, then Mitch, wishing them good luck before turning to stand beside Mitch to form the greeting line. Not daring to so much as glance into Justin's eyes again, she stood stiff, staring directly ahead. It didn't do her a bit of good, as he continued to torment her in that low, deep, nerve-rattling sexy voice.

"My permanent place is not as far away. In Montana," he murmured, his head so close to hers she felt his warm breath caress her ear. "But I have a temporary place here, as I know you do. Conveniently, both places are at the very same location, that beautiful old Victorian house."

Hannah was genuinely shocked. "Maggie's apartment? I...I couldn't, wouldn't dream of it!" she softly protested, suddenly realizing she had not said no to *him,* but rather to meeting him at Maggie's adorable little flat on the third floor.

"Of course not," he agreed, drawing her startled gaze just as he smiled at Karla who settled in line next to him. His eyes still gleamed with a sinful light. "But I haven't the least hesitation in using the roomier apartment on the first floor for some fun and games."

Fun and games. The overused expression, following the tired line of your place or mine, didn't sound as worn-out and dated coming from Justin's sensuous mouth. Truth be told, the soft invitation sounded much too tempting.

At a loss for a coherent retort, Hannah felt a wave of relief as she turned her head to find the first of the guests, Justin's parents, who were laughing and crying and hugging Maggie and Mitch in turn.

Justin merely lowered his head closer to her, his whispered words tickling her inner ear and every nerve ending in her body. "I'll be moving in for a couple of days tomorrow, right after Karla and Ben vacate."

Hannah had to suppress a visible tremor as his tongue swiftly speared into her ear.

"Feel free to visit at anytime…day or night," he murmured, increasing the tremor a hundredfold. "Come early…and often—" he chuckled at her quick, indrawn breath, "—and stay late…like a couple of days."

Thank goodness, at that moment Justin's father swept her into a celebratory embrace, as she found it difficult to pull a comeback from her mush of gray matter. The man was nearly as tall as his three sons, but not as strong as them, and not nearly as ruggedly handsome as Justin—darn his too-attractive hide.

His mother, a lovely woman, and almost as tall as Hannah took her hands and leaned forward to kiss her cheek. "You look beautiful in that dress, Hannah," she said, delicately dabbing at her eyes with a tissue. "Both of you do, you and Karla."

"Why, thank you," Hannah responded, lowering her head to kiss the older woman's still smooth cheek. She had liked Mrs. Grainger from their first meeting. "Maggie picked the color. She insisted I search until I found the perfect dress."

"And you did. It's a perfect color for so soon after the holidays," the older woman said, smiling as she stepped into Justin's waiting arms. "It's lovely on you."

Wrong on both counts, Mom, Justin thought as he swept his mother into a hug and planted a kiss on her cheek. That dark green was great against Hannah's blond hair and creamy complexion any time of year. And she didn't look merely lovely, she looked ravishing. And as for it being lovely on her, he'd rather see it off her. And he intended to…soon.

Naturally, Justin didn't say any of that to his mother. She just might have decided to step in and protect the lovely Hannah from her "bad boy" son.

He complimented her instead. "As always, you not only look wonderful, Mother, you smell terrific, kinda sexy. I'll bet Dad loves that scent."

"Justin Grainger!" His mother sounded shocked, but she couldn't quite control the amusement twitching the corners of her lips. "Behave yourself."

"He doesn't have a clue how to do that," his father drawled, the glimmer in his eyes similar to the light dancing in his son's. "But, you know what?" he said, drawing his wife from Justin's loose hold. "He's exactly right. I do think that perfume's sexy. It turns me on."

His mother gasped and proceeded to scold her grinning husband. Justin thrilled to the soft sound of laughter from the woman by his side. He smiled at Hannah.

"They're a trip, aren't they?"

"I think they're perfect together." Her returned smile caused sudden heat and potentially embarrassing sensations in all parts of his body.

"I think we'll be perfect together, too."

"To quote a wise woman I recently met, 'Behave yourself, Justin,' before you embarrass me," she said sternly, giving him a brief, pointed look at one particular part of his anatomy, "As well as yourself."

He laughed aloud, he couldn't help it. This gorgeous woman thoroughly delighted him.

Hannah simply shook her head in despair of him and turned her attention to the line of waiting guests. Then she ignored him until the last couple of guests had finally departed.

Thinking her advice prudent, at least until he got her on the dance floor at the reception, Justin conducted himself like the perfect gentleman throughout the boring ordeal of being prodded and pushed into position by the fussy photographer during the snapping of the wedding pictures.

While he drew impatient with his self-imposed restraint, and at the seemingly endless procedures, he still was distracted and amused by the quick, suspicious glances Hannah winged his way every so often.

Although he felt at the point of busting loose, Justin maintained his circumspect demeanor during the time-honored rituals of the start of the reception. He didn't even suggest that Adam again change partners with him as the wedding party made their entrance.

Toasts were raised, seemingly never-ending toasts. As best man, Justin gave the first one, and even managed to deliver it without firing one risqué shot at Mitch. Adam stood up after him, and followed his lead of propriety. It was their father, the unrepentant, rugged seventy-five-year-old zing-tosser that scored with a couple of sly innuendoes.

Braving their mother's startled and annoyed expression, Justin joined his brothers and the guests in laughter. He was happy to notice that Maggie, Karla, his sisters and even the tempting Hannah were laughing.

Within seconds, at a teasing, endearing smile from his father, his mother gave in to laughter, too.

It set the mood for the celebratory party. Growing impatient to hold Hannah in his arms; Justin remained stoic throughout the rest of the preliminaries.

There was dinner. A buffet fairly groaning with the weight of the food. Servers stood behind the long table, slicing roast beef, baked ham and roasted turkey. Then there was an array of all kinds of hot vegetables, salads and fruits.

Would this never end? Justin wondered, filling his plate then only picking at the food. Not anytime soon, he concluded, hearing the announcement for the bride and groom's first dance.

The first dance ended and the frontman for the small band called for the attendants to take the floor. Schooling himself, Justin swept Hannah into his arms and onto the floor, keeping a respectful distance between them.

She gave him a wary look, as if recalling the way he had held her the night before.

Justin offered her a polite smile. "Did you enjoy your dinner?" he asked, his tone every bit as polite as his smile. "I noticed you didn't take very much to eat."

Hannah still looked wary. "I really wasn't hungry."

"I suppose you didn't notice, but I wasn't, either." He smiled at Adam and Karla as they danced past. "At least, I wasn't hungry for food."

"Justin." Her voice was soft, stern. Her gaze narrowed on his. "Are you going to start up again?"

"Oh, honey, I've barely begun." He grinned. "May I see you back to the house?"

Her eyes glittering defiance, she raised her chin. He was tempted to take a tasty bite of it.

"No. Thank you." She gave him a superior, mocking smile. "I have my own car."

Releasing her hand, Justin took a half step back,

feigning shock. "You mean, my brother didn't send a limo for his prospective bride and her attendant?"

"Of course not. Why should he? I rented a large SUV. And he did have the limo to bring them here from the church."

"Even so, I'd have sent a limo for my intended." His eyes refuted his self-righteous tone. Reclaiming her hand, he whirled her around.

"And do you have an intended hidden away somewhere?" She was slightly breathless from his sudden quick movement. A becoming color bloomed in her cheeks.

Justin was intrigued, wondering if his swirling action had caused her pink breathlessness, or if it had sprung from her question. "No." He gave a fast and sharp shake of his head. "No intendeds for me." He lifted a dark, chiding eyebrow. "If there were, I wouldn't be here, now, wanting to make love with you."

She made a sound that to him was part gasp, part sigh. He waited for a response from her, feeling breathless himself.

At that moment the music ended, and she slipped out of his arms and damned near ran to the bridal party table.

* * *

For someone who was usually calm and collected, Hannah was feeling more than a little rattled. Rattled, excited and annoyed.

No intendeds for me.

What was he trying to tell her with his emphatic statement, the quick negative shake of his head? He had no use for women? Hannah gave a silent but definite "Ha!" Justin obviously had one use for women.

Just then, Maggie found her. "Hannah, I want you to come with me." Her friend grasped her arm, tugging to get her moving.

Trailing along, thoroughly confused by the urgency in Maggie's voice, Hannah asked, "Where are we going…and why such a hurry?"

"We're going up to the suite Mitch reserved for us for tonight," Maggie explained—kind of—continuing to tug on Hannah's arm.

"I don't understand." Now she was more than confused.

"Of course you don't." Maggie exhaled as the doors to the elevator slid together after they stepped inside. "I want you to help me out of my dress."

"Me?" Hannah could only stare at her in disbelief. "Maggie, isn't that Mitch's job?"

"Yes, yes, I know all that." Maggie waved the question aside. "But Mitch is the one who asked me to give you another heads-up." The doors swished open, and Maggie swished into the corridor. "Besides," she added over her shoulder, "I would like you to take my dress back to the house for me."

"I'd be happy to take it with me." Tired of trailing in her friend's wake, Hannah strode forward to walk with her to the suite. "Heads-up about what?" she asked, with wide-eyed innocence, as if she didn't know damn well it would concern Justin somehow.

"Justin." Maggie unlocked then flung open the door and ushered her inside.

Who would ever have guessed? Hannah thought, resigned to hearing more negative tidbits about Justin's character, or lack of same. She sighed, might as well get it over with. "What about Justin?"

"Well…" Now, after having given Hannah the bum's rush from the reception room, Maggie hesitated.

"He's a wanted felon?" Hannah asked, facetiously.

"No, of course not." Maggie tossed an impatient look at her. "Apparently, he's something of a…uh…philanderer. You know, the no-strings, love-'em-and-leave-'em type."

Big shocker. Hannah had figured that one out for herself. If she hadn't, she wouldn't have been about to bid good-night to Maggie and Mitch, wish them happiness, give them both a congratulatory hug and head for the nearest exit.

"I suspected as much," Hannah said, with self-imposed equanimity, walking around Maggie to unhook and pull the waist-length zipper on her dress.

"You did?" Maggie swung around to face her. "How?"

Hannah actually contrived a reasonable-sounding chuckle. "Dearest friend, Justin has been making…shall I say…explicit suggestions to me since the rehearsal supper last night."

"Aha," Maggie crowed. "Mitch was right. He said he thought Justin was hitting on you. That's why he asked me to clue you in."

"I appreciate the concern." In point of fact, even though she had figured Justin wasn't looking for a real relationship, Hannah wasn't at all sure she did appreciate the concern, or the information. She gave a frowning Maggie a serene smile. "Where is your bridegroom, by the way?"

"Oh my gosh," Maggie yelped. "He'll be here any minute. If you don't mind," she said, stepping out of the dress, "I'm going to toss this into the bag and toss you out of here so I can get ready for him."

Laughing with genuine amusement, Hannah retrieved the long, heavy plastic dress bag and held it open while Maggie slipped it onto a padded hanger and beneath the garment bag.

"Okay, I'm outta here."

"Wait," Maggie ordered, stopping Hannah as she turned toward the door. Bending to a low table, she scooped up her bouquet and shoved it into Hannah's free hand.

"What are you doing?" Hannah demanded. "You're supposed to toss that to the single women downstairs." She tried to hand it back to Maggie, who refused to take it.

"What single woman?" Maggie backed away. "As far as I'm concerned, *you* are the only single woman here…which means, you'll be the next bride."

"But, Maggie, you know there is no—"

"I know, I know, but who knows what's in the future? Mr. Right might be just around the corner." Laughing at Hannah's skeptical expression, Maggie backed up another step. "Will you just take it and get out of here?"

Hannah heaved an exaggerated sigh. "Okay, you win. But only because I don't want to be here to cramp his style when Mitch arrives."

"Thanks, love," Maggie fervently said, rushing to Hannah to give her a hug. "For everything, especially being my friend. I'll call you after Mitch and I get back."

"I'll be waiting," Hannah said, holding the bag up from the floor as she moved to the door. "Be happy." She smiled, opened the door, then turned back to murmur, "Love you."

Maggie's return smile was misty. "Back at you."

Five

Avoiding Justin as she made her escape, Hannah didn't breathe fully until she locked the door behind her in Maggie's cozy attic flat.

Nervous, edgy, both afraid—and secretly hopeful—that she'd hear Justin rap at the door any second, she carefully hung Maggie's dress away before removing her own dress. After a quick shower, Hannah slipped into her nightshirt and robe, then proceeded to collect her stuff. She was leaving, going back to Philly, first thing in the morning.

She was *not* running from Justin, Hannah kept telling herself, knowing all the while she was lying. She knew, without a shred of doubt, Justin would not force any issues or hurt her in any way. Why she was convinced he would honor her decision, whatever that might be, she didn't know, but she felt certain she was right.

So, if she was not running from fear of Justin, what was she running from? She was attracted to Justin, fiercely attracted. She had never, ever wanted a man, his touch, his kiss, his possession as much as she wanted Justin Grainger.

It scared the hell out of her.

He scared the hell out of her.

Not physically. Emotionally.

As sure as Hannah was that Justin would never physically harm her, she was equally sure he could devastate her emotionally.

She had been warned. Justin himself had told her he was the family "bad boy," and to protect her, Mitch had instructed Maggie to inform her of his brother's love-'em-and-leave-'em reputation with women.

Perhaps, Mitch had had a heart-to-heart with his wayward brother because, by 2 a.m. he had neither rapped on the door nor rung Maggie's phone.

Hannah knew the exact time, because by 2 a.m., she had not slept, had not so much as closed her eyes. Her restless, wakeful state had nothing to do with not having heard from him, she assured herself. She absolutely did not feel let down, disappointed…damn near bereft.

Sigh. She had done a lot of sighing.

Somewhere around 4 a.m., well, actually, 4:14 to be exact, Hannah faced the cold hard fact that Justin had been amusing himself by teasing her, stringing her along. For all she knew, he simply might have been deliberately coming on to her to rile his brother Mitch.

If that had been Justin's aim, he had scored a direct hit. Problem for Hannah was his barb had scored a direct hit on her, as well.

Her own fault. She had walked fully conscious into the cross-hairs. Served her right if she was feeling the sting of his arrow. She deserved the piercing stab in her chest. She had known full well that his make on her was all about sex, anyway.

So, the hell with Justin Grainger. She'd forget him in no time once she was back in Philly, back to her real life of work and friends.

But first she had to get some rest. She had a lot

of driving in the morning to get to the airport in time for her flight. Sleep, stupid, Hannah scathingly told herself. Clenching her body against the aching emptiness inside, she shut her eyes tight, denying the sting burning her eyelids, and concentrated on the word sleep.

Her alarm went off at seven, approximately one hour and twenty minutes after she had finally drifted off.

Groaning, Hannah levered herself off the cot and stumbled into the bathroom. Even though she had showered last night, to get an early start this morning, she pulled off her nightshirt and stepped under a spray of tepid, wake-up water.

It helped, but not a helluva lot. Heaving a deep sigh, followed by a wide yawn, she brushed her teeth, applied a layer of concealer on the dark half-moons beneath her eyes, and finished with a light application of tinted moisturizer and blush to each cheek.

Frowning at her image in the mirror above the sink, Hannah left the bathroom, made up the cot. Deciding to grab something to eat in the terminal concourse, she skipped breakfast for a fast get-away. Quickly dressing, she stomped into foul-weather boots, pulled on her coat, gathered her baggage and sent a final glance around the cozy flat, checking that everything was in order.

Swallowing another sigh, which she adamantly refused to admit was of regret, Hannah left the apartment and clattered down the stairs to the second-floor doorway. Yanking open the door, she stepped into the hallway and practically into the arms of Justin Grainger.

"What kept you?" he said, a lopsided smile on his smooth, clean-shaved face.

Startled, rattled, Hannah stared at him. "Wh–what?"

"I thought you'd never get it together this morning." His warm gaze caressed her face, settled on her mouth. "I heard your alarm go off all the way down two flights of stairs—what the hell have you got, anyway, a miniature Big Ben?" Before she could open her suddenly tingling lips to reply, he caught her by one arm to lead her along the hall to the other stairs. "I hope you didn't waste time eating. I've been holding breakfast for you."

"But...but..." Hannah stammered. Dammit, she never stammered. "Why?" she demanded, allowing him to relieve her of her suitcase and carry-on with the other hand as he urged her down the stairs and to the open door of the apartment where Karla and Ben were staying.

"Why not?" he asked, ushering her inside and firmly closing the door behind them.

More unsettled than she would have believed a man, any man could make her, Hannah ignored his question to ask one of her own. "Where are Karla, Ben and the baby?"

"They left before daylight. I helped them load the SUV. They're going to visit her folks in Rapid City before heading back to the ranch," he explained.

"So, why were you holding breakfast for me?" But before he could respond, she went on, "And how did you know I'd agree to have breakfast with you?"

Justin held up one finger. "I thought you might be hungry." He grinned—too darned sexily—and held up another finger. "I didn't know. I hoped. Will you?"

He had done it again. Thrown her off track. "Will I..." she blurted, before she collected her senses. Never in her adult life had a man held the power to so fluster her.

"Share a meal with me." His grin turned into a sensual smile; his lowered voice was sheer temptation. "Among other even more satisfying pleasures."

"I, uh…" Damned if she wasn't stammering again. Grabbing a quick breath, she stammered, "I…really…I don't…uh…think that…would be wise," she finished, all in a breathless gush.

"Maybe so," he drawled, in that same low, tempting tone. "But it would be fulfilling …for all our hungers."

"I know." Hannah blurted out without thinking, amazed at herself for doing so. "But that's beside the—"

"No, that *is* the point," he interrupted, setting her bags aside to cradle her face in his warm palms. "I want to be with you so bad I ache all over," he murmured, lowering his mouth to within a breath of hers. "And I feel, no, I know you want to be with me every bit as badly."

"How…" Hannah swallowed. Her voice was barely there, because suddenly her throat was tight, dry. "How do you know I want what you want?"

"Ahhh, sweet Hannah," he whispered, his breath slipping between her slightly parted lips and into her mouth. "Your eyes give you away." His mouth skimmed across hers, setting off a sensation that sparkled throughout her entire being. "Admit it…" His voice gathered a wicked, teasing thread. "So we can get on with other things, be-ginning with breakfast, which I can smell is ready."

It wasn't until he mentioned it that Hannah caught the mouthwatering aroma of freshly brewed coffee, meat sizzling and something she couldn't quite identify, but which tantalized her taste buds.

"Okay," she said, giving in, not to him, she told herself, but the rumble of emptiness in her stomach. "I'll have breakfast with you." Chastising her weakness, she hurried on, "But then I must get moving or I'll miss my plane."

"There'll be other planes." Very softly, very gently, he touched his mouth to hers.

Hannah couldn't answer. She couldn't breathe. His half kiss had turned the sparkle inside her to tongues of flame.

She stood mute while Justin lifted the strap of her handbag from her shoulder and slid her coat from her arms. She didn't protest when he stashed her coat, handbag and two cases into a small closet. Turning back to her, he smiled, melting what felt like her fire-charred insides, and held out a long-fingered hand.

"Come…let's have breakfast."

* * *

Hannah was well and truly stuffed, pleasantly so. Cradling her second mug of coffee in her hands, she sat back in her chair, replete, one hunger satisfied.

"More?" Justin raised one dark brow, smiling at her over the rim of his coffee mug, reigniting another, even more basic hunger inside her.

"Good heavens, no." She returned his smile, if a bit shakily. "Thank you. Everything was wonderful."

"You're welcome." He lowered the mug; his lips were moist from the beverage and much too appealing. "And thank you, I'm glad you enjoyed it."

"I certainly did. Do you cook a lot?"

"Not often, I admit, but I can cook."

"A man of many talents?"

"Oh, honey, you'd be amazed."

Always before, Hannah had resented a man calling her honey, yet, somehow, coming from Justin, it didn't bother her. The fact was, she rather liked it.

"Refill?" he asked, raising his mug.

"I don't think so." She shook her head before swallowing the last of the coffee and setting her mug on the table. Hannah stood, telling herself to get moving before she gave in to the desire to stay and indulge herself. "I've got to go home."

"Why?" he asked with a grin. "I was tempted to say—Home is where the heart is—but," he shook his head. "I decided that was a bit too obvious."

Though she really tried, Hannah couldn't contain a smile. "And practically everything you've said to me, every suggestion you've made, wasn't obvious?"

He pulled a long face—an attractive long face. "And here all the time I thought I was being subtle."

She burst out laughing. "Subtle? Justin Grainger, you are about as subtle as a jackhammer."

"You deeply wound me." His words were belied by the devilish light in his eyes. He set his cup aside and started toward her. "Is that any way to being an affair?"

"Affair?" Hannah felt a thrilling jolt. "We, uh… we're not beginning an affair." She took a step back. He took two steps forward. "We hardly know each other." She held up one hand…as if she actually believed that would stop him.

Of course it didn't. Justin kept moving, slowly backing her up until her spine made contact with the kitchen wall. He raised his hands to cup her face. His palms were warm, gentle. His long fingers stroked her cheekbones.

"Justin." Hannah would have drawn a deep breath, if she could have found anything other than the most shallow wisp of air. "Don't." Her breathless voice was a mere half-hearted whisper, hardly a deterrent.

Still, Justin paused, his mouth within inches of hers. He sighed, as if held motionless by that one word don't. "Oh, sweet Hannah, don't tell me no," he murmured. "If I don't kiss you soon, I'll explode."

Hannah raised her hand to his shoulders to move him back. She felt the muscles grow taut beneath her suddenly gripping fingers. And then, amazing herself with her boldness, she slid her hands to the back of his neck, grasped his hair, and pulled his head to hers to devour his mouth.

Justin did a fantastic job of devouring in return. Holding her head still with gentle fingers, he angled his mouth over hers. His tongue outlined her lips, teased the sensitive inner skin, before exploring deeper, engaging her tongue in an erotic dance.

Hannah could barely breathe, and she didn't

care. His mouth was heaven, his tongue a seeking, probing, ravenous instrument of sensual torment.

His hands deserted her head to glide down her spine, cup her bottom, draw her to the fullness of his body. All rational thought dissolved, swept away by a torrent of sensation, part agony, part pleasure, all terribly exciting and arousing.

He could have this effect on her with one kiss? Hannah marveled, in an obscure corner of her disintegrating mind. What would making love with him do to her?

On the spot, without having to give it a moment's thought—which was good, since she couldn't think anyway—Hannah knew she had to find out, possess him while she experienced his possession of her.

"Hannah, sweet Hannah," Justin groaned into her mouth, lifting his head to stare into her pleasure-clouded eyes. "You can't kiss me like that then tell me you must leave, that we're not beginning an affair."

"I know," she admitted in a raw whisper.

Justin drew back another inch to study her expression. "You want me, don't you, sweet Hannah?"

She didn't answer at once, but stood staring

back at him. Able to breathe a little, and almost think, Hannah was struck by the realization of having lost count of the times he had called her "sweet Hannah." She had been called many things in her life, from "squirt" by her older brother, to "the cool one" by her friends, to "beautiful," even "stunning" by hopeful lovers but never "sweet." If anybody had said she was sweet, she'd have bristled, been annoyed. Babies were sweet, not mature, adult women.

So, then, why did she melt at the endearment murmured through Justin's so-tempting lips?

"Hannah?" The thin, sharp edge on his voice yanked her from her muddled reverie.

She blinked. "What?" Then she remembered his question. "Oh…yes," she answered with complete honesty. "I do want you, Justin," she confessed, spearing her fingers into his thick dark hair.

His soft laughter had a joyous ring. Releasing her bottom, Justin flung his arms out to his sides. "Then take me, sweet Hannah. I'm all yours."

Hannah accepted his invitation by pressing her mouth to his.

Without breaking contact, Justin moved Hannah away from the wall, through the small dining room and in the direction of the bedroom.

Drowning in multiple sensations, Hannah was only vaguely aware of his arms curling around her waist, holding her entire body tightly to his. But she was fully aware of heat rising inside her at the feel of his hard muscles against her softer flesh.

Entering the bedroom, Justin shut the door with a backward tap of his bare foot. Still without breaking the kiss, he carried her to the side of the bed. Setting her on her feet, he released her, stepped back and brought his hands to the hem of her sweater.

Trembling with need, Hannah raised her hands and the sweater swished over her head, landing who knew, or cared, where. She was fumbling with the buttons on his shirt when an errant but important realization stilled her fingers.

"You need to know that I'm not on any kind of birth control. I haven't used anything for over two years now."

He frowned at her statement. "That's pretty risky, isn't it?"

"Not at all." She shook her head, a bittersweet smile shadowing her lips. "I…haven't…er…indulged—" She broke off to shake her head once more. "You know."

"You haven't had sex in two years?" His voice, his startled expression, hovered somewhere between amazement and disbelief. "Are you serious?"

"Yes." She sighed.

His expression turned pained. "You don't like sex?"

She had to smile. "Well, I don't dislike it." She sighed again. "It's just that," she lifted her shoulders in a hapless shrug when his frown deepened to a near scowl. "I haven't felt attracted…that way…to a man, any man, since I ended a relationship a little more than two years ago."

"Why did you end the relationship?" he asked, in a tone that said he wasn't sure he really wanted to know.

"It was mutual," she answered. "It simply wasn't working for either of us."

"What wasn't working?" His gaze probed intently into hers. "The sex?"

"Well…yes," Hannah confessed, lowering her eyes to the allure of his half-naked chest, suddenly aware of her own near nakedness. "I owe it to you to admit that I fear I may be, uh…unresponsive." She drew a deep breath before rushing on, "I've never had an orgasm."

"You're kidding."

Tired of feeling like a feminine failure, Hannah lifted her head and boldly stared straight into his shocked eyes. "No, I am not kidding. Dammit, do you think any sane woman would kid about something so serious?"

"No, I suppose not," he agreed. Then he asked, "You said you wanted me. Did you mean it, or were you just experimenting with me?"

"I meant it." Hannah's tone was filled with conviction. "I do want you."

"Good," Justin purred, the flame of desire flaring again in his eyes. Lowering his head, he brushed a taunting kiss over her mouth. "Then let's get on with it, see if we can't give you that orgasm."

The mere brush of his mouth robbed her of breath, sent her senses whirling.

"What about...um," she said between quick breaths, "protection?"

Justin smiled. "Luckily for us," he said, shoving his hand in a jeans pocket and retrieving a foil-wrapped package, "I *do* practice safe sex."

Six

Hannah lay where Justin had placed her, right in the center of the queen-size bed and watched as he stretched his long length next to her.

"Hannah, Hannah," he murmured. "What am I gonna do with you?"

She gasped and opened her eyes in wide innocence. "You need instructions?"

Justin laughed gently. "That does it, sweetheart. Now you are really gonna get it."

"Really, really?" Hannah curled her arms around his neck to bring his mouth back to hers.

She was thoroughly enjoying herself, never before had she teased and laughed while making love. "Will I like it?"

"Let's find out," he whispered, taking command of her mouth with his.

Deepening his kiss, he slid a hand over her shoulder, down her chest to the rounded slope of her breast. Gasping, Hannah arched her back, seeking more of his exciting touch. Growling into her mouth, he cupped her breast, found the hardening peak with his fingers.

Heat flowed like molten lava from the rigid peak to the core of her femininity. Hannah was on fire. She couldn't breathe but she didn't care. She wanted more and more.

Squirming to get closer to him, she lowered her arms and pulled him tightly against her straining body. Her hands made a tactile exploration of his broad back, his narrow waist, his slim hips, his long well-muscled thighs.

She needed something…something.

"Slowly, sweetheart," he softly said, his lips following the trail laid out by his hand. "We have all day." His tongue darted out, electrifying her as it flicked that aching peak. "There's plenty of time."

That was easy for him to say, Hannah mused,

moaning deep in her throat at the exquisite sensations his tongue sent quaking through her. She was on fire, every inch of her burning for…that elusive something.

Grasping his hips, she urged him to her, arching in an attempt to align their bodies. Resisting, holding himself back a few inches from her he slid his hand down the center of her quivering body.

"Justin." Hannah cried out as his stroking hand found, delved through her mat of tight blond curls and into the very core of her.

"Justin!" she cried out again, her voice now a near sob, as he parted the delicate folds to explore the moist heat within. "I…I…please!"

"Please what, sweet Hannah?" He delved deeper as he raised his head to her mouth, spearing his tongue between her parted lips, capturing her gasping breaths.

She arched her hips into his tormenting hand, and slid her mouth from his. "I need…need…" she paused to pull some air into her lungs.

"Me?" he whispered enticingly, slipping the tip of his tongue into her ear.

"Yes, I need you, your body…now!"

"At your service, sweet Hannah." Continuing to tease her by gliding his tongue to the corners of her mouth, Justin settled himself between her thighs.

Hannah immediately embraced him with her legs, urging him closer, closer. She gave a hoarse cry when he thrust his body deeply inside her. He set a quick, hard rhythm. Holding on to him for all she was worth, she arched back her head and strove to match his deep strokes. It was a very short ride.

The fire inside her blazed out of control. Hannah felt the unbearable tension quiver, then snap.

"Justin!" Her voice was raw, strangled as her body convulsed around him. In reaction to the sheer pleasure pouring over her, and without conscious direction, her nails scored his buttocks, thrilling once more when he attained his release, growling her name, over and over.

Pure ecstasy. Hannah wanted to tell him, thank him, but at first she couldn't find the breath. Then, when her breathing evened enough to speak, before she could put the thought into words, she succumbed to the sleep that had eluded her during the long night.

"Hannah?" Getting control of his own breathing process, Justin lifted her sweat-slick head from her equally moist breast to look at her. Her eyes were closed, and she looked serene, disheveled but serene. She was breathing at a normal sleeping rate. "Knocked you clear out, did I?"

Smiling, he disengaged, lifted his depleted body from hers. Stretching out beside her, he drew her soft, pliant body to his, pillowing her cheek on his chest.

"Ahhh, Hannah, sweet Hannah," he murmured, not wanting to wake her. Well, with the swift response of his body to the satiny feel of hers, he actually did want to wake her, but he held himself in check, letting her rest.

She'll need it, he thought, rubbing his cheek against the silken, tangled mass of her hair, his body growing harder at the memory of her long blond tresses spread wildly on the pillow in the throes of passion.

And Hannah was passionate. Justin could still hear the echo of her voice pleading with him, her nails raking his skin, crying out to him in the intensity of her orgasm.

Her response had triggered the strongest, most shattering orgasm he had ever achieved, he thought, aching to repeat the experience.

Good grief, were Hannah's former lovers complete idiots? How could they not be as fired up—

roasted, in fact—as he had been to her quick, passionate sensuality?

A shot of sheer male satisfaction flashed through Justin as he realized he was the first man to bring Hannah to ultimate completion.

And ultimate was the only way to describe it. She lay thoroughly satiated and relaxed in the protective cradle of his arms, one of which was growing numb. Justin didn't care. Ignoring the sensation and the discomfort of his hard body, he closed his eyes.

"Sweet, beautiful, Hannah," he whispered, kissing the top of her head as he drifted into a light doze.

The afternoon sun rays were slanting into the room when Hannah woke. She felt good. No, she mused, yawning. She felt wonderful…but hungry. No, that wasn't quite right, either. She felt famished, in another part of her body as well as her stomach.

She made a tentative move in the confines of Justin's caging embrace, sliding her body against his.

Justin. A thrill skipped up her spine at the memory of what they'd shared. With his mouth, his hands, that strong hard body, he had given her a gift beyond her wildest imagination. Not only in her delicious release, but by freeing her fears of being frigid.

"I was beginning to think you had died."

His breath tickled her scalp, his low, intimate tone tickled her libido. "For a moment there, I think I did." Tilting back her head, she smiled up at him and nearly melted at the tender expression on his handsome face. "Isn't that what the French call it. The little death?"

"Yeah." His mouth curved invitingly, a flame springing to life in the depths of his eyes. "Wanna do it again?"

"Yes, please," she said, sliding her free hand up his chest to toy with one flat male nipple. His response was so swift it was breathtaking.

Grunting like a caveman, he heaved himself up and over her, settling her flat on her back. Precisely where she wanted to be at that moment. She opened her legs for him.

"Not so fast, sweet Hannah," he said, laughing down at her as he lowered his head to hers. "You had your way with me the last time. This time it's my turn."

She pouted at him. Still chuckling, he crushed her pouting lips with his hungry mouth.

This time the little death was even more intense; the release, mind and body shattering. Never had Hannah expected to feel as if she were soaring above the clouds. Talk about a natural high! Justin's slow, fantastic loving had brought her to the point where she had actually screamed in response to the sensations of joyous bliss.

Hannah might have been embarrassed by her uncontrollable outcry, if Justin's shout hadn't almost immediately followed her own. Still buried deeply inside her, he lay, spent and relaxed, his head pillowed on her breast. Moving beneath him, she rubbed her leg over his buttock and down the long length of his muscular thigh.

He murmured something against her breast, letting her know he was alive, if not altogether awake.

"I'm hungry," she said, sliding her fingers into his hair, combing through the sweat-dampened, long, tangled strands.

"Are you trying to kill me, woman?" he muttered, raising his head to stare at her in feigned astonishment. "I'm in my thirties, you know, not my late teens."

Hannah giggled. "I thought I felt something stir awake inside me," she lied, laughing into his teasing eyes.

"You thought wrong. It's out for the count." He grinned, rather leeringly. "It'll take a while before I'm ready to spring into action again. Do you think you can bear the wait?"

"I guess so." She sighed, then grinned back at him. "But I don't know how much longer I can bear your weight."

Justin groaned and rolled his eyes. "Give me strength. The woman's tossing puns at me now," he groused, lifting his body to roll over, sprawling next to her.

Hannah gave an exaggerated sigh of relief. "That's better." Arching her back, she stretched the stiffness out of her arms and legs. "I'm hungry."

"You said that." He grinned and looked down at the front of his body. "And I explained that—"

"For food, *man,*" she taunted, getting back at him for twice calling her woman. She wrinkled her nose in distaste. "So drag your so depleted carcass off this bed and help me get something together to eat."

"Slave driver," he complained, laughing as he practically leaped from the bed. "I'm not doing another damn thing, bossy *woman* until I shower and shave." Circling the bed, he scooped her body up into his arms and headed for the door. "And you, sweet Hannah, are going into the shower with me."

Smothering yet another giggle, Hannah curled her arms around his neck and rubbed her face against his shoulder. "I've never showered with a man before," she softly confessed.

Justin stared down into her eyes. He shook his head, his expression compassionate. "You've never done a lot of fun things with a man, have you?"

"No."

"Did you enjoy your, er, first thing?" He arched his brows, then wiggled them.

Hannah laughed, feeling her cheeks grow warm. "Immensely," she admitted. Darn it. What was it about this man, anyway? She hadn't blushed since…hell, she couldn't recall ever having blushed.

"Then, trust me, sweetheart, you're going to enjoy this, too," he promised.

He was dead right. Hannah thoroughly enjoyed

every minute of the playful splashing, lathering, caressing, kissing beneath the spray of warm water. Who knew how long they would have remained there, if not for the audible grumbling sound of hunger from her stomach.

It was almost as much fun drying each other off.

Clean, but still naked as a newborn, Hannah dove back under the covers while Justin shaved. When he walked boldly naked into the bedroom, she unabashedly watched, admiring his lean, muscular and magnificent body as he stepped into briefs, jeans and pulled a cable-knit sweater over his head.

"See anything you like?" he asked, arching a dark brow over laughing gray eyes.

"Actually, I like the whole package," she readily admitted. "You're a very attractive and nice man."

"Boy, that last compliment is a relief." He heaved a deep sigh. "For a minute there, I thought you wanted me only for the pleasure of my body."

"Well," Hannah said teasingly. "There's that, too."

"Thanks. Hey, aren't you ever coming out from hiding? I thought you were hungry."

"I am. But I have no clean clothes here." She

made a face at their clothing scattered around the bed. "I'm waiting for you to be a gentleman and fetch my suitcases."

"I knew you were a slave driver," he muttered.

Justin was back in moments. He set the bags next to the bed, then stood watching her.

"Out," she ordered, flicking a hand at the door.

"But I wanna watch," Justin said, in tones similar to a petulant little boy.

"Are you some kind of voyeur?" Hannah asked, grabbing a pillow and throwing it at his head.

He ducked. The pillow missed him by inches. "No." He grinned. "But you watched me. Hell, I could feel you watching me. It was like a touch. And now I want the privilege of watching you."

"You don't have time to watch me," she countered, enjoying the banter. "I told you, I'm hungry."

"Then I suggest you get your tush in gear and get dressed." He moved back to prop himself indolently against the door frame. "Because I'm not budging."

Giving him a narrow-eyed glare that only brought a wolfish grin to his lips, Hannah flung back the covers and stood. "All right, then, dammit. Watch your fill."

Laughing softly all the while, Justin did watch, his appraising look missing nothing as she dug through the largest of the cases. Secretly thrilling to his caressing gaze, Hannah took her sweet time stepping into almost-there panties, fastened the front closure of her bra, wriggled into hip-hugging jeans and shrugged into a turtleneck sweater.

"You are one absolutely stunning woman from head to toe, sweet Hannah," he said in near reverence.

"Thank you," she whispered. Feeling her face grow warm again, this time with pleasure, she turned away, opening the other bag to search out footwear. Like him, she didn't bother with shoes, slipping into satin ballerina slippers.

In the meantime, Justin moved to open a dresser drawer, making do with a pair of heavy-duty socks to keep his big, narrow feet warm.

He held out his hand to clasp hers. "Now, let's go rustle something up for lunch—" he shot a look at the dark beyond the window "—or supper." He laughed. "Hell, for all we know, it may be a midnight snack."

"Not quite," Hannah said, letting him lead her from the room. "I looked at the clock. It's only nine-fifteen."

"Only, she says." He groaned, and fumbled for the light switch as they entered the kitchen. "We haven't eaten since early this morning. We're both ravenous…and the woman says it's *only* nine-fifteen."

Hannah laughed, at him and at herself. She must be losing her mind, she decided happily, because she not only didn't mind him calling her woman, she was beginning to like it. No doubt about it, her mind was starting to disintegrate. She masked her laughter with an exaggerated groan at the sight of the table still cluttered from their breakfast.

"Yeah," Justin agreed, propping his hands on his hips. "It's a mess. Tell you what, sweet Hannah. I'll make a deal with you."

She gave him a skeptical look. "What kind of deal?"

He frowned and shook his head in sad despair of her. "You have a suspicious mind, Ms. Deturk."

"Damned straight, Mr. Grainger," she retorted. "What deal?"

"Here's the deal. I'll get dinner, if you'll clean up the breakfast debris."

"Deal," Hannah accepted at once, fully aware

she was getting the better end of the arrangement. Crossing to the table, she went to work, while Justin went to the fridge.

"That was delicious," Hannah commended Justin, raising her wineglass in a salute. "You're a very good cook."

"Either that," Justin said, inclining his head and raising his own nearly empty glass in acknowledgement of her compliment, "or you actually were famished."

"I was," she admitted. "But that doesn't mean I'd have praised anything you set in front of me." She grinned. "I'd have eaten the meal, but I wouldn't have praised it, or your culinary skill."

"I wouldn't go so far as to call it a skill. I simply can manage to prepare a reasonably palatable meal. Now, my mother, she's a skilled cook."

"I like your mother, by the way," Hannah said. "She is a lovely woman. I admire the way she handles her husband and her overgrown sons…all three of whom I also like."

"Three?" He appeared crushed. "Just my father, Adam and Mitch? What about me? Don't you like me?"

Hannah's expression and tone went hard and serious. "If I didn't like you, Justin, do you really believe for one minute I would be here with you now?"

"No." He gave a quick shake of his head, his voice as serious as hers had been. "No, Hannah. I don't, for even a second, believe you would be here now, if you hadn't found something about me to like." The seriousness fled, and the gleam sprang back into his eyes. "What is it that appeals to you? My body? My…"

"Is fantastic," Hannah interjected, holding back a laugh. "And you use it to advantage."

Justin arched a brow but continued with what he had started to say, "My personality?"

She mirrored his dark arch with her lighter eyebrow. "I didn't know you had one."

He laughed.

Her pulse leaped and her senses freaked. How was it possible for one man's laughter to cause such exciting sensations inside her, Hannah mused, loving the feelings, yet scared of them at the same time.

"I like you," Justin offered the unsolicited opinion. "I like your gorgeous body, too."

"I kind of figured you did," she responded wryly.

"But I'd like to do a further exploration of the terrain." He grinned...more like leered. "Just to be sure."

"Uh-huh." She eyed him warily. "But that will have to wait. My plane left hours ago. I've got to phone the airline, see if I can book another flight."

"You've already missed your flight," Justin pointed out, his voice soft, persuasive. "Why can't you wait till morning to call and reschedule?"

"I, er..." She faltered at the brazen look of renewed passion in his eyes. At her hesitation, he shoved back his chair and stood.

"Come on, let's get the supper things cleared away," he said, collecting his plate and cutlery.

Rising, Hannah began to follow his example. "And after the supper things are cleared away, we'll go to the bedroom...."

"Good," he flashed a self-satisfied grin at her.

"To pick up the clothing we discarded and scattered all over the bedroom floor."

"Yeah, yeah," he muttered, not meaning one yeah.

Ten minutes later Justin found himself hanging the damp towels on the mounted wall racks in the bathroom. "You know, this could have waited till morning, as well," he called to Hannah, who was busy neatly folding their clothing.

"Yeah, yeah," she mimicked his agreement. "But you'll be thanking me tomorrow."

In truth, Justin did thank Hannah in the morning, but not for remaining resolute about picking up their stuff. He thanked her with words and caresses and deep, searing kisses for what he swore was the most fantastic night of his life.

Seven

"**W**hat about Beth?" The gleam in his eyes grew brighter. "Didn't you like her?"

It took a few minutes for Hannah to make the connection. She and Justin were in the middle of breakfast. This time he had cooked oatmeal, served with brown sugar. He was watching her, waiting for the dawn of comprehension to break over her sleep- and sex-fogged mind.

"Oh, your sister, Beth." Hannah felt like a dull wit. At least she hadn't said, "huh?" "I like her, very much. She stopped by Maggie's apartment a few days ago. We had a nice chat. Besides being warm and friendly, she's a gorgeous woman, a striking combination of your mother and father."

"Yeah, she is," Justin agreed, popping another spoonful of cereal into his mouth. After swallowing the oatmeal, he downed half the orange in his glass. "Adam's wife, Sunny, is no slouch either."

Nodding, Hannah took a ladylike sip of her juice. "She's lovely, and their daughter, Becky, is absolutely adorable. I immediately fell in love with her."

He chuckled around the last of his cereal. "She has that effect on everybody." He arched a quizzical dark eyebrow. "You like kids?"

"Very much." Finished eating, she dabbed her mouth with the paper napkin she had spread over her lap, and gave him a teasing smile. "Some of my best friends have kids."

"So," he said, getting up to fetch the coffee carafe to fill their cups. "What about you?"

Frowning, Hannah gave him a blank look. "What about me?"

"Don't dodge, sweet Hannah," he chided. "I've told you about myself. Now it's your turn."

Her mind may have been a little slow that morning—apparently a wild night of unbelievably fantastic sex had that effect on her—but it hadn't come to a complete stop. "You did no such thing," she retorted. "You quizzed me about my opinion of your family."

"Well, I sure couldn't give you my opinion of your family, since I haven't met them."

"Now who's dodging, Mr. Thinks-He's-So-Clever Grainger?" She grinned as she mimicked his one eyebrow lift.

He took a careful sip of his steaming coffee and grinned back at her. "Okay, what do you want to know…all my deep, dark secrets?"

"Do you have any?"

"No."

Hannah laughed, she couldn't help it. She just loved… Whoa, hold it. Loved? Don't go there, Hannah, she cautioned herself. Avoid that word like the plague.

"Are you really the bad boy your mother called you?" she asked. Not that she believed he'd confess to her all about his philandering ways.

"Of course not. I'm worse."

"Indeed. In what way?"

"You know," he drawled, "I don't know what you do for a living, but you should be in police interrogation."

"I'm in marketing," she said wryly. "And don't try changing the subject. It won't work. I want to hear all the lascivious details."

"Lascivious?" Justin tilted back his head and laughed. "You are really something, woman."

Woman. Again? Time to drag the knuckle-dragger into the twenty-first century. "Yes, actually, I am something. And don't call me woman. My name is Hannah."

He looked astounded. "You're not a woman? Damn, you could have fooled me. Yesterday morning and last night. Mostly last night. And I'll call you woman whenever I want to."

"Okay." Hannah pushed back her chair and stood. "I'm out of here." Turning away, she walked to the phone mounted on the kitchen wall.

"Wait a minute." His hand covered hers on the telephone receiver, holding it still.

She hadn't even heard him move.

"Hannah, sweetheart," he crooned into her ear. "I was only kidding. What are you doing?"

"Precisely what I said I was going to do today," she said. "I'm going to phone the airline to book another flight, hopefully for tonight or tomorrow morning."

"Hannah," he murmured, his voice a low, coaxing siren song. Releasing her hand to cup her shoulder, he turned her into his arms. "Don't go."

She raised her eyes and dropped her guard. His gaze was shadowed, compelling. Oh, heavens, she had to get out of there, away from him, because if she stayed with him...she could wind up being hurt. Hannah knew her thinking was right and yet. And yet...

"Hannah." Justin slowly lowered his head, to brush her mouth with his. "Don't go. Stay here, with me, for a week, or at least a few more days."

His tongue outlined her lips, and Hannah was a goner. Against her better judgment. Against everything she had believed about the folly of a rushed relationship, she knew it was too late to stop, too soon to bolt.

She wanted more of him. It was as simple and frightening as that. Surrendering more to her own needs and desires than to Justin's plea, Hannah raised her arms, curling them around his strong neck to draw his lips to her hungry mouth.

"You said you had been married."

"Hmm," said Justin.

Hannah couldn't see his face, since she lay tightly against him, her cheek resting on his chest.

Justin's angled body was curled almost protectively around her. The fingers of his one hand
played with a strand of her long hair. The protective position of his long body sparked a memory
of the night of the wedding reception.

After leaving Maggie in the bridal suite, Hannah had returned to the hotel lobby and gone
straight to the coat-check counter. Draping the
garment bag containing Maggie's gown over the
counter, she exchanged her high heels for the boots
she had worn earlier. Shrugging into her coat and
toting the garment bag and the shoe bag, she considered slipping away, before Justin began looking for her.

She started for the lobby doors, but with a sigh,
changed direction to go to the banquet hall where
the reception was being held. Hannah had been
brought up the old-fashioned way. Good manners
dictated she say goodbye to Justin's family, thank
his parents—whom she had learned had footed
the bill for both the rehearsal dinner and the reception—for a lovely time at both events.

Peeking inside the hall, Hannah's determination
faltered. Justin was standing next to the table, talking and laughing with his father and Adam, and
looking far too tempting.

She was on the point of turning to leave when little Becky had come up to tug at his pant leg. Gazing down at her, his laughter changed to a tender smile, and instead of kneeling to talk to her, he bent down, his body curved protectively over her. With her pretty little face turned up to her uncle, Hannah saw her mouth move, saw Justin's move in reply before, with a laugh, he swept her up into his arms and headed for the edge of the crowded dance floor.

Hovering in the doorway, Hannah had watched, expecting Justin to whirl Becky around the floor. He hadn't. Setting her on her feet, he'd bowed like a proper gentleman, taken her tiny hands in his and danced her onto the floor.

For some ridiculous reason the sight of Justin, so careful and caring of his niece, had brought a lump to Hannah's throat and a hot sting to her eyes.

With a firm shake of her head, a stiffening of her spine—and her resolve—Hannah had used those few precious seconds while the music played to pay her respects to the Grainger family, then steal away from the hotel, and Justin.

Hannah was brought back to the present when a thought struck her. "Justin, do you have children of your own?"

Heaving a sigh, he rolled onto his back, spreading his arms wide in surrender. "No, Hannah." He opened his eyes to look at her, his expression somber. "Angie…my ex-wife, said she wanted to wait a little while before starting a family." His lips twisted, as if from a sour taste in his mouth. "Before the 'little while' was up, she put on her running shoes and sprinted away with another man." He made a rude, snorting noise. "Would you believe, a traveling computer-software sales rep? Pitiful, huh?"

"I'm sorry," she said in a subdued tone. "I shouldn't have pried."

"No." Justin moved his head back and forth on the mattress; the pillow had somehow wound up on the floor. The icy look in his eyes had thawed…somewhat. "It's okay, Hannah, you may ask anything that comes to mind."

"Did you—" Hannah hesitated, before taking a chance of making him angry, bringing back the frost. "Did you love her very much?"

He managed a slight smile. "We didn't know each other very well at the beginning. You could say it was a whirlwind thing. But yes, at the time, I loved her."

Despite his omitting the words *very much*, Hannah had to fight to control herself from betraying the sharp twinge of pain in her chest. "Are you still in love with her?" It would explain his love-'em-and-leave-'em attitude toward women.

"No." He stared directly into her eyes, his voice firm. "You want the truth?" he said, not waiting for a reply before continuing, "I realized I wasn't really in love with her a month after we got married."

She frowned. "But then…" She broke off in confusion.

Justin moved his shoulders in a shrug. "She was hot, and I was horny."

Hannah didn't know quite how to respond to his frank admission, so she circumvented that particular subject. "Have you ever truly been in love?"

"No," he answered with blunt candor. "Have you?"

Hannah smiled. Turnabout was fair play, she supposed. "No," she said, equally frank and candid. "But, like you, I thought I was for a time." Her smile turned into a small grin. "But unlike you, instead of a measly month, I believed that I was in love for almost a full year."

"So, what happened? That no-orgasm thing?"

Hannah felt her neck and face grow warm. This blushing was getting pretty damned annoying. Her expression must have revealed her feelings, because he grinned in a manner of sheer male hubris. She really couldn't challenge him on it, for he certainly had cured that *thing*. Many times.

"Partly," she admitted, on a sigh. "But that wasn't the major issue."

"What!" Justin exploded, jackknifing up to sit facing her. "Was he an idiot…or were you?" As before, often before, he didn't allow her time to answer. "Not the major issue? If you believed you were in love, I would think it would be the most important issue."

"Yes, I believe you would," Hannah said, her tone patient, her silent sigh sad. "Justin, there are more things to a relationship than sex, at least if there's any hope of the relationship lasting."

"Yeah, yeah," he brushed off her scold. "Compatibility, similar likes and all the rest of that jazz. But good sex is a very large component, and great sex even more so."

Yes, indeedy, Hannah thought, without a trace of humor but with a large amount of disappointment. Justin Grainger definitely was sexually motivated.

She sighed again. "Turned out, we weren't very compatible," she explained. "He was altogether career oriented. He ate, drank and slept his career, and it got worse with every move he made up the corporate ladder. There was no time for fun, friends, long, deep conversations."

"Or even the fun of longer, deeper, lovemaking," Justin interjected.

Hannah chose to ignore his opinion, then doggedly continued. "Understand, I was recently out of college and devoted to the marketing business I was getting off the ground. But I was often able to leave my business concerns in the office when I locked up for the night."

"And he couldn't do that?"

"No." She shook her head, at the same time wondering why she was bothering to explain all this to him when they obviously weren't going to be seeing each other again after she returned to Philly and he went back to breed horses in Montana. But she soldiered on, "I didn't simply quit, you know. I tried to make it work. I even learned to cook, a chore he knew I wasn't exactly crazy about."

He laughed.

She bristled. "Well, I never could understand why anyone would put so much time and effort into preparing an elaborate meal for someone to consume in fifteen minutes, leaving the cook to clean up afterward."

Justin laughed harder. "I'm sorry. I'm not ridiculing you."

Hannah glared at him. "Then what's so damn funny?"

"The fact that you've put my own feelings about the culinary art so elegantly into words." He had brought the laughter to a more acceptable grin. "If I want an elaborately concocted meal, complete with fine wine and candles on the table, I'll go to a fine restaurant and let an expert prepare it."

"My sentiments exactly," Hannah concurred, grinning back at him, not for a minute realizing that they were in the midst of the kind of deep conversation she had just complained about being missing from her previous relationship. Maybe that was because she never considered she and Justin ever would be in any kind of relationship...other than the physical one they were briefly conducting.

"So, what do you say we consign whoever-he-was to the dull life he deserves and get on with our own pursuits?" His grin slid into an invitingly sexy smile.

"Which are?" she asked, suddenly aware of

them sitting there, naked to the waist, and the thrill of expectation dancing along her exposed spine.

"The dreaded kitchen duty first." The sexy smile reverted back to a grin. "Then a shower." He hesitated. "And I think it's time I stripped the bed and tossed these sheets into the washer."

"Okay." Though she readily agreed, Hannah was disappointed. Drat the man and his sensually teasing ways. "I'll remake the bed."

"You're on." Springing from the bed, he scooped up his crumpled jeans and put them on before reaching for the same sweater he'd worn the day before.

Quickly sliding from the bed, Hannah picked up the robe he had earlier flung aside, and slipped into it, belting it securely, while admiring the back he turned away to gather his clothes.

Justin Grainger was a magnificent specimen, his broad muscular back, his slender waist, the tightness of his butt, the long muscles of his thighs and calves. She sighed. Hell, she even thought he had handsome feet!

Pathetic, she chastised herself. Who the devil ever thought of a male's feet as handsome?

She did, that's who, and the realization was pretty damn scary. Hurrying out of the room, Hannah kept telling herself what she was feeling was simply a strong physical attraction, a very strong physical attraction. Nothing more.

Working smoothly together as they had the day before, Hannah and Justin had the kitchen clean in less than twenty minutes.

"Know what?" Justin said to her as she was rinsing out the dish cloth. "I'm hungry."

Dropping the cloth into the sink, Hannah turned to him and pointed out the obvious. "We just finished clearing away the breakfast things."

"Yeah, I know," he agreed, favoring her with that blasted devil smile. "But have you looked at the clock?"

Naturally, Hannah shot a glance at the wall. The clock read 1:44. Unbelievable. She and Justin had finished breakfast somewhere around nine. For some weird reason, knowing the time made her aware of the hollow feeling inside her. She shifted her gaze back to him.

"You know what?" She pulled his trick of forging ahead without waiting for a response. "I'm hungry, too."

He flashed his most sexy smile. "Good. Let's grab some lunch."

Within ten minutes, again working easily together, they sat down to a meal.

Where before they had cleaned up the kitchen in compatible silence, this time they chatted away about this and that, nothing earth-shattering, simply kitchen talk.

From the kitchen they returned to the bedroom to gather the dirty laundry. They had no sooner set foot inside the room when Justin placed a hand on her arm, stopping her in the process of bending to start collecting clothes.

"You know what?" he asked again, and once more going on without pause, "I think it would be a waste of that invitingly rumpled bed." He raised that brow and flashed that wicked smile. "Don't you?"

Hannah wanted to say no. She really did. But her vocal chords and tongue wouldn't cooperate, and what came out was a hushed and breathless "Yes."

Later, lying replete and boneless beside him, Hannah silently marveled at the sexual prowess of the man holding her firmly against him. She loved the feel of his warm skin against hers, his breath ruffling her hair, his hands smoothing, soothing her back with long strokes of his hand. She gave a soft, contented sigh. Could she possibly love...

Don't go there. Hannah repeated the order she had given herself once before. This was merely fun and games. A few days out of the ordinary.

Allow yourself a few more days of physical indulgence, then run for home as though your very emotional stability depended on it…for it just might.

Spurred by her introspection, Hannah rolled out of Justin's arms, off the bed and grabbed up her robe. "I'm taking a shower," she announced, making a bee-line for the bathroom.

"Hey, wait," Justin barked, coming after her.

He was too late. She flipped the lock jut as he reached for the doorknob.

"Hannah," he pleaded with a soft laugh. "Let me in."

"You've been in," Hannah dared to playfully remind him. "A lot. And I loved every minute of it," she conceded, smiling at his exaggerated groan. "Now I want to have a long shower and shampoo my hair. I'll see you in about a half hour…if you're lucky."

"A half hour?" Justin shouted. "What the hell am I going to do for a half hour?"

"I'm sure you'll figure something out." She turned the water on full force to drown out any reply he might make.

Hannah felt wonderfully clean as she stepped from the shower. She also was rather proud of herself, as she had finished five or so minutes faster than she had promised Justin.

Holding her robe around her, she entered the bedroom. The room was empty, not a half-naked, too-attractive man in sight. To her surprise, not only was the floor clear of their clothes, the bed had been stripped and remade.

The man in question continued to amaze her. Whoever thought Mr. Philanderer would turn out to be so domesticated?

Taking advantage of the moment or privacy, Hannah dug in her suitcase for a clean set of clothes. When she was dressed, she stepped into her slippers.

Feeling warmer, and relatively protected by the clothing, Hannah plugged in her blow dryer and went to work on her hair with a round brush. She was making progress, the long strands no longer dripping, when Justin breezed into the room.

"The sheets are in the washer. It'll shut off in about fifteen minutes." He went to a dresser to remove fresh clothing. "As you'll note, I remade the bed."

"And now you want applause?"

He grinned. "No, a kiss will do for a reward."

"I don't think so." She shook her head.

Up went the eyebrow. "You don't trust me?"

"Not for a heartbeat." Trying not to laugh at his sorrowful expression, she grabbed her brush. "You get your shower, while I finish drying my hair."

He heaved a deep, noisy sigh. "You're one tough lady, sweet Hannah. You know that?" Grumbling loudly, Justin strode to the bathroom.

Never in a million years would Hannah have believed she could have so much fun with a man. She had hardly even laughed with—Well forget that one. He had been much too serious and full of himself, among other things.

Giggling Hannah decided on the spot that she would stay on, perhaps until the end of the week with Justin. She felt relaxed and happy. Why not enjoy his company, the fun and laughter, if only for a few more days?

After all, once the few days were over, she'd be flying back to her real life in Philadelphia. Justin would be heading back to his ranch in Montana.

They'd probably never see each other again.

The thought was oddly depressing.

Eight

Hannah was home in her apartment in Philadelphia. It was Sunday. She had flown into the airport late the previous Friday and had been home for a week and one day.

She had yet to hear a word from Justin.

Well, what had she expected? Hannah asked herself, making a half-hearted attempt to dust the living room. They had spent five days together. Five wonderful days that had left her so relaxed, her assistant had noted it the moment she had walked into the small suite of offices Monday morning.

"You look positively glowing," Jocelyn had exclaimed. "Were you in South Dakota, or did you hide away somewhere in some exclusive spa?"

Hannah had to laugh. Actually, she felt terrific. "No spa, I promise I was in South Dakota the whole time."

Jocelyn leveled a measuring look at her. "Well, something put that sparkle in your eyes. A man?"

Hannah knew her soft sigh and satisfied smile gave her away. The warmth spreading up her throat and over her cheeks was answer enough. Damn her new propensity to blush.

"Aha!" Jocelyn crowed. "Was he handsome? Was it romantic? Was he great in bed?"

"Jocelyn, *really*." Now Hannah's cheeks were burning. "You know I'm never going to answer such personal questions."

"Sure." Jocelyn grinned. "But I don't need a blow-by-blow—" she giggled "—pardon the pun. Your expression says it all."

Hannah blinked, startled. "It's that obvious?"

"Yes, boss. I'm sorry, but it is. You needed a break."

That was Monday. This was Sunday. Hannah was no longer amused, or glowing. She was hurting inside, and she feared the tiny lines of tension were about to make another appearance.

But then, she had known all along that their moment out of time couldn't last. What had she been secretly hoping for, that Justin would be on the very next flight east, following her back?

No, she hadn't hoped for that, even secretly.

But one phone call just to find out if she had arrived safely would have been nice, not to mention thoughtful. Had she really believed Justin was thoughtful? Hannah chided herself. Just because he helped her prepare meals, pick up their clothes that were forever flung without care to the floor, smooth the bedding that was inevitably rumpled? Because the last time they had made love there had been a sense of desperation? And because his goodbye kiss had been deep, lingering, as if he couldn't bear to stop?

Hannah knew better. At any rate she should have. They had played house, she and Justin, like little kids. Okay, not exactly like kids.

Hannah shivered at the memory. It had been fun, playing house together. It had been more than fun, it had been wonderful, an awakening of her senses and sensuality.

Tears misted her eyes. Why the hell had she

gone and done something as stupid as fall in love with him? For she *had* fallen in love with Justin, no strings for me, Justin, philanderer extraordinaire.

Not fair, Hannah, she told herself, swiping her eyes with her fingertips. He had never made any promises. He had been up-front with her, had offered her nothing more than fun and games. She had gone into the affair with her eyes open. She had no one to blame but herself for the empty feelings of pain and longing she was experiencing now.

Life does go on, Hannah assured herself, and so would she. There was no other choice. She had friends, a career, a business to run... a living room to dust.

Justin was on the prowl, roaming the house, unsettled and cranky. Karla would attest to it; she had been witness to his moodiness. She was beginning to eye him warily, as if uncertain what he might do.

It was the weather, he told himself, staring out the window at the nearly foot of snow on the ground that was growing higher in the driving blizzard. He felt trapped, that's what was bugging him, he thought, turning away from the scene.

Justin knew damn well his restlessness had nothing at all to do with the inclement weather. He had been raised in Wyoming, and had lived in Montana for almost ten years, had taken over the running of the ranch soon after he had graduated college. Snow, ice, winter and spring rains hadn't bothered him, except in regard to worrying about the horses.

But Justin knew full well that the animals were in their stable stalls; warm, fed and watered by Ben and the rest of his ranch hands.

"Can I get you something, Justin?" Karla asked, as he stalked into the kitchen.

Wondering what in hell he was doing there, Justin said the first thought that jumped to mind. "Is there any coffee in the pot?" It was a dumb question, and he knew it. There was always coffee in the pot. It wasn't always freshly made, but he had never demanded fresh, although he preferred it that way.

"Yes." Karla smiled at him as she opened a cabinet and took down a mug. "I just made it." She shook her head when he reached for the mug. "Sit down, I'll get it for you."

Not about to argue with the woman who prepared some of the best meals he had ever tasted,

Justin moved to the table, collecting a carton of milk as he went by the fridge.

The coffee was exactly as he liked it, strong, hot and freshly brewed.

"Would you like something to go with that?" she asked, carrying her own mug to the table. "Cookies, a slice of pie or coffee cake?"

Ever since Ben had brought Karla to the ranch as his bride, there were always cookies in the pantry and pie in the fridge. He liked her coffee cake best...although her apple pie was also delicious.

Justin glanced at the wall clock. It was several hours to go until suppertime. "Couple of cookies sound good. Do you have any of those oatmeal, raisin, walnut cookies?"

Karla laughed and headed for the pantry. "As those are both Ben's and your favorite, I always keep a supply on hand. I baked a double batch yesterday."

While Karla was inside the large storage room, Ben strolled into the kitchen from the ranch office, where he had been checking stock on the computer. In effect, Ben had virtually taken over the running of the ranch, leaving Justin feeling superfluous and adrift. He didn't resent Ben...how could he resent a man for doing a great job, especially when the man was next thing to a member of the family?

No, Justin didn't resent Ben. He simply felt useless.

"Where's my bride?" Ben asked, going straight to the cabinet to pour a cup of coffee for himself.

"Ran off with the milk man," Justin drawled, sipping carefully at the hot brew in his mug.

"Neat trick." Ben grinned as he strolled to the table. "As we don't even have a milk man."

Justin waved a hand in dismissal. "Minor point."

"You rang, Your Lordship?" Karla emerged from the pantry to favor her husband with a smile. "Was there something you wanted from me?"

Ben flashed a wicked grin. "Yeah, but this isn't the time or place. The boss is watching." He jerked his head at the plate she was carrying. "I'll settle for some of those cookies you've got there."

Their affectionate banter created a hollow sensation in Justin's midsection. Telling himself it had nothing to do with one Hannah Deturk and the bantering, laughter and tender moments they had shared, he attempted to fill the hollow place with cookies. His ploy didn't work.

Through the long, seemingly endless days that

followed, nothing worked. Including Justin. Leaving the majority of the ranch responsibilities to
Ben, Justin brooded and prowled the house like a
hungry mountain lion.

Hungry was the key word, and it had nothing
to do with his stomach. How often had he reached
for the phone, to place a long-distance call to
Philadelphia? Justin couldn't remember, but he
knew damn well why he had never actually lifted
the telephone receiver.

What could he say to Hannah? I miss you, and
I'm hard as hell? Yeah, he derided himself. That
ought to turn any woman's mind and will to molten lava. And Hannah wasn't just any woman. Oh,
no. Sweet Hannah was her own woman, a fact she
had made abundantly clear to him from the beginning.

Sure, she had agreed to spend a few days of mutual pleasure with him, Justin conceded. And the
pleasure had been mutual, of that he had no doubt.
For a man who had not so much as stayed a full
night with a woman since his marriage ended, the
pleasure had been intense, teeth-clenching ecstasy.
As for Hannah, well Justin felt certain that not
even the most skilled of actresses could have faked
the depth of her response.

Still, their shared desire, and compatibility out of bed, had not kept her from leaving when she said she would.

Without saying it aloud, she had made it abundantly clear that she had a life back east and she wasn't about to change it. Her determination to leave was unshakable. Despite his murmured plea for her to stay a while longer and the implied enticement of his last kiss, she had whispered a farewell, slid behind the wheel of her rental vehicle and driven away without looking back.

Unaware of heaving a heavy sigh, Justin stared out the window. The blizzard had long since blown itself out, but the temperature had not risen above the twenties since then. The snow remained, the unrelenting wind driving it into five-foot and higher snowbanks.

Damn, other than the inconvenience of getting back and forth from the house to the stables, Justin had never minded the snow before. What in hell was wrong with him?

"Why don't you take a vacation?" Ben's voice broke through Justin's thoughts. "Someplace where the sun's shining and the temp's in the eighties. Find yourself a woman. You're workin' on my nerves, and you're starting to worry Karla."

"I'm working on your nerves and making Karla edgy?" Justin said in a soft, tightly controlled voice to keep from snarling at the man. "Maybe you and Karla are the ones needing a sun-filled vacation."

"Not us," Ben denied. "Karla and I are happy here, sunshine or not."

Justin lifted an eyebrow. "And you think I'm not?"

"Oh, gimme a break, Justin. I've known you a long time, remember?" Ben shook his head. "In all that time I have never seen you like this, stalking about the house, staring out the window, sighing every couple minutes, not even when Angie took off with that smooth creep."

"I sigh every couple of minutes?" Justin drawled in feigned amusement, feeling a twinge of alarm and ignoring the reference to his ex, because *that* wasn't important. The strange sensation was. "I'll think about it," he said, ending the conversation by turning back to the window.

"Okay, I can take a hint," Ben said with a short laugh of resignation. "I'll mind my own business."

"I appreciate it."

Justin only vaguely heard Ben's chuckle as he left the room. Staring out, he didn't see the barren scene of winter white on the other side of the window. An image had formed in his mind, an image Hannah had drawn for him with her description of Pennsylvania. The verbal picture she had given him was of a different landscape, a vision of rolling countryside, lush and green, bathed in sparkling spring sunlight.

Blinking, he frowned, then turned and strode to his bedroom. Going to his desk he opened his personal laptop, and went onto the Net. He had some research to do.

Several hours later Justin shut down the computer and picked up the phone to call the company pilot in charge of the ranch's helicopter. After asking the pilot to pick him up at the pad a short distance from the house, he pulled a bag from the closet and dumped enough clothes into it to last him a couple of days.

Following the near ennui he had been experiencing since he had returned from Deadwood, the rush of anticipation he was feeling was invigorating.

Justin placed another call before striding briskly from his room. He had what he figured was an interesting and potentially very profitable idea he needed to discuss with his brother, Adam.

His battery recharged, Justin gave a brief explanation to Ben as he drove him to the landing pad. The chopper was already there, blades slicing through the frigid air.

"Not to worry," Ben assured him. "I'll take good care of the horses."

"I know you will." With a wave goodbye, Justin headed for the helicopter.

"By the way," Ben yelled over the roar of the spinning blades. "You look and sound like your old self again."

Near the end of the second week of February, Hannah faced up to the suspicions she had been mentally dodging for close to a week, suspicions induced by the vague feeling of queasiness she had in the morning, the slight tenderness in her breasts. Needing more proof than just symptoms, she stopped by a pharmacy on her way home from work.

The strip from the particular home pregnancy kit she had purchased turned the positive color. Not an altogether complete confirmation, Hannah knew. There had been cases where the strip results had proved wrong, but…it definitely required a visit to her doctor.

How could it have happened? Not even in their most heated, impromptu and wild love play, had Justin forgotten to use protection.

Of course, no one ever claimed the protective sheaths were infallible, Hannah mused as she studied the inside of her freezer, trying to decide what to have for dinner.

Having heated in the microwave the frozen meal she'd chosen Hannah sat in front of it, considering the options available to her should her doctor's examination prove conclusive.

Sliding the plate aside, Hannah laid her fork on the place mat and picked up the cup of green tea she had brewed for her dinner beverage, instead of her usual coffee.

Coffee. She sighed. She loved coffee, especially in the morning, all morning…several cups of coffee, regular, not decaf.

Hannah knew she would have to forgo her favorite drink if she decided to—

Oh, hell. Hannah took another sip of the tea. It wasn't bad tasting. It wasn't coffee, but actually was rather good as far as substitutes went.

That is, unless she chose an alternative. The thought set a wave of nausea roiling in her stomach. She gulped the tea in hopes of quelling the sensation.

She couldn't do it. Though she supported a woman's right to choose any of the options, Hannah knew that she really had only one option. Should the doctor confirm her pregnancy, Hannah was going to have a baby.

A baby. Visions of soft blankets and tiny booties danced through Hannah's mind. A fierce rush of protectiveness shot through her, and she slid a hand down over her flat belly.

Her child.

Justin's child.

The sudden realization was both thrilling and somewhat frightening. How to tell him?

Justin had been up-front with her from the beginning. He had wanted nothing from her except a brief physical affair. Their affair had been the most wonderful experience Hannah had ever known. Of course, she hadn't considered the possibility of falling in love with him.

Over the days they had been together, Hannah had learned a lot about Justin. Yet at times she felt she hardly knew him at all.

As a lover, she couldn't imagine anyone his equal. There were moments when his voice was so tender, his touch so gentle it brought tears to her eyes while at the same time setting her body on fire. And there were other times when his voice was raw and ragged, his touch urgent, his lovemaking fierce and demanding.

And Hannah had reveled in every minute of both approaches.

Then there were the periods when all they did was talk, sometimes teasingly, other times seriously.

Hannah had learned that Justin was honest to a fault. When he shared something of himself with her he was blunt and to the point. Not a bad quality to possess. She knew a woman had betrayed his trust and that he had no intention of walking that route again.

She also knew Justin liked kids. He had confessed to Hannah that he adored his niece, Becky. But Justin had never mentioned a desire for children of his own, other than to say his ex had wanted to wait a while before starting a family.

If the doctor confirmed her pregnancy, Hannah didn't know whether or not to inform Justin. After all, she reasoned, if Justin had any interest in a child of his own, he wouldn't have been so scrupulous about protection.

For all the good it had done them.

Still, he had a right to know he had fathered a

child. It was her duty, as an honest person, to let him know.

She just didn't know how to tell him.

Nine

Valentine's Day. The day for lovers. Hannah not only didn't leave work early, she worked over an hour later than usual. She even skipped lunch. Tired, only vaguely hungry, and not so much as considering a restaurant, especially on this special day for sweethearts, she went straight home.

Her heart skipped many beats as she stepped from the condo's elevator to find Justin propped languidly against her door. A bag was on the floor next to his crossed ankles.

The bag, along with the very sight of him filled

her with a flash of hope that he had come to Philadelphia because he realized that they belonged together.

Gathering her senses, and applying her common sense almost at once, Hannah told herself to play it cool until she heard from his lips the words she desperately longed to hear. How easy it would be for her to then tell him of her pregnancy suspicions.

Heaven help her, he looked…wonderful, like the horseman he was. With his Stetson, heavy wool jacket, jeans and slant-heeled boots, he looked exactly as he had the first time she'd seen him.

"Hi."

The low, intimate timbre of his voice nearly stopped her breathing completely. Damn his gorgeous hide. She had to repeat to herself her cautioning advice to play it cool.

"Hi." Hannah was amazed by the steadiness of her own voice, her ability to speak at all, as her throat was suddenly dry. "What are you doing here?" Door key at the ready, she aimed it at the key hole. No minor feat, considering the tremor shaking her fingers.

"I came to see you. Are you going to invite me in?"

"Yes, of course, come on in." Hannah walked inside with as much decorum as she could muster. "I didn't mean what were you doing here, at my apartment," she said, not sure if she was making conversation, or babbling on in response to the sudden attack of nervousness coursing through her. "I meant what are you doing here, in Philadelphia?"

"Well," he said, grinning as he shrugged out of his jacket, removed his hat, "I wanted to see you. Though that isn't the only reason I'm here, in the northeast."

Hannah's spirits soared at first, then took a nosedive, her hopes going down in flames. Still, she maintained her composure and took his jacket and hat and hung them away in the coat closet. The flight bag she set behind the nearby chair.

"I see." She tried to match his casual tone and didn't quite make it. "Well, I'm glad you stopped by," she said, dredging up a shaky smile to hide the sting of pain burning inside. "So," she held on to her smile for dear life. "Why else have you come east?"

"I'll tell you after dinner…" Justin hesitated, frowning. "You haven't had dinner, have you?"

"No," Hannah shook her head. "I worked late and didn't feel up to the crowds in the restaurants tonight."

"Oh." He nodded, then raised a dark brow. "You eat out often?"

Hannah wanted to scream at him. Didn't the man know that it was Valentine's Day? And what difference did it make to him whether or not she ate out often? This was only an afterthought visit, anyway.

"Occasionally," she answered, smothering the curse and a sigh. She gestured for him to sit down. "Would you like something to drink?" she asked, too politely, certain that if he said coffee she'd throw up.

"No, thanks." He sat down on the plush lounge chair. "I'll wait for dinner."

Did he actually expect her to cook for him? He'd wait until the cows came home, she fumed, using one of her father's favorite expressions. Hannah gave him a level stare and mirrored his eyebrow action. "I hope you realize that there will probably be long lines at all the better restaurants tonight," she said, making it perfectly clear she had no intention of providing a meal for him.

"I don't need a restaurant." His smile was knowing, making her aware he understood her unsubtle hint. "I've ordered dinner to be delivered here."

The audacity of the man. Why didn't it surprise

her? Everything inside him radiated audacity and…and…sheer male sensuality.

Stop that train of thought immediately, you dimwit, Hannah ordered herself. Stick to the subject at hand. "How did you know I'd be in town?"

"I didn't." Justin shrugged, then laughed that deep, thrilling, damnably exciting laugh that set her pulses racing. "But I figured I'd take a chance. I'll tell you all about why I'm here while we eat."

"But…" Hannah began to ask him how he had gotten past the security guard in the lobby, only to be interrupted by the buzz on the intercom from that very same man.

"There's our dinner," Justin said, moving to the intercom beside the door. "I'll take care of this. You go set the table."

You go set the table, Hannah grumbled to herself, whirling around to do as he ordered. As he ordered. Who the devil did he think he was?

Hannah had finished setting the table except for the water glasses she had retrieved from the cabinet. But she didn't know whether he wanted water with whatever it was he had ordered for dinner or if he'd prefer wine, which of course, she couldn't have. She set one glass on the table and was filling the other glass for herself from the refrigerator's water dispenser when she heard him open the door and speak to a delivery man. The distinct aroma of pizza wafted through the apartment.

To her amazement, instead of bringing on a wave of queasiness, the smell made her mouth water and her stomach rumble with hunger.

Carrying a large pizza box with one hand and a white paper bag in the other, Justin walked jauntily into the kitchen, his smile more appetizing than the smell of the food.

"Dinner is served, madam," he said, carefully sliding the box onto the table. "This," he added, holding the bag aloft, "is our dessert."

Someday, maybe, hopefully, you'll get your just dessert for being such a rogue, Hannah thought, but simply asked aloud, "What do you want to drink to go with it?"

"Beer?" he asked.

"Yes." She turned to the fridge.

"Beer with the pizza, and coffee with dessert."

Her stomach twitched in protest. Wishing he hadn't mentioned her previously favorite beverage, Hannah took a can of beer from the fridge and moved to the table to reach for the glass at his place.

"I don't need a glass," Justin said with a dismissive wave of his hand, popping the top while seating himself in the chair opposite hers. "Sit down and serve the pizza."

Starting to seriously resent his assumed right to order her around, Hannah fixed him with a fuming look. "You know, you could have served it while I was getting your beer."

"No, I couldn't," he said with a smile, indicating the box with a nod of his head. "The opening's in front of you. And in case you haven't noticed, the lid's taped shut."

Hannah couldn't decide if she wanted to laugh at his obvious teasing, or toss her glass of water at him. She did neither. Drawing the box closer, she broke the paper tape and lifted the lid.

The delicious aroma hit her first, making her almost groan with hunger. Then two other factors struck her, making her gasp in surprise. The large crust had been worked into a heart shape, and the words, Sweet Hannah, had been formed with small slices of pepperoni.

She laughed with delight. It was the strangest, most wonderful Valentine's gift she had ever received. "Wherever did you get this?" she asked.

"The pizzeria a couple of blocks down. I told the counter man what I had in mind. Turns out, he owns the place and he smacked his hand against his forehead and said, and I quote, 'Why didn't I think of that? I coulda made a bundle.' I told him to keep it in mind for next year." He grinned. "Are you ever going to serve it?"

Hannah pulled a sad face. "Must I?"

"Only if you want to eat…and don't want me to starve to death at your kitchen table."

"Well, in that case, I suppose I'd better." Laughing, if rather weakly, Hannah scooped up a slice and slid it onto his plate. "May I ask what gave you the idea in the first place?" she said, serving herself a slice.

"Hmm." Nodding, Justin murmured around the big bite he'd taken into his mouth. "I came up with the idea when I decided I wasn't in the mood to stand on line at a restaurant, at a candy store or a florist," he said after swallowing. "Hey, this is pretty good." He followed that with a swig of beer. "And I wasn't in the mood because I was tired after driving around since early this morning." He took another big bite.

Ready to bite into the slice she had served herself, Hannah paused, unable to resist asking, "Why have you been driving since early this morning…and where?"

* * *

Before responding to her questions, Justin polished off his slice and held his plate out for another. His hesitation wasn't because he was that hungry, although he was, but because he was carefully choosing the words of his explanation.

"Actually, I've been driving around for two days. I flew into Baltimore the day before yesterday." Justin couldn't miss the tightness that stiffened Hannah's spine, so he rushed on. "I picked up my rental car, checked into a hotel, then went to keep an appointment with a real estate agent."

She frowned. "Here? In Baltimore?"

"Yes. You see, I'm doing some scouting for Adam. We're thinking of investing in a horse farm here in the East, to breed Thoroughbreds. The agent found farms available in several states and set up appointments for me."

"What states? And why here in the East?" she asked, frowning.

"Maggie told me there were a lot of horse farms out here." He answered her second question first.

"Well, Maggie should know," Hannah said. "She was born in Berks County."

Justin nodded. "So she said. She suggested Virginia, Maryland and Pennsylvania." He polished off a third slice of pizza, grinning as he again held out his plate to her.

Hannah shook her head as if in disbelief of his capacity for food, but slid another slice onto his plate.

He plowed on. "I started in Virginia, where there were two possibilities. From there I drove into Maryland, where there were three. I stayed in a motel in Pennsylvania last night and got an early start this morning. I toured one in Lancaster County, another two in Bucks County, and the last one in Berks, in the Oley Valley."

"Oh, I've been there," Hannah said, patting her lips with a paper napkin. "My assistant is a dedicated antique-shop crawler. I go with her every so often, and one time she drove through the valley, to Oley Village, I guess that's what they call it. It's not very big, but charming."

"I didn't get to see the village or town, or whatever it's called. But the valley is beautiful, even in winter. And the property I looked at has definite possibilities." He arched a brow, wondering at the tiny, wistful smile that quirked her lips. "I'm ready for my coffee now."

"Of, of course, I forgot," she said, sliding her chair back and rising. "What's for dessert?" she asked, moving to the automatic coffee unit set on the countertop.

"You'll see," Justin answered, puzzling over her odd expression as she prepared the coffee. His puzzlement deepened as she filled a red enamel teakettle then put it on to boil and took a flower bedecked porcelain china teapot from the back of the stove and a box of teabags from the cabinet. She placed a couple of bags in the pot.

"You're not having coffee?" He didn't try to hide the surprise in his voice; he had firsthand knowledge of her passion for coffee…among other passions. He had to turn his mind to something more mundane when he felt his body stir in reaction to the sensual direction of his thoughts. "What's with the teapot?"

Hannah gave a careless shrug of her elegant shoulders. "I've developed a liking for green tea lately," she said, not looking at him as she concentrated on pouring the now boiling water into the teapot. "It's supposed to be very good for you, you know."

"Not for me," Justin said dryly. "I'll stick with my coffee…and beer."

"Well, here's your coffee," Hannah said, in a strangely choked voice. She set the steaming mug on the table, before going to the fridge for milk.

"Thanks," Justin said, pondering her odd behavior; Hannah had held the mug out in front of her as if she was afraid it would attack her. Weird. He took the carton of milk she handed him, and watched her as she returned to the countertop for the teapot and a mug.

"I don't understand," she said, obviously avoiding his gaze, as she carefully poured the pale tea into the mug. "Why would Adam be interested in another horse farm for the company, when you already have the ranch?"

"At the ranch, we breed and train Morgans, primarily for the rodeo circuit. And, as I already mentioned, we're thinking about branching out, breeding and training Thoroughbreds."

She took a delicate sip of her tea, grimaced, set down the mug and added sugar. "How many more farms are on your schedule to look at? Any other states?"

"No more states, no more farms," Justin said, singeing his tongue. "Damn, that's hot, I felt it burn all the way down," he added, reaching across the table for her half-full water glass. "Do you mind?" His hand hovered above the glass.

Hannah shook her head. "Help yourself."

Justin did, soothing the sting with a gulp of the

cool water. "I'm scheduled to fly out of Baltimore on the red-eye tomorrow night."

"Oh, I see. Are you flying home to Montana, or to Wyoming to report to Adam?" Hannah's expression didn't alter by even a shadow. She looked as she had the first time he met her, mildly interested but cool and composed. Detached.

Justin felt a wrenching disappointment. He knew, better than anyone, that beneath her facade of cool, composed detachment, a spark lay in wait to blaze into roaring flames of passion.

Dammit to hell! Why was she in hiding from him? For she was in hiding. He had sensed it the minute she had stepped from the elevator and had seen him by her door.

"To Wyoming to confer with Adam, then back to Montana," he said, working hard to control the anger and frustration building inside him.

"So you're driving back to Baltimore tonight...or have you booked a hotel here in the city?"

Justin couldn't read her expression, as she had raised her cup to her mouth, concealing the lower half of her face from him. But her voice was even more detached, cooler. The distant sound of it fanned the flame of his anger. What was she playing at, looking, speaking as if they were nothing more than casual acquaintances, when it had been less than a month since they had been passionate lovers?

Well, Justin decided, getting to his feet and circling the table to her, he wasn't about to play along. He had been missing her something fierce from the moment she had driven away from him in Deadwood.

Hell, he had tossed and turned every night, even dreamed about holding her, caressing her, kissing her. Damned if he was going to walk away without tasting her.

Coiling his hands around her upper arms, he drew her up, out of her chair, pulling her body against his.

"Justin...what..." Hannah began, her voice no longer cool, but surprised by his action.

"I think you know what," he murmured, sliding his arms around her to bring her to him, and lowering his head to crush her mouth with his.

He had meant it to be a forceful kiss, but the instant his lips made contact with hers, he gentled, drinking in the taste, the scent, the feel of her. It was like coming home, where he belonged.

The alien sensation rattled Justin deep inside.

After the blow Angie had delivered, he'd never believed he would feel such a way again.

Justin was on the point of lifting his head, breaking his near-desperate contact with her mouth, when Hannah curled her arms tightly around his neck and speared her fingers into his hair.

Needing to breathe, Justin raised his head just far enough to gaze into Hannah's eyes. "No, I am not driving back to Baltimore tonight, nor have I booked a room here in the city," he said between quick indrawn breaths. "I was hoping you'd let me spend the night here. With you. In your bed."

"Justin, I...I..."

Her eyes were warm, almost misty, the way they had looked every time she was aroused. Hannah wanted him, maybe almost as much as he wanted her. Justin knew it. Relieved, he silenced her with the brush of his mouth, back and forth over hers.

"Hannah," he whispered against her parted lips, into her mouth. "I'm on fire for you. Come to bed with me."

"Justin..."

He silenced her again, damn near terrified she was going to refuse. He ached, not only from the steadily growing, hardening of his body, but inside. He stifled a groan when she pulled her head back.

"Justin, wait, listen," she pleaded, her fingers tangling in his hair, hanging on as though she was afraid he'd let her go. "We haven't cleared the dinner things away—or had dessert."

He laughed, because it sounded so…Hannah. And because the exultation filling him had to escape.

He smiled and rested his forehead against hers. "It wouldn't be the first time, sweet Hannah. As we did before, many times before, we can clean it up later. And we can have the dessert for breakfast."

"Dessert for breakfast?" She pretended shock.

Laughing softly, Justin began an exploration of the fine, satiny skin of her face with his lips. "What I brought will do fine for breakfast, or for dessert after breakfast."

Laughing with him, in a sure sign of her surrender, she tickled his ear with the tip of her tongue. "I have never heard of dessert for breakfast."

Justin's body nearly exploded at the moist glide of her tongue into his ear. "Errr…Hannah," he said in a rough croak, "You'd better lead me to your bedroom before I lose control and take you right here and now."

"As if," she retorted, grinning as she pulled away from him, grabbed his hand and started through the living room to a short hallway. "You've never lost control."

"There's always a first time, sweetheart," he said, raising her hand to his mouth to press his lips to her fingers. "And I'd sure hate to embarrass myself in front of you."

Entering her bedroom, Hannah turned her head to give him a wry glance. "That…or are you possibly afraid your loss of control would give me a sense of womanly power?"

"Oh, sweet Hannah, you have no worries in that department," Justin said, shutting the door behind him and twirling her around into a tight embrace, letting her feel her power in his hard body. "You've got womanly power to spare."

Minutes later, their clothing tossed in all directions of the room, Hannah lay naked, eager, in the center of the queen-size bed that had felt so large, cold and empty for weeks. Also naked, Justin stood next to the bed, tall and proud and magnificent, his turbulent gray eyes watching her as she watched him sheathe himself in delicate protection.

The image would haunt her after he was gone. She knew it, would pay for it, but for now, Hannah could think of nothing except having him beside her, inside her, loving her...if only for this one more night.

She held her arms up to him in invitation. He came to her, stretching his long body next to her own. His mouth hot on hers, his hands implements of exquisite torture.

He couldn't wait, and with a murmur of need he slid his body over hers, settling between the thighs she parted for him. She couldn't wait, either. Wrapping her long legs around his waist, she raised her hips in a silent plea.

Justin's possession of her was fast and hard, exactly as she needed it to be. Their zenith was reached in shuddering, spectacular unison. Though Hannah wouldn't have believed it possible, the climax was more intense, more thrilling than any previous one she had experienced with him.

She loved him, loved him with every living cell within her, as she would love his child, their child, after Justin was gone. For then, weeping silently,

Hannah decided she would never again be a receptacle for his convenience. She just couldn't bear to be one of the women "the bad boy" visited every so often.

Holding him to her, inside her utterly satisfied body, Hannah drifted into the deepest sleep she had known since leaving him in Deadwood.

Ten

Hannah woke up at her usual time. A creature of habit, she needed no alarm. She was still tired. She really hadn't slept very much. She ached, but pleasantly so. Twice more during the night, she and Justin had made love.

It had been wonderful. No, it had been more than wonderful. It had been heavenly. Between periods of short naps and long, slow indulgences of each other, they never found time to venture out of the bedroom to clear away the dinner clutter.

Yawning, Hannah pushed back the covers Justin had haphazardly drawn over them after their last romp, and moved to get up. A long arm snaked out to curl around waist, anchoring her to his side.

"Let me up, Justin," she said, trying to pull back. "I still have to clear the kitchen table, eat something and get ready to go to work."

His arm held firm, and he rested his cheek on the top of her head. "Take the day off." His voice was low. "Stay with me until I have to leave for Baltimore."

Hannah was tempted. Lord was she tempted. But mindful of the vow she had made to herself after their first frantic bout of sex—for that's all it had been, at least for him, she reminded herself— she steeled herself against his alluring suggestion. "I can't." She shook her head and pushed his arm away. "I can't leave my assistant on her own today."

"Why not?" His sleepy voice threatened to undermine her resistance. "You did when you went to Deadwood."

Taking advantage of the momentary easing of his hold, she slipped out from under his arm. "I know, but then I had laid out all the upcoming projects, explained my ideas in detail. There are things pending that need my personal attention."

While speaking, she had collected her clothes as she made her way to the connecting bathroom.

"Hannah, wait." Justin jumped from the bed, attractive as sin in his nakedness. He reached for her.

Dodging his hand, she stepped into the bathroom, locking the door before calling out to him, "You can have the shower when I'm done." She turned on the water full blast to drown out the sound of his muttered curses.

Exhausting every curse word he knew, Justin stood stock-still next to the bed, staring at the locked bathroom door. Hannah was closing him out, exactly as she had tried to do last evening. Frustration, anger and an emotion too similar to fear to be acknowledged burned inside him.

He didn't get it. He just didn't get it...or her. One minute she was cool and remote, the next sensual and hungry for him. During the night Hannah had freely displayed how badly she wanted him, again and again.

So what happened between the last time they made love and this morning? And, dammit, they *had* made love, not merely had sex, whether or not she wanted to admit it, either to him or herself.

Shaking his head in bewilderment, he moved

around the room picking up his clothes. They'd have to talk about it, about their relationship, for, like it or not, that's what it was shaping up to be, not a one-night stand, not a slam-bam-thank-you-ma'am, but an honest to God relationship.

It scared the hell out of him. Nevertheless, an in-depth discussion was definitely called for here. He would have to make another stab at convincing her to take the day off.

Hannah had never showered and dressed so fast in her life. Her hair still damp, she twirled it all into a loose twist at the back of her head and anchored it with a few well-placed hairpins. Sighing in longing and regret for what might have been, she turned with steadfast determination and went to the kitchen. Justin stood by the kitchen table, and with a nod she indicated that the shower was all his.

She had the table cleared and wiped, dishes stacked in the dishwasher, the coffee brewing, the tea steeping, bacon sizzling and eggs whipped, ready to pour into a warming frying pan by the time Justin walked into the room.

"We forgot to say good morning." His soft voice crept across the kitchen to slither up her spine.

Gritting her teeth against a shiver, Hannah returned his greeting. "You're just in time," she said with calm detachment, dumping the egg mixture into the pan. "If you want to help, you can set the table." Without turning to look at him, she dropped four slices of bread into the toaster. She jumped when he plucked the spatula from her hand.

"I'll do the eggs," he said, his voice and his body too close for her comfort. "Since you know where everything is, it's better if you set the table."

"Okay." Hannah was glad to escape, if only to the wall cabinet a few feet from him. After setting two places at the table, she went to the fridge for orange juice and milk. "Do you want jam for your toast?"

"Do you have peanut butter?"

"Yes," she said, surprised that he also liked the spread on his morning toast.

"Natural or sweetened? I don't like the sweetened stuff."

"Neither do I," she said, removing the jar from the fridge.

Other than the odd remark here and there about the food, they ate in silence, each into their own thoughts. Feeling edgy, Hannah saw him raise a brow when she glanced at the clock for the third time. But he didn't comment on it…until after he had his coffee and she her tea.

"I think you should take the day off," Justin said, his voice laced with determination.

"I already told you I wouldn't do that," she retorted, her voice equally determined.

"We need to talk." Now his eyes were cold as gray ice.

Getting up, Hannah carried her barely touched tea to the sink, dumped it and rinsed it before replying. "No we don't. I need to leave for work." She walked from the room to the coat closet. "And you need to drive to Baltimore." She pulled on her coat and grabbed her purse.

"Dammit, Hannah," Justin said, his tone bordering on a shout. "Listen to me." He reached out to take her arm, to prevent her from walking out the door she'd opened.

Her nerves and emotions raw, her mind screaming at her to get away before she succumbed to agreeing to be one of his now-and-then women, Hannah avoided his hand as she spun around to confront him. "I won't listen to you, Justin." She was hurting, and wanting to hurt him back, if that was possible, she lashed out at him. "I have to thank you for giving me so much please," she said sarcastically. "But it's over now. You belong in Montana, and I belong here. Whether or not Adam sends you back here, I don't want to see you again."

"Hannah, you don't meant that." He sounded genuinely shocked. "You can't mean it."

"I do mean it," she insisted, fighting tears and a desire to punch him...hard, for hurting her so much. "I've got to go now." She backed out through the doorway. "I'd appreciate it if you would lock the door as you leave." With that last parting shot, she slammed the door on his stunned face.

Justin was mad. He was more than mad, he was furious. He just couldn't decide who he was more furious with, Hannah for cutting him dead, or himself for getting too deeply involved with her in the first place.

Dammit, who needed her, anyway? Certainly not him. The last thing he needed was a haughty, overly independent woman. Hell, there were plenty of warm, eager and willing women out there.

Justin repeated the assurance to himself all the way back to Montana and throughout the following three weeks. He repeated it to himself while he was working, when conferring about the horse farm in Pennsylvania they had decided to invest in, but mostly when he prowled the house at night, unable to sleep for thinking about her, aching for Hannah.

Why the hell had he been so stupid as to fall in love with her? Why had he allowed himself to fall for the Hannah that was not always cold and haughty, but sweet and hot, a tiger in his arms.

Justin knew when he was beaten. To his amazement it didn't even bother him that he'd finally fallen in love—real love. He decided he'd have to do something about it, something more than he had originally planned on back in February.

Going to the phone, Justin placed a call to Adam, his fingers tapping an impatient drumbeat as he waited for his brother to come on the line.

"What's up?" Adam said.

"We need a family meeting about this horse farm in Oley, Pennsylvania."

"Wait a minute, we've already bought the property," Adam said. "And it was your idea to begin with. Don't tell me you changed your mind and want us to back out of the deal when we're just days away from settling it."

"No, no, I haven't changed my mind about the property," Justin reassured him, "only about who we send east to manage the farm."

"Not Ben?" Adam sounded shocked.

"Not Ben," Justin concurred. "I know for a fact that Ben really doesn't want to relocate and that Karla doesn't want to move so far from her family."

"Then who the hell do you have in mind?" Adam demanded. "One of the men on the ranch?" Before Justin could get a word in, Adam added, "Is there another one of the men capable of running a Thoroughbred farm?"

"Yeah. One," Justin drawled, thinking the answer should be obvious to Adam, of all people.

"Who?" Adam snapped impatiently.

"Yours truly, brother mine," Justin said, grinning when he heard Adam sigh.

"I'll call a meeting," Adam said. "Of course, Beth will send her proxy, as usual."

Justin was now chuckling. "To me, as usual."

"Goodbye, Justin." Adam hung up.

Justin laughed out loud, inwardly praying for success in the East Coast endeavor. Not with the farm—Justin felt confident he could succeed with that. Hell, without conceit he knew he was nearly a damn genius when it came to horses. No, the challenge was convincing Hannah that he was the man for her. His plan had to work; he'd make it work...somehow.

It was the middle of March. The days were growing milder. Instead of taking the bus as she usually did, Hannah had begun walking the two-plus miles back and forth from her apartment to her office. The exercise and fresh air were good for her.

Without conscious thought, Hannah's hand slid down in a protective gesture over the small rounded mound of her growing belly. Her pregnancy had been confirmed by her doctor. Her due date was in mid-October; another season, another life.

A thrill shot through Hannah at the thought of the tiny person awakening inside her body. She hadn't felt any movement from her baby yet, but she knew it would not be long before she did.

Hannah had told Jocelyn the day after she had seen the doctor. Over a month ago.

"Does the father know?" her assistant asked, her expression a mixture of stunned delight.

"No," Hannah admitted, shaking her head. "I don't think he'd want to know."

"Not want to know?" Jocelyn said indignantly. "What kind of a user is the son—"

"Jocelyn," Hannah interrupted her, unwilling to hear her curse Justin. "I knew what I was getting into. What Justin and I had was just a fling." She managed a wry smile. "One might say a close encounter of the sexual kind. He never asked for anything more and I expect nothing from him. This is my baby. I'll take care of it."

"And I'll be right beside you," Jocelyn said staunchly, giving Hannah a reassuring hug.

Although Hannah had taken full responsibility for her pregnancy, she still had nagging doubts about not telling Justin. Not to seek financial support for his child—she didn't need his money. She just felt that he had every right to know he was to become a father.

Justin loved children. He would make a good father...if he cared to do so. That was the dilemma Hannah was feeling.

Arriving home refreshed from the brisk walk, Hannah kicked off her shoes and went straight to the phone. She had to tell him, she'd never be able to live with herself if she didn't.

After getting his ranch's number from information, she punched it in and forced herself to breathe normally. It was difficult, especially with the phone continuing to ring. Finally, when she was about ready to hang up, an unfamiliar voice answered.

"Yes, is Justin there, please?" she asked, wondering why Karla hadn't answered.

"No, he isn't," came the brisk reply. "Would you like to leave a message?"

Declining the offer, Hannah pressed the disconnect button, then stood staring at the instrument in her hand, unsure what to do next. Blinking against a sting of tears, she hung up the phone just as the doorbell rang.

Doorbell? Her doorbell never rang without her being notified by the security guard in the lobby.

Hannah hesitated, puzzled by the oddness of the situation. The bell rang again.

Hannah went into the living room and looked through the peephole. She went absolutely still.

Justin.

The bell rang once more, quick, sharp, as if punched by an impatient or angry person.

Drawing a deep, steadying breath, Hannah disengaged the lock and pulled the door open. She backed up as he aggressively stepped forward.

"Justin…" She had to swallow to moisten her bone-dry throat. "What are you doing here?"

Dropping the same bag he had carried before,

he walked right up to her and caught her face in his hands, holding her still.

"Dammit, woman," Justin said, his voice rough. "I love you, that's what I'm doing here. I didn't want to love you. I didn't want to love any woman, ever again. But I do love you." His voice softened to a gentle purr. "Oh, sweet Hannah, I love you. I want to marry you." His stormy gray eyes grew bright with that heart-melting devil light. "And if you don't say you love me, too, want to marry me, live with me and have my babies, I'm going to curl into a ball of misery on the floor and cry for a week."

"Only a measly week?" Hannah was already crying, and laughing.

"Well, maybe two," he conceded, lowering his head to hers. "But I'd rather not. Hannah, sweetheart, say it. Say you love me before I go completely crazy."

"I love you. I love you. I love you." Tears poured down her face. "Oh, Justin, I love you so much I could die from it."

"Don't you dare. We've got a lot of living and loving before us. And there's no better time than now to get started."

Holding her tightly to him—as if he'd never let her go—he kissed her, deeply, lovingly, reverently.

Pure joy bursting inside her, Hannah flung her arms around his neck and kissed him back with all the love and longing she had tried so hard to reject. She moaned in soft protest when Justin lifted his mouth from hers.

"We'll get back to that in a minute," he murmured, gliding his tongue over her lower lip in silent promise. "But I have to ask you something."

Hannah reluctantly opened her eyes. "What?"

"Will…you…marry…me?" Justin asked.

"Oh." Hannah felt a tingle do a tango down her spine. "Well, yes, of course. Was there any doubt?"

"Oh, boy," he groaned, in feigned dismay. "I have a feeling I'm in for trouble with you."

"Yes, you are," Hannah replied happily. "And I with you, but…won't it be fun?" She pulled slightly away before saying, "I said I'd marry you, Justin, and I will. But there is one possible problem."

He arched a brow. "Like…what?"

"Like…you run a ranch in Montana," she said. "And I run a business in Philadelphia."

He shook his head. "No problem."

"But…" she began in protest, afraid he'd ask her to give up the business she had worked so hard to get up and running, and even more afraid she'd agree to do so.

"Honey, let me explain," he interjected. "When I was here a few weeks ago, I didn't just stop in to visit you for a quick bout of sex at the end of my business trip."

"You didn't? Tell me more. Spill your guts, Grainger."

He laughed. "You're something else, sweetheart, you know that?"

"Yeah, yeah." Hannah flicked a hand at him. "Get on with the explanation."

"The idea of our company buying a horse farm in the East wasn't Adam's, it was mine."

"Really?" She frowned. "Is that important?"

"I think so." Justin smiled, pulling her over to the sofa where they both sat. "At my suggestion, the company bought the farm in the Oley Valley. We made settlement yesterday." He paused.

"Go on." Having an inkling of what was coming, she held her breath.

"I'm going to manage it."

"Oh...oh," she cried, almost afraid to believe it. "You're relocating?"

"Yes."

"I can keep my business? Commute?"

"Yes, sweet Hannah." His smile grew a bit shaky. "You can keep me, too, if you want."

"If? If?" Hannah exclaimed, moving into his waiting arms. "Try to get out of being kept."

Holding her tight, as if afraid to set her free, he pressed his forehead to hers. "Oh, sweet Hannah, I love you so much, so very much."

"Oh, Justin. I...I have something I must tell you, something I think is wonderful. I'm pregnant."

"You're pregnant?" Justin asked, his gray eyes starting to gleam. "You're pregnant!" He whooped, laughing. "I'm going to be a father!"

"You're not angry?" Hannah asked.

"Of course I'm not angry. I'm thrilled." He frowned. "Did you know about this when I was here before?"

She nodded. "I knew how you felt about marriage," Hannah defended herself. "I was afraid to tell you, afraid you wouldn't care or that you would think I was trying to trap you."

"Wouldn't care?" Justin appeared stunned, as though he'd taken a blow to the head.

"I...I did finally call you," she said softly, trying to placate him. "You weren't there."

"No one said I had missed a call," Justin said. "When did you call?"

Hannah wet her lips and lowered her eyes. "A couple of minutes before you rang the bell."

"A couple of—" Justin broke off, shaking his head. "You know, sweetheart, I don't know whether to kiss you senseless or shake you senseless."

"You'd better kiss me," she advised demurely. "You can't shake me in my delicate condition."

"Okay." Lowering his head, he took possession of her lips...and her heart.

* * * * *

SECOND-CHANCE HERO

BY
JUSTINE DAVIS

Justine Davis lives on Puget Sound in Washington. She says that years ago, during her career in law enforcement, a young man she worked with encouraged her to try for a promotion to a position that was at the time occupied only by men. "I succeeded, became wrapped up in my new job, and that man moved away, never, I thought, to be heard from again. Ten years later he appeared out of the woods of Washington State, saying he'd never forgotten me and would I please marry him. With that history, how could I write anything but romance?"

Chapter 1

"I diverted a plane to pick you up, should be there within the hour."

Already diverted a company plane? John Draven took a deep breath before answering his boss, Josh Redstone.

"You seem awfully sure I'm going."

"I already apologized," Josh said.

He had said, not very convincingly, that he was sorry to interrupt Draven's time off. Draven had refrained from pointing out that you couldn't interrupt what hadn't yet begun.

"I'm on leave." He repeated what he'd said when Josh had first called.

"And you still will be. I just need you to do this one thing first. This is something only you can handle," Josh said.

Only he could handle? From what Josh had told him, it was a simple case of sabotage, from someone among the population of ten or so thousand who apparently didn't like the idea of Redstone coming to that unnamed little cay off the coast of Belize. Nothing any one of the team couldn't handle.

Draven felt how tightly he was gripping the phone. He frowned. Relaxed his fingers. Yet another sign, he thought. He'd always been able to separate inner tension from bodily reaction. But not now. And that was what had gotten him into this.

"Besides, when you're done with this problem at the construction site, you can stick around. Do some diving. The Belize reef is one of the best dive spots in the world."

So that was Josh's master plan, he thought. Force him to relax. Josh was big on that kind of thing, making sure his people took care of their spirits as well as their bodies.

"I know," he said.

And he couldn't deny that diving had already been on his list of things he might consider for this supposed leave of absence. He hadn't been pleasure diving in a long time. For the past several years, all his dives had been work-related, whether it was simply checking the function of an underwater system, or doing a hull check for explosives on a Redstone vessel that had been too long in port in a volatile part of the world.

The idea of days of simply drifting in the warm waters off the Central American coast held a definite appeal. Under water the world above barely existed. Down there it was peaceful, quiet and fascinating, the only predators the ones you knew on sight. Unlike that world up top, where they sometimes came in disguises so clever you didn't find out until it was too late.

Now he knew he was in trouble. He never thought of things like that. He resisted the urge to blurt it all out to his boss. But how could he tell the man who trusted him with the safety of the empire he'd built, "I nearly slugged a guy for just mouthing off?" Or "I lost control and threw a chair through a window?" Or worse yet, "I nearly blew a job and got one of our own hurt, because I couldn't keep a grip on my temper?"

"Look," Josh said, "you go, contact our people, handle what you find—no matter what it is—and then you're on your own."

That one phrase triggered Draven's radar; they knew what the problem was, so what did "no matter what it is" mean? He didn't feel capable of handling anything at the moment. He didn't even have the energy to ask for details. But he owed Josh Redstone a great deal. He also knew Josh would never trade on that, and wouldn't ask this of him unless he really thought it was necessary.

And Josh Redstone wasn't often wrong.

When he hung up and went to get his largest duffel bag, he knew he'd been manipulated. But it was Josh, so he couldn't bring himself to resent it. They'd come a long way since the day he'd shown up at a ramshackle hangar in Iowa to tell Josh his brother's dying thoughts had been of him. He'd quickly seen what Jim had meant when he'd said Josh was a dreamer, that he'd either do glorious things or nothing, but not end up in between.

Glorious had obviously been the choice. Tiny Redstone Aviation, riding on the wings of Josh's self-designed Hawk 1 jet, had quickly grown into a varied, global entity worth more than Draven could even wrap his mind around. Yet Josh Redstone was the most genuine, unassuming and generous person Draven had ever known, and he was not a man who was easily convinced of the goodness of anyone. He'd seen too much, dealt with too many of the opposite ilk.

Draven put the bag on the bed and turned to his laptop, already booted up and on his small desk. While he searched for the data he wanted online, he searched his memory for what he knew about Belize from a brief visit to Belize City years ago. Redstone had done a project or two in the area before, and he'd read the informational data. Population well under a million. Airports minimal with paved runways, and only one with a runway length of over fifteen hundred meters. The inevitable drug trade in that part of the world had a solid foothold, with the threat to grow.

But they had an abundance of natural treasures, not just the diving Josh had mentioned. Tourism was the answer to many of the country's woes, and they knew it. And were promoting it, widely. So it was easy to find out what concerned him at this moment: the weather. Eighties, he read on the Web site, this time of year. Humid. Rain frequently, usually better than six inches in July. That would get better in August, they promised.

He shut down the laptop and slipped it into the case. He put the case in the duffel bag, followed by his shaving kit, a few short-sleeved T-shirts, khakis and jeans, one lightweight jacket and, just in case he had to do any midnight recons, a set of black jeans and matching long-sleeved shirt. His hair was dark enough that he didn't worry about covering it, but it was long enough to get in his eyes, so he threw his usual knit cap in more to control it than cover it. He added a camouflage paint kit and a few other odds and ends he thought might come in handy. He did most of it without much thought; it was routine to him, and he usually had a good sense of what might be needed.

The problem with that was that it gave him too many free brain cells to think with. And as seemed typical lately, he couldn't seem to stop himself from thinking about the last thing he wanted to remember, his meeting with Josh two days ago. Draven knew he would never forget the look on the man's face when he realized what Draven had handed him was his resignation.

Draven had been face-to-face with some of the most vicious humans on the planet, and he'd felt nothing like the unease he'd felt then. He saw the moment when Josh shifted from shock and concern to determination, and when the barrage began, he'd been ready.

"Are you sick?"

Not physically. "No."

"Someone else sick?"

Josh knew there was no one else. "No."

"In legal trouble?"

If only it were that simple. "No."

"Financial?"

Redstone paid him more than he could ever imagine spending in his life. "No."

"Do you want out of the field? A desk?"

He'd go insane, locked up inside all day. "No."

Josh looked at the letter again. Read it as if the wording had somehow changed. Then he looked back at the man standing at parade rest in front of him. When he spoke again, it was in the soft voice Draven had been dreading.

"We've been together a lot of years, Johnny. You've helped me build Redstone into what it is. Don't you think I deserve a little more than 'It is with great regret I tender my resignation?'"

"Yes."

Draven's voice had been as gruff as Josh's had been soft. Nothing in his life or career had been as difficult as quitting on the man he admired most.

They'd finally compromised on this unwanted leave of absence. So as long as he wasn't officially unemployed, he was still Josh's man.

Finished packing, he slung the duffel over his shoulder. He locked the door of the small studio apartment behind him, not that there was anything of real value in it. He wasn't there enough to make him want to invest in much. Most things he

personally valued were tucked away in his locker at Redstone, although none of them would matter much to anyone
else. If you didn't count the shares of Redstone he owned,
and the investment portfolio Harlan McClaren had built for
him, the most expensive thing he owned was the laptop he'd
just packed.

That and the holstered weapon at the small of his back.

He strapped the duffel on the back of his motorcycle.
He'd long ago sold his last car. For the same reason as the
apartment, it didn't make sense to let a car sit and depreci-
ate when he wasn't around to drive it. The serviceable bike
had enough power, was reliable and didn't have the name,
chrome or flash that made it a theft target. Suited him just
fine.

When he pulled through the security gate at the airfield
utilized by Redstone Security for scrambling to various parts
of the worldwide Redstone empire, he rode to the back of the
unmarked Redstone hangar. He unlocked the small door with
his code, and rolled the bike inside. He parked it in the back
corner, then trotted up to the loft where the lockers were.

He didn't think he'd need heavy firepower, but given the
part of the world he was headed to, and the reason, he needed
something. He'd take the 17-round Glock he was wearing,
and a smaller backup just in case. He added a satellite phone
and a couple of boxes of ammunition, glad yet again for the
convenience of not having to fly commercial.

On the thought he heard the roar of a jet engine, unusual
enough at this small airfield to tell him there was a good
chance it was his ride. He stepped outside just in time to see
a sleek gray-and-red craft land dead center with a feather
touch and nary a bounce.

His brows furrowed. This had to be it, they were the Redstone colors, but…

"Holy skyrocket," he breathed.

It was the Hawk V. It had to be. No markings, just the tail number, but the unmistakable color scheme of Redstone. And a cutting-edge design, smaller than the biggest Hawk, the recent Hawk IV that Josh personally flew, but also sleeker and more efficient. It was still in prototype stage, although two had been completed and were undergoing intense testing.

One, apparently, was about to make a test trip to Belize.

"Well, shoot, Josh," Draven said to himself with a grin, "all you had to do was say the flight was on this and we could have saved a lot of time and talk."

He went back to get his gear. By the time he locked the door behind him, the jet was coming to a halt on the apron beside the hangar. And a small fueling truck was already in sight, heading their way from the big storage tanks.

A few moments later the gangway came down, dropping out of the sleek side of the craft like some loading ramp on a futuristic spaceship. He got his second surprise when the pilot hit the steps.

"Tess?"

The petite, dark-haired woman with the pixie haircut came down grinning at Draven. "You think I'm going to give anybody else the chance to test drive this baby?"

He grinned back at her; Tess was one of the few people outside his own security team who had his complete and total trust and respect. She was the best fixed wing pilot he'd ever seen, and was almost as good with a helicopter. She'd been with Redstone even longer than he had, and had flown in and out of some of the most difficult spots on the planet, under sometimes even more difficult conditions.

Even under fire. The first time he'd flown with her, when Josh had sent her to fly Draven and Redstone point man Noah Rider out of a Colombian jungle where Rider had been exploring the possibility of opening a branch of Red-

stone Research and Development, utilizing the local vegetation in an effort to produce cheaper medical products. The
fact that it might also stabilize the area, and perhaps give
them a path other than the illegal drug trade to follow, was
one of the side benefits that tended to accompany Redstone
projects.

But the local insurgent guerillas had quickly decided the
presence of globally known Redstone was not going to help
their cause, and would quite likely hurt their drug business.
Draven had seen helicopter evacs in war zones that had taken
less fire than Tess had that day. But she'd kept on coming,
never wavered, had held the ship rock steady as he and Rider
had scrambled aboard. She'd had them out of there in seconds. Only when they'd landed safely in neighboring Brazil
did they see the results; it was going to take some time to
mend the bullet holes in that chopper. They all knew how
lucky they'd been that they hadn't been blown out of the sky,
and Draven and Rider knew who to thank that they were still
alive.

When Tess had taken over the personal flying for Josh,
who had reluctantly given up flying himself on business
flights so he could work en route, no one had been surprised.
It would take one hell of a pilot to get Josh Redstone to surrender the controls. And Tess Machado was exactly that.

Draven gestured at the plane. "So, is she all she's supposed to be?"

"And more," Tess said. "Faster, more efficient, with
greater range even on some of those questionable fuels we
find some places."

"Quite a résumé."

She nodded. "Josh designed it after Ian Gamble came up
with a new composite material that's incredibly strong, with
a higher stress point than any traditional material."

Draven lifted a brow. "You mean he didn't come up with an impossible design and then tell Ian to make it work?"

Tess laughed at his description of one of Josh's typical approaches to inspiring his people. Amazingly it worked more often than not. Draven knew that was because of the caliber of people Josh hired, and the loyalty he inspired in them, but sometimes it still amazed him.

"No, although it did require some breakthrough construction techniques. But this plane is going to bring the price down to within reach of people who never thought they'd be able to afford a private or company jet."

Draven's mouth quirked upward at one corner. Tess laughed again. "I know, I know, I sound like a promo brochure or something."

"You love what you do. That's beyond price," he said.

He knew when Tess's smile faded and her gaze narrowed that his voice really had sounded as solemn as he'd thought.

"John?" she asked quietly. She was one of the few people, even at Redstone, who ever used his first name.

He didn't respond. Instead he flicked a glance at the fuel truck. "Might want to keep an eye on that fueler. He's looking more at the plane than watching what he's doing."

For a moment longer Tess kept looking at him, making it clear she knew he was dodging her tacit inquiry.

"I'll go make sure he isn't putting avgas in," she said, and turned to walk toward the fueling truck.

The fueler shifted his attention to her, with a look of male appreciation that Draven completely understood. The kid was probably about eighteen, and Tess was...well, however old she was, he didn't really know. But twice that kid's age, anyway. But it didn't really matter. She was a very attractive woman, period.

He started up the gangway into the plane. As a prototype still unscheduled for production, the interior lacked the usual

Redstone amenities and was only roughly finished, but he'd flown in much worse. And he guessed the cockpit would already be finished with all the gadgets and controls that Josh felt were standard. First and foremost Josh was a pilot. Even if it did give his insurance agent heart palpitations when he elected himself test pilot to put some new design through its paces.

Draven wedged his duffel under one of the half-dozen standard airline seats that were temporarily bolted in place. He then headed back to confirm his earlier guess. He'd been right, the cockpit was a finished work of art, and he smiled to himself.

"Like it?"

He turned to see Tess standing there, smiling. "More important, do you?" he asked.

"He's topped himself this time," she said, gesturing at the banks of dials, screens, switches and other controls. "If something's not here, it hasn't been invented yet. Enhanced vision system so you can see through heavy weather, and at night. The latest GPS, of course, and collision avoidance system. Ground proximity warning, integrated hazard avoidance system, map displays that move as you do, you name it, it's here."

"No weapons?" he asked dryly.

She grinned. "Got a jamming device for incoming missiles, will that do?"

"I suppose it will have to," he said in mock resignation.

"Hey, we got an order from a place in Asia I can't even pronounce for a Hawk IV to serve as their Air Force One because of that jammer. And there are advancements on this new plane that the commercial aviation industry won't see for years."

"Because Josh isn't afraid to take the risks." She was as passionate about this plane as Josh himself was.

"No, he's not. Not in his work."

It was Draven's turn now; he hadn't missed the undertone in her voice. "Tess?"

"Got your gear aboard?" she asked, dodging the silent inquiry just as he had hers. He let her; he could hardly do otherwise, considering.

"Yes."

"Belt in, and I'll give you a takeoff you'll never forget."

"Mind if I sit up front?"

She looked surprised. He couldn't blame her. Usually he was busy with mission plans on a flight to a job. He didn't tell her he hadn't wanted this mission to begin with, and was trying to avoid thinking about it, he who rarely avoided anything. He'd once been told, by a well-meaning woman, that it was because he didn't care enough about anything but his work to need to avoid it, and he supposed that was true. He'd seen and done too much in this life to let down his guard that much.

"Fine," she said, gesturing to the copilot's seat.

The takeoff was all she'd promised and more. The plane was both fast and quick, two very different things when it came to small planes. It was also nimble and powerful, as she showed when she banked for a three-sixty turn and straightened out all while still climbing.

"You're lucky," she said when they leveled out. "This'll only be about a five-hour flight."

"I'm also lucky," he said, "because if I was flying commercial, I'd be headed for Houston or the East Coast to make a connection, and would get to Belize sometime tomorrow."

"I can guarantee you'll get there sooner than that," Tess said.

Thanks to the distraction of the new plane and Tess's enthusiasm for it, the flight passed quickly enough. The

Hawk V performed faultlessly, and Draven was in a more equable state of mind by the time they touched down at Goldson International Airport, where all private planes were required to land in Belize.

But he was back to being edgy again by the time he'd rounded up water transport out to the island temporarily known as Redstone Cay, where the project was being built. And after he transferred from the second boat to the third—he suspected the captains were brothers, and shared the wealth with this method—he was wishing he'd just hired a seaplane, even if it had meant waiting for a couple of hours.

What they were going to need, he thought, was their own airstrip. Then at least people could get there directly, maybe even get an exception to the rule about private planes having to go into Belize City. They could—

An airstrip.

Draven's mind slammed to a sudden stop. Josh had never said exactly what stage of building they were in, had only referred to "the Redstone Cay Resort project." Draven hadn't asked, because it didn't really matter to him, his equipment would be the same regardless, until he got on scene and assessed.

An airstrip.

It made sense. Whenever Redstone built in a hard-to-reach location, particularly an island, an airstrip was often the first thing to be built. It made getting people, supplies and equipment there so much easier that it was well worth the effort and expense. And who was their premier airstrip overseer?

But it couldn't be, could it? It was too soon, too soon after the earthquake and her hospitalization? She should still be recuperating, going through therapy and rehab. Shouldn't she?

Not the way my luck's running lately.

He groaned inwardly, nearly certain now.
An airstrip.
God help him, Grace.

Chapter 2

Grace leaned back in the office chair that tended to roll to the left. She suspected the floor in the construction trailer wasn't level, but hadn't gotten around to doing anything about it yet. She'd been too busy trying to figure out who it was who had decided they didn't want an airstrip built here.

Grace O'Conner sighed. She'd done the right thing, calling the home office for help. She could design an international airport, handle most aspects of getting it built and in a pinch fly at least a prop plane in and out of it, but this was beyond her. She didn't have the training to deal with this kind of thing, and she knew it. She'd also known that what was happening was too much for the single security guard they had had up to now. He had been hired locally, with the assumption that no more help would be needed at this early stage of the project.

But as Josh Redstone had told her when she'd made the call—it still disconcerted her that the man frequently answered his own phone—no one expected her to build the airstrip and police it, too.

Odd, she thought. She had a beautiful place to work in, great weather and the full support of the mayor of the small town down the beach a couple of miles, grandly called Matola City. He'd even thrown a welcome party for them in his own home. But while her last project had been a much welcomed airfield nearly destroyed by an act of God, this one was under attack by man. And she had no idea who.

After that act of God in Turkey, she'd spent hours buried in that pile of rubble with nothing to do but try to ignore the pain and think about dying, and what would happen to Marly, her daughter, if she did. As the pain had gotten worse and no help came, her thoughts had become crazier, and she had begun to talk out loud just to assure herself she was still alive. And she bargained with God, who, if he really had caused that earthquake, had a lot to answer for. She'd sworn never to put herself in jeopardy again if he would just let her live to take care of her daughter.

And now, every time that missing foot began to ache, she was reminded of how lucky she was to be here to feel even that phantom pain, lucky that she hadn't died under that pile of fractured brick and mortar.

The form that luck had come in still haunted her dreams, but she tried not to think about it, at least not all the time. It was done, she was alive, and grateful for it.

Wearily, she rubbed at her forehead, where a headache was beginning to build. Maybe she should have listened to them after all. Here she was, on a sparsely populated sandbar of an island off Belize, battling mosquitoes, beetles the size of Volkswagens and who knew what else, when she could be sitting at home with a glass of iced tea and a nice book to read.

Like an invalid?

Just the thought stiffened her spine.

She made herself get back to business. She wondered if what was happening was bigger than simply not wanting an airstrip built, if perhaps whoever it was simply didn't want Redstone here at all. She knew that wasn't impossible. Many people who hadn't had any firsthand experience with Redstone found it hard to believe that the company really was all it was reputed to be. Once they'd dealt with them they knew the reputation was well earned, but there were still doubters. And despite the small population, she supposed there could be at least one of those here on Redstone Cay.

Of course, she knew that what was more likely was that whatever slime controlled the local drug trade was the one behind all this. They'd warned her it was a rampant problem in this part of the world, but she'd hoped that here, on this quiet, almost isolated cay, it would be minimal.

And not for the first time she felt a qualm; one of the reservations she'd had about bringing Marly down here was just that. There had not been a drug problem with her daughter yet—that she knew about—but the fourteen year old had been teetering on the edge of real trouble long enough that Grace couldn't help wondering if it was only a matter of time.

She heard the roar of a motor, one she'd come to recognize. She got up and glanced out the window, and saw the bright orange and white cigarette-style boat coming into view from the direction of the mainland. There were only two occupants, both male, one considerably taller than the other. It looked like Jorge Nunez at the wheel, and he was gesturing in the general direction of the dock.

She went back to the desk and picked up her walkie-talkie then headed outside. She slipped her sunglasses from the top of her head to her eyes as soon as she was down the steps; she'd learned early on to protect her blue eyes from the near-equatorial sun.

She headed toward the dock, curious. She paused as someone in a hard hat waved at her from the heavy equipment enclosure. The area had been empty two days ago, but now that the rain had swept through and the weather promised to hold, the fleet of graders, backhoes, earthmovers and compactors had moved in. They'd even been, with typical Redstone efficiency, two days ahead of schedule.

And that same night they'd had their second incident of sabotage. The first, a bucket of paint tossed over gravel to be used as a base, had been minor enough they'd written it off as petty vandalism, but this one had nearly cost them a very expensive piece of machinery. Sand in the fuel tank did not make for efficient running or much longevity. If someone hadn't noticed the tiny pile of sand on top of the filler pipe, they might have started the bulldozer and ruined the engine.

It appeared someone really didn't want this job finished.

The man started toward her, and after a few steps she saw it was Nick Dwyer, the foreman of the entire project.

"Ms. O'Conner," the man said, touching a finger to the edge of his yellow helmet as they stopped a few yards from the chain-link enclosure.

"Nick," she said with a nod; she'd not seen the grizzled veteran of three of her projects yet this morning. Then, with a smile, she added, "Even after all the work we've done together, I still can't get you to call me Grace, can I?"

He smiled back. "No, ma'am. You're my boss, and it doesn't seem right."

She studied him a moment, remembering. His smile faded.

"I know," he said quietly. "Time was I didn't show you that respect."

"Time was," she answered, looking steadily at his weathered face, "you didn't know I deserved it."

The smile returned. "And that's part of the reason you do," he said. "Because you know it has to be earned. And by God, you did it with that Alaska project."

"Thanks, Nick."

She couldn't deny that airstrip at Redstone Sitka had been a problem from the beginning. Building anything in Alaska was a challenge, but building an airstrip there had its own unique problems. There was the permafrost; they'd had to move the proposed site for the strip because the original location was too poorly drained. Drainage was always a problem, but at an Alaskan site, it meant ice was mixed with the finer grained sediments, which was a recipe for disaster. The last thing she'd wanted was to lose the strip to frost heaves, slumping or anything else.

So she'd come up with an idea that involved a different kind of base and a new freeze-resistant soil stabilizing compound Ian Gamble had come up with, coupled with an interlocking surface system that could expand and contract more freely. And it had been a success. Better than five years ago and constant testing had shown it was holding up better than she'd dared hope.

Nick turned to head back to the equipment, then turned back. "Oh, tell your little girl she can have that 'dozer lesson she wanted. This afternoon, after work hours."

Grace knew she was gaping, but couldn't help it. "Lesson?"

Nick nodded. "She's been asking the guys, but they wouldn't until they cleared it with me." Then, as the obvious registered, he frowned. "You didn't know? She said you said it was okay."

It was one of those moments as a parent she hated. Did she openly catch Marly in the lie, and further alienate her? Or let her get away with this one, because at least she was showing an interest in being here?

Or an interest in being able to mow the whole thing down, she amended ruefully, admitting with reluctance that she could no longer say with certainty what would be out of the realm of possibility in her daughter's behavior.

"I'll get back to you on that," she told Nick.

She let out a sigh as Nick left and she continued her trek to the dock, where the racing boat was nearing the dock now. Just getting Marly—who at fourteen was hardly a little girl anymore, in stature or attitude—here had been a major undertaking. The fact that people traveled from all over the world to vacation in this tropical, crystalline water place hadn't made much difference in her complaining about not getting to spend the summer with her friends, although now that they were here, it was hard to tear Marly away from the beach.

And those friends were exactly why she wanted her daughter away for a while in the first place. She'd seen Marly slip further and further away from the close relationship they'd once had, and while she was willing to cede some of that distance to the process of adolescence, Marly had gone beyond just that. And Grace wasn't about to let her go any further. She could only hope she hadn't already let her go too far.

She pushed the persistent worries out of her mind, and focused on the new arrival. The man with Jorge, carrying a large duffel bag, jumped nimbly onto the dock before the boat had even come to a halt or been tied off. Jorge gave him a grin and a thumbs-up, then roared away, kicking up a wake that sprayed his former passenger from the knees down. The man didn't seem to mind, or even notice.

She noted how he moved as he walked the length of the dock toward the beach. She paid more attention to that these days, comparing her own impaired stride to those of intact people, trying to see where she might improve. But never in her life would she try to imitate this easy, powerful stride; even before she'd lost her foot she wasn't built right for that walk, it was far too masculine.

Because of her concentration on his movement, she didn't really see his face until he was much closer. When she finally shifted her gaze, her breath caught in her throat. On some level, her gut knew instantly. It clenched, sending a wave of shivering sensation through her.

Her brain took longer to process what she was seeing. It ticked off each element, from the longish, nearly black hair to the wicked scar that slashed down the left side of his rugged face. And most of all the haunting and haunted green eyes that appeared in her dreams, startling her awake with the fear that she was back in that pile of rubble, pinned, dying and alone.

She had never expected to see that face again. Had decided long ago she never wanted to. It wasn't that she wasn't grateful. Or that he was hard to look at. Her reaction had little to do with what he looked like, or the fact that when she'd first seen him she'd thought him a harshly beautiful angel come for her.

To her, this man was a creature of nightmare. Her nightmare. The nightmare that had never completely ended.

And the creature was indeed coming for her.

Despite knowing she was likely here, Draven winced inwardly at the sight of Grace at the foot of the pier. Standing there, she looked much different than when he had last seen her, pale and bruised and hooked up to machines in a hospital bed.

Standing.

It finally got through to him. She was standing there, on her own two feet. Well, one of her own, and one of Ian Gamble's; the new prosthetic foot he'd designed was rapidly becoming a marvel in medical circles, Draven knew. He'd read the data as soon as he knew she'd be getting the foot.

Made of graphite and titanium, yet incredibly flexible, it had built-in biofeedback microprocessors that could read the angle, direction and intensity of the strain put on the foot every tenth of a second. It could adjust almost as quickly as a natural foot to different walking speeds and conditions, making it much more stable than previous prostheses.

And then she started walking toward him, and he was reminded yet again just how good Ian Gamble was. It took him a moment to realize he was fixating on that to avoid the rush of awareness flooding him. She was walking, and walking easily, less than six months after the removal of her mangled foot.

He should have thought of this long before it had come to him in the plane. The same strength that had allowed her to survive three days pinned under a pile of concrete had also sped her through the rehabilitation process. He'd even known how fast it had gone, because he had requested constant updates. And the bills; he and Redstone had made certain she'd gotten the best. He marveled at the ease of her gait, noting there was barely a trace of difference between the natural foot and the prosthesis. If he hadn't known to look, he would never have seen it. Not for a while, anyway.

Of course, that could be because he was distracted by the sight of her. She'd cut her hair, and the short, wispy, windswept dark locks suited her. And bared a neck he'd never realized was so long and graceful. She was thinner after her ordeal, but when she pulled off her sunglasses, her blue eyes were just as blazingly bright and alive as they'd been when he'd uncovered her in that mound of debris.

He hadn't been at all surprised when Josh had sent the order for all available Redstone personnel in the country to respond to the small town struck hardest by the earthquake.

He hadn't been surprised when he arrived to find most of them, knowing their boss, were already on their way anyway. Nor had he been surprised when they refused to give up, digging through collapsed buildings, scouring every damaged structure in the gradually fading hope that someone else, anyone else, would be found alive.

He had been surprised to find someone alive. They'd been on the verge of turning loose the cadaver dogs when one of the searchers had sent up a shout of discovery.

He stopped the recollection with the discipline of years of training. Despite his long, hard history there were not many things John Draven dodged—or that gave him nightmares—but the memories of this woman, and what had happened to her, were at the top of his short list.

When she was close enough that he could see her expression, he realized she was startled to see him. *I know the feeling,* he thought. He wasn't, however, startled by her reaction. He was certain he was the last person on earth Grace O'Conner wanted to see again. Ever.

When they were face-to-face, she didn't speak. She just stared at him in a way that told him she was remembering, probably too clearly, their first encounter. He couldn't blame her for the look in her eyes, for the pain he saw there. He could understand the horror that was reflected in the blue depths.

What he couldn't explain was the feeling in his gut, that kicked by a mule feeling he'd once experienced in the literal sense.

"Grace," he said, not sure if he meant her name or the demeanor she'd exhibited under the most horrendous conditions.

"Mr. Draven," she answered, and he was amazed at how the formality stung.

Quickly he quashed the feeling, and took her lead. "You

weren't expecting me," he said, his tone as formal as hers had been.

"No."

The terseness of her response gave him his answer. She wanted nothing to do with him—and he couldn't blame her.

"I will stay out of your way as much as possible. I'll be gone as soon as the situation here is resolved. Can you tolerate that?"

For a moment he thought he saw puzzlement furrow her brow. But it was gone before he could be sure, and she spoke briskly. "I can tolerate anything that enables me to get my job done."

He nodded. "That's why I'm here."

"Then let's get going. You have a saboteur to find, I have an airstrip to build."

He noticed the tautness of her muscles as she lifted an arm to put her sunglasses back on. She turned with seeming ease on the rough gravel surface of the graded area, and he wondered if she was trying extra hard to show no sign of her changed body. Of course, he'd never seen her before the earthquake, so he had no way of knowing. The only thing he'd been aware of was that she did damn fine work, all of which he'd seen after the fact.

Get back on task here, Draven, he muttered to himself.

He started after her, since she appeared to be heading for the construction trailer, his own destination. He ordered himself not to watch her walking ahead of him, but then decided it wouldn't hurt, that he could give Ian a firsthand report on how one of his inventions was working under real live conditions, something the brilliant inventor—and husband of one of Draven's own top operatives—might appreciate.

Suddenly Grace stopped and turned around. For a split second he thought she might have been aware of his gaze on her, or perhaps just checking to see if he was looking. As any red-blooded male would. He guessed, despite recent events, he must still qualify, because he had to admit he'd been enjoying the view. She was wearing black jeans and a vivid blue tank top in the Belizean warmth. They weren't snug, but nothing could disguise the feminine curves.

"Are you here officially?"

It took him a moment to process, and once more he had the thought that he was not functioning at full capacity. "Officially?"

"Do you want the crews to know you're here?"

"You haven't told anyone?"

"No. I thought you might want to get the lay of the land first. Our local guy quit, after the last incident, so they know Redstone security will be coming. But that's all. They didn't know it would be John Draven."

She said it as if the announcement of his name alone would solve the situation. Which, on occasion, it had.

"Let's keep it that way for a while. I'm just the security guy they were expecting," he said. He took out a card, scribbled his cell number on it and handed it to her. "If anything happens when I'm not around," he explained, then asked, "what are the chances someone on the inside is involved?"

He liked that her response wasn't immediate but thoughtful.

"Slim. Very. Most of these people have worked for Redstone, and some of those for me, on several projects. But I never say never."

Cautious. He liked that, too. She wasn't blind. Redstone hired the best, let them do what they were hired to do, backed them up and paid them what they deserved, earning the kind of loyalty mere money couldn't buy. It was the foundation of the Redstone empire, and anyone who worked there long enough not only came to believe it, but live by it.

But every now and then a bad apple slipped through.

There had been some recently, and it had put everyone more on their guard. He wondered if, even tucked away in the hospital, she knew that, and that was why she was wary, or if it was just a natural trait. Not that it mattered, he told himself, as long as she was.

"Do you have any questions?"

She stopped and looked over her shoulder at him. "I figure you know what you're doing, or you wouldn't have the reputation you have. I'll just follow your lead."

Grace O'Conner left him standing there, and vanished into the trailer.

"Don't call me that!"

Draven's brow twitched, his only visible reaction to the young girl's angry tone and mutinous expression. He'd run into her on his first recon of the site, and had known immediately who she was.

"How'd you know my name anyway? And who I am?"

She had Grace's eyes, he thought. Her hair was a medium-brown rather than Grace's gleaming sable, and she moved with that gawkiness of adolescence rather than Grace's easy…well, grace, he thought, but the eyes were definitely the same deep blue.

"It's the name on your passport," he said mildly.

He'd seen a copy of the document in the files he'd gone over during the flight. And it was a good thing he'd guessed she was the only child on the project; she certainly didn't look anything like the smiling, cheerful child in the passport photograph. Usually it was the other way around, and it was the photo that was stiff and stern looking.

"I don't care what that thing says." She folded her arms across her chest in a message even someone who'd never heard of body language could read. "I hate that name and I won't answer to it."

"Something wrong with Marilyn?"

The girl gave an ungracious snort and rolled her eyes. "It's bad enough my mother got named after some fairy-tale-type princess, why did she listen to my grandmother's suggestion and stick me with the name of an old-time actress who killed herself?"

"I see."

He didn't, really. He didn't see or know anything about kids her age. Especially girls. They were a foreign species to him. But if she was a typical example, he was amazed any teenager survived to adulthood without being killed by their parents. His own parents had given up on him fairly early, but he'd long ago realized he probably deserved it. He'd been out of control. He'd needed more regimentation than his rather free-spirited parents had been able to provide. They'd been horrified when he'd joined the army, proud but still puzzled when he'd become a ranger, but in the end, even they had admitted it had been the saving of him.

"Ms. O'Conner, then? Or should I just say, hey, you?"

"I don't use that, either!"

He was striking out, it seemed. Which didn't surprise him, given that the only teenager he'd ever dealt with had been his cousin, who had suffered a serious case of hero-worship for the ten-years-older cousin who came home in a uniform.

"Just because my mother—" she emphasized the word with an anger that startled him "—dumped my father and his name, doesn't mean I will. I'm more loyal than that. I hate being here instead of at home with my friends, and I hate her!"

Ah. Apparently sabotage wasn't the only problem Grace was dealing with.

"'Hey, you, it is, then.'" Tired of the sparring, he turned to go. To his surprise, she called out, in a tone that seemed almost apologetic.

"I'm Marly. Marly Palmer."

He looked back over his shoulder. He gave her a slight nod, but added, "If your mother approves."

As easily as that the anger was back. "Everything's always subject to her royal approval."

"It's in the mother job description."

She scowled at him.

"And I don't envy her the job," he muttered, and turned away again.

He resisted the urge to look back at her, then wondered why he'd felt the urge at all. But he couldn't resist the idea that formed in his mind.

Did Grace's daughter want to go home so badly she'd resort to sabotage?

Chapter 3

Draven came awake instantly at the sound of what had to be at least a 500 horsepower Caterpillar motor. With that innate sense of time he'd always had, he knew he'd only been asleep an hour or so, which would put it at about midnight. Midnight, and someone had fired up a piece of equipment worth hundreds of thousands of dollars. A piece of equipment that could likely do hundreds of thousands of dollars worth of damage.

He rolled to his feet from his bedroll on the construction trailer floor. In a split second he had pulled on the slip-on boots he'd long ago gone to for just this reason, and was running. He'd already planned his route to various areas of the project, in case he had to do just this, respond in a hurry and silently.

He got within sight of the chain-link equipment enclosure just in time to see a huge piece of machinery, with a couple of fits and starts, roll through the open gate. Whatever it was, it was at least ten feet tall and thirty feet long, with a large set of wheels in front and a smaller set trailing the body in back.

Hunkered in the shadow of a wheeled bulldozer, he couldn't see into the elevated glass cab of the machine, although whoever was handling it seemed to have smoothed things out. He started to stand when he caught a movement on the ground from the corner of his eye.

There were two of them.

He reached for the gun at the small of his back and drew it out. He hadn't bothered to unclip the holster, since he wanted the weapon close at hand. Besides, he was used to sleeping with it. Or rather, dozing with it, since it also served the purpose of keeping him from getting too comfortable when he needed to be on guard. He held the lightweight Glock in his left hand. He and, at his insistence, all his people, were as skilled as possible with either hand.

Then something about the man on the ground caught his attention. He was wearing a hard hat.

Draven thought fast. What were the chances somebody from the outside bent on mischief would bring or risk stealing a hard hat? Or even think about it? For that matter, did their saboteur really think no one would notice what he—or they—were doing, starting up a machine that could be heard for hundreds of yards down the beach?

Unless they were complete idiots, they'd know the people on the site would be on guard by now. And while he couldn't discount the idiotic possibility, his gut was telling him something else was going on here. Especially since the machine was now moving smoothly, driven by someone with experience. Not that one of the people living on the cay couldn't know how to run the thing, but still…

The man on the ground moved, turned slightly as he watched the big machine roll by. And when he saw the profile Draven relaxed slightly, enough to slip the handgun back in the holster. It was foreman Nick Dwyer. Draven recognized him from the file he'd studied on the plane. He'd worked for Redstone for nearly two decades, and he was near the bottom of Draven's suspect list, and only on it at all because he had access to every part of the project.

Draven started walking, openly now. Over the noise of the big diesel Nick didn't hear him approach, so when he spoke the man jerked slightly in surprise.

"A little midnight work?"

"Oh! Oh, no, it's just...Ms. O'Conner."

Draven blinked. "What?"

Nick gestured at the machine. "She just wanted to see if she could still do it." He studied Draven for a moment. "She lost her right foot, you know. That bad earthquake in Turkey."

"I know." He didn't tell Nick he'd been there. He didn't tell anyone. It was the only job he'd ever tried to keep secret.

The man nodded. "She was very good on the loader, the compactors—well, on most of the rigs—before, but she hasn't had the chance to try since she got that new mechanical foot thing. She didn't want to try it in front of the whole crew, just in case." The man glanced at the moving machine and grinned. "But I'd say she'll do just fine."

Draven stared at the huge, yellow machine, trying to picture Grace at the controls. It was difficult if he thought only about her size and beauty, but if he remembered the toughness that had gotten her through three days buried alive, and the determination that had hurried her through rehab and back to work, it was easier.

"She's always done that?" he asked, nodding toward the machine.

"Every project I've been on with her," Nick replied. "She says she doesn't like ordering others to do things she can't or won't do herself."

"Fits," Draven said.

"Redstone? Yeah, she does. Mr. Josh got a good one there."

He'd meant more than just Redstone, meant that it fit with what he knew of her personally, but he didn't elaborate. It was clear the man already had a great deal of respect for Grace, and Draven suspected he'd find the same reaction among most people she supervised or worked for or beside.

He tried not to think about the emotions that must have been churning in her before she'd tried this, afraid Ian's miracle might not help her get this far.

But it had, and at that moment he thought he heard a yelp of joy over the sound of the humming diesel.

Grace woke up just before five, trembling. She hadn't had the dream in weeks, hadn't had the suffocating sensation jolt her awake, but it had returned last night. It wasn't hard to figure out why; the appearance of John Draven explained many things, including the recurrence of her nightmare.

Now if she could just explain the sudden leaping of her heart that seemed to occur every time she saw him. Earlier, during her self-imposed driving test, she had been able to write her reaction off to excitement at how well her new foot worked, at how quickly Ian Gamble's invention had adapted, in only a few minutes learning what feedback she needed to control the grader.

When she had whooped in victory and turned to raise a triumphant fist to Nick, and seen John Draven's unmistakable tall, lean figure standing there, she'd been startled, that's all. She hadn't known he was still on-site, had assumed he'd gone for the night.

But that didn't explain why she was relieved that he left before she turned the grader around and brought it back.

"Seems like a nice guy," was all Nick said when she asked

if that had been the security man, just to make sure she hadn't been way off in her certainty about who had joined him.

But now she'd been revisited by the nightmare she'd hoped gone forever, although the Redstone counselor had warned her some form of it would likely be with her for a very long time. Draven's presence was obviously dragging up those quashed memories, and she knew from long, sad experience that there would be no going back to sleep for a while.

She sat up and swung her legs over the side of the queen-size bed. She still wasn't quite used to the layout of the big, almost luxurious RV Redstone had set up for her use, so she turned on the low-wattage night-light.

The bedroom in the rear of the converted bus was spacious, with a slide out that did away with any feeling of being cramped. Marly had tried to negotiate for the bedroom for herself, wanting privacy with typical teenage urgency. Grace had agreed easily, with the proviso that since the bedroom had the only shower Marly mustn't complain about being awakened when her mother had to use it before dawn. That had quickly changed the girl's mind.

Now Grace was wishing she'd left well enough alone and let the girl have the room uncontested. Right now her daughter was using the foldaway bed up front, and while it was quite comfortable, it also had access to the outside door, and with Marly in her current frame of mind Grace wasn't too happy about the idea that the girl could sneak out and she'd never know.

With a sigh over the travails of single-parenting a teenage girl, Grace reached down and massaged the stub of her lower leg. It needed to toughen up more; even though she assiduously followed the doctor's instructions on keeping it dry and protected, just the nature of her work stressed flesh and machine to the max. Bless Ian Gamble for thinking about comfort as well as his amazing programming and biofeedback chip; she knew she would never have come as far as she had without the extra thought he'd given to all aspects. A true Redstone man, she thought, and gave thanks once more to Josh Redstone for seeing the brilliance beneath the absent-minded professor exterior.

She smiled slightly as she thought of what it must be like to be married to such a man, and about what had to be a very unusual relationship. Samantha and Ian Gamble were an unlikely but clearly successful pair; everyone at Redstone knew how crazy they were about each other. An inventing genius married to a highly trained and efficient Redstone security agent—

And there she was, back to Draven again. The security team was his creation, most said it was his life, and some said it was also his soul.

Trying to shake off thoughts of the man who haunted her nights but whom she thanked by day, she stood up. She reached for the crutch she used at night from where it leaned against the nightstand. She could hop to the bathroom, but in an RV, even a well-built one like this, it tended to make enough vibration to wake Marly up.

She splashed some water on her face, as if that would wash away the remnants of the dream. She knew better, but at least she felt as if she was doing something.

She would look in on Marly, she decided. Then she'd just get dressed for work. She was due in about an hour anyway, and she could always find something to catch up on.

"Catch up, what a concept," she muttered to herself as she went to the door between the bedroom and the rest of the motor home and pulled it carefully and quietly open.

A moment later she was through the door and standing beside the converted sofa, her heart hammering as what she'd feared since they'd arrived greeted her.

Her daughter was gone.

Chapter 4

She knew Marly had made it to bed. She didn't go to sleep herself until the girl was tucked in for the night. Marly told her it was childish, and Grace had managed to disconcert her by telling her that her mother had the right to be childish if she wanted to be.

She leaned down and felt the bedding. Cool. Well, as cool as it ever was in this tropical climate. But while the pillow held the impression of Marly's head, there was no body warmth left. And the clothing she'd had on earlier was gone, instead of tossed on the floor in the girl's usual manner. There was no way to know when she'd left. Nor did it matter. What was important now was finding out where her daughter was.

And when she's back, I'm going to read her the riot act about scaring me like this, Grace promised herself. She didn't know how much more of this she could take. It had to stop. But nothing she'd tried so far had had much effect, and she was nearly out of ideas.

She grabbed the cordless telephone, got balanced on her crutch, then hastened back to her room to dress while she made some calls.

Draven didn't think he was imagining the flurry of unusual activity. A construction site was always a busy place, but there was something else going on here. Something different than the usual routine this early in the morning. He watched the various people scurrying around, noticed the pattern of the activity and saw who was pointedly absent.

When he was sure, he headed for the equipment enclosure to find Nick.

"What's missing?" he asked without preamble.

Nick frowned, then the expression cleared. "You mean who. You didn't hear yet, I guess. Ms. O'Conner's little girl is gone."

"Marly?"

Nick gave him a curious look. "You met her, then?"

"Briefly," Draven said, his tone wry.

Nick grinned. "'Bout all most of us can take. She's been giving her mom a real hard time. But we all think an awful lot of Ms. O'Conner, so we're looking."

And that, Draven thought, said it all. Then, like throwing a switch, he clicked into investigation mode.

"She have any ideas?"

Nick shook his head. "They haven't been here that long, so she doesn't know where the girl might go. Lots of places to hide out and not be found on this island, if that's what you want to do."

"Any sign it was involuntary?"

The man looked startled. "You mean...kidnapped? No! Nothing like that. Not here. Why, they only have a part-time cop, or constable, whatever they call it, because they don't have any crime."

Draven thought of the reason he was here; they had some crime now. "Until now."

The man blinked as it registered. "Yeah. I guess." Nick gave Draven a sideways look. "I suppose given your job, you have to think that way. I mean about kidnapping and such."

Draven gave a half shrug in answer.

Nick shook his head. "I wouldn't like that much."

Sometimes neither do I, Draven thought. But right now there were more questions to ask.

"When was she last seen?"

"Last night," Nick said, "around one-thirty, when Ms. O'Conner went back after trying the grader. The girl was there then."

"Discovered gone when?"

"Around five, when she got up."

Early riser, Draven thought. Of course, on a construction project, most people were.

"What's been searched?"

"We've covered most of the site," Nick said. "Don't know where to go from here."

"The beach," Draven said, not putting into words the ugly possibilities there.

"Okay."

"Higher ground, too. Sometimes people want to see what they can see."

"Yeah, good," Nick said, his mood clearly lightening now that there was a plan of sorts.

"Any vehicles missing?" Draven asked.

Nick looked startled. "Don't know, but I'll check. You think she'd take one of the pickups? She doesn't have a license yet. I don't think she's old enough."

"If she's the type who'd take a vehicle, no license wouldn't stop her."

"Good point," Nick said with a grimace. "I'll check for anything missing."

Draven nodded. "The inflatable," he said, referring to the gray Zodiac runabout they used for supply runs to the mainland. "Make sure it's still at the dock."

"Didn't think of that, either," Nick said, eyeing Draven with even more respect.

"Where is...Ms. O'Conner?"

"Went into town, to look."

Draven nodded. When the man had gone, he walked back to the construction trailer, thinking all the way. He'd been involved with missing persons before. Often, in fact. When the son of the Redstone Human Resources director had vanished, Josh hadn't hesitated to call up the troops. It was part of working for Redstone.

That one had ended happily, with the child being found safe, but others hadn't. Reeve Fox, one of his best agents, had been on a leave of absence for nearly a year because they hadn't found one in time. She'd found the body in pieces strewn across a garage floor, and simply hadn't been able to deal with the brutality of it.

Of course, he thought as he went up the steps into the trailer, he hadn't been asked to help with the missing girl. But Grace was part of Redstone, and Redstone took care of its own. Josh would expect—and accept—no less.

Grace disconnected her call and put her cell phone back in her purse. She'd contacted Nick to tell him to call off the search, that Marly had been found. Safe, thank heavens, although the sound part was questionable just now, after what she'd been told.

She continued on her way to pick up her wayward daughter. Moments later she arrived at the town center office she'd been in once before, a holdover from the colonial days when

Belize had been British Honduras. She went straight to the office of Mayor Colin Remington, who sometimes also seemed like a holdover from those days. He had been delighted that Redstone was coming to his little island. She couldn't blame him, Redstone was welcomed almost everywhere they went.

Now the mayor had tactfully excused himself so she could speak to the other man in the room, although at the moment she was speechless, unable to quite believe what she'd heard.

"She what?" she finally managed to say.

"I'm afraid it's true," the man in the wrinkled uniform said with apparent reluctance, gesturing at the spread of makeup, perfume, magazines and candy on the desk.

Grace was stunned, and just stared at the man for another long moment. Thin, bowed, very tanned legs emerged from the khaki-colored shorts that were a concession to the tropical climate. Above the left breast pocket of the matching shirt there was a small brass tag, slightly crooked, that proclaimed him M. Espinoza.

Espinoza cleared his throat and said, "I'm sure it's just a misunderstanding, that she meant to pay."

Grace wheeled around and looked at her daughter. "You stole all this?"

The girl glared back at her. "What of it? They weren't worth buying. They don't have any good stuff here in bumbleville."

Anger spiked through Grace, and she reined it in with an effort. "I have put up with your moods, your rudeness, your sullenness and your temper. I've put up with your self-involved, it's-all-about-me attitude. But I will *not* tolerate stealing, sneakiness and arrogance."

Marly's smirk vanished.

"There are some forms to be done," Officer Espinoza— or sergeant, apparently, judging by the three striped chevrons on his sleeves—said quickly, before the girl could respond.

"Fine," Grace said, and quickly sat down in the chair the man indicated. She wondered if she should sit on her hands before she could grab her child and shake her silly. She simply could not allow that attitude to continue. Her daughter might not like her right now, but she *would* respect her.

She just wasn't sure how to make that happen.

With a sigh she picked up the papers, wondering how they'd gotten to this state. They'd always been so close, Marly had always confided in her, but now—

When the door to the office opened, Grace looked up, expecting to see the mayor coming back, with the ever-present smile of a man happy to be living in paradise. Instead her breath jammed in her throat as John Draven walked in.

Nick must have told him, she thought. But why was he here?

Draven took over the room as surely as if he were a foot taller than his already solid six feet. Even Espinoza straightened up, looking at the newcomer warily, as if sensing something that told him this was a man to pay attention to.

Or be on guard around.

The words echoed in her head, and she didn't know why she'd thought them. She caught herself gaping, and quickly lowered her eyes. She wound up focusing on his feet, but couldn't seem to stop herself from scanning upward. He wore a pair of faded jeans over boots with what looked like a crepe sole. For skulking around, she supposed. The jeans were snug, but not tight, and tucked into them was a tan T-shirt with the sleeves ripped out, baring tanned, leanly muscled arms. His chest seemed impossibly broad to her beneath the knit fabric. The overall impression was one of leashed power, and she didn't think she was alone in that assessment; Espinoza was practically standing at attention now. Clearly she wasn't the only one being affected by the sheer power of John Draven's presence.

She flicked a glance at Marly, who looked more wary than anything as she frowned as if trying to figure out why Draven was here. And with her recently developed self-centeredness, how it was going to affect her.

Exactly my question, she thought as he spoke to Espinoza first.

"Sergeant," he said, holding out a hand that the man took rather gingerly. "I'm Redstone security. I'm hoping I can help with this situation."

She noted he was speaking genially, unlike the brisk, businesslike tone she usually heard from him. She also noted he didn't give his name. She knew Redstone security preferred a low profile, and could see the reasons for it, but she hadn't realized they even tried to keep their names quiet.

"Excellent!" Espinoza appeared vastly relieved to be able to hand this over to someone other than her; male chauvinism was apparently alive and well in this part of the world. And Draven obviously knew it.

"With your help, I'm sure we can wind this up and keep Miss O'Conner out of any further trouble."

"Mr. Ayuso, he is willing to not press charges if he gets his property back and I can assure him the child will be properly dealt with. Children, they need discipline."

"That they do," Draven said, almost cheerfully. "I needed it so much I joined the army."

Espinoza laughed. Grace was in no mood for all this male bonding, however fascinating she might find it under other circumstances. She flicked a glance at Marly, who looked both wary and disgusted, no doubt because she didn't like being referred to as a child.

"I've signed these," Grace said, inserting herself back into the process. To heck with male chauvinism, *she* was Marly's mother. "What else do I need to do?"

Espinoza seemed to ponder her question.

"I'm sure there will be some sort of appropriate punishment," Draven said, although he was still looking at Espinoza, not at her, or Marly. "It wouldn't be right to just let this slide."

Espinoza suddenly grinned, and she wondered what on earth Draven had done that she couldn't see. The sergeant nodded in almost fierce agreement.

"We could put her in our cell," he said, "but I confess, it's not a nice place. The local wildlife has no trouble getting in. You know, iguanas, boas, rhino beetles and the like."

Marly sucked in an audible breath at that.

Grace was fairly certain Espinoza was staging this for Marly's benefit. What part Draven was playing, she didn't know. But because it was working she kept silent, as if she were considering that cell.

Her daughter stared at her, looking astounded. "Mom?"

Grace steeled herself against the shock in her daughter's voice. "Any other options?" she asked after a moment.

"I suppose," Espinoza said thoughtfully, looking at her now, "we could consider house arrest." He lifted a grizzled brow at her. "You have a house?"

Her mouth quirked slightly. She quashed it; she didn't want Marly to think she found anything about this even slightly amusing. "It's on wheels, but yes."

"But you are a very busy woman," he said. "Who will make certain that she stays where she's supposed to?"

She guessed things like monitoring bracelets hadn't made their way out here yet. She grimaced inwardly; they likely hadn't been *needed* before. Until her recalcitrant daughter had arrived to disrupt their little paradise.

"Her father could be involved, perhaps?"

Grace stifled a bitter chuckle. "Not likely."

Marly made a tiny sound, one that tore at Grace's heart, and she didn't dare look at her daughter's face. She knew

what she would see there, and she couldn't bear it just now.
Not on top of everything else. And again she thought of a
special place in hell for heartless fathers like her ex-husband.

"She can be secured at our job site," Draven said.

Espinoza turned back to him. The man seemed very relieved to simply hand things over to Draven. She imagined
it was an effect he found very useful on occasion. She wasn't
sure she didn't feel just that way herself.

"You will be responsible for her?" Espinoza asked eagerly.

"No." Draven turned then, looking at Marly straight on.
When he spoke, his voice was frosty enough to cool even
Marly's temper. "She'll be responsible to me."

The girl's eyes widened. For a moment she simply stared
at the man towering over her. Then she looked at Grace.

"Mom!" She yelped it this time, a near-desperate tone in
her voice.

"If you wanted her help," he said, his voice softer but no
warmer, "you should have rethought the way you've been
treating her."

Grace stiffened. What did he know about it?

Marly started a retort, then stopped. Finally she just muttered, "I don't have to listen to you."

"Your decision. But actions have reactions. Decisions
have consequences. About time you learned."

He was back to his curt, concise sentences, and Grace
suddenly saw why he did it. In part, anyway. Marly had
opened her mouth to protest, but closed it again the moment
he spoke in that clipped tone. Once she was silent, he turned
back to the sergeant, who appeared fascinated by what was
happening. As, she confessed to herself, was she. She decided
then to just let this play out. Perhaps a new element added to
the mix might produce better results than she'd had so far.

"What else?" Draven asked Espinoza.

"Restitution to Mr. Ayuso, the store owner would be first."

"I'll take care of that right now," Grace said, reaching for her purse.

"No."

Draven's tone was sharp. Her hand stopped and her head snapped around, her gaze narrowing as she looked at him. "What?"

"Marly will pay it back herself."

"I don't have that kind of money," Marly yelped. "If I did I would've bought the stuff in the first place."

Draven just looked at the girl. "Would you have?"

Marly lowered her eyes, and Grace knew lack of money wasn't the reason for this. Her hand fell back to her side.

"You'll work for the money. We'll decide later what you'll do and how much you'll be paid. You'll bring the money to Mr. Ayuso yourself. In installments. Minimum of once a week."

"How'm I supposed to do that?"

"How did you get here today?"

"I walked." Realization widened Marly's eyes. "You can't expect me to *walk* here every week!"

"You did today."

Outrage made the girl sputter. Grace wasn't sure how she felt about it herself; it was one thing for her to be upset with her own daughter, and something else entirely for this man to be so hard-nosed with her. She was Marly's mother, she should have the final say. But he had the girl's attention, which was more than she'd been able to accomplish recently. And that had to be the bottom line, more than who did it. So she kept silent, hoping she wasn't making the wrong choice.

Things happened quickly after that. She signed some papers, trying not to let her eyes tear up as she realized that but for the kindness of a shop owner she'd met only once,

her daughter would have had a criminal record. Then she accepted a copy of the list of the stolen items, showing a total
cost that surprised her until she realized the prices no doubt
reflected the complications of getting products out here—
or the prices of the Nunez brothers, she amended wryly.

She also asked for and got the phone number for Mr.
Ayuso, although Espinoza reminded her that while cellular
service on the cay was good because of the new tower that
had been built, landline phone service was unreliable.

"Redstone will be upgrading that," Draven said.

Espinoza gave him a wry look. "That will be good for
your facility, but I doubt it will help Mr. Ayuso."

Draven smiled. Grace realized she'd never actually seen
him smile before. It was charming, and pure Redstone mu-
nificence. It also made her heart do that crazy leap again.

"I meant for the whole island."

Espinoza blinked. "The whole island?"

"New system, from the ground up. Underwater cable
from the mainland."

Espinoza's jaw dropped. "But why would you do that?"

"Because Redstone believes in improving the lives of
those who welcome us."

"The golden touch balanced by the golden rule," Grace
said, quoting the motto the media had hung on Josh Redstone
long ago. It had been mocking then, but over the years he'd
shown by undeniable example that it fit.

"St. Josh," Marly muttered.

Draven spun around to face her so quickly that Grace
jumped and Marly gasped.

"Not. Another. Word."

His voice had gone from cold to icy. Grace couldn't see
his expression, but if Marly's widened eyes and sudden pale-
ness were a reflection of it, she was probably better off.
Again she felt the urge to leap to her little girl's defense. But

she'd nearly snapped at her daughter herself for her words and tone when Josh Redstone had done nothing but help them.

Marly looked at her, eyes full of pleading and indignation. The pleading made her waver, but the indignation when she was so clearly in the wrong, here and in the whole situation, decided her. She'd let Draven play this out. Her tactics of patience and indulgence certainly hadn't been working.

"Let's go," she said.

Draven kept looking at the girl. "Perhaps she should walk back. Get used to it."

"No," Grace said. "I want her within my sight for the foreseeable future."

His gaze flicked to her then, and she thought she saw a glint of approval there.

"Good point," he acknowledged. "With who?"

Grace didn't miss the change in his voice. He was asking much more than a simple logistical question. She answered the unspoken query.

"You. You heard Sergeant Espinoza. You're in charge."

Marly made a tiny movement, but she kept her mouth shut. That alone gave Grace the strength to hold steady when her daughter looked at her as if she'd betrayed her.

"I will always, always love you," she said softly, "but right now you're not very likable."

Marly lowered her gaze, and Grace's stomach knotted.

By the time they got back to the site, Grace had worked herself into quite a state wondering if she had just made the biggest mistake of her daughter's life. But she soon had a distraction.

They'd been hit again.

Chapter 5

Grace walked out onto the pier, looking down into the crystalline water. Marly walked beside her, also watching. They stopped a few feet short of where Draven and Nick were in deep discussion. Although she was glad the girl had trailed along automatically to the site of all the activity, so that she could keep an eye on her, she didn't want her overhearing anything that might frighten her. So far she'd managed to keep her worries about the sabotage from the girl, passing it off as just local mischief, and she'd like to keep it that way as long as possible.

She peered into the water. It was hard to judge how far down the Zodiac was, but she knew it had to be at least twenty feet deep here where it had been slightly dredged, because a couple of the small cargo boats that had pulled in here drew at least seven or eight feet and had been able to dock at low tide.

She looked up to ask Nick what had happened. At that

moment a movement caught her eye and when she looked, coherent thought fled.

Draven had kicked off his boots and peeled off his shirt. She knew she was gaping at him, but couldn't stop herself. It took her a moment to get past the muscular, ribbed perfection of structure and notice the collection of scars that marked the tanned skin.

"Wow," Marly said, her first words since they'd left town. "He's buff, but, man, he's beat up."

"Yes," Grace agreed absently.

Since he wasn't even glancing their way she continued to stare as he walked to the edge of the pier at the spot where the Zodiac had been tied up. She'd never been so aware before of how a man was put together. Perhaps, she thought, because she'd never seen one put together so well before.

Stop it! she ordered herself. She couldn't believe she'd even thought that.

He dove into the water in a clean, controlled arc that barely sent up a splash.

"That'd win a dive meet," Marly said; apparently Draven was no longer—or wasn't yet—on her most-hated list.

He went straight down to the inflatable, his image oscillating along with the boat's as the water rippled. He swam around it, checked the outboard motor that was half buried in the soft bottom, touched the side tubes in several places. Once he even dug into the sandy seabed, to see the bottom of one of the tubes. Then he checked the mooring line, hand-over-handing the length of it until he reached the end.

"Damn, how long can that boy hold his breath anyway?"

Grace heard Nick's exclamation, which voiced what she'd just been wondering herself. But finally, with the bitter end of the mooring line still in his hand, he headed back up.

When he broke the surface, Grace expected to hear an explosive gasp for breath. Instead it seemed as if he were barely breathing hard. Without even a pause he tossed the rope up to Nick. As Draven slicked back his wet hair, Grace glanced toward the ladder that went from the water to the deck of the pier, some twenty feet behind them, where Draven would have to go to get out, or swim the hundred feet to the beach.

When she turned back, he was already on the pier.

Marly said a word Grace would normally have chastised her for. "Did you see that?"

"No, I didn't," she admitted, forgoing the motherly instruction for the moment.

"He came up out of that water like a dolphin, high enough to grab the edge of the pier. And just *pulled* himself up like it was nothing!"

"Stay here, please," she told her daughter, and headed off the instant protest with a simple glance toward Draven.

Great, she thought. *I finally find somebody who can control her, and it has to be him.*

She buried her emotions as she joined the others, and asked briskly, "What happened to it?"

"Very large, very sharp knife."

"Reparable?"

"More than it's worth," Draven said with a shake of his head.

The movement drew her eyes to the water streaming off the dark strands of hair and over that body that had taken her breath away. Up close the scars were even more prominent, a long, heavy, puckered mark across his belly, a round indentation that she recognized as probably a bullet hole and a thin one down his left arm that looked like the one on his face. She'd seen a worker sliced by a sharp blade once, and the scar had looked like that. A knife fight?

She shuddered, and with an effort yanked her unruly mind back to the matter at hand. "Did anyone see anything?"

Nick shook his head. "Not a thing."

"Probably came underwater," Draven said.

"So we don't know when, either," she said.

"No," Nick said. "We don't know how long it's been down there. Nobody even noticed it missing until he—" he gestured at Draven "—told me to check on it."

"You told him to check on the inflatable?" she asked.

He nodded, flicking a quick glance at Marly, telling Grace just what Draven had suspected, that her daughter might have taken the boat. The thought of what could have happened if she had, with her very limited experience with boats, made Grace's stomach churn. It could have been Marly's lifeless body he'd gone into the water for.

She suppressed a shudder. With a tactfulness that surprised her, he began to issue instructions to Nick, giving her a chance to recover her composure.

"Search the site for the weapon. Any wet clothes stashed. I'll head that way." He gestured up the beach.

Nick nodded. "Think maybe he went into the water up there?"

"Too visible the other way."

She saw what he meant; the brush was heavy there, providing lots of cover. To the south was mostly open sand, with the vegetation far enough back from the waterline to make it hard to get out there without being spotted.

Draven reached for his boots, started to pull one on, then obviously realized his still-wet feet were going to be a problem. He grabbed his T-shirt off the pier and used it to dry his feet. And only then did Grace see what had been covered by the shirt: a deadly looking handgun in a holster with a belt clip lay on the boards of the pier.

Even as she stared at it, he picked it up and clipped it on

the back of his wet jeans. She realized how long she must have been gaping by the fact that he'd gotten his boots back on and she hadn't even realized it.

She watched him head up the beach, walking as smoothly on the sand as on a paved road. She shouldn't have been surprised about the gun, she realized. Of course the head of Redstone Security would be armed. Probably at all times.

Probably the first time she'd ever seen him, her harsh angel had been carrying a gun.

Too bad there hadn't been anyone or anything to shoot, she thought. *Just an earthquake. A natural disaster.*

And a very personal one for her.

Draven saw the light still on in the construction trailer when he got back to the site just after 10:00 p.m. He'd found a spot north of the pier where the brush had looked trampled, but nothing else. After that, he'd gone into town and engaged in casual conversation with a few people, slipping in some low-key questions and getting some interesting answers. With some thinking to do, he headed back to the site.

He went up the steps and pushed the door open, not expecting anything untoward because the light was on at this hour, but his hand on the butt of the Glock nevertheless.

Grace was sitting at the desk she used, and it was her light that was on. She had some design drawings spread out in front of her, and something labeled Wind Study, but she wasn't looking at any of them. In the split second before she heard him and turned around, he'd seen her slumped shoulders and her head cradled in her hands.

A sudden, aching feeling flooded him. It was unfamiliar to him, and when he finally recognized it as the need to comfort, he was stunned.

"It will be all right." The words were out before he'd even realized they were coming.

"Marly will be," she said, obviously not realizing the momentousness of what had just happened. "She's a good kid at heart, she's just having a tough go right now."

"Teenager," he said succinctly, and was rewarded with a slightly wobbly smile.

"Yes, but with her it's more than just that." She jammed her fingers through her hair. It should have messed it up, he thought, but instead it just seemed to make it more sexily tousled.

Sexily?

His own startling thought ricocheted around in his mind, and he could almost feel it chewing its way through neurons long inactive.

Damn.

Hastily he spoke again, hoping her answer would give him time to reel in that unwanted, unwelcome and poorly timed thought.

"More?"

Grace sighed. "That bit about her father, in the mayor's office?"

"I heard."

"We went that route once. Marly was angry because I wouldn't let her...I forget, do something that her friends were doing. She said she wanted to go live with him, even though he hadn't even talked to her in months. I said, 'Fine, call him.' She did."

"He didn't want her," Draven said softly.

"No. And he told her so, very bluntly. She never told me exactly what he said, but it was something about why would he want to ruin his lovely new life by having a brat around." She sighed again. "I still feel guilty over that one."

That made no sense to him. "You?"

"I had a pretty good idea what he'd say. I should never

have let her ask him. I knew she'd be hurt. I guess I just got tired of her yelling about how much better her life would be if she lived with her father."

"Some fantasies need to be ended." He thought about the name he'd seen on the passport, the name he assumed was her father's. "You can't live in them."

She leaned back in her chair and looked up at him. She seemed to be studying him with a new intensity. "I expected you to say something simple like 'She'll get over it.'"

"She will."

She rolled the pen she held between her fingers. It seemed a nervous gesture in a woman who projected such calm.

"I never had the chance to thank you for your help today," she said finally.

"Not necessary."

Her mouth quirked. "You are the proverbial man of few words, aren't you?"

He lifted one shoulder in a half shrug.

"It bothers you?" He knew his brusqueness bothered some, was misinterpreted by others, but the people whose opinion mattered understood it was just his way.

"No," she said. "It's really rather efficient."

He blinked. That was a new one. Of all the comments, gibes and observations he'd ever gotten on the subject, there had never been one that was actually a compliment.

"Besides, I know you *can* speak in full sentences. I've heard you."

He smothered the beginnings of a smile. "Yes, ma'am. Even went to college."

"Now there are some term papers I'd like to read," she said, startling him once again.

"Tossed them," he said, the image of her reading that long-ago work rattling him in ways he didn't fully understand. "Profs and I were rarely on the same planet."

She grinned at that, and that he'd managed that warmed him far too much. "I can imagine."

He walked over to the corner of the trailer and pulled out his bedroll. She glanced at the small bundle, then at him, brows furrowed.

"You're sleeping here?" she asked.

He nodded. "It's easier."

"I'll finish up quickly, then."

"Don't rush." He pulled out the spare chair beside her desk, reversed it and sat, crossing his arms over the back. "Working late?"

"Just going over some things. I had to spend some time with the mayor this afternoon, showing him around, so I'm a little behind."

"On what?"

"Inventory, mostly. I need to be sure we have all the supplies and equipment we need, since without the inflatable there won't be any quick runs to the mainland, or over to San Pedro on Ambergris Cay. Frankly, Jorge Nunez charges too much to use that speedboat of his."

"Not a problem."

"What?"

"Josh is sending a replacement inflatable and motor, plus a backup."

"He is?" she asked.

"Should be here by tomorrow."

"Oh."

She was silent for a moment, and he wondered if she was bothered by being cut out of that transaction.

"Didn't mean to step on any toes. I was already on with him, so I asked."

She blinked. "What? Oh, no, I wasn't thinking about that. I should have asked myself, I guess. But I was feeling responsible for the thing being destroyed."

"Josh doesn't work that way."

"I know. But I still felt I should have stopped it somehow."

"You're not responsible for everything and everyone. Just getting this field built."

"And my daughter."

"Yes."

She seemed to hesitate, then spoke again, lowering her gaze as if she couldn't look at him when she asked her next question.

"Why did you help today?"

"You're Redstone."

"Yes. But Marly isn't. Why did you help her?"

"She'd argue that I didn't."

A smile flickered again, but she wouldn't be distracted. "Yes, she would. Why?"

Did she not remember? he wondered. Had the trauma wiped out the memory of what she'd wrung from him that day? Should he say something generic, to avoid reminding her of it? Should he lie by omission?

He gazed down into blue eyes he'd first seen looking up at him from a pile of devastation. They'd been full of pain and fear that day, but nothing could vanquish the fierce life he'd seen there. And he knew he couldn't lie, even by omission.

"I promised you."

Her eyes widened, her face paled and she dropped the pen onto her desk. "Oh, my God."

"You remember."

She sucked in an audible breath. "I remember everything about that day." Her gaze narrowed. "And I remember it exactly. I asked you to take care of my daughter when I…"

"Died." He said it bluntly.

"I was sure I was going to."

"I know."

"But I didn't."

"No."

"Thanks to you."

He grimaced. "At great cost to you."

She shook her head as if that were negligible.

"But I didn't die, so keeping that promise is unnecessary."

The twitch of his mouth got through that time.

"The fact that you did not die does not release me from that promise."

She blinked. "Wow. When you do the complete sentence thing, you don't mess around."

He wanted to grin, but was fairly certain it was inappropriate for the seriousness of the subject. "I understand that you don't like me, of all people, being responsible for your child. And I understand why you feel that way, after…what I did that day."

"That building was about to come down and you knew it. It *did* come down, barely two minutes after you pulled me out."

"Most of you," he said tightly.

"So that's it," she said, as if in sudden understanding.

"I should have found you sooner, would have had more time to get you out."

"You did what you could." Her eyes darkened. "I won't say that I don't have awful memories. Or that seeing you doesn't bring them all back."

Draven felt his stomach clench as she put what he'd known had to be true into words. But he appreciated her honesty.

"I'll stay out of your sight whenever possible."

"Fine. I'll manage, then."

He let out a breath he hadn't been aware of holding. He didn't understand, had never understood, why this one had gotten to him. He'd splinted bloody broken bones, picked debris out of an exposed brain, cut bullets out of living flesh. All in conditions as bad as or worse than the aftermath of an earthquake.

But it was this one that haunted him. It had been bloody, long and agonizing. And she'd stood it better than most. She'd lain there, trapped in that debris, and barely let out a moan.

Even while he was sawing off her foot with a field knife.

Chapter 6

Draven took a long pull on the cold beer, having to admit to himself that it somehow tasted better, sitting at this outdoor bar surrounded by tropical plants. He didn't drink much, and when he did it was usually in circumstances like this, where there was a greater goal to his drinking.

The bartender was making something for a local, a drink that seemed to consist mainly of several varieties of rum and a tiny splash of some thick red substance whose identity he didn't want to hazard a guess at. The man took it and wandered back to the table where his friends were gathered. Draven wondered if he'd be able to walk when he finished the thing.

This was the only tavern on the island, so eventually about half the population came through. He saw some that already looked familiar, including Mr. Ayuso from the store where Marly had started her criminal career.

"Quiet place," he said when the bartender came back.

"Come on Saturday nights," the man said, flashing a smile that showed two gold-trimmed teeth. The national flag proudly displayed behind the bar told Draven he was likely from bordering Guatemala, the country that still claimed Belize as its own.

Draven smiled back. "Sometimes quiet's nice."

The man nodded, and went back to drying the glasses he had lined up on the varnished surface.

"Saw your mayor out for a walk," Draven said.

"He likes to be seen," the bartender said neutrally.

Draven gave him a grin that told him he understood the subtext. "He was complaining about some guy he called *el mercader.*"

The man's hands stilled. "The merchant. Yes."

And people react just like that when you mention him, Draven thought.

"So," he said in a buddy-to-buddy tone he'd developed long ago, "is he really as bad a guy as Mayor Remington made out? A big drug dealer?"

The man glanced around, then stared at Draven for a moment, as if to assess how much it was safe to tell him.

"You are from the Redstone people?"

He nodded.

"They are doing good things here. My business will be much better."

"That's generally how it happens, yes."

The man went back to drying his glassware. "Let us just say that if a person in Belize City wants something…stronger than what I sell here, that person would likely go to *el mercader.*"

"I feel sorry for Sergeant Espinoza, then. The mayor seemed to be riding him pretty hard."

The man frowned for a moment at the idiom.

"Pushing him to do something," Draven clarified.

"Ah. Yes, it is true. But Miguel Espinoza, he is not a fool.

He does what he must, but he knows it could mean his life to go up against *el mercader* alone."

Or was he reluctant to push because he knew someone else was responsible? Draven wondered. *Perhaps even Espinoza himself? Being the law made a great cover.*

"Besides," the bartender added, "*el mercader,* he never does business here on the cay, where he lives."

"Does he live here in town?"

"Oh, no," the bartender said, clearly grateful for that fact. "He lives on the far end of the island, in what they call the lap of luxury, I think? In the house his father built. And his home, it is very well guarded.

"His father?"

The man nodded. "He is the son, you see, of the original *el mercader.* His father was even more feared. Very brutal. Some of us even thought the son might change the business to something…"

"Legitimate?"

"Yes. That's the word. He went away to school in the United States, and when he came back there were many arguments between he and his father. So we had hope. But it came to nothing."

Draven changed to inconsequential topics as he finished his beer, then tipped the man nicely but not so much as to make it seem as if he were paying for the information. He wanted it to appear as if he'd had only normal curiosity about the local drug dealer.

He walked back to the edge of the small town thoughtfully. Mayor Remington's theory was indeed the most logical, that *el mercader* was behind the sabotage at the airstrip site. Obviously anyone in his particular line of work wouldn't be happy about the coming of radar and flight plans, and the other equipment that comes with a modern airfield. It would make sense that he try to stop it.

Draven reached the edge of town, and continued on several more yards. Once out of sight of any buildings, he
glanced around to be certain no one was showing any interest in him. Then he pulled off his shirt and tucked it into the
back of his jeans, arranging it to cover the Glock.

Then he ran the two miles back to the site at a blistering
pace. When he got there, he added the length of the beach,
pushing himself even harder on the soft sand. He stopped at
last, jogged a bit to cool down. Then he peeled down to the
trunks he'd worn underneath his jeans and took a plunge in
the water, never getting too far from his clothes and the
weapon they covered, up on the beach. Feeling loose and
warmed up, he grabbed his clothes and headed back to the
site to track down his new charge.

"I'm tired," Marly whined.

"Hmm."

The girl tried again. "It's hot."

"Yes."

"I want to go swimming."

"When you're done."

"I can't finish this in one day!"

Marly's voice was escalating, and Grace had to smother
a chuckle as she watched from out of sight. She found
Draven's verbal style amusing, and as she'd said, efficient,
but it was driving the teenager crazy.

"Your choice," Draven answered, making it clear in those
two words that there would be the promised consequences.

Marly swore, a crude word Grace hated to hear coming
from her little girl's mouth. But before she could step forward to speak, Draven dealt with it neatly.

"That's another hour."

"That's not fair!"

"Life isn't."

The girl glared at him, then turned on her heel and stomped back the way she had come, toward a pile of native plants she'd obviously been assigned to sort. It was part of the price of building here, that the plan had to include returning the site to as natural a state as possible.

"You're being a little tough on her," Grace said as she came around the corner of the trailer.

Draven turned to look at her. "Yes," he agreed, surprising her. It took the wind right out of her sails.

"You don't think too tough?"

"She has options." He paused, then added, "You, too."

"What are my options?"

He gave her that half shrug she was coming to know. "She goes back."

"Back?" she asked, thinking he meant back home to the States. And then it hit her. "The police, you mean. That's no option."

"Better than the other."

"What other?"

"Give up. Let her keep on that path."

She winced. He nodded.

"It's long, twisted, evil and sometimes deadly."

Grace knew he was right, but it still stung. But the vision he painted with those stark words hurt so much more. She swallowed hard, sucked in some air and tried to keep her voice level.

"I've been trying for over a year to get through to her. Nothing I did worked. At least you have her attention."

He looked at her for a long, silent moment. Then he nodded. He started to turn away, apparently to go back to whatever he'd been doing when Marly had interrupted him to complain. And then he looked back at her, an odd expression on his face.

"She'll be all right," he said.

"Thank you," she said, wondering why he looked like saying it was painful.

Draven fingered the scar on his face as he stood in the dark, contemplating his sleeping quarters. He caught himself doing it, and yanked his hand away. Most of the time he forgot the scar was there, at least until somebody reminded him. Few people were tactless enough to do it in words, but their eyes gave them away. The widening in shock when they first looked at him was hard to miss.

He didn't know why he was aware of it now. But it had become more frequently lately, in his mind yet another sign that he was not the man he'd been.

I wish Josh would just let go, he thought.

But he knew better. Josh Redstone was careful about who he chose, but once you were in, he'd go to the wall for you.

Even if—especially if—you couldn't do it for yourself.

Which apparently he couldn't, he thought sourly, since he was standing here like an idiot pondering things that had no answers, something he normally didn't do much.

Which just proved yet again that, at least at this point, he wasn't normal.

Yanking his uncharacteristically unruly mind back to business, he contemplated his surroundings. And the standing orders from Josh; Redstone Security was not the police. *Thank goodness,* Draven thought; he knew a lot of cops, and nearly all of them felt handcuffed by the system they were trying to work within. So while they weren't limited in that way, Josh's policy was if they came across something criminal, they handed it over to the authorities.

Unless one of their own had been hurt. Then, for Josh, all bets were off.

But no one from Redstone had been hurt here. Yet, at

least. So Draven's job was to keep it that way, and secondarily to keep the job going. That obviously meant stopping the vandalism. Whether that process included finding out who was behind it and turning them in, or simply making it too risky for whomever it was to continue, was up to him.

Decision made, he went into the trailer to grab his bedroll, came back out and tossed it up on the roof of the trailer. He hoisted himself up after it, spread out the blankets, and stretched out on them. He left his boots on this time, thinking if something happened he'd have to jump in a hurry.

But he'd be able to hear better outside, and the spot gave him a better view all around. They didn't know when the Zodiac had been sunk, but the other strikes had come at night, so he would be on guard. At least this close to the equator he didn't have to wonder when sunrise was. The sunrise and sunset were nearly always somewhere between five-thirty and six-thirty.

He looked up at the tropical sky, felt the warm breeze on his skin and thought of the other places he'd spent nights like this. Places that were much more unpleasant, inherently much more dangerous.

His cell phone vibrated against his side, and he took it out. A glance at the screen told him it was Redstone headquarters. The timer also told him it was nearly midnight here, so nearly eleven back there. It seemed odd that there was only an hour difference in the time zones; this place seemed much farther away than that.

He flipped the phone open and answered.

"Draven."

"News?"

Ah. St. John. "Still only a few incidents. Minor, except for a Zodiac."

"I heard."

"News?" he asked in turn. Josh had once said listening to them talk was like listening to Morse code, only in English. He supposed that wasn't far wrong.

"Info checks out. The nickname's known in Belize, Guatemala, couple more. So far, research hasn't uncovered the real name."

The man known as *el mercader* was very careful, then, if the Redstone research team hadn't been able to dig that up. Very careful.

"They will. Eventually," Draven said. They always did. But he still wasn't convinced the man was their problem. It was just too predictable.

Things become predictable by happening frequently, he told himself, *so don't discount any possibilities.*

"Need anything?"

To not be here, Draven answered silently.

"Not for this," he said, and disconnected. If Josh had told St. John, or if, in that disconcerting way the man had, he simply knew about his resignation, then he'd understand the blunt answer. If not, then it didn't matter.

Something else Josh had said that morning when he'd tried to quit came back to him. He'd asked if Draven thought he would let his top man go without a fight.

"St. John might have something to say about that ranking," he'd said.

"St. John is nobody's man," Josh had replied. "If he walked out tomorrow I wouldn't be surprised. But you..."

And just like that, Josh had hit his most vulnerable point. He, and Redstone, had earned Draven's loyalty. And that was the real reason he'd let Josh revoke his leave.

Draven laid back down on the bedroll. He tried to think about the job at hand, but the end of that scene was jabbing at him. The stiff, formal way he'd said to Josh, "I can no longer do my job adequately."

Josh's mouth had twitched, and in the lazy drawl that fooled so many into thinking he was less brilliant than he was, he said, "I've got news for you, my friend. You've *never* done your job just 'adequately.'"

While the compliment, coming from this man, pleased him, it made it all the more impossible to explain why he had to quit.

He couldn't trust himself anymore.

He didn't sleep but dozed, waking regularly to look and listen. He'd always slept very lightly, and his years on the edge had only honed the habit to a fine edge, where the slightest thing out of the ordinary would bring him fully awake and alert. Occasionally there was the sound of some night creature moving, but his subconscious processed and categorized the sounds without truly waking him.

When it happened this time, it took him a moment to realize that it hadn't been a sound that had awakened him. He kept his eyes closed and listened, but heard nothing. He drew in a deep breath to hold it, so his own breathing wouldn't mask any slight sound. And it was then he got it; the faintest, merest tinge of a smell.

Propane.

He was up and moving in an instant. He dropped from the roof of the trailer to the ground and took off to the west in a low, swift run.

The only thing that used propane on the site was the power generator, and it was some distance away, tucked back behind some shrubbery to minimize the noise during the day while it ran to charge the batteries on all the self-contained housing units and motor homes, and power whatever else needed to be run. At night it automatically switched off in the interest of peaceful sleep for those staying on the site.

The propane smell got stronger as he got closer, until it was so strong he knew he was going to have to be careful.

The stuff could be lethal if you breathed in enough of it, but it would make you light-headed long before that. And he needed to be thinking clearly.

He was thankful for the breeze that had wafted the heavier-than-air gas up to him. He didn't want to think how ugly the explosion could be at the slightest spark. And if the leak hadn't been found before the timer tried to fire the engine in the morning, just the spark plug could do it.

He crouched down behind the bushes that masked the generator from the rest of the site. He listened, but still heard nothing. He slipped around the shrubbery and over to the big, metal housing-encased machine.

It took only a minute to find the problem. The line running to the generator from the five-hundred-gallon tank had been cut. With the valve still open, the gas was escaping at a steady rate.

In a moment he'd found the valve and turned it off to stop the flow. That done, he retreated, heading into the breeze for some clean air. Once he was sure he'd cleared out his lungs, he did a search of the surrounding area. He found some footprints, but had no way of knowing if they were from a suspect or one of their own. They were from bare feet, which might indicate a local, except that many of the crew took advantage of the mild weather to free their feet from heavy work boots or shoes when they were off shift for the day.

He also found a broken branch on one of the bushes. It looked fresh enough to have been done tonight. He continued in the direction suggested by the break, and found more of the bare footprints here and there until he reached the road. Whoever it was, they hadn't been in a hurry; the steps were evenly spaced and at a comfortable walking distance. Closer together than his own strides, so likely the suspect was shorter, but there was no sign he'd been running or even walking fast.

Likely he parked a vehicle and walked in. A quick, silent slice and he was done. Back in the vehicle and gone. And smart enough—or lucky enough—not to pull the car or truck off onto the shoulder and leave tire tracks in the soft ground. Combined with the bare feet instead of recognizable shoe prints, he was leaning toward smart.

Which took this whole thing into a different ballpark.

He searched the area thoroughly, but found nothing else he could connect to the incident. He made his way back to the propane tank. He found and shut off the timer switch so it wouldn't try to turn the generator on before they got the line repaired. Then he turned his thoughts to what to do next.

He could simply sit here and wait for the breeze to dissipate the remaining fumes.

And hope like hell nobody had the need for a midnight cigarette, he thought.

Or that nobody turned on an electrical switch anywhere near a buildup of the heavy gas. Or started a vehicle. Or any one of the numerous things that could spell disaster in the presence of propane vapor. With the moisture here in the tropical air static electricity thankfully wasn't likely, so simple movement shouldn't be a problem.

But if something did go, an explosion could follow the gas trail back to the source, and if that big tank went up it would leave a crater the size of a large asteroid hit, and they'd all probably be buried in it one way or another.

The other option was waking everybody up to warn them. Of course, if he did that, their first instinct would be to turn on a light. And while the chances were slim the buildup was heavy enough that far away for that to cause an explosion, he couldn't say there was no chance at all. He couldn't even go around and disconnect the battery power for each rig, for fear of causing an arc.

He could just check for any low pockets where the gas might have accumulated. But he wasn't sure how sensitive his nose was, if he would still be able to smell well enough after taking in so much of the vapor. But it was better than doing nothing, he thought.

He'd start with Grace's motor home. He told himself it was only logical that he start there because it was the closest.

By the time he got back to the site, he almost had himself convinced.

Chapter 7

Grace tried to slow her racing heart with deep breaths. She listened for a repeat of the sound that had awakened her. She heard nothing, but knew something had awakened her.

Marly again?

She reached for her crutch, got up and went to the doorway to peer into the other room. Her daughter was facedown on the foldaway bed, snoring softly, no doubt exhausted from the work she'd done today. It was a new experience for the girl, working that hard physically, and Grace couldn't help thinking it would do her good.

But that didn't tell her what she'd heard.

She crept past Marly and unlocked the front door of the motor home. She grabbed the flashlight she always kept handy, thinking the heavy, metal tube would serve as a weapon if necessary. It wasn't until she'd eased the door open that she remembered the inflatable, and realized a flashlight wouldn't be much defense against the kind of knife that had sunk it.

She was considering retreating and locking both her and
Marly safely inside when she caught the faintest whiff of
something on the air. She'd been on enough sites that used
generated power to recognize it quickly.

Propane.

Fear spiked through her. She'd once seen a tanker carrying the fuel explode after a collision, and it was not a thing
she ever wanted to see again. The resultant fire had literally
burned through the asphalt roadway, and left the truck itself
a melted pile of unrecognizable metal.

She had no choice now, she had to find out why she was
smelling it all the way over here. She pulled the door open
and went quickly down the two metal steps.

And nearly screamed when a huge, dark figure suddenly
loomed up in front of her.

"What are you doing?"

Draven. It was Draven.

She repeated the knowledge to her once-again hammering heart, but it didn't seem to be listening. She had to gulp
for air before she could answer.

"Testing my heart rate, apparently," she snapped, straining to keep her voice low to avoid waking Marly.

"Sorry."

She decided to drop it there; she supposed skulking
around in the dark was part of his job, after all.

"I smelled propane," she said.

He nodded. "Line's been cut."

She let out a compressed, disgusted breath. She'd been
hoping it was some sort of malfunction or normal kind of
leak. "You shut the valve?"

"Yes."

"Another big knife?"

"More likely the same one."

"In the same hands?" She knew he couldn't be sure, since

no one had yet been seen, but she wanted his gut feeling. She suspected it was rather finely tuned by now.

"If I had to guess, yes," he said, confirming her own thoughts.

She turned her head and took a deep breath, then turned the other way and did the same.

"It'll be clear shortly," he said. "Stuff lingers."

"Are we safe now?"

"Not enough left to be a problem without direct ignition, I don't think."

She nodded. "I'll have Chuck Carlson fix it in the morning. He's good with that stuff."

He nodded in turn, then gave her a quick look up and down. "I'll watch till it's clear. Go back to bed."

For the first time, she realized she was standing here in front of him in just the old T-shirt and boxer shorts she slept in. And the shirt was worn thin, which made it comfortable but didn't hide much.

"Oh. Yes. I will," she said, feeling as if she had suddenly developed a stammer.

He nodded, and turned to go. Then he stopped and looked back at her.

"Next time, Grace, stay put and call me. It's my job, not yours."

She flushed, but hoped he couldn't see it in the darkness. "I'm not used to having to call someone." *Or someone to call,* she added to herself.

"Get used to it," he said.

And then he was gone. Grace went back inside, intending to head back to bed. But her legs felt suddenly weak, and instead she sank down onto the passenger's chair at the front of the motor home and felt herself tremble.

"It's the stress," she whispered. "That's all."

And it just happened to get worse when he was around. Because of what she associated with him. That's all.

After a few minutes, she checked once more on Marly, and went back to bed.

The heavy equipment was fine, Nick told him in the morning.

The propane line was fixed and the entire system had been checked, Chuck Carlson said.

The new inflatables had arrived right on schedule just before noon, and Draven had gone back underwater to attach and activate the motion alarm he'd asked for, which had come along with a few other things in the shipment with the boats.

The first thing he heard when he pulled himself out of the water was a young voice from behind him advising, "You're a mess."

He slicked the water out of his hair before he turned around to see Marly studying him—or rather his scars—intently.

"You're late," he said.

"You didn't tell me a time."

"I said morning."

"It is," Marly protested.

Draven glanced at his diver's watch. It was one minute to noon. "You skate the edge, don't you?"

She gave him a mutinous look. "What edge?"

"The edge," he said, his tone ominous, "of my temper."

"Oh." She apparently decided to cut her losses and dropped it. "What happened to you?" she asked with the bluntness of youth, indicating his scars.

"Which time?"

Her mouth quirked, as if she wanted to smile but wouldn't allow herself. "All of them."

"Knife, gun, shark and bomb."

Her eyes widened and her eyebrows shot up. "Shark?"

"Shark," he confirmed.

"Which one?"

"Guess."

She looked him up and down, her gaze halting on the semicircle of marks on his right calf. "Your leg, right?"

"Right."

"Wow."

"Didn't think so at the time."

Again the smile threatened, a little more of it getting through this time.

So, there's hope, he thought.

The momentary softening didn't last. A moment later she had her arms crossed in front of her, and was glaring at him.

"What do I have to do today, Mr. Boss?"

He studied her for a moment. He looked past the bluster in her tone, and the challenge in her posture. He saw what hovered beneath the façade, saw it and knew it for what it was, because he'd seen it so often.

He'd planned on more manual labor to drive the point home, but he suddenly changed his mind.

"Help," he said.

"Who?"

"Me."

She blinked. Then, suspiciously, "Help you what?"

"Set some traps."

It worked. She looked interested despite herself. "Traps?"

He nodded. "Surveillance cameras. Alarms. Trip wires. Snares."

With each word her eyes widened more. "Me? You want me to help with that kind of stuff?"

"Problem?"

"No! Beats sorting weeds, that's for sure."

The smile broke through completely then. And her enthusiasm grew when she realized he'd seriously meant for her to help, not just hold things for him. He used her to test the field of view for the cameras around the perimeter of the site. When she asked why no wires, he explained about the transmitters Ian had developed, and that all the images would be recorded back in the trailer.

"Taped?"

He shook his head. "Digital. New system." He gave her a sideways look. "Developed by the same guy who did your mother's foot."

The girl frowned. She was still angry with her mother, it seemed. He was very glad he didn't have to deal with that teenage moodiness. It was tough enough handling the little contact he was having.

Once the cameras were in place and turned on, he started out on the more primitive stuff.

"A trip wire? You mean like people trip over?"

"Yes. And they pull one end out of a box with an alarm."

"And that sets it off?"

He nodded. "And in this case, does a little extra."

"Extra?"

"Heard of a dye pack? In a bank robbery?"

"You mean the thing they put with the money that sprays the robber?"

"Exactly."

She looked at the little box they were setting up. "You mean these have those?"

"They do."

The smile became a grin. "Cool! What color?"

He blinked. Looked down at the alarm box.

"How are we gonna know what color to look for?" Marly asked with a touch of impatience.

"Good point," he muttered, and picked up the packet to read it. "Purple."

"Hey, my favorite color!"

"Congratulations. You can pass the word."

"Really? You mean to the crew?"

He nodded.

"Cool," she said again. He wondered what two "cools" in less than a minute were worth in teenage coin. "So what do I tell them? Watch for any purple people?"

He couldn't stop the corner of his mouth from twitching. "Pretty much."

"And report to you if they see any?"

He nodded. "No matter what their explanation is."

"Okay. What's next?"

"Lasers," he said.

She seemed to have given up trying not to grin. "Co—"

Draven held up a hand to cut her off. "Cool," he said.

"Yeah," she said, the grin getting even wider.

She helped him sight the laser beam projectors and the receivers, something he could have done by himself but it would have taken twice as long.

"So do they have those red beams like you see in the movies? And if you break the beam, it's set off?"

"No, and yes."

Her brow furrowed. "No red beams?" She sounded disappointed.

"Not visible. Defeats the purpose."

"I guess it would," she said, although she still sounded let down.

When they were done with the lasers, she stood back and looked at where they'd put them.

"A lot of people walk through here all the time. Aren't they going to go off all the time?"

"Only on at night, like the inner set of cameras. But, yes, I'll be jumping at false alarms a lot."

"Then why do it?"

"Only takes one real one."

"I guess," she said, but she looked doubtful, as if running to false alarms wasn't the idea she'd had of his job.

When they were done there, she helped him carry the camera monitors into the trailer.

"Why four?" she asked as they lined them up on a counter at the back of the trailer. "We put up sixteen cameras."

"Four zones," he said. "Perimeter, beach, two in the actual construction area."

"The ones that will be off at night? 'Cause everybody's always walking around?"

He nodded.

"Four cameras in each zone?" she asked.

He nodded again as he started to hook up the first monitor.

"Then…each screen is divided into four pictures? Or do they rotate?"

He stopped and looked at her. "Divided. Know why?"

She thought a moment. "So you can always see all the cameras?"

"Exactly."

He gave her a nod of approval. This time her smile wasn't one of amusement, it was one of pleasure.

She watched closely as he connected the first and second monitors. When he started on the third, she turned the fourth so she could see the back. She seemed to be poking at the wires, and then he realized she was trying to wire it. He opened his mouth to stop her, but then stopped himself. She'd done fine on the other stuff, she was obviously bright, so he let her continue.

She was still fiddling with it when he finished, but he said nothing. He saw her glancing at the others, as if to confirm she'd done hers the same way. Then she stepped back and looked at him, silently inviting him to look.

He didn't.

"Let's fire them up," he said.

She stared at him. "Aren't you even going to look?"

He met her gaze. "Do it right?"

"I think so."

"All right, then."

The girl's jaw literally dropped. He'd trained enough new agents over the years, and enough ranger candidates in the army, to recognize he'd found a key here.

And when they turned on the monitors and they all worked, Draven gripped her shoulder for a moment and said, "Good job."

She smiled up at him. He felt how thin her young shoulder was under his hand. So fragile. And for the first time in his life, he thought he understood a little bit about parents who would do anything to protect their child.

They had a morning of peace. No more incidents, the grading had actually started, and Draven had time to enjoy watching Grace in her element. He'd done all he could do for now, with the cameras and other gear now installed and working. He knew that, but he was still wound up. He wasn't sure why, but he knew better than to deny the feeling. He'd learned early on that when his gut started screaming, it was usually about something his head hadn't figured out yet.

So, figure it out, he ordered himself.

He walked down toward the water. Since they faced west here, he could see the sun on its downward arc, and the water was reflecting the golden light. It would get darker, more orange as it continued the plunge. He dropped down on the sand, drew up his knees and rested his crossed arms on them.

He stared at the incoming surf. It wasn't big here, the reef took care of that. But the rhythm was the same, the sound as soothing as everywhere on the water. But it wasn't soothing him. It was doing nothing to ease the edginess he was feeling.

He heard faint sounds behind him and glanced over his shoulder. With an inward sigh he saw something approaching guaranteed to only increase his tension.

Grace.

She was wearing a pair of loose, almost flowing pants and a short, sleeveless sweater, both in a shade of blue that nearly matched the distant stretches of the sea. The outfit seemed to suit the location; she looked cool and tropical at the same time.

She had an almost bemused expression on her face as she came to a halt beside him.

"Do you mind?" she asked, gesturing toward the empty sand beside him.

He did, but he couldn't say so. Besides, he knew she wouldn't voluntarily seek him out unless there was something she needed to say. So instead he nodded, and she sat beside him. Smoothly, he noticed. She went down on the knee of her intact leg first, then went the rest of the way. She'd obviously figured out ways to do most things smoothly.

The breeze caught a gleaming strand of her dark hair, and she reached up to push it out of her eyes.

"You cut it." Yet another lapse, he thought. He didn't usually voice such things, merely observed and filed away.

"The prosthesis takes time in the morning. Something had to go."

He just looked at her while he processed that unexpected bit of information. He wondered if she realized what that simple act said about her. That she was practical, yes, but also that she was adaptable, flexible, willing and able to make the best of a difficult situation.

He wondered if she'd realized how good that haircut would look before she'd seen it.

"Suits you."

"I like it," she said. "It's easier, cooler and my hair's healthier."

And it makes your nape the sexiest thing on the planet.

He jerked his head back toward the water, as his thoughts careened out of control again. He didn't want her to see the sudden rise of heat reflected in his eyes. He wasn't sure he could hide it; it had been so long since he'd had to try.

And another sign, he thought. He who had the poker face that was second only to St. John, had lost that as well. He wasn't getting better. He was getting worse. True, he wasn't really on the promised leave, but this wasn't exactly a high-stress case.

"If I'm bothering you," she began.

Oh, you are, he muttered to himself. "No," he said.

"You looked deep in thought."

"Was. I'm too edgy. Feel like I overlooked something."

"I doubt that."

He gave the half shrug. "Trying to figure out what they'll try next."

She seemed to ponder that. "What would you do?"

"What?"

"You're the best at this. What would you do if you were on the other side?"

He drew back slightly. In fact, he often did just that, but he hadn't expected her to come up with it.

She mimicked his one-shouldered shrug. "It just seemed logical that by now you'd know how they think."

"You're right."

For a few minutes they sat in silence. It should have been comfortable, in this beautiful setting, but he felt as tightly wound as if he were heading into a fight against stacked odds. He didn't know, wasn't sure he wanted to know, if it was the situation or her presence that was making him feel this way. But the way he kept glancing at her, his own thoughts about her incredibly sexy nape rolling around in his head, told him which was more likely.

"Thank you," she said.

Yanked out of that particular reverie, he reassured himself that he hadn't really said that about her sexy neck aloud, so she couldn't be talking about that. It wasn't something she'd thank him for, anyway. Hardly.

He started to speak, then stopped, wondering when he'd started to feel everything she said needed an answer from him. With most people he simply let them talk until they got to the point, then answered if necessary, but with Grace he felt oddly compelled to respond to it all.

He compromised by staying silent but lifting an eyebrow at her in query.

"Marly. She's changed, especially the past two or three days. She's excited, enthused, maybe not cheerful but at least not sullen. And she's talking, even to me."

"Amazing."

Her mouth quirked before she added. "She's almost human again."

"Scared."

She drew back slightly. "What?"

"She's scared."

Grace frowned. "Of what?"

"Losing you."

Her eyes widened. "Losing me?"

"Almost did," he pointed out. "And she already knows her father doesn't want her."

"But she didn't lose me. And that's one of the reasons I brought her with me to this job, so she'd know it's normally not really dangerous."

"What shouldn't happen doesn't register when what did happen is taking up all the room."

Her gaze turned inward, as if she were searching for truth in his words. Probably wondering where he got off espousing theories about her child. Or any child.

Finally she gave a slow, thoughtful nod. Still, it was another moment before she spoke again. "But if she's afraid of that, then why is she pushing me away?"

He gave her the half shrug. "Trying not to need you so much, for when she does lose you."

She stared at him until he did something he rarely did; he dodged her steady gaze by turning his face back to the sea.

"For a guy who says he knows nothing about kids, you're awfully wise."

"Some things are universal."

"Like trying to avoid pain?"

"I've seen people who could withstand the worst kind of physical pain run like hell from the other kind. They don't want to be on either side of it, so they make sure nobody gets close enough to hurt or be hurt."

There was a long moment of silence, long enough to make him tense. When she spoke, in a soft, gentle voice, he knew he'd been right to be wary.

"Are you one of them?"

He drew in a breath. Made himself look at her. Made himself hold that steady gaze.

"Yes."

She didn't look surprised, only as if something she'd suspected had been confirmed. He supposed his reputation in this area preceded him almost as much as his reputation with Redstone Security. No one, but no one, got really close to John Draven.

He wondered why he'd admitted that to her. Why he had told her something that he normally wouldn't even talk about at all, to anyone. When he realized it was by way of a warning, his gut knotted. He could only hope she would heed the warning and keep her distance.

Because the longer he spent with her, the less certain he was that he could.

And then she startled him by asking one more question, one no one else had ever asked. Ever dared to ask.

"Do you like it that way?"

He was saved from having to answer that one.

A bone-shivering yell came from the direction of the construction site.

So much for peace.

Chapter 8

It was easy to spot the scene of the incident once they were back on the site. Most of the crew was clustered around the area where the building supplies for the very small, single gate terminal that would eventually be built were kept. As they got closer, they saw that there was a man on the ground, with Nick and two others kneeling beside him, and several others leaning over him.

Grace started to run, and on the soft ground he saw the first real evidence of her injury. He doubted she would welcome an offer of help, so he smothered the instinct. Once she got on more solid ground her stride evened out and she picked up speed.

When they got there they found Chuck, the man who'd fixed the propane line, lying on the ground amid a pile of cinder blocks. A couple of the men were still dragging the blocks off of him, so Draven had to assume he'd been at least partially buried under them. But he was conscious, talking to Nick, and recognized Grace when she knelt beside him.

"I'm okay," he said, but his face was pale and he winced when he sat up.

"I'll take him into the clinic in town," Nick said. "The doc there's a Brit. He'll check him out."

"Just get him out from under all this," she ordered, the sharpness of her voice the only outward sign of the strain Draven knew she had to be under.

His glance flicked to her. This was eerily reminiscent of the earthquake, and her own trauma of being trapped under building debris. It had to be sending hideous images racing through her head. Yet she stayed right there, her hand on the injured man's arm, assuring him he would be all right and that everything would be taken care of.

He'd always known she had physical courage. She wouldn't have come back the way she had if she didn't. But what she was doing right now showed serious mental courage, and he marveled at her strength.

He couldn't help thinking of their talk on the beach, when he'd as much as admitted he himself was an emotional coward. He felt even more of one now, witnessing this. True, in his case it was mostly habit and knowing that his work didn't make for stability for anyone involved with him, but he couldn't deny that not getting burned was a side benefit.

Reminding himself it was time to get back to work, he also knelt beside Chuck.

"What happened?" he asked.

"I saw the stack of cinder blocks leaning," he said. "One near the bottom had gotten pushed way out of line. Stupid, I tried to push it back and the whole thing came down."

"See anyone else around?"

"No."

"Anyone leaving?"

"No. Ouch," he said as, the last of the blocks cleared now,

Draven began to check for broken bones by pressing his ribs. "We were done for the day. I was heading to sign out."

Draven nodded and continued his inspection. He'd lost track of how many times he'd done this over the years, checked for injuries. Too often, he thought.

"Nothing obviously broken," he said.

"Except maybe that hard head," Nick joked.

"Yeah, yeah," the injured man said in exaggeratedly insulted tones. But Draven guessed that if he hadn't still had his hard hat on, they might be looking at something a lot worse than scrapes and bruises.

Draven stood up and nodded at Nick. "He's all yours."

One of the others had run to get a truck. There was a brief dispute while Chuck convinced Nick that he didn't need to lie down in the back, he could sit up just fine, then Draven watched as the crew helped get the injured man into a vehicle for transport to the small clinic in town. When Redstone was established, they'd provide an ambulance for the clinic, but for now they were on their own. He didn't think the man's condition would require anything they couldn't provide, or he would have called Redstone for an airlift.

Grace closed the door of the truck, reached in and patted Chuck's arm and told Nick to call as soon as they knew anything. Draven guessed she was not accompanying her crewman only because Nick was already going. She felt the same loyalty to them that they felt for her.

When the vehicle had pulled out and the crew began to return to what they'd been doing, Draven and Grace headed for the trailer. Grace needed to make a report to Redstone headquarters, and he wanted to check the video monitors.

"Do you think this was more of the same?" she asked.

"I don't know. This one was daytime. Not an obvious booby trap."

"Obvious?"

He nodded. "Whoever it is, wants us to know. So we'll know more is coming if we don't stop."

She stopped walking and turned to face him. "You mean they don't want to slow the project down, they want to shut it down?"

"That's my guess."

She let out a sigh. "So much for my clever idea."

"Idea?"

"I had myself half convinced this drug king or whoever it was just wanted time to move and after that things would calm down."

She gave him a sideways look, as if expecting him to call her a fool.

"Not a bad theory," he said. "But no sign of *el mercader* packing up the china."

"You've checked?"

He nodded. "Lot of money sunk into that compound of his. And he's worked at keeping his nose clean here."

"So he won't give it up easily."

"No. If it is him."

"You don't think it is?"

"Not convinced yet," he said, leaving it at that. They began to walk again.

"So, do you think this was an accident?"

"Could it have been?" he asked in turn.

She considered that, then reluctantly said, "Yes, it could have. We don't usually have accidents like that, but I can't say it doesn't ever happen."

"Reserve judgment on this, then."

She nodded as they reached the trailer and went up the stairs. To his surprise Marly was there, and when they stepped inside she whirled on them.

"Where have you been?" she yelped. "I've been waiting and waiting so I could tell you."

"Don't be rude," Grace began, but stopped when Draven held up his hand.

"Tell what?" he asked the girl.

After a triumphant glance at her mother, she looked at Draven and said, "I found something!"

"Found?"

She nodded excitedly. "I've been looking at the recordings, from the cameras."

"What did you see?"

"I'll show you!"

Eagerly she picked up a DVD case from the table that held the monitors. She seemed nearly giddy as she ran over to her mother's desk, sat and pushed the disc into the drive on the computer. The software started up automatically, and quickly a small image appeared on the screen. For a moment it was simply the camera view of the area where the accident had happened.

"This was the day we put the cameras in," she said. Then the picture flickered and steadied again.

"The block," Grace said.

Draven nodded. In the clip, the huge load of cinder blocks was clearly visible. As was the block Chuck had talked about, far out of line with the rest. Looking at it, it was easy to see how the entire thing had toppled.

"So you see, it was already crooked by the time we turned the recorders on. And I figure most of the guys would notice that, just like Mr. Carlson did, so he must have been the first to see it, so it couldn't have been that way long, maybe just since the night before."

She finally stopped, probably because she had to take a breath, Draven thought. When Marly realized both adults were staring at her, she didn't start up again. She stared back, waiting, her body wiredrawn with excitement.

"The propane," Grace whispered.

Draven nodded. "Same night."

"It could have been a diversion rather than an attack?"

"Both," Draven said.

"We'd better look around for anything else like that stack of blocks, then," Grace said. Then, to her daughter she continued, "That was great, honey. And you were clever, to figure that out."

The girl only shrugged.

Draven nodded in agreement with Grace's assessment. "Good job," he said.

At his words, the girl beamed. Grace shot him a sideways glance. The difference in reactions couldn't have been more blatant. He felt like telling the girl she was being beyond stupid, if she cared more about the opinion of some man she'd known all of a few days over her mother's. Especially when that man was him. And that mother was Grace.

He didn't dare look at Grace. He had a feeling this was the teenager trying to manipulate them, or at the least manipulate her mother, and he didn't want to play into her hands.

"Now you can get an early start on sorting the last of those plants in the morning."

She looked so crestfallen he wondered how any parent ever hung on to discipline.

"Oh, to be doing a nice, plain, gravel runway," Grace said rather glumly.

"You always say that," Nick said with a chuckle.

She smiled. He was right. And she also knew it was a sign of how much she'd relaxed that she'd slipped into the old habit.

And it was all thanks to Draven. The string of uneventful days had stretched into a week now, because of all he'd done. Chuck was back at work with a clean bill of health, no more accidents or sabotage incidents.

And a lot had been accomplished. Clearing, grading, leveling, it was all done. They were nearly at the point of putting down the first layer, the cement-treated base. Then would come the reinforced concrete layer, and finally a layer of extra-strength concrete made that way by a new additive the Redstone lab had come up with.

If it lived up to the advance billing, the runway should last twice as long as previous structures, with minimal cracking and half the maintenance, before it had to be resurfaced. And if it did that, the commercial applications for airports and roads were tremendous. They could save the public millions of dollars over the long term.

"Are you going into town for the mail?"

Grace turned to look at her daughter. Despite her changing attitude toward Draven, she still hadn't let go of her resentment toward her mother, as evidenced by the abruptness and impatient note in the question. And her body language; the crossed arms and the angle of the chin practically shouted that she hated even talking to her.

With an effort Grace kept her voice even. "I may. Later."

"Can't I just get a yes or no?"

At the waspish tone of her voice, Nick cleared his throat and muttered something about a delivery and excused himself. He didn't quite run, but Grace guessed it was a close thing.

"Congratulations, Miss Congeniality," Grace said. She'd tried, but she was tired of being singled out for her own child's scorn.

"Hey, it was just a question. I can't help it if he didn't like it."

Grace reined in her temper and bit back the retort that was on the edge of her tongue. "Aren't you supposed to be working?"

"I don't care. I've had it. The other day was fun, with the cameras and stuff, but now he wants me moving rocks."

So, her rapport with Draven was conditional. As long as she liked what was happening, she liked him.

"If you quit, you're going to have a hard time finishing paying back Mr. Ayuso."

She shrugged. "You can pay him. You were about to anyway, before *he* stopped you."

Grace went very still at the way she said it. "That was a fast turnaround. Just days ago Mr. Draven was your pal."

Marly snickered. "Is that what you call him?"

"No. It's what you should call him."

The shrug again. She was getting mightily tired of them, both this one and Draven's one-shoulder version.

"Whatever," the girl said. "He doesn't really like me. He doesn't like kids at all."

"He isn't comfortable," she corrected, "because he hasn't been around them."

"Right." The girl waved her hand, in a gesture indicating how little she cared. "So, when you get the mail, you can pay the shop guy."

Grace took a deep breath. Despite the fact that the change apparently hadn't lasted, there had been a change, which was more than she'd been able to accomplish on her own.

"No," she said. "No, I can't."

"What?"

"You heard me. You keep saying you're not a child anymore. Handling your own responsibilities is part of that."

"Fine!" Marly snapped. "Just fine. I should have known I couldn't count on you."

"To love you, protect you and be a parent, you can always count on me. To help you get off easy when you mess up, or be your buddy instead of your mother, no. I've tried that. And I don't like how it came out."

The girl muttered something under her breath, something Grace couldn't make out. She let it pass, deciding one battle at a time was all she could handle. But when her daughter turned on her heel and marched off in an obvious snit, she felt a wave of near exhaustion overtake her. Nothing wore her out like conflict with the child she loved so much, but sometimes wanted to send away until she turned eighteen.

Maybe she would go in and get the mail, she thought. It wasn't her job, but she enjoyed it so did it anyway. It had only been a couple of days since she'd been in to the small post office window in the back of the general store, but there likely were some things for the crew. Nick in particular had a loving wife who constantly sent him whatever she thought would feel like a bit of home to him.

She decided to go, hoping the drive might clear her head. She checked to see if anyone needed anything. Everyone except Draven, that is; she felt better if she simply avoided him altogether. It had been difficult to approach him on the beach. And not just because every time she saw him all those awful memories flooded back. It was also because this was a setting for love, for romance, and the very idea made her uncomfortable.

She took one of the pickup trucks that wasn't needed at the moment. When she started it, the radio came on to a Caribbean station out of Belize City. The music was upbeat and she left it on, thinking it might help lift her spirits. By the time she pulled out onto the main road, she was already feeling better.

Chapter 9

"Seen Grace?"

The man on the grader shook his head. "Not in the last hour or so."

Draven felt an odd sort of pressure building inside him. This was the third person he'd asked who hadn't seen Grace for too long for his comfort. He'd checked the trailer, and her motor home, and everywhere work was going on, all the places she would usually be. Nothing. It was out of character for her, and any change in routine right now made him edgy.

Not that she had to check in with him anytime she went somewhere. She'd left the site before, for this errand or that, and he hadn't known. But she'd not been gone this long before.

Nor, he thought suddenly, had it bothered him. Not like this, anyway. But right now her simply being out of sight was bothering him. And he wasn't sure why.

So, figure it out, he told himself. And his own thought reminded him of what else he needed to figure out, what Grace had said to him on the beach.

He set off to check the perimeter, as he did often during the day. He did his best thinking off by himself, and right now he had the feeling his best thinking was what he needed.

"I've told Sergeant Espinoza he must go after *el mercader,* but he has not done anything. I begin to wonder why," Mayor Remington said, wringing his hands.

"I'm sure you have," Grace said.

"I cannot tell you how upset I am, that this man is on my island to begin with, let alone that he is interfering with your work."

Interfering wasn't the word she'd use, not after that too-near miss with Chuck, but she didn't say so. It also wasn't "his" island; Redstone owned from the border of the airstrip site south. But again she said nothing. The man was obviously upset, and she didn't want to make it worse.

He had flagged her down as she was walking through the grocery store to the post office window at the back. He looked as if he'd been wadding up what hair he had, and his shirt was damp with sweat. Of course, why he would wear a rayon shirt in this climate was beyond her.

But she knew he was genuinely concerned, so when he asked she told him, yes, they'd had more incidents since he'd last heard, but nothing recent. Redstone Security, she told him, had taken care of that.

"You're certain? *El mercader* is very clever."

"Redstone Security is the best," she told him. *And Draven is the one who made it that way.* "I'm not worried any longer, so don't you worry."

She felt a little ridiculous, reassuring the mayor, but it was true. She felt the project was much safer now. Draven had seen to that.

"Good," he said. "This airstrip will be a good thing for my island."

"Redstone will be good for your island," she promised.

She managed to break free of him then, and continued back to pick up the mail. The clerk, a friendly woman named Yvette, greeted her cheerfully, and said, yes, they had some mail waiting. While the woman gathered it up Grace asked about her granddaughter, always guaranteed to bring on an excited stream of chatter and a display of the latest photographs. She responded enthusiastically, exclaimed appropriately, which wasn't difficult; the child was a little beauty with huge, dark eyes.

Coming had been a good idea, Grace decided as she walked back to the truck with the armful of mail. She felt much better now, just getting away for a while. Although she was a little concerned about Sergeant Espinoza after what the mayor had said. She'd have to mention it to Draven.

She got into the truck and set the mail beside her. She started the engine and quickly rolled down the windows to let the heat that had built escape. After she fastened her seat belt, she checked the box addressed to Nick before starting out, to make sure it was secure on the seat.

She smiled, wondering what his wife had sent this time. There were always magazines from home, which Nick handed off to his eager co-workers, usually some home baked cookies—he wasn't quite so generous with those—and a selection of miscellaneous things that often had more than one crew member sighing for home.

Funny, people came to this tropical place from far away, thought of it as paradise and were reluctant to leave. But her crew was homesick. It was different being here for work, she supposed. And being away from family always took a toll. She'd seen more than one marriage crumble under the strain of constant travel. Including her own.

Of course, that had been only one of the problems she and Russell had had. He hadn't liked her choice of careers, either. Although he never actually said it, she suspected he'd wished she was in a more traditionally feminine field. And he had continually sniped at Redstone, in the manner of a person trying to raise himself up by tearing down better people.

But the most critical problem had always been the simple fact that he no longer wanted to be a father. Or Marly's father, she amended, not that it made any difference. His indifference to the girl who tried so hard to win his approval, who was still trying even in the face of his total rejection, hurt Grace more than anything Russell could ever do to Grace herself.

She smothered a sigh; this was old, worn ground and there was no point in going over it again. With an odd little start she realized that this could be credited to Draven as well; since the sabotage had started she'd been too distracted by that to spare even a thought for her ex. Until now.

She pondered this as she drove back to the site. So much had changed since Draven had come here. Just like it had the first time he'd come into her life.

Sometimes she wondered just how accurately she remembered that day. She'd spent so much time trying not to, but some images seemed inescapable. And one of them was Draven's face when he'd told her what he was going to do. She hadn't realized until much later how unusual that was, for him to show any emotion at all.

He certainly didn't now, she thought. She could never be sure what he was really thinking. Not that it mattered, of course, but—

The truck backfired. The loud crack made her jump. That must have made her jerk the wheel, because the truck suddenly careened sideways.

No, not a backfire. A blowout. A tire.

She barely had time to realize it before, with a sickening

lurch, the truck began to roll. The slope wasn't steep, but it was enough. Her seat belt dug into her as the passenger side hit the ground. Side. Top. Other side.

And in that moment she remembered the lagoon at the bottom of the slope.

There was no sign of any disturbance along the perimeter, but Draven kept walking.

What would you do if you were on the other side? Grace had asked.

What would he do? If, say, this airstrip was being built by the drug lord, and his assignment was to stop it by whatever means necessary? And so far, attacks on the project hadn't worked? What would he do?

He stopped dead in his tracks. His stomach plummeted. He should have realized this long ago. It was the final vicious piece of evidence that proved he was past it, that he shouldn't be here at all. There was no excuse for this not occurring to him until now.

He knew exactly what he'd do next if he was that guy on the other side. He'd go after the one person whose removal would bring everything to a halt.

He'd go after Grace.

He headed back to the work site at a run, leaping shrubbery and fallen trees. The trailer was still empty, and there was no sign she'd been back here. He started looking for Nick. If anybody on the crew knew where she was, he should. Unfortunately he was also sometimes hard to find. Being a typical Redstone employee, he ran every piece of machinery there was, wherever and whenever it was needed and the regular operator wasn't available.

He was heading for the compactor he'd last seen Nick running when he caught a glimpse of Marly sitting beside the native plants she was supposed to have finished sorting so the replanting could start. He changed directions abruptly and headed that way.

"Where's your mother?" he asked when she looked up as he got within a few feet.

"I. D. K. and I. D. C."

Her tone was immediately recognizable as sarcastic, but it took him a split second to translate the verbal shorthand into "I don't know and I don't care." Exasperation at her shot through him.

"No time for your moods. Where is she?"

She looked startled by his words, or the fierceness of them. "How should I know? She's the one who keeps me on a leash, not the other way around."

Draven knelt down to get on her level, well knowing the effect his stare had on people when he wanted it to. And he wanted it to now.

"When you're being a bitch, you should be on a leash."

The girl's eyes widened and she drew back. And then she met his gaze and paled. She wasn't too young to see it, he thought, that thing in his eyes that made people far more dangerous than this girl quail. He supposed he shouldn't use it on a child, but this was too important. He'd use whatever he had to use.

He asked again, in a deadly quiet voice. "Where is she?"

"She…might have gone to get the mail. In town."

He stood, and turned to go without a word. Then he looked back, not sure why he felt the need to try again to get through to this child.

"While you're sitting there, maybe you should think hard about what your life would really be like without her."

He caught up with Nick. The man confirmed what Marly had said, that the last thing he'd heard under discussion was a trip to town for the mail.

"But that was well over an hour ago. If she went, she

should have been back by now." Unlike Marly, Nick was quick to pick up on Draven's growing tension. "What's wrong?" he demanded.

"Just my gut," Draven said.

"You think she's in trouble?"

Draven hesitated. He wasn't one for involving civilians in his work. But if Grace had been gone for an hour on an errand that should have taken fifteen minutes, there was only one answer to Nick's question. And it might take more than one person to logistically handle.

"Possible," he said.

Before he could say any more Nick was off the machine and pulling off his work gloves.

"Let's go," he said, and headed toward the area where the auxiliary vehicles were parked.

When they were in the last pickup truck, before he started the engine, Nick looked at Draven.

"You got some kind of weapon?"

"Yes."

Nick studied him for a moment, and Draven wondered if he'd deduced that was why he was driving, so that Draven could keep his hands free.

Nick left it at that, to Draven's relief, and they started to move.

If the cay had traffic cops they would surely have been after Nick on this run. Draven was glad; it saved him from having to ask the man to step on it.

"We see Yvette first?" Nick asked at the edge of town.

"Post office?"

"Such as it is," he answered.

"Look for the truck first, then there."

Nick nodded. They drove the main street, checked the few side streets, with no luck. Nick glanced at Draven, who nodded to indicate the post office was next.

Draven followed as Nick led the way through the small store that seemed to carry everything from produce to hammers. The woman behind the counter in the back smiled as they reached the window, and said hello to Nick.

"Hi, Yvette," the man said. "You seen Ms. O'Conner?"

"Grace? She was just here this afternoon."

"When?" Draven asked, only aware of the tension in his voice when he saw the woman frown.

"Just after lunch. Maybe…one?"

Damn, Draven thought. *Definitely over an hour ago.*

"Did she say where she was going?" Nick asked the woman.

"No. I thought she was going right back." She smiled at him. "She had picked up your package, and said she knew you'd be anxious to get it."

Nick at least remembered to thank the woman; Draven was already halfway to the door.

The size of Matola City was an advantage in this case; Draven took one side of the main street and instructed Nick to take the other. Within half an hour they'd hit every open business and service, only to come up empty. No one else seemed to have seen Grace.

"Now what?" Nick asked.

Draven felt a qualm as the man looked at him for the solution. He was used to this. It was who he was. Redstone people looked to him for answers to things like this. When the darker side of real life intruded into their world, it was John Draven they turned to for help. But in this instant, at this moment, he didn't know what to do.

Never in his adult life had he felt like this. In the service, or with Redstone. No matter what the situation, he'd always been able to *do*. Something.

It's finally happened, he thought. He'd shut down completely. Just as he'd feared. Just as he'd expected.

He'd just never expected it to be at a time when he desperately didn't want it to happen. That's what he'd been trying to avoid by quitting.

"What should we do?" Nick asked.

Draven's stomach clenched, the only response from a gut that was usually utterly reliable in coming up with strategy. Something. Anything.

If your gut's silent, use your head, he ordered himself. Draw on experience. He had enough of that. What would he normally do in this situation?

"Backtrack," he said. "Trace her route."

Nick nodded as if Draven had come up with the best possible plan. He trailed after Nick as he headed back to their vehicle, feeling as if he were doing it because he couldn't think of anything else to do.

Draven sat in the passenger seat, thinking he'd never felt so much like exactly that, a passenger. He was no longer the man in charge, no longer the go-to guy. He'd known it was coming. And perhaps he should have known that when it hit, it would be at the worst possible time. He should have—

"I think I see something."

He looked up as the truck slowed down.

"Over there," Nick said, pointing.

Draven looked. He saw what the man meant, the disturbance in the dirt at the edge of the road.

"Stop," he said.

Before the truck had stopped rolling he was out and heading for the place Nick had spotted.

Tire tracks. There were tire tracks on the shoulder. Tracks that showed every evidence of a skid. And just over the lip of the road he could see the tops of shrubs that had been bent, twisted, smashed.

His breath jammed in his throat. He had to force himself to take that last step to look down the slope. Force himself, because he knew what he was going to see at the bottom of the slope. And when he got there, he saw it.

The truck Grace had been driving.

Upside down.

Cab under water.

Draven heard a shout just before he hit the water. He ignored it. He was focused only on that upended truck, as he had been throughout his mad, crashing race down the slope. It didn't matter that logic told him it had happened too long ago. It didn't matter that logic told him if she was inside, she was dead. After all, she'd been written off before and had survived.

He was at the truck in seconds; the water wasn't deep, but it was deep enough to drown in. It was also murky. Unlike the water of the sea, the lagoon water was stationary enough for various plant organisms to flourish. He got to the cab. It had dug into the silty bottom a few inches. On some level his mind was registering that the silt had had time to settle, but he refused to let the significance of that in.

He grabbed the sill of the window and pulled himself down, trying not to stir up the bottom and cloud the waters. He knew the moment he got even with the portion left exposed that he'd never be able to get inside. He couldn't even be sure Grace could have gotten out.

He didn't want to look but knew he had to. He had to.

The cab was empty.

"Now you just hold on there," Nick said, grabbing Grace's arm and pulling her back from the water's edge. "That boy can hold his breath a mighty long time."

"But—"

"No sense in you going back in there, not when you're lucky to have gotten out."

"It's not that deep," she said. "If the truck hadn't rolled upside down, I would barely have gotten wet."

"Then you don't need to worry about him, do you?" Nick said, nodding toward the water.

Grace opened her mouth, stopped and frowned at him. "That was sneaky."

Nick grinned. "Yes, wasn't it? I— Ah, there he is."

Her head snapped around just in time to see Draven's head pop up, and hear him take in a gulp of air. The kind he hadn't needed diving to the sunken inflatable the other day. He hadn't been down that much longer, but obviously he'd used more of the air he'd stored in his lungs.

He got to where he could stand up in waist-deep water, lifting his arms to slick his dripping hair back and clear the salty water from his eyes. Grace stared at him, thinking all those wet T-shirt contests over the years had been held for the wrong gender. Her fingers curled into her palms.

And then he saw her.

He went very still. As usual his expression betrayed nothing, but she saw his chest rise sharply, then heard, even from where she stood, the long, soft exhalation.

"I shouted," she said, feeling a bit guilty that he'd plunged right past her and she hadn't realized what was happening until it was too late and he was already under. She supposed her reactions were still dulled from the shock.

He walked up out of the water and stopped before her. He seemed to hesitate, then reached out and gripped her shoulders. The heat of his hands made her feel suddenly chilled wherever he wasn't touching her.

"You're all right?"

She nodded. "I got out right away. I had the windows open, so all I had to do was find up."

He closed his eyes for a moment.

"It's not deep," she continued. "I could see sunlight."

He muttered something under his breath that she couldn't catch. He opened his eyes and slowly, as if it were a tremendous effort, released her. She tried not to protest the loss.

"Lucky," he said.

"Yes," she agreed. She glanced at Nick. "I was more upset about your package than anything."

"Good grief, girl," Nick said. "That doesn't matter. You're safe, that's what counts. What happened anyway?"

"A tire blew," she said.

Nick frowned. "A tire? Everything's got new rubber on it. I'm really careful in hot climates, you know that."

"Yes, I know. But I heard the pop when it went, and then the truck just careened sideways. I tried, but the shoulder wasn't wide enough for me to get it straightened out."

"Well, damn," Nick said. "When we get back, I'll check all the tires on the auxiliary vehicles, to make sure—"

"Don't bother."

They both turned to look at Draven.

"What?" Nick asked.

"The other tires are fine. The one that caused the crash was fine."

"But it blew," Grace explained again, wondering if perhaps he'd not heard her right, water in his ears or something. "I heard it."

"What you heard," he said grimly, "was a shot."

Chapter 10

"But I can't—"

"You can and will."

Draven spoke in that same grim tone he'd used when telling her the tire hadn't simply blown, when he'd realized someone had tried to hurt or even kill her. It reflected exactly how he felt, how he'd felt since the moment when he'd seen the truck upside down in the water.

She'd taken a shower to rinse off the residue from the lagoon. He'd liked that she hadn't worried about anything else, but had simply come out of the motor home's bathroom in a pair of cutoff jeans and a bright blue T-shirt, with her hair wet and slicked back, her face scrubbed clean... and sans the prosthetic. Clearly she wasn't bothered by him seeing her without it, but then, considering, why should she be?

They'd done a nice job cleaning up his mess, he thought. The end of her leg was tidy, and looked healthy. Even the scars weren't that noticeable now, merely pink instead of the angry red he'd last seen.

She was using a crutch, resulting in a hop-and-swing-type motion that was in stark contrast to the ease with which she used the artificial foot. He wondered if the prosthesis had been damaged. If it had been, they'd deal with it later. Redstone would ship out a new one if necessary.

"I can't just stay off the project!" she protested now.

"You'd rather stay off it by dying?"

She paled slightly, but her chin came up in stubborn determination. "We have a schedule to keep."

"You won't."

"What?"

"If you're not safe, there is no project."

Her brow furrowed. "What are you saying?"

"Safety of Redstone personnel is job one."

He wasn't exaggerating. Josh put nothing above the safety of his people. When the Redstone Bay resort project had been taken over by terrorists from a neighboring island, the entire security team had been sent in. When a Redstone bookkeeper's child had been kidnapped, it was Redstone Security who had effected the rescue. And he had personally gone after Redstone's own Harlan McClaren, the famous treasure hunter who had been the first to believe in and financially back Josh, when one of his famous expeditions had gone sour in Nicaragua.

Shutting a project down until it was safe again—or forever, if necessary—was hardly out of the realm of possibility for Josh.

"You stay off-site unless there's something both urgent and that can't be delegated or handled on the phone."

"According to who?" she asked, her tone suspicious.

"Me," he said bluntly. "Next. You go nowhere without me."

"Nowhere?"

"Nowhere."

"Please, sir," she said in a voice dripping with sarcasm, "may I go to the bathroom by myself, like a big girl?"

"Depends."

"On what? You?"

She was building up a good mad; he could feel it. It wasn't surprising, given her narrow escape. She'd proven before that when she was knocked down, she came up fighting. He'd once thought of her as a quiet sort, maybe even shy. But he realized now that his impression was wrong, that her quietness had to have been because she had focused all her energy and considerable drive on getting well fast. Because this woman was no shrinking violet, in any way. She was standing up to him now in a way few ever did.

He tried to keep his voice level but, uncharacteristically, some tension crept through as he ticked items off.

"I'm going to move your motor home."

"Why?"

"Higher ground. And more isolated."

"Isn't there safety in numbers?"

"Don't argue with me, Grace."

"I'm not arguing," she protested. "I'm asking a simple question."

He reined in his temper, something else he'd never had to worry about before.

"I want it situated so that I know anybody coming toward it is looking for you, not just wandering or lost or looking for someone else."

"And if they are?"

"I'll handle it."

"How?"

"My problem."

"No, it's—"

He cut her off, and continued to count off his instructions.

"You go nowhere without me. You go nowhere I haven't checked first. If I don't like it, anything about it, you don't go or I go in with you. I stay till you're done."

"Does that include my bedroom?" she asked sweetly.

Heat blasted through him, so fast and fierce he nearly wobbled on his feet.

"Don't tempt me," he muttered under his breath. And then, as his body clenched, he added silently, *Please, don't.*

She looked at him, the faintest spots of color flaring on her cheeks, and he realized she'd heard him. She looked at him, her eyes wide. She looked at him as if she didn't hate the idea of tempting him. As if it didn't repulse her.

He told himself it was shock, shock from her crash, shock that he would say such a thing. But the only one who seemed shocked was he himself; he never—ever—did things like this, not with a protectee. Which is what she had suddenly become.

He didn't know how to deal with this. It never happened to him. He felt many things for the people he protected or helped for Redstone; he even liked many of them.

But he'd never felt anything like this.

"Look," he said, his unaccustomed emotions making him resort to slow, complete sentences. "I wish it wasn't me. You'd be better off with somebody else, especially since I'm running at about half speed. But I'm what you've got."

Her brows furrowed again. "What's wrong?"

God, he couldn't believe how he was rattling on. *Cut to the chase,* he ordered himself.

"You've got to cooperate, Grace, because right now I'm all that's between whoever wants to shut this down and you. And Marly."

She gasped, and he knew she hadn't thought that far ahead, hadn't realized that if she was in danger, it was possible her daughter was, too. He knew he had to take advantage of that. He had to use any tool that would work.

"Whoever it is tried to kill or at least badly hurt you," he said softly.

"Maybe not me, specifically, maybe…"

Her voice trailed off as he looked steadily at her. It was natural to deny the possibility that someone actually had tried to murder you, but he didn't have time to work her through to acceptance right now.

"You, specifically," he said. "And if they're willing to do that, why would they stop short of using your daughter as leverage?"

"Who's going to use me as leverage?"

They both jerked around as Marly stepped into the motor home. The girl looked at Draven, and as if he'd asked, said, "I finished, okay? I came in to clean up."

He nodded, not knowing what else to do. Using Marly to scare Grace into cooperating was one thing, scaring the child was something else.

"What kind of leverage? What are you talking about?" Marly persisted. And then, belatedly, she seemed to realize her mother's state. "Why are you all wet? And your foot, you never take it off in the middle of the day."

Grace shot Draven a warning look he couldn't misinterpret. "I took a little dip, so I rinsed off the salt."

The girl frowned. "You don't do that, either. You never take off work to play."

Only then did she seem to notice Draven, too, was soaking wet. He hadn't taken the time to hit the shower in the hut set up for the crew; he'd been too focused on getting Grace to cooperate.

"And you," Marly said, "don't know *how* to play."

At that succinct assessment of them both, the girl muttered something that sounded like "Whatever," and turned her back on them both to walk toward the bathroom. Apparently forgetting about the leverage question. Judging from Grace's look of relief, that was a good thing. Right now, he'd take anything that made her happy, as long as it also made her cooperate.

"I'm going to be your shadow, Grace. You're going to have to live with it. It's the only way to keep you and your daughter safe."

There was a whoosh of air as the door of the bathroom was yanked open. "Safe?" Marly's voice was sharper, and they clearly weren't going to get off so easily this time.

Someone had told him once about the selective hearing of teenagers, that they heard only what you didn't want them to hear, but he'd never seen it in action before. He should have waited until the bathroom door was shut tight.

Feeling guilty that his lack of knowledge about kids had caused this, he tried to fix it, to go along with Grace's obvious desire to keep today's incident from her daughter.

"A precaution," he said.

Marly looked from her mother to him, then back to her mother again.

"You really think I'm stupid, don't you?"

Her voice was soft, not angry as it usually was. There was an undertone even Draven recognized as a young girl's pain, and would have even if he hadn't noticed the sudden glistening of the girl's eyes as tears brimmed.

Grace's eyes, he thought, and wondered what it must be like to look at another human being and see parts of yourself. He'd never thought about it before, but when he did now, all he could picture was a dark-haired boy with those same eyes. And that rattled him enough to keep him silent. Grace needed to deal with this anyway. And would do a much better job of it than he would.

"No, Marly, I don't think you're stupid at all," Grace finally said. "I know you're not. But I'm your mother. I'm supposed to protect you."

The girl stepped back into the room, her gaze now fastened on her mother's face.

"So there is something to protect me from," she said. She flicked a glance at Draven, but only for an instant. "And it has to do with you both being wet, doesn't it."

It wasn't a question. No, Marilyn O'Conner was hardly stupid. Draven waited. It was up to Grace now to decide what and how much to tell the girl.

"There's a chance," Grace began, "that these little incidents on the project aren't accidental."

"No kidding," Marly said sourly. "You think I didn't notice everybody being so jumpy? What's that got to do with you being all wet, and him, too?"

Something about her reaction and tone made Draven take the girl off his mental suspect list. Unless she'd gotten tangled up with somebody in the short time they'd been here, he didn't think she was connected.

Grace sighed. "I didn't get wet intentionally. The truck and I...ended up in the lagoon outside of town."

Marly blinked. "How did—" She stopped. Draven saw her figure it out, saw her face pale. "Somebody ran you off the road?"

Grace took in a deep breath. Draven could see she didn't want to tell her about the shot, but didn't know how else to explain.

"In a manner of speaking," Draven said. "She wasn't hurt, but we're going to be very careful from now on."

Marly looked at him. "Why are you talking funny?"

It was Draven's turn to blink.

"What?" He definitely wasn't used to the twists and turns of the teenage mind.

"You never talk like that. Like a regular person."

"Thanks," he said, his mouth twisting wryly.

Marly shrugged and let it go. "What do you mean, careful, and who's we?"

"Those present," Draven said.

"And?" Marly prompted for the answer to the first part of her question.

Draven glanced at Grace and waited. After a long moment, during which Marly looked from one to the other as if their silent stares were a tennis match, Grace finally let out an exasperated-sounding breath of resignation.

"Go ahead," she said. "Tell her."

Great, he thought, imagining the teenager's reaction to being told she was to be more restricted than before. And he wasn't stupid, either, he knew perfectly well this was Grace's way of letting her own aversion to this whole thing be known.

Get it over with, he told himself. And rattled off the same list of limitations and orders he'd given Grace.

The girl's eyes widened with every statement. And when he was done, to his surprise, all she said was a very quiet, almost meek, "Oh."

"Any questions?" he asked, still a bit startled at her non-reaction.

She shook her head.

"Comments?"

She met his gaze, with more steadiness than some grown men he'd encountered. "Just that I thought about what you said."

He'd said so much to her—uncharacteristically—that he had no idea what she was referring to.

"This afternoon," she clarified.

It hit him then. *Maybe you should think hard about what your life would really be like without her.*

Apparently she had been thinking, if this was her reaction instead of the expected explosion.

"Are you moving in here with us?" Marly asked him, sounding quite open to the idea. He quashed the images that flashed through his mind, and hedged a bit when he answered.

"You'll be seeing me a lot more."

"Where are you gonna sleep?"

It was all Draven could do not to look at Grace. The possibilities that Marly's words brought to mind were vivid and breath-stealing. And he couldn't seem to stop them.

"Outside," he managed to say. "Hear better."

Marly frowned. "Where?"

"On the roof," he said.

And again he didn't dare look at Grace, for fear she might have noticed how gravelly his voice had gone. But he was so focused on not looking at her that the additional words he'd been thinking slipped out aloud.

"For now."

For a third time he didn't dare look at Grace, but he heard her sudden intake of breath. She'd heard, all right. But Marly didn't seem to notice anything unusual. After a moment when she seemed to struggle to take it all in, she turned to face Draven.

"Were they really trying to hurt her?"

Truth, lie or half-truth? The options raced through his mind. But as he stood there, looking at Grace's eyes reproduced in her child's face, he knew there really was only one option.

He nodded.

The girl bit her lip until he could see it turn white where her teeth dug in. "Were they trying to kill her?"

"Maybe. Put her out of commission, most likely."

She absorbed this, pondered for a moment. Then words burst from her, almost explosively.

"Hasn't she been through enough?"

This time he did look at Grace, in time to see a near-startled expression cross her face at her daughter's words. Or at the intensity of them.

"Yes," he said. "She has. That's why we're doing this."

Marly thought about this, too, but not for long. Then she nodded. "All right."

She started toward the bathroom again, then came back and gave her mother a swift hug. Without another word she turned back and continued on her way. When the bathroom door finally closed behind her Draven let out a long, relieved breath.

"Don't know how you do it," he said under his breath.

"It's a challenge," Grace said as if he'd spoken normally, reminding him of the other muttering she'd heard. Those two words that had betrayed the lascivious road his thoughts had barreled down without warning.

He fought down the urge to explain, telling himself nothing he could say could change what she'd heard. Besides, he didn't know what the explanation was, and it didn't seem wise to make something up just now.

"I'm going to go dry my hair," Grace said.

He barely breathed until she was gone into the bedroom, closing the door behind her. Then he let out all the air in his lungs, grateful she'd let the subject drop, that she hadn't called him on his uncharacteristic and no doubt thoroughly unwelcome comment. If there was anyone she'd be less likely to want to share a bed with, he couldn't imagine who it would be.

Maybe her ex-husband, he thought wryly. But nobody else.

A hair-dryer started to hum noisily in the bedroom, joggling him out of his reverie. That had never happened before, either, this drifting off into crazy thoughts about things that he had never dwelt on before. Just another symptom, he told himself, wishing yet again that Josh would have simply let him quit when he'd wanted to instead of pushing until he'd agreed to the bargain that had landed him here. Here, with the one woman he had never been able to forget.

He made himself move, leaving the motor home and heading back over to the trailer. He picked up his bedroll, stuffed his things back in the duffel bag, already planning where he was going to move the motor home.

And wondering, on top of everything else, when he'd become such a coward.

Chapter 11

"That has to be finished by tomorrow. The paving has to start," Grace said into the phone, her voice a bit edgy as she paced.

Draven couldn't hear what was said on the other end of the call, but she was quickly apologetic. "Sorry, Nick. I'm just frustrated."

There was a pause while she listened again. From his seat at the small table, Draven glanced over at the sofa where Marly sat with the control for her video game player in her hands. Her hands were in constant motion, and the images danced across the television screen before her. She had on a headset for the sounds, ordered to do so by Grace so that she could work on the phone.

"I know it's for the best," Grace said into the receiver, "but I don't have to like it. Yes. Tonight's fine for a report." Then, with a grimace, "I'll be here."

She disconnected the call, but kept pacing the floor. She

tapped a finger against the phone receiver as she bit her lip and thought.

Draven yanked his gaze away; the last thing he needed was to watch her nibble on that soft, full lip. It only made him wonder what it would feel like to do it himself. And that idea did things to his gut that he couldn't explain.

After a couple further circuits of the floor, from kitchen to living area and back again, Grace finally tossed the phone down on the counter. It clattered and slid across the granite.

And then she turned on him.

"I hate this!"

"I know," he said quietly.

"How am I supposed to run this project long distance?"

"You're doing fine."

"Fine? Hardly. We're doing concrete, which is a lot different from just rolling out some asphalt. I need to inspect the final grading, check the status on the drainage system, oversee the relocating of the native vegetation, then I—"

He held up a hand, but she was on a roll and it took her a moment to stop.

"Never said you couldn't go out. Just not alone."

"Oh." She sounded a bit deflated, as if she'd been building up to an explosion and felt denied.

"Now?" he asked.

"Yes," she said. Then she glanced at Marly, who was intent on maneuvering some CGI character through a maze, and back at him.

"She'll have to come," he said.

"She'll love that," Grace muttered.

But to his surprise, the girl took the interruption of her play rather quietly. After a heavy sigh, she shut off the game console and the television, pulled on some thick-soled shoes Draven couldn't see how she walked in. Then she stood up, indicating she was ready.

Grace was looking at her daughter warily, as if still await-ing an explosion that hadn't been averted but merely delayed. Draven wondered what it was like to live that way, never knowing if, when or how the explosion would come, or what the trigger would be.

It sounded exhausting.

As they went about Grace's tasks, Draven shifted his mode. Through some strings Josh had pulled—there wasn't a businessman on the planet more respected than he was in law enforcement circles—the Redstone team had been through training given by several federal agencies, includ-ing the Secret Service presidential detail. They'd learned about bodyguarding from the best, and they put the knowl-edge to use on a regular basis. And they'd done well enough that the service had tried to recruit them, even knowing the likelihood of anyone leaving Redstone was slim.

He scanned the area constantly, close in first, then mid-ground, then the perimeter. Anything that moved got atten-tion until identified. If it shouldn't have moved, it got inspected, once turning up a sizable lizard, and once a howler monkey that proceeded to earn its name by chewing him out fiercely for disturbing it.

That at least got Marly to smile. But of course she decided immediately that she wanted it for a pet. Draven told her he wasn't about to catch it, he liked his fingers the way they were. He left it for her mother to talk her out of it; he wouldn't even know where to start. Although he guessed the first night the thing started howling at two in the morning she'd change her mind in a big hurry about its suitability for pethood.

As they crisscrossed the site and covered Grace's list, none of the crew commented on the new arrangements, or on his constant presence, and he wondered if Nick had put the word out. Not that it mattered, really. More eyes the better. It would only make a difference if the problem was inside, and he didn't think it was.

Of course, maybe he just didn't want to believe that, since they'd had so much of that lately. It was a rarity for somebody within Redstone to turn on them; any bad apples usually never made it in, or if they did, were quickly ferreted out.

By the end of the day, Draven realized he had underestimated Grace's stamina. She went from job to job relentlessly, rarely stopping for longer than a minute or two. She also clearly had a tremendous amount of information stored in that clever brain of hers; rarely did she have to consult the clipboard she held for data or dates.

When they got back to the motor home that evening, and Grace had gone to the shower, Draven sat watching Marly start up her video game once more. Watching her much more closely than was necessary, in an effort to keep his mind off of the sound of the shower, and the images the running water brought to his unruly mind.

Watching wasn't enough. Desperate for a stronger distraction, before Marly could turn the game on he asked, "Ever seen your mother at work before?"

"Paperwork, office stuff, yeah. But not like this."

"Pretty impressive."

"She's smart," the girl said with a shrug that said even smart people could be a pain as a parent.

She went back to her game. Draven heard the shower stop, and the door on the other side open as Grace went into the bedroom.

Wrapped in a towel? he wondered.

Naked?

His breath jammed in his throat and stayed there. When he finally remembered how to breathe it was all he could do not to gasp audibly.

Then Marly stopped in her installation and turned to look at him again. It took more effort than he could ever remember having to make to compose his expression. But he did it; the last thing he needed was this child-woman realizing he was sitting here heating up over erotic images of her mother.

"Is it that drug guy?" the girl asked.

He hesitated. Hesitated a moment too long, because Marly flared up at him.

"I'm sick of being treated like I'm a child! Do you think I don't know what really happened out there? That somebody *shot* at her?"

Uh-oh, he thought. "There was no need for you to know, it would only scare you more—"

"Don't *patronize* me! I'm not a baby."

"Never thought you were."

"I don't need to be protected from the truth. I expect that from my mother. She's always been that way, but you're supposed to be some real tough guy. You should be honest, too, but you're as bad as she is."

"Take a breath," he suggested when the tumble of words finally stopped.

She said a word he didn't think girls her age were supposed to know. Then she tossed her game controller on the couch and stomped toward the door.

"Marly," he said warningly.

She ignored him and yanked the door open.

"You're not going anywhere," he told her.

She said that same word again, this time in a physically impossible instruction about what he could do with himself. And started out the door.

He caught her before her foot even hit the first step. His arm around her waist, he swung her off her feet and back into the room. She yelled, and started to struggle. She kicked, and flailed her arms. Landed a couple of glancing blows he barely felt, a couple of solid ones that stung, although he never loosened his grip.

He dragged her back in and shut the door as she screamed at him to let her go.

"Marly!"

His head snapped around at the sound of Grace's wild yell as she came barreling through the bedroom door. She was wielding what looked like a heavy metal flashlight in one hand, clearly ready to use it as a weapon.

Draven froze in an odd sort of awe at the sight of her, all maternal fierceness as she flew to the rescue of her cub. Even Marly went still.

Grace skidded to a halt as she took in the scene. The towel, he thought, almost numbly. It was the towel. She was dressed from the waist down, but a blue towel was still wrapped around her upper body.

The arm holding the flashlight dropped. With the movement, the towel dropped, too. For an instant he caught a glimpse of the ripe, full curve of one breast, tipped with soft pink, before she grabbed the towel and pulled it back into place.

"What's going on?" she demanded.

My blood pressure's going through the roof, for one thing, he thought, listening to his pulse hammering in his ears. That image, that brief flash of feminine flesh, was burned into his memory. He had a feeling he'd be seeing it on an endless loop when he tried to sleep tonight.

This is insane, he thought. He'd seen breasts before. He'd seen them on strangers. On women he was involved with. He'd seen more than just breasts. But nothing had ever affected him the way that split-second glimpse of luscious curve had. Nothing.

"Will you let go *now?*" Marly demanded.

He shook his head as if to clear it, and released her. The girl staggered slightly as her feet hit the floor, righted herself, then spun to glare at him.

"Someone," Grace said, in a voice as grim as any he'd ever heard, "had better start explaining here. Fast."

Marly crossed her arms, still scowling at him, and obviously with no intention of talking. He would have laughed at himself, at his reluctance to face this furious woman, if he hadn't been so busy trying to figure out what to say to her.

"A disagreement about what she needs to know," he finally said. "Made her forget she doesn't go out alone."

Grace's gaze flicked from Draven to her daughter and back. "Need to know what?"

"The truth!" Marly snapped. "You should try it some time."

Grace blinked. "What are you talking about?"

"Nick told me what really happened at the lagoon."

Grace winced. "Oh."

"You didn't think I should know you'd been shot at?"

"I wasn't. It was the truck. The tire."

"Whatever. You could have been killed either way."

"I wasn't."

"So that makes it okay to lie to me?"

"I didn't exactly lie."

"Oh, yeah, like you'd buy that from me."

Draven felt a bit like a spectator at a Ping-Pong match. But he was glad that the girl's resentment had shifted to her mother. Not that he didn't feel sorry for Grace, bearing the brunt of it now, but she at least had practice at it. He had no idea how to handle teenage anger.

"You're right," Grace said. "I wouldn't buy that from you. I apologize."

"Yeah. Well. You should have told me the truth."

"I didn't want to scare you."

Marly glanced at Draven, who had begun to edge slowly backward, toward the door, thinking the last place he wanted to be was in the midst of this family discussion. Especially this female family.

"He said 'need to know,'" Marly said. "Did you ever stop to think that I might *need* to know? What if I saw something, or someone, but I didn't know to say anything?"

She had a point, Draven thought, and he could see Grace realized it, too. Marly glanced at him again before continuing her argument.

"He said 'leverage,' too, that somebody might try to use me on you. What if somebody did, because I didn't know to avoid them, or get away?"

Grace sighed. Her mouth quirked. She looked at Draven. "Don't you just hate it when they're right?"

"Irritating," he acknowledged, barely keeping his mouth from quirking.

"Score!" Marly yelped, as delighted now as she'd been angry before. Draven shook his head, wondering how Grace kept up.

"You two work this out. I'm going to make a call."

He left them there, Grace telling her daughter the whole— well, most, he supposed—of the real story. He stepped outside, relieved to be out of there.

At least, he thought he was relieved. But he had to admit that watching them, and seeing how Marly had reasoned out and won her case, had been oddly pleasing.

As for that glimpse of soft, lush breast, pleasing wasn't the word. It was a very long way past simply pleasing. He was still aching from his response to it, and had the feeling he would be for a long time.

It was going to be a very, very long night.

Chapter 12

Grace rolled over onto her left side. Not that it was going to help, she was sure. Right side or left, back or stomach, covers or none, nothing seemed to matter.

She pounded her pillow into a more comfortable shape, not that she really thought that was going to help, either. She'd gotten close to sleep, repeatedly, so close she could nearly taste the blissful oblivion, but she always jolted wide-awake again before she'd floated away.

Sleep was clearly not on the agenda tonight.

With a sigh she rolled onto her back. She yawned, then listened for any sound from above her, but heard nothing. She'd heard nothing since Draven had climbed up to the roof, reminding her that the sundeck section where he was sleeping was right over her head.

It had to be the stress. Stress over the project, which was normal, stress over the sabotage, which was not. And stress over becoming a target, which most certainly was not. That had to explain why she was in such an uproar.

But it didn't explain why she was so vividly aware of the presence of John Draven, mere feet away, the only thing between them the relatively insubstantial barrier of the motor home's roof.

She felt herself blush in the darkness of the bedroom. She was sure he'd been looking at her when the towel had slipped. She had no idea how much he'd seen, but that he had seen at least a flash, she was sure. And that was certainly more than she was comfortable with.

But she'd been so terrified when she'd heard Marly's scream that she'd reacted instantly and instinctively. Covering up had been the very last thought in her head. Not when her daughter was in danger. She had simply grabbed the nearest thing that could possibly be used as a weapon and run.

She wasn't sure now what she'd thought when she'd raced into the other room of the motor home and seen Draven hanging on to her daughter as she flailed wildly. She remembered noticing that he was doing it easily, despite how strong she knew Marly could be when she was going at full tilt, as she obviously was.

But whatever she'd thought, it hadn't been that her daughter was in any danger. Not from Draven. And the certainty she had about that had surprised her.

With a sigh of surrender she sat up and turned on the bedside light. She'd read her book for a while, she thought. If it didn't hold her interest, then maybe it would put her to sleep.

And maybe it would keep her mind off of the man who was now just above her.

Probably sleeping soundly, she thought wryly.

She picked up the novel she'd purchased in the general store a few days ago. She was so exhausted she couldn't even recall exactly what it was about, so she read the blurb on the back of the thriller again. She wondered if it would live up to the enthusiastic billing.

Generally she was too tired at the end of the day to read more than a page or two, but tonight being tired didn't seem to have much to do with it. With that perversity her mind sometimes had, she couldn't keep her eyes open to read, yet when she again gave up and turned out the light, she still couldn't fall asleep.

She felt an odd sort of hum that seemed to fuzz her head from the ears up, telling her she'd gone beyond mere weariness. Not for the first time she wished the brain came with an off switch.

With your luck, you'd never get it turned back on, she told herself, and flopped back onto her back once more.

She straightened the tangled sheets yet again, then stretched her body as if that would help. She was disconcerted, as she often was, by her brain telling her it was feeling the texture of the sheet against her right foot. It was as real as if the foot were still there, and nothing could convince her brain it wasn't. The therapists and doctors had told her that might never go away, and she wondered how long it would take to stop startling her. She wondered—

A loud, electronic shriek shattered the quiet.

Grace nearly echoed the shriek as she sat bolt upright. Even as she did, she heard a faint scraping sound from the roof, then something hitting the ground beside her window. Draven, she thought, already moving.

"Mom?"

Marly's voice was sleepy and tentative from the other room. Grace rolled out of bed and grabbed her crutch to save time. It could be a weapon, too, if she needed one, she thought as she hurried into the other room.

"I don't know what it was, honey, but I'll find out," she

reassured the girl, who was sitting on the edge of the sofa bed rubbing at her eyes.

"I know what it is," Marly said, then yawned.

Grace stopped in her tracks. "You do?"

The girl nodded. "'S one of those trip wire things we put up. They're alarmed."

"Trip wire?"

Marly explained about the security devices Draven had arranged, sounding rather proud of her part in the setup. Grace hadn't known about that part of it; when Marly had told her they'd set up alarms, she'd not thought of anything that simple.

"I wonder what set it off," Marly mumbled, clearly still groggy with sleep.

"I don't know."

The teenager stood up, gawky and long legged in her rock band T-shirt. "Should we go look?"

Grace nearly gasped aloud at the very idea of her little girl setting out into the night in this foreign place to check out what had set off an alarm of any kind. She wasn't real thrilled about the idea of doing it herself, although she would if she had to.

But she held her tongue for the moment. She and Marly had at last reached a tentative truce last night, after Grace had been as honest as she thought she could be with the girl. And more honest than she'd wanted to be; the urge to protect was very strong. She didn't want to blow that peace now, but there was no way she was letting the girl outside until she knew it was safe.

Which also meant she herself was going to have to stay inside, because if somebody with malicious intent had indeed tripped that wire, she wouldn't leave Marly here by herself.

"Mom? Shouldn't we see what set it off?"

"Mr. Draven's already check—"

She broke off as the sound of the earsplitting claxon halted abruptly. The silence seemed almost eerie after the volume of the noise. She looked at Marly.

"Do they shut off automatically?"

The girl frowned. "I'm not sure. But I don't think so. The wire pulls out a pin, and that sets it off. I think you have to put the pin back in to shut it off."

Which meant that Draven—or somebody—had gotten to where the alarmed trip wire was.

"We'd better go," Marly said. "He's all by himself. If it really is the bad guy, he could get hurt."

"So could you," Grace pointed out, although she was a little concerned herself at the uninterrupted silence.

She told herself firmly that it would take a lot more than one bad guy to seriously hurt John Draven. He'd been a legend at Redstone for longer than she'd been there. His exploits were common knowledge, and he was one of the first things she'd heard about when she'd started her job.

And after the earthquake, she hadn't been at all surprised to learn that the man who had pulled her out, the dark, intense, scarred man who had maimed her in the process of saving her, was the legendary Draven.

"Mom!" Marly said, "you promised not to be so overprotective."

"Stopping you from going out after a possible saboteur who's also possibly armed is hardly being overprotective," Grace said sternly.

"But—"

Grace held up a hand. "Let me get my foot squared away, and if he's not back by then, I'll reconsider."

The girl agreed, reluctantly. So reluctantly that Grace left the bedroom door open as she prepared, so she could hear if her daughter gave in to temptation and the door opened. She dressed quickly, then started on the foot, forgoing the lengthier preparations of lotion and powder in the interest of speed. As time ticked on with no sign of Draven returning, she was getting anxious herself. Or else she was catching Marly's eagerness.

Finished with the foot, she slipped on her other shoe, then stood up, grabbed the flashlight she'd nearly beaned Draven with and headed back into the living room where Marly was impatiently waiting by the door. The moment she saw Grace she reached for the knob.

It turned and the door swung open before she ever touched it. Marly gave a startled exclamation and jumped back. Grace's hand tightened on the flashlight and she started to raise it and step forward.

Draven stepped into the room. In a split second he seemed to assess their relative positions and actions. Grace thought she saw something glitter in his eyes when he looked at her flashlight. But then his gaze settled on Marly. Steadily. Unwaveringly.

"Going somewhere?"

"Mom wouldn't let me go see if you needed help," the girl complained.

"Good," he said.

Marly flushed. She whirled away and flounced down on the rumpled sofa bed. "Fine," she muttered, clearly stung by his words.

Grace thought she heard him draw in a breath. Was dealing with Marly getting to him? When he spoke, his voice was kinder than she had expected.

And it was a complete sentence.

"I need to know if I see someone out there at this hour it's not one of us."

Marly looked up at that. "Oh. Okay, I get it. You don't want to shoot the wrong person."

Another breath. "I don't *want* to shoot anyone."

"Oh." She sounded almost disappointed. After a moment she asked, "What set it off?"

"Your furry buddy."

"What?" Marly frowned, then grinned. "The monkey?"

"None other."

"So this was one of those false alarms you were telling me about?"

"So it seems."

"Well, darn it. I was hoping we'd finally caught the bad guy."

"Me, too," Draven said, making Marly's grin widen.

"Maybe next time," she said, and this time Grace almost grinned at the unsubtle encouraging note in her daughter's voice.

"Maybe." Draven's voice was solemn, and Grace liked him for not laughing.

This time when she went back to bed, Grace expected to be too wound up to sleep. But instead, as if that burst of energy expended when the alarm had sounded had taken the edge off, she was out within moments of her head hitting the pillow. She slipped quickly into a deep sleep, dreamt vividly about things that made no sense but mostly involved the man who had haunted her dreams for months now.

She became restless in the middle of one of these dreams, one in which they'd been alone, and instead of falling the towel she'd had wrapped around her after her shower had simply dissolved into thin air, leaving her breasts bared to a pair of masculine green eyes that, in her deluded state, turned hot with desire. So hot that instead of lifting her hands to cover herself, she straightened her posture, arching her back slightly, as if in the dream she wanted to thrust her breasts toward him. Offer them.

When the trip wire alarm blasted her awake again, she woke up with a cry. She told herself it was merely being startled out of sleep, but some part of her felt a sense of loss that the dream had ended, at that moment.

That realization rattled her so much that it took her a moment to focus on what was happening outside her too-erotic dreamworld.

Be glad it ended before the rejection, she thought, and forced herself to concentrate on reality.

Had she heard Draven leaving the roof again? She couldn't be sure; she'd been too soundly asleep and too slow to wake up to know if she'd heard those sounds again. But she knew Marly would be awake again, and she wasn't confident enough that Draven's words had taken to simply trust her not to do anything foolish.

Once more she got up and put herself back together, telling herself that she was going to start sleeping with the prosthetic foot on if this kept up.

And dressed, she added to herself as she pulled off her sleep shirt, which reminded her of the dream and sent a fierce blast of heat through her that made her sway slightly. Her nipples tightened at the memory of that vivid image, and she ached in a way she never had before.

It scared her, and she made herself hurry to finish and get out to Marly.

The girl was huddled by the door, but she hadn't gone out. She glanced up as her mother came in.

"Bet it's the monkey again," Marly said.

"Most likely," Grace agreed; at this point she'd go along with anything that would keep the girl safely inside the motor home.

They hovered near the door, wondering what was going on out there. And Grace had to admit she didn't like sitting back and waiting for the big, strong man to handle this. It wasn't in her nature. She was an expert in a field that was dominated by men, and while she always tried to get along, she had never deferred to them.

Unless, of course, they knew more than she did. She was confident, but not stupid.

And Draven, she thought, knew a heck of a lot more about what to do out there than she would ever know. More than she ever wanted to know.

Once she remembered that, she felt herself calm slightly. He was the expert, and by all accounts one of the best in the world at what he did. He would handle this, and he didn't need any help from her, and he certainly didn't need any interference from a teenage girl. His job was to protect the project, and by circumstance he'd gotten pulled into protecting them as well. So while he was doing the first, the least she could do was help with the second.

"Boy, he's not getting much sleep tonight, is he?"

Grace looked at her daughter. "No. No, he's not."

In fact, now that she thought about it, he probably hadn't gotten much rest since he'd been here. She knew he spent a lot of the night watching the surveillance monitors, so he was starting out at a loss. When he did sleep, at first he'd been in the construction trailer, on the floor. Then on the roof of the trailer, and now on the roof of the motor home. Hardly conducive to sound sleep.

Of course, that was probably why he was doing it. She'd bet he didn't want to get too comfortable, for fear he'd miss something, some sound, or movement, or like the other night, the smell of danger.

"Mom?"

She snapped out of her reverie and looked at her daughter. "What?"

"Did you know him before he came here?"

Grace tensed. She'd never told her daughter exactly what

had happened during and after the earthquake. Marly had been staying with Grace's aunt Charlotte during that time, since Grace hadn't wanted to take her to a part of the world that wasn't the most stable. So by the time Redstone had flown her home to the States, she'd buried the incident in her mind while she concentrated on her rehab.

She looked at the girl, who met her gaze steadily. Grace remembered her daughter's plea to be told the truth, remembered that she'd had some very good reasons for it.

Perhaps she had a right to know this, as well.

"Mr. Draven is the man who pulled me out of that building after the earthquake."

Marly's eyes widened and her mouth opened in shock. "He's the guy? Why didn't you tell me?"

"I try not to think about it very often," Grace said. It was the honest truth; until Draven had shown up here she spent a great deal—probably too much—of her energy every day not thinking about it.

And then he'd arrived, and it had become impossible. His presence was just too big, too much, she simply couldn't ignore him. He took up too much space, too much air.

He was too...too, she thought.

"Well, yeah," Marly said, "but, jeez, I wish I'd known."

"Why?" she asked, curious.

"I woulda been nicer, maybe."

Well, hallelujah, Grace thought.

"How come he's not friendlier to you?" Marly asked.

"I don't know. I think that's just the way he is, that's his nature." She thought about it a moment, then wondered aloud, "Or maybe not. I suppose it's possible that I'm not a very enjoyable memory for him, either."

"Why? I'd think saving somebody's life would make you feel good."

"I'm sure it does. But in some cases there's a downside,

too. Sometimes to save someone you have to do things that aren't pleasant."

Marly frowned. "You mean your foot? But why would that bother him? I mean, if he got you out in time, before the building—" The girl stopped suddenly, and her eyes got huge once again. "Oh, wow. Your foot…"

Grace looked at her, not denying or confirming the implication, wondering if there was a way to continue to avoid this.

"He did it?" Marly asked, her voice barely above a whisper. "He cut it off, right there?"

Grace sighed. She'd never told the girl, knew she'd always assumed her foot had had to be amputated later on in the hospital. She hadn't felt it necessary to correct that impression, in fact had chosen not to, to avoid giving the child any more nightmares than she was already having. But now she didn't seem to have any choice; it was the truth or a face-to-face lie.

"There was no choice. It was the only way to get me out in time. He knew the building was about to collapse. That we had only minutes. Maybe seconds."

Marly shivered as she stared at her mother.

Now that she'd started, Grace decided she might as well finish. "He risked his own life. He would have been killed, too, if that building had come down. But he stayed, to get me out."

"No wonder you seem so twitchy around him. Now I understand."

You only think you do, Grace thought, fighting down the rush of color that threatened to flood her face as the memory of her dreams came back to her when Marly said the word *twitchy.* That was a good description of it. She was twitchy, all right, but it had nothing to do with her foot. And everything to do with the man who had separated her from it.

She told herself it was only natural, to feel, or imagine you felt, some sort of attraction to the man who'd saved your life. That's all it was.

"And now I understand why he's so weird around you," Marly said.

Grace fought down the wave of aching sensation and focused on her daughter. "What?"

"He must really feel like crap, having to do that to you."

Grace was so startled by the idea her daughter expressed that she neglected to object to the language. She had never thought of that, never thought it was even possible. Draven seemed so invulnerable, impervious to the frailties that plagued ordinary mortals.

She couldn't believe that, however bloody and awful what he'd done to her might have been, that he hadn't seen and done worse in his years with Redstone, or with the military before that. Something had to have put that look in his eyes, the look that chilled even the coldest of souls. You didn't get that way by growing daffodils.

"I sort of doubt he feels that badly about it," she said. "As I said, there was no choice."

"I'll bet he does," Marly insisted. "I bet it gives him nightmares, just like us."

Grace tilted her head to look at Marly. "You still have nightmares?"

That shrug again. And an embarrassed expression as she muttered, "Sometimes."

The girl had never admitted to that before. Grace was fairly certain she'd had some nasty dreams, as she herself had, after she'd first arrived home. Too many times she'd found the girl up walking around at odd hours of the night. And her bed had been a tangled wreck in the mornings, as if she had tossed and turned all night.

But Marly had always denied it, insisted she was fine,

with that affected, blasé attitude of the young teenager. Grace hadn't believed it at the time, and had kept watching her daughter carefully. The nighttime excursions and restlessness seemed to have eased as time passed, but still—

This time it wasn't the alarm that split the nighttime quiet. It was a shot.

Chapter 13

He didn't come back.

Grace stared at the door as if she could make it swing open by sheer force of will.

"Mom?"

Marly was sounding more upset with every query. But she couldn't leave the girl alone, not with somebody out there with a gun.

Of course, it could have been Draven, shooting. Despite his comment to Marly about not wanting to shoot anyone, she was certain he would do whatever was necessary. She was a little surprised at how much faith she had in that, but there it was. She supposed all that telling herself he had the reputation he had for a reason had finally sunk in.

"It's his job, Marly. He's the expert."

"What good does that do if somebody gets the drop on him?"

At the phrase Grace reminded herself to more carefully monitor her daughter's choices in entertainment.

"Being the expert is what keeps that from happening," she said.

"But what if that shot was at him? Like…like a…a sniper or something!" Marly, not having her mother's knowledge of who and what Draven was, asked anxiously. "What if he's out there hurt, bleeding, maybe even dying?"

Grace had to admit her daughter's frightened words sent some ugly images through her head. But she couldn't quite wrap her mind around the idea of the mighty John Draven being taken down like that.

But, once again she had a point. The bad guys could always get lucky, she thought. It happened. Cops got shot all the time, even with all their training.

"Mom, come on!" Marly was nearly shouting now.

"You heard what he said," Grace said, afraid the girl was going to bolt in a moment. "He has to know anybody moving is the bad guy."

"You think half the crew isn't out there after hearing a shot?"

Grace stared at her daughter. When had she gotten so logical? And when had she herself apparently lost the capacity to think clearly? At least, when it came to Draven.

Probably the moment he stepped off that plane, she muttered inwardly.

"You're right," she said aloud, earning a flash of a smile from Marly. "But we're going to stay in the main quad until we find out what's going on. No straying out to the edge, even though that's where the trip wires are. All right?"

Marly hesitated, but then nodded.

She had been right, Grace realized, soon after they stepped outside. Several outside lights were now on, in addition to the high-intensity spots over the heavy equipment

enclosure that were always on all night. And she could see
men moving in and out of the pools of light.

"Over there," Grace said, pointing to where a silhouette
against the brighter lights appeared to be Nick. "Let's go see
what he knows."

Marly grudgingly followed her, muttering all the way that
they should be out looking for Draven instead. Grace registered this, and wondered when the man had become so important to the girl, despite their disagreements. For a guy who
insisted he knew nothing about kids, he'd certainly made an
impression on this one. Perhaps she was the one who should
be learning from him when it came to relating to her daughter.

"Hell of a way to wake up in the middle of the night,"
Nick said when he saw Grace approaching. "Oops," he added
when he saw Marly behind her. "Sorry."

"Don't apologize. It seems she has her own vocabulary
to apologize for," Grace said dryly.

"Yeah, yeah," Marly muttered. "Where's Draven?"

"Mr. Draven," Grace corrected automatically.

"Yesterday he said to call him Draven," Marly protested.

"Haven't seen him yet," Nick said, cutting off the incipi-
ent argument. "Must be out prowling around."

She glanced at Marly, then asked Nick, "You don't think
he might be hurt? That shot…"

"Nah. He's the toughest man I've ever met. He knows his
stuff. If anybody's hurt out there, I'd lay odds it's the guy
behind all this nuisance."

"How can you be sure?" Marly asked.

Nick looked at the girl. "Honey, that man went into the
jungle of Nicaragua and pulled out some warlord's prime
prisoner, all by himself. You think he can't handle some
two-bit drug dealer's flunky?"

Marly stared at Nick. "He did?"

"And single-handedly rescued the entire Redstone staff when some extremist in the Philippines grabbed them to try to blackmail Josh into using his influence to get their friends out of jail."

The girl was gaping now, like a youngster who has just gotten the first glimpse of a much bigger, wider world than was encompassed in her own narrow view.

Grace knew Nick had been telling those tales to reassure Marly, but in the process he'd managed to reassure her a bit as well. But as long as there was no sign of Draven, she wasn't going to be certain he was all right.

It was only natural that she feel disturbed, she told herself. After all, the man was part—a very big part, much bigger than she herself—of Redstone, and they truly were all one family. And he'd come here to protect her project, so of course she felt guilty that he might be hurt in the process.

Not to mention the fact that she owed him her life. How could she not be upset at the prospect?

"You and the crew stick close by here until we know for sure. I don't want anybody…getting hurt," Grace told him, first hesitating, then omitting the phrase "anybody else."

"Yes, ma'am," Nick said, a bit fervently. "I'm not big on getting shot at."

Grace looked at Marly. "Let's go over to the trailer. You're good with those security monitors and recordings, let's see if we can see anything."

Brightening at the prospect and, Grace hoped, at the compliment, Marly nodded quickly and started that way. Grace followed this time, vaguely aware that her leg was protesting the extra time on her feet tonight. She was comfortable with the prosthetic, but that didn't mean the stump of her leg had completely toughened up yet. She might have to give it a rest if this kept up.

Marly trotted up the trailer steps and opened the door.

"Hey!" the girl yelped.

Fear shot through Grace. She leapt up the two steps in one move, landing on the artificial foot. Ignoring the pain that stabbed through her leg, she yanked Marly back.

And then she saw what had startled the girl.

Draven.

Alive, well and sitting at the monitors calmly scanning recorded images.

Draven had turned when he'd heard the noises outside, hand reaching for the weapon at the small of his back. It was probably just Nick, he'd seen the lights go on over there, but he wasn't big on taking anything for granted. It was one reason he was still alive.

When he saw who was there, he realized he shouldn't be surprised. He should have known the girl wouldn't be able to stay put forever with all this activity going on.

When Grace pulled the girl aside and put herself in front of her, he was puzzled for a moment.

When Grace swore at him, something he'd never heard her do despite provocation, he was more than puzzled, he was startled.

"I don't think my mother would appreciate the characterization," he said mildly.

"Then she should have taught you better manners!"

"Grace—"

"Did it never occur to you that we all heard that shot?"

"Of course—"

"Or that none of us knew where you were?"

"The alarm—"

She swore at him a second time. "Damn it, Draven, we didn't know if you were lying out there bleeding to death or what!"

He blinked. "Me?"

"Even the great Draven isn't invulnerable," she snapped. "For all we knew, that shot had hit you. For all we knew, you were dead."

"Not likely," he said, more than a little stunned by the turn this had taken.

Grace stared at him. High emotion was roiling in her eyes, and he wasn't sure why. There was a trace of lingering fear, yes, but any mother would feel that way, wouldn't they, hearing a shot and having their child in the vicinity?

He couldn't think of any other explanation for her state. Of course, he could barely think at all, looking at her. The only thing that was clear in his mind was that Grace, angry, was the most incredible thing he'd ever seen in his life. He told himself it was because he knew up close and personal how close she'd come to dying, that seeing her so alive and vibrant now was just a spectacular comparison.

But on some level, someplace buried deep inside, he knew better. He knew it was more than that. Knew there was something within him responding to her in a way he'd never felt before. He knew it. Just like he knew he could never acknowledge that fact.

At a loss for what else to do, he tried to reassure her. "It would take more than a guy with lousy aim and a popgun to do any real damage."

She continued to stare. Then, when she finally spoke again, he winced inwardly.

"Kryptonite?" she suggested, in that sweet voice that he'd learned meant it was time to tread very carefully.

Marly giggled, taking the edge off the confrontation.

"I never said I was a superhero." His voice sounded stiff even to his own ears.

"Contrary to your reputation?" Grace said, her voice still carrying that tone that made him wary.

Draven wasn't sure what to say. After a moment's pondering he decided the best course was to say nothing just now. Let her take the lead, answer only what he had to and hope she calmed down. He wasn't sure exactly what had her so wound up anyway.

"What happened?" Marly asked. "Was it the bad guy this time?"

With a wary glance at Grace, Draven answered her. "It was somebody. The alarm scared him off."

"Did you hit him?"

He frowned at the girl's obvious enthusiasm. "I never got close enough to even throw a punch."

"I meant shoot him," Marly explained.

"Sorry to disappoint," he said, "I never drew my weapon."

"Oh."

She did sound disappointed. Again. He guessed he just wasn't living up to her image. But there really had been no point in trying to shoot back when the man had fired at him. Besides the fact that he didn't want to start a running gun battle here on the site. He preferred to choose his own ground for that kind of thing.

He'd heard the round whistle past his ear. Realized right away that if he'd ducked left instead of right, he'd likely be dead, a round buried somewhere in his head. He'd wondered if the shooter was that good, or just lucky. Logic told him if it was somebody connected to *el mercader,* it was skill. If not, all bets were off, it could go either way.

Crouching below the level of the brush, he had worked his way toward the hollow he thought the shot had come from. He had a feeling the shooter was long gone, that the round he'd capped off had been more warning than anything else, but that was another thing he didn't take for granted.

"Did you see him?" Grace asked.

"Not well," he said. "Enough to see he was male, thin and

wiry. Not too tall, maybe five-eight or nine. But I got a look at his car."

"What was it?"

He looked at her, a vision of her finding it and confronting the driver shooting through his mind and making him cringe inwardly.

"You've got to promise—both of you—" he added with a glance at Marly "—that if you see it you do *nothing*. You let me know and you stay away. Period. No exceptions. And that goes for the crew, too. I don't want anybody getting hurt here."

"Yeah, yeah," Marly muttered.

"She promises," Grace said. "And so do I. Nick will get the word to the crew."

After a moment, Draven realized he had little choice. The more eyes looking for this guy, the quicker they'd find him.

"Light-colored four-door, maybe off-white or a light yellow. American make. Older, kind of beat-up, with big, square taillights. Got a clatter in the engine, like it's got a bad valve."

And he would remember the sound if he ever heard it again. He'd listened to it pull away, his eyes closed to concentrate on the sound, committing the sour note to memory. He had a good ear for machinery, and knew he'd recognize it.

"Did you get the license?" Marly asked excitedly.

"Partial," Draven said, stifling the twitch of his lips at her enthusiasm. "There was some mud on the plate, covering a couple of the numbers."

"Can you still check it, like the cops do? And find out who owns it?"

"It's harder with only a partial, but it can be done." His mouth quirked. "But there aren't that many cars on the island in the first place. Be faster to just look for it."

"Oh." Again that disappointment in the girl's voice. But

Draven didn't mind; at least things had calmed down. Enough that he felt safe in pointing out that they weren't supposed to go anywhere without him.

"But you were gone," Marly said in response. "How could we go with you?"

Now there was teenage logic, Draven thought. "You weren't supposed to go at all," he said.

"But we were worried," Marly pointed out in turn.

"You both were safest staying in the motor home."

"Us?" Marly scowled at him. "You are *so* dense!"

He drew back slightly, wondering what had brought that assessment on.

"Did it never occur to you," Marly asked, in a startlingly adult-sounding voice, "that it was *you* we were worried about?"

Something slammed into his chest with the force of a fist. "Me?" he asked.

Or tried to, the word came out very oddly, almost like a startled squeak. He looked at Grace, who was watching him steadily. He saw something in her eyes that tightened the knot that was making it hard to breathe.

"Is it that strange," she asked softly, "to think somebody might actually worry about you?"

Yes, was the answer that came to his lips, but he bit it back. It sounded too damned pitiful.

"Don't worry about me. It's my job." He managed to keep his voice fairly level.

"They're not mutually exclusive," Grace said.

"They should be," he said, not liking how gruff he sounded, but seemingly he'd lost control over that, too.

He didn't want to think that simply coming here and facing the woman who haunted him—for he'd finally had to admit to himself that it was Grace herself who haunted him, not what he'd had to do to her—had so shaken him. Didn't want to admit she had that much power over him. Especially knowing she had never intentionally done a thing to wield that power. Probably didn't even know she had it.

How could she know? To her, he was eternally connected to her nightmare, what had to be the worst trauma of her life. How could she know, and why would she care if she did know, that it haunted him, too? What right did he have to be preoccupied about it? It was her body, her life that had been irrevocably changed. He'd walked away, as he had countless times before.

Only now was he facing the possibility that while he might have walked away, he'd never really left it behind.

And for the first time in his life and career, he wanted to quit in the middle of a job.

Chapter 14

Draven had changed, somehow.

Grace considered this as she looked at him across the motor home's table. Marly was in the bathroom, where she was sure the girl would take at least an hour on her new, experimental beauty regimen. It tugged at her heart; her little girl was growing up. And it was going to be a battle, the wisdom of age combating the ignorance of youth, bouncing her back and forth between near-adult acumen and childish lack of judgment.

But she had to go through it, and there was nothing Grace could do about it except be there. So she turned back to the silent man sitting across the table. This had become somewhat of a routine since that day at the lagoon; she would get up, fix coffee, and the smell drew him in.

There was something different about him since last night, when the alarms had sounded. It wasn't anything obvious, anything she could pinpoint. He went about his work as before—and still not sleeping enough, she thought—and acted the same as he always had.

But there was something in the way she would catch him looking at her, watching, as if she were...something he was trying to figure out.

When he'd first arrived it had been painful just to look at him, to see that rough, angular, scarred face and remember the first time she'd seen it, looming over her, at that moment the most welcome sight in the world. Her salvation, her deliverance from death. And then the dispenser of agony.

Now, if she was honest, she'd have to admit part of the difficulty of having him here was based in the attraction she felt. *And because you're embarrassed to even look at him, after that dream you had,* she told herself sourly.

She looked out the window and somewhat wistfully remembered the time when she'd been free to come and go as she pleased. And how it felt to not be worrying about the job, a constant concern now.

She didn't think she'd made a sound, but he looked up from the cup of coffee he held. It was still the strongest stuff she'd ever tasted, but she supposed he needed it that way to keep going as he did. She'd have been facedown in the dirt long before now. But it was starting to show, she thought. Finally. His eyes were as vivid and alert and wary as ever, but there were shadows beneath them, painted there by the lack of sleep.

When she poured her own coffee, she only poured a half a cup and then diluted it with hot water to make it drinkable. He'd told her she didn't need to make it stronger for him, he appreciated her simply making it. But it was easy enough to doctor her own, and she felt it was the least she could do.

She heard the shower start, and knew her daughter would be in there until the hot water ran out. And now, she knew, was her chance to bring up what had been bothering her ever since Marly had said it.

"May I ask you something, about that day in Turkey?"

He didn't move, but somehow she thought he'd tensed. She picked her next words carefully.

"Does that day...bother you?"

He looked up then. "Bother me?" He gave a short, hard laugh. "Bother isn't the word I'd use, no."

She had to know if Marly's theory was wrong—she didn't think she could bear to make a fool out of herself by assuming he even thought about that day much at all.

"What word would you use?"

He held her gaze for a long moment. Her heart started to pick up speed, and she wasn't even sure why. She thought she saw hints of a battle taking place in his head, and wondered if it was some very rare moment when he let something show, or if she was possibly getting better at reading him.

"Please," she said. "It's important to me."

A muscle in his jaw jumped. She tried not to read too much into it, tried not to think that it really meant so much to him that he couldn't speak of it.

"Haunt," he finally said.

She sucked in a breath. Marly had been right. "Surely you've seen worse things."

He nodded. "And done worse. But never to a civilian, an innocent."

She got up then. She faced him, standing tall and straight, her head up. "I'm standing here, alive and well," she said with emphasis on the last word, "because of you."

"Ian Gamble," he said.

"Yes, him, too, but if not for you, I wouldn't have been around to try out his new foot. I wouldn't be here at all."

He gave that half shrug again, as if he were very uncomfortable with the turn this had taken.

"Grace—"

"No, let me finish. I know there was no other choice. I understand that." She paused, to let him know she knew there was a big difference, then she added firmly, "I *believe* that."

He was staring at her. And she saw in those green eyes that *haunt* was indeed the word; it was as if she could see a string of countless nights fraught with images as ugly as her own.

"How can you do that?" he said at last, and there was an undertone in his voice that she'd never heard before. It sounded almost like wonder. "I cut into your living flesh, sawed off a part of your body, caused you horrific pain and hardship for the rest of your life."

"You may not believe this, but it's truly not like that anymore. There are so many who are worse off. I kept my knee, do you have any idea how important that is?"

He shook his head, slowly. "I maimed you and you're… absolving me? Forgiving me?"

It was worse than she'd feared, Grace thought. She spoke quickly, putting all the sincerity she felt into her words.

"There's nothing to forgive. You didn't cause any of what happened. You only did what had to be done. If you hadn't, I'd be dead. I would never see my daughter grow up, and she would be stuck for the rest of her life with only a father who didn't want her."

He lowered his eyes then, staring into his coffee cup. She thought she heard a breath escape him. This was more emotion than she'd ever seen from the man, and it was rattling her almost as much as it was apparently rattling him. She took another deep breath and let the words unroll.

"I can't say I don't have painful memories, that you're not connected to them. No, I'm not the same woman I was, and perhaps there's not a man on the planet who can look past the physical change, but that's all right. I don't need that. I love my work, my daughter and my life. That's more than many have. And it's thanks to you that I have any of it. So I wanted you to know how grateful I am."

He was looking at her as if shell-shocked. His expression alone told her how much he had assumed about what she felt about what he'd had to do. If she'd realized, she would have done this much sooner.

And it both amazed her and gave her hope that it had been her little girl who had figured it out.

Draven went from camera three to camera four, checking for any problems. This was his second trip, because he didn't trust himself. He'd made two circuits of the perimeter, too, because he'd repeatedly caught himself off in the ozone somewhere, and right now he didn't trust his autopilot.

He wasn't often shocked. Or stunned. Grace O'Conner had done both.

Hell, she'd blown him away.

He knew he would never forget the way she'd stood there and given him total absolution. His head had known what she'd said was true; it had been the only thing to do, but he had never expected her to see it that way. He'd expected to be the star in her nightmares for the rest of her life.

When she'd seemed to relax a little around him, he'd assumed it was simply practice, that since he'd practically taken up residence she'd gotten used to him. He'd never considered that she actually might not hate him for what had happened that day in Turkey.

And now he was reeling. Because now, without the buffer of the negative feelings he'd assumed she had, he had to admit she'd gotten to him. Gotten to him as no one ever had, in a very personal way.

He stopped in his tracks as a stunning thought hit him.

Once again what Josh had said came back to him. *Handle whatever you find—no matter what it is.*

Draven had thought at the time there'd been an odd sort of emphasis on those particular words. He hadn't known why then, but now he was wondering if somehow, in that amazing way Josh had of reading people, he'd known something. If he'd sent Draven here on purpose, knowing Grace was here. If he'd sent him here to deal with the demons he hadn't even known the source of himself. If that was what Josh had meant when he'd said only he could handle this.

He wouldn't put it past his boss to have done just that. It was just the kind of thing Josh Redstone would do. He'd have to have a word with him when he finished here. Asking him for help was one thing, manipulating him was something else again, something he didn't take kindly to.

He filed away the notion and went back to work. He checked the mount on the camera closest to the water, making sure it wasn't damaged from the salt spray and air. He gave it much more attention than necessary, trying to divert his thoughts. He felt as if his mind was working at triple speed, as if too many thoughts and images were careening around inside his skull, bouncing off each other and the walls and never slowing down enough for him to catch and process them.

He was not used to feeling like this. About anything. That it was a woman shook him. He'd been attracted to women over the years, had occasionally acted on the feeling. But the bottom line was still that he'd never met a woman he couldn't leave behind.

And I sure as hell don't want to start now, he thought. Especially a woman with a child he could barely deal with.

As if any woman would take you on in the first place, he reminded himself.

The two serious relationships—God, he hated that
word—he'd ever had had both ended for the same reason:
neither woman could deal with his work. Whether it was the
work itself, and the demands it made, or the fact that it was
his first priority, he didn't know. Probably both, he thought
as he finally moved on to the next camera.

Or maybe it was simply him. There was no denying he
was no prize for any woman. He had few illusions about himself. He knew he was a loner, a hard case, blunt, pragmatic
to the extreme, with far too many rough edges. And his job
meant long hours and lots of travel, was sometimes risky and
a few times deadly.

But above all, he knew he didn't have a romantic bone in
his battle-scarred body. And Grace deserved the exact opposite of all he was—and wasn't. She was gutsy, smart and
beautiful, and many other things he admired. More woman
than a man like him had any right to.

He nearly groaned that he was even thinking about such
things. But how could he not, after what she'd said?

*…perhaps there's not a man on the planet who can look
past the physical change.*

Didn't she know how beautiful she was? Still was, no
matter what had happened? Didn't she know that her missing foot was nothing when the rest was so beautiful and the
brain was quick and sharp enough to keep any man working all the time just to keep up? That her courage dealing
with what had happened to her made her even more incredible, more sexy?

Heat shot through him, a stabbing, piercing claw making
his body clench until he almost doubled over. He nearly
gasped at the force of it. It had been a very, very long time
since he'd wanted, truly wanted. Hell, he wasn't sure he'd
ever wanted like this. And was even less sure that he was
going to be able to keep it under control. He had the feeling

he was going to be glad there was a teenager around to force him to keep a leash on this ferocious need. Because he had to keep it leashed. Just because she'd forgiven him didn't mean Grace would have any interest at all in getting involved with the chaos that was his life. And his mind. And the emotions he didn't want to admit to even having.

Yeah, you're a pretty messed up package, he thought wryly.

He forced himself to pay attention to the matter at hand. He needed to be doubly sure everything was in place and working. Whoever it was, Draven didn't think their culprit was going to give up easily.

He wanted to adjust the outer perimeter cams; the recorded visuals at the time of the alarm trip had shown only a shadowy figure with some sort of hat pulled down and hiding his features. When he'd tripped the wire and the alarm sounded, he'd jumped, startled, and the hat had flown off. He'd grabbed it and run, which was why he was already getting into the car when Draven had gotten there.

He might need to install some floods, at least on the perimeter cams, he thought. The extra light would have made this guy plainly visible. He'd have somebody send them out. If he'd thought of it earlier, he could have had them come along with the other delivery he was expecting.

Which reminded him to check the time, and he glanced at his watch. The boat should be reaching them any time now. He picked up the pace and finished his inspection, better able to concentrate now that he had a reason to hustle. Then he headed down to the dock.

He wanted to make this pickup himself, so he could go over the situation thoroughly, but didn't want to leave Grace and Marly unguarded for too long. With a little luck, no one else would notice the arrival for a while, and he could still get the briefing done.

When he was within sight of the cove, he saw that Jorge Nunez and his offshore racer were already in sight. By the time he got down to the pier, the powerful boat had slowed and was sliding neatly toward the docking area. Draven walked down to meet it, and when Nunez tossed him the mooring lines, he tied them neatly off on the cleats bolted to the pier decking.

Nunez waved as his passenger bent to grab up a duffel bag that looked much like Draven's own.

"On my way to Ambergris," the man in the captain's hat said, referring to Ambergris Cay, the largest and most developed island off Belize's coast.

"I have a charter out to the reef. A load of divers, very rich," Nunez added with a grin.

That would make it a profitable afternoon, Draven thought; Belize's reef was the second largest in the world, after Australia, and you could spend hours there without realizing. He nodded in understanding that the man was, for once, on a schedule, but kept his eyes on the young man who tossed the duffel bag onto the pier and leapt fairly agilely up after it.

Once he was on the pier, Draven freed the bowline. Without prompting, the young man did the same with the stern. Nunez waved again and was off, leaving a swirling wake behind him and kicking up a rooster tail of spray to mark his course.

The new arrival held out his hand. "Mr. Draven."

Draven shook hands briefly, noting the grip was strong but not challenging.

Kieren Buckley looked much as Draven had remembered from his Redstone interview. Only slightly shorter than he himself, lean but muscular, with sandy-brown hair he wore in a buzz cut that reminded Draven of his own service days. He had the small goatee that seemed to come standard with twentysomethings these days, sparse enough that Draven thought he'd look better without it.

But what Draven had noticed first about him was his eyes. Not the color, which was an amber sort of brown, but the calm alertness in them, and in his entire stance. He'd clearly been nervous about the interview, but he'd met Draven's eyes steadily, and that was a make or break point with the head of Redstone Security.

"You made good time," Draven said.

"Yes, sir. Went like clockwork."

"Redstone," Draven answered simply.

"Yeah, I'm beginning to see that."

"You finish reading the file?"

He nodded. "On the plane."

"Good. Ready?"

"Absolutely. Thanks for asking for me."

Draven gave him a sideways look. "St. John tell you what the job was?"

Buckley nodded.

"That doesn't bother you?"

"No, sir. I'm sure there's a reason, or you wouldn't be asking."

He could have been sucking up, but Draven didn't think so. And Redstone people always got the benefit of the doubt, even the new ones.

"Doesn't hurt to be in paradise, either?" Draven suggested.

Buckley shrugged. "I'm a cool-weather, mountain kind of guy myself, but this is nice for a change. What's the setup here?"

"Redstone owns the south two-thirds of the island. Matola City, such as it is, is about two miles north. At the far north tip of the cay is a guy you'll need to know about, but we'll get into that later."

Buckley nodded. "What's first?"

Draven's mouth quirked. "You meet the family," he said. "I'll fill you in as we go."

He led the way, giving Buckley the layout of the site as they went, pointing out the various work and storage areas, and the construction trailer. He told him about the situation up until now, including Grace's close encounter with the enemy.

"She's the one who got hurt in that earthquake in Turkey, isn't she?"

"Yes," Draven said succinctly.

"I heard about her. Guess she's one tough lady."

You don't know the half of it, kid. "She is," he said.

When they got to the motor home, he knocked. Marly pulled open the door.

"Mom's in the…"

Her voice trailed away as she spotted the man with him. Her young face betrayed her every thought as she gaped at the handsome young man.

That should keep you occupied, young lady, Draven thought, with no small amount of satisfaction that his choice had had the desired effect. He'd figured a girl Marly's age couldn't help but react like this to the good-looking kid only ten years older than she was. When he'd made the call to Redstone headquarters, he'd intended to just let St. John decide who to send, but then he'd remembered the young man he'd personally interviewed, and made his own selection.

"Hi," Buckley said. "You must be Marly."

Apparently dumbstruck, the girl just stared at him. Finally she managed to nod.

Buckley jerked a thumb at Draven. "He didn't tell me you were cute."

The girl's color deepened and her eyes went even wider. *Smooth,* Draven thought. *This just might work better than I'd even hoped.*

"I…what…who are you?" Marly finally managed to ask.

"I'm Kieren Buckley," he said cheerfully, with a grin that made the girl blush. "I'm your new babysitter."

Chapter 15

"He's what?" Grace asked.

"He's going to watch out for Marly. She's his only assignment."

Grace looked dubiously at the young man her daughter was talking to so fervently, a few yards away. To her he looked barely older than the fourteen-year-old herself.

"What is he? Sixteen?"

Draven's mouth quirked. Either he was relaxing, Grace thought, or she really was learning to read his slight expression changes.

"He's twenty-four," he said.

She barely managed not to gape at him. "Twenty-four? That's twenty-four?" She felt ancient, looking at him and realizing he was ten years older than Marly.

"The older you get, the younger they look," Draven said as if he'd read her thoughts. She couldn't tell if he'd been teasing or simply voicing an observation; his voice was dead-pan, as was his face.

"He's a trained Redstone agent," Draven said, obviously trying to reassure her. "And if it makes you feel better, he was also a cop in L.A. for a couple of years."

"Why did he leave?"

"That's his to share or not. I can only tell you it wasn't anything negative. He wasn't fired, asked to leave or guilty of any misconduct."

"Oh." She eyed the new arrival warily, then looked back at Draven. "I can trust him with her?"

"You can."

"You know what I mean?" she asked, not certain if he understood all the ramifications of entrusting a fourteen-year-old girl to a young man she'd never met. A very handsome young man.

"Yes. He's completely trustworthy. In all areas."

She considered this for a moment. Then realized if Kieren Buckley was Redstone security, he'd been vetted within an inch of his life. The L.A.P.D. background check likely paled in comparison to what Redstone put him through.

She looked over at the pair again, thinking she'd never seen her daughter blush so much. And she was actually giggling. Marly was not just laughing, but giggling, in a girly sort of way Grace couldn't remember ever having heard from her daughter before.

Grace's mouth twisted into a wry smile. "He's too darn cute. Every adolescent girl's dream. She's going to get a crush on him."

"I'm counting on it."

Grace's head snapped around. "What?"

"I'm counting on it," he repeated. "Better chance she'll cooperate, stay with him."

Grace stared at him. "And stay safe," she said softly.

He nodded.

She shook her head in wonder. "Don't ever tell me again you don't understand teenagers."

"I don't. But I've seen the reaction he gets."

"From girls?"

"Women, too."

She glanced back over at the two, this time studying Kieren's perfect features. "Too pretty for me," she said.

When she turned back, Draven was studying her intently. She felt a blush rising to her own cheeks as she realized that could have been interpreted as expressing a preference for more rugged looks.

Looks, for example, like his.

Well, it's true, she admitted inwardly. *You've never been attracted to the pretty ones.*

And Draven was many things; strong, powerful, mysterious, scarred, competent and tough, but there was no way you could call him pretty. Not even good-looking, that was too bland. He was much more than that.

She thought for a moment, trying to come up with the right word, and nearly blushed again when the only term that came to mind was *magnificent.* But she wasn't sure that wasn't the perfect description.

"I would give a great deal," he said in a voice so soft it wouldn't carry beyond her ears, "to know what you're thinking right now."

Caught, Grace lost the battle with the rising blush, and felt the heat of color flood her face.

With the blunt honesty that sometimes got her into trouble, she muttered the only thing she could think of to say. "And I'd give more for you not to know."

She got up then, and hastily went back inside the motor home before he could say anything that would embarrass her further.

If that was possible, she thought ruefully.

She retreated to the bedroom and sat on the small, built-in settee that served as a chair, and in her case, too often a clothes basket. She wasn't surprised to realize she was trembling slightly.

She felt as if her world were spinning out of control. She was in danger, and because of that Marly was in danger, too. Yet she felt safe, protected, because of Draven. That she owed that feeling of shelter to the man who was connected to the worst nightmare of her life was an irony she didn't have the slightest idea how to deal with.

She had even less idea of how to deal with the fact she could no longer deny. She was attracted to him. Attracted in a way she'd thought herself long past, even before the damage to her body. Attracted in the way her pain and panic-racked body had responded in the first moment she'd looked up out of the rubble and seen him, in the way her mind had labeled him a harshly beautiful angel come to save her. Before the encounter had turned to torment.

She'd been truly surprised to find out Marly's guess had been right, and he'd expected her to hate him for what he'd had to do that day. And she'd meant every word she'd said, that she knew and believed he'd done what had to be done, and she was grateful. Grateful that she would see her daughter grow up, go to school, hopefully find her passion in life. Maybe marry someday, perhaps even have children of her own.

Grandchildren, Grace thought. Now there's a scary thought. You really are getting old if you're thinking about *that.*

But even that didn't bother her as much as it once had. Once she'd been confronted with the prospect of never growing old at all, the alternative seemed much more inviting.

She heard the phone in the other room ring. With an effort she reeled in her thoughts and stood up.

The ringing stopped. A moment later there was a tap on the door.

"Grace?"

Draven. She hadn't even heard him come in. But then, she'd already seen that he could move quieter than a cat.

"I heard it," she said as she opened the door. He was standing there with the cordless handset, which he now held out to her.

"It's Nick," he said.

She nodded and took it. "Yes, Nick," she said into the receiver.

"We'll be ready to start the first pour right after lunch."

She never missed this stage, and didn't want to start now. She looked at Draven. "I need to be there."

He nodded, and she told Nick she would be there in an hour. When she'd disconnected, Draven took the phone from her.

"You can do whatever you need to, go wherever you want now, as long as I'm with you. Buckley can handle Marly."

Her mouth quirked. "I'm sure he can."

She hadn't really realized what his calling in Kieren meant as far as her own freedom was concerned. That it was going to make it possible for her to resume her normal work habits.

At least, as normal as anything could get for her with John Draven glued to her.

The images that brought to mind threatened to send her scampering back to her bedroom until the blush faded again. Not that her bedroom was the best place to go to quash her rowdy thoughts.

"Lunch," she said abruptly. "I've got some Caribbean jerk chicken in the fridge. Sandwich?"

"You don't have to cook for me."

She knew he meant it; she wasn't sure what he did for meals, but he'd certainly never asked her.

"I said fridge. No cooking involved. For which," she added, "you should be grateful. My repertoire of edible food is limited, I'm afraid."

He gave her that half shrug she was starting to look at almost affectionately. "Nobody should be expected to build airports and cook, too."

She smiled at that, and decided to just fix the sandwiches. A few minutes later she had two rolls piled high with the local concoction of meat rubbed with spices, and "jerked" apart rather than cut into tidy slices. She'd grown to enjoy the particular blend that was available in Matola City, a recipe from Mr. Ayuso's mother.

That thought reminded her of Marly's escapade in the man's store, and something else she had wanted to say. She put the plates on the table, added a couple of glasses of lemonade and sat down, gesturing at Draven to join her. When he did, and had taken a bite, she spoke.

"I wanted to thank you."

"For what?" he asked after he'd swallowed.

"Everything. But right now, for Marly. Keeping her out of any further trouble."

The shrug again.

"I've been able to concentrate on my work better, not having to worry about her." She didn't mention the new distraction he himself was providing.

"Should be easier now, with Buckley."

She nodded. "Thanks for that, too. I appreciate the one-on-one for her."

He looked at her over the sandwich. "But not for you?"

She lowered her gaze to her own sandwich, still on the plate. "I didn't mean it that way."

"Having a bodyguard is tougher than being one."

She'd never thought about it that way. But then, she'd never really thought about it at all. At least, not in reference to herself.

"Anyway, thanks for bringing him."

Again the shrug. "I can't do the other part of my job and keep both of you safe, too."

"Find who's sabotaging us."

He nodded.

She hadn't thought of that. "I guess you haven't had much chance to work on that," she said.

"It's not at the top of the list."

She knew what Josh Redstone's priorities were. "Redstone people ever and always first," she quoted.

Draven nodded. "Doing what official or government agencies are supposed to handle comes in after all that, although Josh has no problem with us helping out if requested or needed. Of course, if somebody hurts one of his own, all bets are off."

Josh himself had told her that, when he'd first hired her. For the first time in a very long time, she'd felt part of a family, as if there were people she'd not even met yet who cared about her and would help if she needed them.

As Draven had. And still was.

"I meant what I said, about the earthquake," she said quietly. "I owe you my life."

"You owe me nothing."

"Same to you," she said.

His brows furrowed. "What?"

"You don't owe me anything. Most especially feeling haunted, whether it's ugly memories or horrible dreams."

He stared at her, for the first time since she'd known him an expression of surprise breaking through. She'd nailed it, she thought.

"They are ugly. And horrible," he said, surprising her in

turn with the admission. "And I don't know why. I've seen worse, done things like that a dozen times. But you..."

He trailed off, and she wondered what he'd been going to say. "I what?"

For a long moment she thought he wasn't going to answer. It was obvious he was battling, whether to speak or stop himself from speaking she didn't know.

"You were the worst," he finally said. "Having to hurt you."

"Why?"

This time the shrug annoyed her.

"You had to have done other things that made you feel that way," she said.

"Once." He stopped, and she waited, hoping her silence would work as it had before. Finally he continued. "When I had to tell Josh his big brother—and my closest friend—had died in my arms in the Gulf."

Grace blinked. This was a story she'd never heard. "Josh's brother?"

"We were on a recon mission. He was leading. Land mine."

The short, brusque words told her as much about his remembered pain as they did about what had happened. And his expression was odd, as if he couldn't quite believe he was talking about this.

Or perhaps, that he was talking about it to her.

"And that's how you met Josh?" she asked.

He nodded. "I tracked him down at the little airport Jim told me he hung out at. Told him. Stayed awhile, to make sure he was okay. Saw the way he was building Redstone. When I left the service, he offered me a job."

"And you've been with him ever since."

He nodded. Then, abruptly, he asked, "What about your own ugly memories and bad dreams?"

As a diversion, it was pretty blatant, but she let it pass. He'd already opened up more than she'd ever seen before.

"I still have them," she answered. "Fewer, farther between, but just as awful when they hit. I don't think you spend that long thinking you're going to die without it leaving some permanent scars."

"You don't. The fact that you're functioning at all is amazing."

"I don't feel amazing," she said frankly.

"You are," he said.

Grace fought down the sudden image that hit her, of him saying she was amazing in another context altogether. A very personal, intimate context.

At least one thing, she thought, *there wouldn't be any surprises. He knows exactly what happened to me, and what's missing.*

She gave herself a mental shake; thoughts like that were not going to help any. She grasped for something else, anything else, to talk about.

"Sometimes," she said, "I feel like I haven't really dealt with it at all. I fight so hard not to let the memories swamp me. Maybe I shouldn't."

"What do you think dealing with it is, except getting control over it?"

Lured by this unexpected openness, she asked, "Have you ever…felt that way? Swamped?"

He went very still.

"Sorry," she muttered. "That was a silly question. You're John Draven, you're always in control."

The sound that burst from him then was an oddly twisted combination of pained laughter and disgust.

"You know what I did, before I came here? I quit."

She drew back, staring at him. "You what?"

"I quit Redstone. I handed Josh my resignation."

John Draven quitting Redstone? That would be second only to St. John leaving, or even Josh himself.

"Why?" she asked, unable to stop herself.

He shook his head, clearly wishing he hadn't let it slip out.

"Why would you leave Josh?"

He swore under his breath. "He asked me the same thing. I didn't know...how that would feel for him to ask that."

"Why?" she asked again.

Again he didn't answer.

"There has to be a good reason. You wouldn't do it unless there was. You quit because...?"

"Because I can't trust myself anymore!"

The words burst from him as if on a torrent of pain, a rush of emotion she was certain he didn't often release. It seemed to suck all the oxygen out of the air, and she had to draw in a deep breath. He wasn't looking at her, in fact was obviously avoiding meeting her gaze, as if it would be too painful to look at another human being and see their reaction to that reluctant exclamation.

"Can't trust yourself?"

"I've lost it," he said, his tone almost bitter. "Fine thing to say to somebody I'm supposed to protect, but, damn it, it's true. Mr. Cool-and-Controlled can't hang on to his temper anymore."

Her forehead creased. "What do you mean?"

"Just what I said. My fuse isn't just short, it doesn't exist. The slightest thing sets me off."

"Everybody has days like that."

He grimaced. "Days I could handle. This has been months."

"Maybe you're just tired. If you usually go without sleep the way you have here, you can't help but be."

"When it interferes with the job, the reason for it doesn't matter."

She frowned. "But it hasn't interfered. You haven't lost your temper here."

"Barely," he muttered.

"Does that matter, as long as you haven't?" she asked, echoing his words back at him. "Besides, if you know you're on a short fuse, you'll be on guard about it. You're probably safer from losing it now than ever."

He stared at her, as if having trouble absorbing her words. She took advantage of his silence to rise and go wrap the second half of her sandwich; she'd made it far too large. And she wanted him to think about what she'd said; it was surprisingly painful to think of this solid, strong man of such legendary cool doubting himself.

She turned to go get her glass to wash, and literally collided with him. Again with that catlike silence, he'd gotten up to bring his plate and glass to the sink.

A little breathless, she reached for the dishes. At the same moment he leaned forward to set them on the counter. She sucked in her breath as they touched once again.

His hands went to her shoulders, as if to steady her, and she wondered if she was really as wobbly as she suddenly felt. And then his fingers tightened, hot and hard on her flesh.

"Grace," he said, his voice gone so low and rough it sent a shiver down her spine.

And then he kissed her.

Chapter 16

He should have known.

The alarms had gone off in his head even louder than the trip wires outside when he'd found himself telling this woman whatever she wanted to know. It had felt like a compulsion, one he didn't even know the source of but that he knew he couldn't ignore. And so it poured out, admissions, pain, feelings he rarely admitted he had to himself, let alone someone else.

Let alone to a woman, especially one he was attracted to. If you could call the fire and fury he was feeling mere attraction.

He'd done quite well at ignoring those alarms, however. Showing once more how out of control he really was. And if he hadn't been sure, the fire that surged in him the moment his lips touched hers would have seared the knowledge into his brain.

He hadn't meant to kiss her. It hadn't even been in his mind. Which was, perhaps, the problem. The urge had arisen out of some deep, primal need, and seemed to have bypassed his brain altogether. And the next thing he knew he was looking down into those incredible eyes of hers, and unable to stop himself.

It was all he could do to keep from ravaging her mouth. It had been so long, and she was sweeter than anything he'd ever tasted in his life. Warm and honey-rich, her lips softened beneath his, and if some part of his mind was startled that she didn't resist, he ignored that, too.

Not only could he not stop, he wanted more. He wanted it longer, hotter, deeper, and nearly shook with the effort to not overpower her and take what he needed so badly. But even as he thought it he realized *overpower* wasn't the word, that you didn't have to overpower someone who wasn't fighting back.

She wasn't fighting.

She wasn't fighting, or even protesting, in fact she was accepting, as if she wasn't surprised at all. Of course, why would a woman like Grace ever be surprised that any man was hungry to kiss her?

"Draven," she whispered against his mouth.

He drew back slightly. "All things considered," he said, "I think you should call me John."

And that in itself should have been a warning, but he ignored it. He reclaimed her mouth, and his hands slipped up to cup the back of her head, to steady her as he deepened the kiss. He felt a shiver of anticipation at the thought of exploring her thoroughly, endlessly. There wasn't a part of her he didn't want to—

The thump of feet on the outside steps sounded like an invasion in the suddenly heated silence. He felt Grace stiffen. With an effort as big as any he'd ever made in his life he did what he knew he had to. He tore his mouth away from those sweet, too-tempting lips.

A split second before the door swung open he made his unwilling hands follow suit and release her. They barely had time to separate before Marly marched in.

Thankfully she appeared too wrapped up in her own agenda to notice anything else. She spotted them in the kitchen, marched—there really was no other word for it—over to them and took a confrontational stance, her hands on her hips and her eyes heated.

When she spoke, her voice was just as angry as her gaze and body language. And it was directed at him.

"I don't need a babysitter, y'know, and I think it really sucks that you told Kieren I did."

They were apparently, he noted, already on a first name basis. That part of his plan had worked, at least. As to this part, this unexpected attack, he wasn't at all sure what to do. Which seemed to be a regular state of affairs for him when it came to Marly.

"It was just a phrase," he began, but she wasn't buying.

"Sure. He's just about the hottest guy I've ever seen, and you tell him to watch me like I'm some sort of child."

"I told him to watch you like you're possibly in danger," he retorted, "which is the truth."

"Babysitting," she insisted.

"Did he say something to make you feel that way?"

"Kieren? No, of course not. *He* would never make me feel like such a baby."

The inference that he would was unmistakable, and Draven smothered a sigh.

"We're going for a walk," Marly said, with an emphasis on the first word that made it clear she was already thinking of herself and Buckley as "we." "I'm going to show Kieren where everything is."

Without waiting for any assent or approval, she turned on her heel and marched out in much the same way as she'd marched in.

Draven watched the girl go, telling himself it was a good thing she'd come in when she had. He wasn't at all sure he could have stopped himself if she hadn't. But that she had, and the way she had, brought home to him once more that whatever he might feel, and even if Grace was willing to settle for what little he could give, he didn't think he could deal with Marly on a regular basis.

"Well, he's certainly charmed her," Grace said shakily.

"Yeah. It's me who can't deal with her."

"You did fine. You usually do with her. Besides, that wasn't really aimed at you, she was just embarrassed and striking out."

He shook his head. "I never know what to say to her."

Grace laughed. "You think I do? This whole parenting thing is a seat-of-the-pants kind of flying."

He shook his head again, more slowly. "I couldn't do it. Not every day, like you do. It would drive me crazy."

She went very quiet, the laugh vanishing, and taking the accompanying smile with it. He felt suddenly bereft, and wasn't quite sure what had happened.

"I understand," she said, her voice as cool as the change in her expression. "It's a rare man who's willing to take on a child that isn't his. I don't think the man willing to take on Marly at this difficult stage of life even exists."

Draven had no idea what he should say to a statement like that, so kept silent. Her expression changed subtly, as if from pain, or maybe resignation. And when she spoke again, her voice was brisk and businesslike.

"Now if you'll excuse me, I'm going to go change to go to the site."

She left him standing there, staring after her, troubled for reasons he didn't even begin to understand.

Two days later he was watching Grace watch the crew frame the walls of the small control tower building when his cell phone rang.

"Draven."

"Two possibles matching your partial plate registered with addresses on the island."

St. John's voice and clipped words were immediately recognizable.

"Go," he said.

"One. A Cecil Bedran. Registration expired several years ago. Check showed he's deceased."

"And number two?"

"More interesting. Current, but according to the record, it's on a 1972 Ford van."

"Hmm," Draven said. There was no way that car had been a van of any vintage. "Name?"

"Business name. Caribe Merchants. Post office box in Belize City."

When he heard the name, Draven's mind made the obvious leap instantaneously. He wondered if he was wrong about *el mercader,* if the drug dealer truly was behind the attacks and had been all along.

"Who are the primaries at Caribe?"

"Layered ownership. We're digging."

The moment he acknowledged the information St. John disconnected. Conversation with the man was always short, and sometimes painfully brief. He talked as if he had a finite number of words to use in his life, so he had to ration them.

"News?" Grace asked, coming up beside him.

"As much as you ever get out of St. John."

"Ah. So the saying's true?"

"What saying?"

"If Draven's a legend, St. John's a mystery."

Draven grimaced, but the expression faded as Grace's mouth curved upward. It was a natural enough smile, but he sensed the same uneasiness he'd felt in the past couple of days.

Ever since he'd kissed her.

"I've heard about him," she said. "Though I've never spoken to him for longer than a minute or two."

"I'm not sure that anybody except Josh ever has," he said dryly.

She smiled again, and again he felt the change in it. She was smiling at the comment, he thought, but wary of who had made it.

By necessity he had gotten fairly good over the years at reading people. And there was no doubt in his mind that Grace had changed. Or rather, her attitude toward him had changed. She was more watchful, more sensitive or more nervous, he wasn't sure which. Like she had been when he'd first arrived, yet different. In any case, it was putting him on edge, because he didn't know what to do about it.

That alone was unusual enough for Draven to bother him. In part it was because he wasn't used to not knowing what to do, but also because he didn't know if it was a continuation of the problem that had made him hand Josh his resignation, or if it was simply Grace herself who had derailed his usual mental acuity.

If he thought about that kiss, the answer to that question was clear.

If he thought about that kiss, the answer to anything else was lost in the heat.

"I need to head back to the trailer," she said. "I have to make some calls."

Unable to speak just then, he nodded, and they started to walk.

They needed to talk, he realized. Or do whatever it was going to take to get rid of this new tension between them.

The moment the thought formed in his head he recoiled inwardly. Was he actually thinking he *wanted* to initiate one of *those* kinds of talks with a woman? Had he gone totally crazy? Volunteering for something like that was way out of his comfort zone. He'd rather volunteer for armed combat.

Hell, those kinds of talks *were* armed combat, and the male of the species was usually weaponless.

"I guess I need to thank you again," Grace said.

Draven stopped in his tracks. Given his current thoughts, his mind shot to the impossible. He'd never been thanked for an unasked-for kiss before—not that there were many in the first place—and he doubted that record was about to be broken.

"Thank me for what?" he asked carefully as she stopped herself and turned to face him.

"Marly."

He let out a breath he hadn't even been aware of holding. "Marly?" he asked, his voice nearly normal now.

"That scene two days ago aside, she's…a different girl. Her old self, almost. But better."

He wasn't sure he didn't like the old Marly better, thorns and all. This new girl, all giggles and sweetness, didn't seem quite real to him. The old Marly had at least been honest. Blunt, angsty and occasionally rude, yes, but honest. He didn't quite trust any change that came about simply by the presence of a good-looking male.

Like you don't trust any change that comes about simply by the presence of a good-looking woman?

His own snide thought dug deep, stinging, and he spoke quickly, before she could ask what was wrong.

"Don't thank me, thank Buckley."

"But he's only here because you brought him."

He shrugged. "Needed another body. I remembered him from his interview."

"And you knew he'd charm Marly."

"Hoped."

"I just hope…" Her voice trailed off.

He stopped to look at her. "Hope what?"

She sighed. "That she doesn't get hurt."

"That was in his orders."

"What was?"

"Making sure Marly didn't get hurt."

Grace chuckled, but it was an odd, rueful sound. "You really don't know much about fourteen-year-old girls if you think that's within his control."

He wondered about the undertone, but he'd already admitted as much, and didn't see that there was anything more to add to her observation.

"He'll do what he can," he said instead.

They started to walk again, until this time Grace suddenly stopped.

"Darn," she said, in a disgusted tone. "I forgot some papers I need to call about the sealer delivery."

She started back. Draven turned to accompany her just as his cell rang again. This time the ID window said not St. John, but Buckley. He'd taken Marly out in the new inflatable an hour or so ago, so Draven let Grace get a little ahead of him before he answered in case Buckley had something to report that Grace shouldn't overhear. If something had happened to Marly, that wasn't the way he'd want her to find out.

"Draven," he answered finally, when Grace was out if immediate earshot.

"Buckley. We're just off the south tip of the island. Marly wants to go to Ambergris Cay, shopping or something. Thought I'd better run it by you first."

What was it with girls, women and shopping? he thought. He wondered if Grace had the same tendency. An image flashed through his mind, of trailing after her in some upscale mall. He should have recoiled at the very idea, but instead he found himself thinking about what watching her shop would tell him about her.

"Sir?"

Buckley's voice was uncertain, as if he thought the connection might have been dropped. Draven again dragged himself out of an uncharacteristic reverie. No matter what had happened between him and Grace, it was no excuse for losing focus.

Belatedly he considered Buckley's question for a moment. He knew Buckley would have had thorough training in all sorts of watercraft, it was part of Redstone's own, in-house academy of sorts. So that wasn't an issue; Marly would be safe with him running the boat, even in unfamiliar waters.

Besides, he knew that Buckley wasn't clearing it with him for that reason anyway; what he really wanted to know was if there was any reason connected to their situation here that they shouldn't go. Ambergris Cay to the south of them was the most developed island in the area, a tourist mecca, and as such was relatively safe. And his gut told him their problem was isolated, confined to this bit of land.

"Stay away from the north end here," he said. "And check in when you're back."

"Right."

"And make sure she pays for everything," he added. "We had a little acting-out problem a while back. Don't think it will recur, but keep on her."

"Yes, sir. Want me to call her mom?"

"No. I'll tell her."

He disconnected the call, and picked up his pace to catch up with Grace, who was just entering the structure that would eventually become the control tower above the small terminal building.

The building exploded into a fireball.

Chapter 17

It was a replay of her nightmare. With different special effects. Instead of the slow rumble of the earthquake that had built until it was impossible to stay on her feet, there was a single, huge flash and boom, knocking her off her feet in the first instant. Her ears were ringing, so much that she could barely hear the galelike rush of the firestorm.

She tried to move. Couldn't. Something was pinning her down. Something hard and heavy lay across her hips. The beam, she thought. The one that was supposed to hold up the terminal's roof. She pushed at it. It didn't move.

She almost screamed.

Just like before, she was trapped.

But this time she could burn alive before anyone got here.

So get yourself out, she ordered silently. She made herself focus, not think about Nick and the others, and who else might be trapped. Or worse. She could do nothing for them unless she got out herself.

She thought she heard a shout, but with her ears still ringing she couldn't be sure. She hoped so; it would mean at least someone else was alive. She looked around as best she could through eyes that were streaming tears in the midst of the smoke, to see what was within reach. Then she twisted, turned, trying to ignore the pain. By turning on her side she managed to raise the beam slightly with her own body. She stretched as far as she could and just managed to reach one of the cinder blocks that had been blown sideways out of the half-built wall. She pulled it toward her. With a tremendous effort she wedged it under the beam. When she rolled back, the pressure eased.

"Now or never," she muttered, and began to struggle to free herself from the still-tight fit.

For an agonizingly long moment, as the fire raced closer, gobbling up whatever fuel was in its path, she didn't think she was going to make it. And then, with a final shove using all her strength, she was free.

She heard the shout again. Her name. She scrambled to her knees, glanced at the inferno that was now a mere yard away.

"Over here!"

Her shout brought on a paroxysm of coughing. She decided to shut up and just get out while she could still breathe at all. But she could barely see, and the heat was getting so intense she was sure the fire was nearly at her. She knew she didn't have time to think about it. She simply had to take her best guess at which way to go and get moving.

She stayed on her knees and crawled. Wished she had something to tie over her nose and mouth to filter the smoke at least a little. She was beginning to feel disoriented. Wondered if she was going in circles. Then a strong hand grabbed her. She looked up through the swirling smoke. And once again the harsh angel was there, hovering, sheltering her, saving her.

"Can you stand?"

Reality snapped back into place. Draven. Of course. Who else would come marching through hell?

Her throat was so raw she didn't trust her voice to speak, so she answered him by standing. She expected him to lead her out, but instead she was suddenly airborne as he picked her up over his shoulder. She let out a yelp of surprise, but it instantly brought on the coughing fit she'd feared.

"Quiet," she heard him say.

Since she could barely breathe hanging upside down over his shoulder, she had little choice but to obey that order.

She closed her eyes against dizziness and the worsening sting of the smoke. The sensation of being upside down only furthered the disorientation she was feeling. She very much didn't want to pass out. She was afraid she'd never wake up again. She had cheated the reaper once before, she didn't know if she could get lucky twice.

She wasn't sure when it started, just became aware that the breath of air she'd just taken had been clean. Smokeless. Life-giving. Even as her somewhat sluggish brain recognized the fact she felt herself sliding to the ground. She tried to stand, but her knees seemed oddly wobbly. And then strong arms caught her under the shoulders and knees and lowered her gently. She opened her eyes and once more it was a flashback to that other nightmare day, only this time she knew the harsh angel, knew he was just a man. An incredibly strong, brave and haunted man.

And that made it seem even more of a miracle than it had been that day in Turkey.

"Are you all right?"

She wasn't sure. Her throat was viciously raw, her eyes bleary from smoke and tears, and she had to try to sense past that and assess the rest of her body.

She hurt here and there; she couldn't deny that. But when

she flexed muscles and bent joints everything seemed to work, with no sudden stabs of pain.

"I think so," she said, barely able to hear her own croak over the steady buzz. "I was trapped. Under a beam." She suppressed a shudder.

Draven said something she couldn't hear.

"Ears," she said.

"I'll bet," Draven said, his voice sounding rough, raspy, as if he'd breathed in as much smoke as she had. Or as if his throat were tight. "You were too damn close to the blast." He paused then, touching her cheek with surprising gentleness. "You saved yourself this time, Grace."

"But you—"

"I just helped you outside. You got yourself out of that trap, and that inferno."

The bigger picture snapped back into her mind. "Marly," she gasped.

"She's fine. Nowhere near the blast."

"Nick," she said, trying to get up. Draven gently but firmly stopped her.

"I saw him outside. He's all right."

"But the framing crew, and the others, they were—" She had to stop to cough, a heavy chest-straining cough.

"We'll find out in a minute," he said when the fit abated. "Look at me."

She did, only then realizing he was streaked with ash or soot just as she was, just not as thoroughly. He stared back into her eyes until she started to feel uncomfortable. Then he put one hand in front of her left eye.

"Keep them open," he instructed.

He was checking her pupils, she suddenly, belatedly realized. "I didn't hit my head," she said.

He didn't answer her. He moved his hand away quickly, then repeated the action with her other eye.

"I've had a concussion before—" she had to stop to cough again "—I know what it feels like. I don't have one."

"No, you don't."

Was he speaking louder than normal, she wondered, or were her ears clearing up? "Then can I get up?"

"No."

"I'm really fine," she said again.

"Just relax."

Only then did she realize he was methodically and gently running his hands over her.

"I don't think anything's broken," she said, her voice still rough.

"No," he agreed.

"Then what are you looking—"

"Blood," he said shortly.

"Oh."

"She all right?"

Although the ringing seemed to be lessening, she hadn't heard Nick approach. She looked up at him, glad to see he looked relatively unscathed.

"I'm fine," she said, feeling a little spurt of irritation when Nick looked to Draven for verification.

"Small burns. Nothing too bad. Probably some bad bruising to come."

"That," she said, "I can pretty well guarantee." She shifted her gaze back to Nick. "What about the crews?"

"They're all…accounted for."

She relaxed, letting out a sigh of relief. But then what he'd said and how he'd said it registered.

"What do you mean, 'accounted for'?"

"I'd say he means he knows where they are," Draven said. "Move your arm out this way. Then the other arm."

She flicked him a glance, wondering if he was trying to distract her. She looked back at Nick, her vision still blurry.

"Was anyone hurt?"

Nick hesitated. He glanced at Draven again, and tension spiked through her.

"You'll get a full report later, I'm sure," Draven said. "Right now we need to get you cleaned up."

Grace scrambled to her feet, catching Draven off guard enough to break free. She felt a little wobbly, but faced him as steadily as she could. She was still blinking rapidly, trying to clear her streaming eyes. She knew she must look frightening, but right now she didn't care.

"I'm responsible for this project, which means I'm responsible for the people on it," she said. She turned back to Nick. "Who's hurt? Do we need an airlift?"

"It's already on the way," Nick said.

In that moment her vision cleared, enough to see the look on his face.

"Oh, God," she whispered. "Who?"

Yet again Nick glanced at Draven. He had apparently become the man in charge, no matter what she said. And as the fire behind them began to finally ebb, she supposed she could see why. This was now his crime scene, or whatever Redstone Security called things like this.

After a quick glance at her, Draven finally nodded.

"Chuck." Nick's voice was tight. "And it's a lot worse."

Grace knew the two men had worked on several jobs together. And she also knew Chuck was one who had asked to be assigned to this job after he'd learned she was the project manager. She felt an aching sense of culpability; she'd never had a serious injury—other than her own—on a job before, not even the one struck by the earthquake. And now one man had been hurt twice.

Besides, she liked Chuck. He'd always been cheerful, worked hard and thought himself very lucky to be working for Redstone.

Nick's eyes were suspiciously bright, and he excused himself before, Grace guessed, he lost control. As he walked away, Grace felt the tiny shivers going through her. It must have been bad, for Nick to react this strongly. Would Chuck be the first death she'd ever had on a project?

She should have stayed on the ground, she thought through the fog of shock that enveloped her. Because right now she felt like she was going to fall down.

"Can you walk to the motor home, or shall I carry you?" Draven said.

She turned her head to look at him, and even that felt slow, as if she were trying to move underwater. "There are things I have to do. He has a wife, kids, they—"

"That will be handled."

"But if they need anything—"

"He and his family will have whatever is necessary, no matter what happens. Redstone takes care of its own."

"But I should call Debra—"

"Josh will call her."

She blinked at that. "Josh? Personally?"

"It's his policy. He is Redstone, and he feels he's ultimately responsible for everyone who works for him."

She felt both sadness at the circumstances, and pride in Redstone, Josh and everything they both stood for.

Draven repeated his original question.

"I can walk," she said. *I think,* she added silently.

She could, she found, but not well. The prosthetic foot seemed to have been twisted slightly, and was no longer properly seated on the stump. After a couple of limping steps she stopped to try to adjust it, although she suspected she was going to have to remove it and start over.

She never got the chance to try. The moment the problem became obvious, Draven literally swept her off her feet. It was the phrase that leapt to her mind; she couldn't help that, nor could she help the flood of color that rose to her cheeks as the other implications of the phrase echoed in her head.

"I can walk," she protested, but it sounded halfhearted even to her own ears.

"Quiet," he said as he settled her in his arms.

His voice sounded rough, and when she looked up at him she saw his jaw was set tightly. She knew his strength, had seen it evidenced, so she knew it wasn't a strain for him to carry her.

At least, not a physical one.

He carried her into the bathroom and gently let her down. Despite her efforts she wobbled. He moved quickly to brace her.

"I'm okay," she said.

He ignored her, and began to peel off her filthy clothes. Startled, she pulled back.

"Just be still," he said, his voice as tight as his jaw had been. There was an undertone in it she didn't recognize, because she'd never heard it before.

She felt herself coloring hotly as he continued, but still noted how gently he touched her, how carefully he pulled her filthy, smoke-and-ash saturated clothes off. She shivered when she was left in nothing but her underwear, but she wasn't at all cold. Embarrassed at the plain, cotton, utilitarian undergarments, perhaps, but nothing fancier was comfortable or practical on a job, especially in this climate.

Odd, she thought with a sort of distant vagueness, that she wasn't at all embarrassed about her foot. How could she be, when this was the man who knew better than anyone but her doctors what she'd been left to deal with?

And then he unhooked her bra, with a slight awkwardness that somehow reassured her. She felt the motion of her breasts as they were freed, and an unusual little sting from a spot on the left one. She looked and saw a reddened spot where an ember or something had given her a small burn.

Even as she looked, she saw Draven's hand move. She sucked in a breath as his strong, tough hand cupped the soft flesh and lifted. She felt an odd tremor through his hands, as if he were trembling. And that reassured her even more. She didn't pull away, couldn't, as a memory of her dream flashed through her head. Instead she barely quashed the urge to push forward, pressing herself into his palm.

Slowly, so slowly she nearly cried out with anticipation, he bent his head and kissed that spot, so gently she felt only the barest brush of his lips.

She wobbled again, but for a completely different reason this time. She felt a shiver go through her, followed by a rush of heat that seemed to pool low and deep. Draven must have felt it, too, because he raised his head and looked at her, his eyes hot with something she had never expected to see in those cool, green depths. Except in dreams...

He began to move quickly then, stripping off her panties and then, after a moment's study, removing the prosthesis as if he did it every day. Again oddly, she didn't feel awkward at being naked in front of him—in fact, judging from that building heat, she instead found it arousing—but only wondered if she was going to be able to hop into the shower.

And then Draven solved the problem by lifting her in his arms and stepping into the shower himself.

"You're going to get wet," she protested.

"Don't worry about it."

"But you're dressed."

"That," he said gruffly, "could be fixed, but I'm not sure you'd like the results."

Again her breath caught as she realized what he was saying. And stopped entirely when she realized that she wanted it. More than she could ever remember wanting anything in her life.

"*I'm* sure," she said.

He went rigidly still. "What?"

"I'm sure I'll like it."

"Grace—"

He stopped as she reached up to cup his cheek. Slowly he let her slip down to the tile. She held on to him for balance…and because she wanted to. He stared down at her.

"Don't, Grace. Don't start if you don't mean to finish."

"I won't," she said. "I mean it."

And then she reached for his hand. Slowly she drew it upward, until it was once more cupping her breast.

She heard him suck in a breath. And then, almost convulsively, his fingers curved around her.

As if making a final effort at warning he said thickly, "Don't count on me to stop unless we do it now. I've wanted this for too long."

Me, too, she thought, unable to speak it with his hand on her. So in answer she balanced against the wall of the shower, took his other hand and urged it toward her other breast.

Draven groaned aloud. Grace felt the rumble deep in his chest before she heard the sound. She pressed closer and felt the surge of male hardness against her. Then she felt a shudder go through him, and the knowledge of his response only stoked the fire building inside her.

And then he began to move. Quickly. Making sure she was safely balanced, he backed up a step and yanked off his own clothes. She looked at his hard, leanly muscled body, at the sleek skin and the scars that marked it. Looked at the broad chest; the lean, flat belly; and below to the thick curls surrounding jutting, rigid flesh. A shiver went through her at the thought of it buried inside her, and the heat within became almost unbearable.

He reached past her and turned the tap. The water turned warm almost immediately, thanks to the proximity of the motor home's water heater. Draven grabbed the soap, but ignored the washcloth on the rack. When she realized why she shivered again; he was going to wash her himself, with his bare hands.

She nearly moaned as he began, his soap-slick hands sliding over her. And then he cupped her breasts again, and slid his thumbs over peaks already taut, and she did moan. He made a deep, guttural sound in response. Then he caught her taut nipples between his fingers and gently squeezed and flicked them until she cried out at the intensity of the sensation.

She thought for a moment she was going to fall, but he steadied her even as his hands slid down her body, rubbing gently, soaping and rinsing in turn. When he reached her legs, she felt the first flicker of apprehension, but he bathed her stump as tenderly as the rest of her, adding a bit of gentle massage that felt wonderful.

He worked his way back up, slowly, so slowly that she was in an agony of anticipation by the time his slick hands slid between her thighs. She knew the fierceness of her own arousal by the ease and speed with which he found the swollen knot of nerves that were already aching for his touch. He circled, caressed and stroked until she knew she was going to explode if he didn't stop.

"Please, John," she begged, not sure what she was begging for.

"Johnny seems right now," he said, and through the haze she was vaguely aware he looked somewhat surprised at his own words.

"Johnny," she whispered, trying it, liking this name that she would never have dared use on her own.

"Relax," he said. "Just let go."

"But—"

He kissed her then, swamping her protest in a wave of

heat so searing she lost all awareness of anything except his lips taking her mouth and his hands claiming her body. She knew her own slick readiness by the way his finger slid into her. Knew how close she was by the sensation of her body clenching around the invasion.

He broke the kiss and swore under his breath as she tightened. She could feel his body tense.

"Not without you," she choked out. "Please."

He shuddered, as if fighting something, and then began again. He stroked her, rubbing that now violently aroused knot of nerve endings. And then he lowered his head and caught one stiff nipple in his mouth and sucked deeply.

Grace heard herself cry out as her body rippled with wave after wave of fiery sensation. And still he kept on, driving her higher, until she was shaking with the force of it.

And then, in one smooth motion, he lifted her, pulled her legs around him and stepped out of the shower. He took her down to the floor with exquisite care. He came down with her and into her in the same movement, driving himself hard and deep, filling and stretching her to the edge of unbearable sensation.

Grace screamed at the hard, driving, huge invasion of flesh into a body already on the edge. And then he moved again, pulling back and driving home again, and she shattered. Some small part of her mind knew she was wild with it; she felt herself buck and twist like some wild thing impaled by incredible pleasure. She grabbed at him, clutched at him, at any part of him she could reach to grind closer, take him deeper.

When he groaned her name as his body surged into her one last time, when she felt him shudder beneath her hands and explode inside her, when he held on to her as if she were the only thing left in his world, Grace thought there was nothing more to be asked of this life.

* * *

Draven woke up, amazed that he'd slept in the middle of the day. Even as tired as he was, that was unusual. And instead of his usual instant alertness, he came back to awareness slowly, in a drifting sort of way he'd never experienced before.

But he'd never experienced anything like what had happened here, either. From the shower to the bathroom floor to Grace's bed, he'd been like some crazed man, starved for something he'd never known existed. Because he'd never known anything like the incredible sensation of sinking into her and feeling as if he'd found home at last, or like the hot, swift passion that had swept them both upward to explode in a firestorm rivaling the one that had nearly separated them forever.

He shied away from the implications of that as he gradually became more awake. He would sort that out later, he thought as he fought off the last groggy remnants of the unaccustomed afternoon sleep. Right now, he had other things to think about. Other things to do.

But one thing was crystal clear to him now, as he lay there holding this gallant, lovely, unexpectedly sensual woman in his arms. He was tired of just reacting. Tired of guarding against instead of solving the problem. *El mercader* had given him the information he needed.

It was time to go on the offensive.

Chapter 18

Grace awoke in the early twilight, feeling oddly energized after her two-hour nap. She would have expected to still feel shaken by the explosion, but with the exception of the expected aches, she felt good.

And some unexpected aches.

The memories flooded back, reminding her of exactly why she felt so energized. For a moment she just lay there as the erotic heat swept over her anew, as if he were still touching her, still caressing her.

As if he were still here.

She jolted upright. Stared at the empty space in the bed next to her. Felt an answering emptiness building inside her. Had he simply gone? Without a word? Gotten what he wanted and casually left her to wake up feeling alone and lost?

Was she suddenly drowning in cliché?

She said it to herself sarcastically as common sense

flooded back in. Everything she knew about John Draven told her he didn't take anything lightly. Just because she was a little emotionally scarred didn't mean she should assume this was any different. Long ago, after realizing her imaginings were so often worse than the reality came to be, she'd sworn not to spend any of her life going to meet a ship full of troubles that hadn't docked yet.

Calmer now, she stretched, wincing when a sore spot protested. Bruises hadn't shown up yet, but she knew they would soon.

She heard a sound from the other room. And chided herself for the way her pulse sped up at the realization that he hadn't left after all.

She got up, pondered what she should do about dressing. After the afternoon they'd spent, naked on her bed and exploring each other in the tropical light, worrying about covering up seemed a bit absurd. But it was still too new, too fragile, so she got out a full set of clean clothes.

She reached for the prosthetic foot, which had gotten fairly grubby amid the smoke and ashes. To her surprise it was clean. She didn't think she was that fuzzy that'd she'd tidied it up and didn't remember, and Marly wouldn't have done it even if she'd been back from her trip to Ambergris.

Which left Draven. John. Johnny, she said to herself, and it made her shiver to remember when he'd told her to use the name she instinctively knew few were given permission to use.

The thought that he had cleaned the prosthesis for her made her feel a tightness in her throat. She couldn't remember anyone doing something like that for her, only to help, without being asked and without expecting anything in return. And he'd clearly felt no qualms, just as his only reaction to the sight of her stump had been to kiss the scars as

the beginning of a sensual foray that had ended with her stifling a scream she was sure would have been heard in
Belize City.

She powdered, put on a fresh stump sock and the foot,
then dressed quickly. She quietly opened the door and
stepped into the main room of the motor home.

And stopped dead.

She knew the man in front of her had to be Draven, but
it was a Draven she'd never seen before. It wasn't simply that
he was dressed in different clothes—black jeans and shirt
and a loose jacket—or that he had his hair dampened and
slicked back, giving him an even more ascetic look.

It was his face. His expression. Always severe, now it
was hard-edged, unyielding, bordering on fierce. And it
was the way he was moving. He always had a tight-knit
sort of grace about him, but now he was moving as if he
barely had a leash on some building storm inside him. She
could sense an imminent detonation, and she had the sudden thought that when John Draven exploded, it was entirely possible that he could do more damage than the pipe
bomb he'd told her had blown up the half-finished terminal building.

When she saw what he was doing, her heart slammed into
her throat.

He was arming himself. Not just the automatic weapon
she'd seen before at the small of his back, but also another,
smaller one in a holster strapped to his ankle.

Then he picked a knife up from the sofa and slipped it into
his boot. A military-style knife that looked painfully like the
one he'd used on her, that day that now seemed so long ago.
But it hadn't been this Draven who had done that. This was
no harsh angel; this was a warrior. A warrior who wouldn't
be stopped by anything short of death.

He picked up something else that looked like a coiled cord

and put it in his left jacket pocket. Something else she didn't recognize, a small case of some kind, went in the other jacket pocket.

He turned then. She thought he hadn't been aware of her presence, but the minute he faced her she knew he'd known all along she was standing there. She felt a shiver go down her spine as a being she'd never seen before looked back at her. The first word that popped into her head was frightening.

Predator.

She swallowed tightly against the sudden dryness of her mouth. She opened her mouth to speak, could think of nothing to say and closed it again.

When he spoke, his voice was a chilly, emotionless thing that matched the expression on his face and the flat, almost bleak look in his eyes.

"I've called Buckley. They're almost back here. He'll take over."

He picked up something else from the sofa and held it out to her. She barely glanced at it before she took it, feeling mesmerized by the changes in him.

"That's a private satellite phone. Dial five-five and you'll have a direct, scrambled connection to Redstone headquarters."

She finally managed to find her voice. "Why do I need that?"

"If anything else happens here, tell Buckley. If something happens to him, you use that."

She looked down at the device, which looked like a slightly oversize cell phone. She stared at it, not wanting to ask the obvious question of why he was giving it to her.

"But you said to call you," she managed to get out.

"I'll be out of touch until I get back."

"Back." She said it flatly as he confirmed her guess. He

was leaving. Leaving to do…something she didn't even want to think about. And before she could stop herself the question came out. "And if you don't come back?"

He didn't even blink. "Buckley will take over."

Just like that. As if this was routine. As if walking into danger that could possibly prove fatal was something he did so often it didn't merit acknowledgment.

And as soon as she thought it, she realized it was quite possibly true.

"What are you going to do—"

The opening of the outer door interrupted the question she didn't really want answered. Marly and her shadow came in, the girl chattering excitedly, Buckley making a very creditable pretense of interest.

Then Marly saw Draven. Even the teenager saw the change. Grace wondered if this was how she had looked when she'd first seen him like this, with that sort of stunned, uneasy expression on her face.

Only Buckley didn't react. Grace wondered if that was because he'd seen this Draven before, or if it was because he could undergo the same kind of change himself. She tried to imagine the golden boy as something dark and dangerous. The image just wouldn't form.

She understood that she was focusing on Buckley to avoid dealing with Draven's transformation. To have the man she had spent the most incredible hours of her life with go from lover to…whatever he'd become was more than she could handle right now.

She told herself she shouldn't be surprised. Hadn't he gone from a gentle, careful and unhurried lover to a fierce, rough and demanding one in the space of an afternoon? That she had reveled in both was something else she couldn't deal with at the moment, in the face of this conversion.

"What are you doing?" Marly asked him, her voice tiny.

"Ending this," he said, and Marly reacted to the changed voice just as Grace had, drawing back slightly.

At last Grace regained her voice, although she guessed it sounded much like her daughter's had. "Where are you going?"

Draven looked at her then. She thought she saw a brief flicker of something warmer in that icy gaze, but it was gone so swiftly she couldn't be sure. But his next word, short and deadly, blasted the thought out of her mind.

"Hunting."

It was a few minutes after Draven was gone that, as if he felt he should say something, Buckley spoke.

"He really is the best."

"I'm sure he is," Grace muttered.

"Don't worry about him. He may be hunting a bad guy, but I'd back Mr. Draven against any five men you could come up with."

She didn't like the fact that her state of mind had become so obvious. And she certainly didn't want what had happened between them to become known until she'd had a chance to work through her roiling emotions.

Especially in front of her too-young, impressionable daughter.

"I'm not worried," she said.

How big a lie that was she wasn't certain. She knew his reputation, and now that she'd seen him in hunting mode, she had to believe it was well earned. But he had given her that phone. To use if he didn't come back.

To use if he was killed.

She fought back the shiver that threatened to ripple through her. She told herself she really shouldn't worry. He knew what he was doing. Hadn't his metamorphosis from lover to predator shocked her into speechlessness?

"He looked...scary," Marly said, still in that tiny voice. "I've never seen him look like that."

"It's part of why he's so good at what he does," Buckley said to the girl. "The people he goes up against see just what you did. And they think twice. Some of them just give up without a fight, after seeing that look."

All Grace could think about was what it had taken in his life to put that look in his eyes.

She'd never felt so tangled up inside. Her memories of this afternoon were colliding with the man she'd seen leave here. She wasn't sure if the two could ever be reconciled. Wasn't even sure she wanted to reconcile them.

But how would she feel if he didn't come back? If something went fatally wrong?

Her mind shied away from that. She told herself he wouldn't be chief of Redstone Security if he made mistakes. That he was capable of handling anything that came along. He was capable of taking care of himself. Capable of resolving any situation. John Draven could handle anything.

While she didn't know if she was capable of handling the simple fact that, fool that she was, she might be in love with him.

Draven tossed the coiled metal line over the ten-foot wood barricade, tugged until the hook on the end grabbed and held. Hand over hand he walked up the wall, then gripped the top and pulled himself up. He checked the other side, picked a spot just big enough behind a hibiscus covered with pink blooms, and went over. He landed with little more than a faint thud, and continued down into a crouch behind the shrub in one smooth movement.

He waited, listening. He'd watched the compound from the roof of an abandoned building a quarter mile away, using one of Redstone Technology's latest compact spotting scopes. The house and three outbuildings—one of them probably a meth lab or something, he guessed—stood just where the island started to narrow toward the point at the north end. The sandbar that extended out from the point curved toward the mainland and disappeared into the turquoise water a couple of hundred yards out.

He'd observed for a couple of hours, noting that there didn't appear to be any guard dogs, and timing the intervals at which he saw any movement of people outside and along the tall wooden barricade that had been built around the five or so acres surrounding the sprawling two-story house.

His next step had been to switch on the infrared feature on the scope, to look for signs of an alarm system. Nothing registered. When he got close enough, he did a physical inspection, again looking for any sign of an alarm. He still found nothing. So either they had something so new he didn't know about it yet, or they weren't worried. Without arrogance, he guessed it was the latter; Redstone usually came up with the cutting-edge stuff, and he was one of the first to know about it.

He timed his arrival at the spot he'd chosen at an unpatrolled moment. He crouched and waited. Saw and heard nothing.

He began to work his way toward the house. Some effort had been made to keep the area clear of undergrowth, but in this tropical place it was a full-time job to just stay even. He was thankful for that, because it offered enough cover for him to make it to the edge of the ornately landscaped area around the glistening pool without being spotted. After that, it didn't matter.

He emerged from the still-wild area into the formal part of the yard, designed by, in his view, somebody with too much money and too little taste. But he had learned early on that it was wise to learn as much as possible about your adversary, and what they chose to live with was information that contributed to that goal. So he studied the garden anyway.

Ornate statuary was everywhere, including several religious icons he found more than a little ironic given that they were gracing the property of a drug dealer. He strolled past a gilded statue of a pudgy cherub with a bow and some tiny arrows that he supposed was supposed to be Cupid, which stood a few feet away from a Madonna that was even more ornate.

Irony, he thought, wasn't a strong enough word.

He reached the flagstone deck around the lagoon-style pool. Drugs still paid well, obviously. He glanced at the house, and the tall, spacious windows on the wall facing away from the coast of Belize and looking at the open sea.

Off to one side, parked on a gravel area, he saw several vehicles, most of them showing the wear and tear of the tropical climate. The fancy wheels he assumed were around must be safely tucked in the large garage he could just see the corner of.

As he went a little farther, he was able to see the last car in the row. He stopped, staring at it. Checked the license plate.

It was the car he'd seen speeding away from the construction site. And the license was not the one registered to Caribe Merchants, but rather the one St. John had told him came back registered to a deceased man.

Had his gut been wrong? Had it truly been *el mercader* all along?

His brain, already in high gear, processed the idea quickly, and he realized it didn't make any difference, he would still be here, handling it the same way.

He stepped out onto the patio and considered the deck furniture that was nearly as elaborate as the statuary had been, chose the least obnoxious lounge of the group. He sat on the edge, glad it was less uncomfortable than it looked.

He swung around to stretch out on the lounge, crossing his feet casually at the ankles.

He relaxed and waited for *el mercader* to notice he was here.

Chapter 19

When the guards finally spotted him, they were so startled that it clearly took them a moment to believe what they were seeing. Draven had interlaced his fingers behind his head as he relaxed on the lounge, making it clear he had no plans to reach for any weapon he might have. It was a gamble, but he was counting on curiosity to keep him alive.

The first thing the men did was draw down on him. That told him their boss didn't believe in taking chances. The fact that they didn't shoot him on sight told him *el mercader* didn't believe in shooting first and asking questions later. It wasn't much, but it was enough to start with.

One of the men spoke into a two-way radio while the other did a perfunctory pat-down search. He found the weapon at the small of Draven's back. Draven didn't wince even inwardly. The two-inch .38 was still strapped to his leg and the Ka-bar knife with the high-carbon, seven-inch blade was still tucked into his boot.

But he also noticed the faintest tinge of purple on the man's hands. Between the presence of the car and the remnants of the dye, he knew this was the man who'd tripped the alarm.

He was escorted rather forcefully into the house. And there he got his second surprise. He'd expected the interior of the house to reflect the same gaudy taste as the outside, but instead it had a completely different feel. The décor was expensive, light colors that emphasized the balminess of the climate and sturdy pieces of furniture that anchored the whole without weighing it down, a classic island effect.

Classic, and classier, was his first thought. The juxtaposition of the outside and inside was startling. And as he was escorted through the house, he wasn't sure what this difference added to his assessment of *el mercader*.

They shoved him into a room that for all the world looked like an English library, complete with dark green walls and floor-to-ceiling bookcases. They tossed the Glock onto the huge, cherrywood desk, in front of the man who sat in the leather executive-type chair. And Draven had to reassess yet again.

He knew what the average person's image of a Central American drug dealer was. Slick, dripping in gold jewelry, dressed in expensive clothes, whatever the stereotype was, *el mercader* didn't fit it. He didn't fit the tacky display outside, either.

Nor, Draven had realized with the first words out of the man's mouth, was he Central American. Draven got most of what he spat out angrily to the two guards, chewing them out for letting him get so far, because it was said in that Americanized combination of Spanish and English known as Spanglish, used mostly by people who had grown up speaking both. And if the near-blond color of his hair was any indicator, his heritage was at least partly on the English-speaking side.

The two men left hastily the moment their boss released them. Draven took a seat in a chair opposite the desk without being asked, and noted that while the man's eyebrows lifted slightly, he said nothing.

"So," Draven said as if he were visiting the new home of a friend, "when did you change decorators?"

The brows lowered as *el mercader* blinked. "What?"

"Inside. Did it used to look like the outside?"

The man drew back slightly. His expression was an odd one, hard to interpret, but Draven thought he saw the faintest twitch at one corner of his mouth, as if he were trying not to smile or chuckle.

"Yes," the man said. "But it left with the woman who produced it. My ex-wife is off to turn some other man's home into a nightmare."

It was, as he'd guessed, the voice of a native English speaker. And a well-spoken one at that.

"Good choice," Draven said, and again saw the mouth twitch. But any trace of amusement vanished as the man leaned back in his chair, looking across at Draven.

"You better have a good reason for being here, *pendejo*."

Draven ignored the last insulting word, thinking instead that it was interesting that the first question wasn't "Who are you?" There was only one reasonable assumption to make, and that was that the man already knew who he was.

"I think so," Draven said mildly.

He waited, letting the silence spin out. He held the man's gaze steadily, knowing it was becoming a contest of who would break first. And knowing it wouldn't be him; he'd done this too many times, with men tougher than this one, men who could afford but wouldn't allow themselves this kind of luxury, for fear it would soften them.

El mercader broke.

"You are Redstone," he said, in the tone of someone expecting to surprise his listener. Since he'd already deduced the man knew who he was, Draven was easily able to keep any flicker of expression off his face, and out of his voice.

"And you are *el mercader*."

This time the twitch broke through to a grin. "Now that we have that clear, I repeat, why are you here?"

"To find out who is hiding behind the nickname."

The grin vanished. *El mercader* tensed, and Draven made ready to move quickly if he had to. But he continued speaking, as if he'd noticed nothing.

"And to learn if he is the one I have to stop."

The man's expression went from antagonism to curiosity in the space of a moment. "Most," he said, "have already decided that."

So, as Draven had figured, he knew that he was the prime suspect. "I'm not convinced," he said.

The man leaned forward, looking at Draven intently. "Why?"

"Because you're the most obvious."

"Sometimes the obvious is the truth."

"Sometimes," Draven agreed.

"What makes you think that is not true this time?"

"Thinking has nothing to do with it."

"Ah. I appreciate a man who trusts his instincts." *El mercader* leaned back in his chair, smiling now. "No, I am not the one you need to stop."

Draven believed him. There was always the chance he was misjudging, and he wasn't one hundred per cent confident in what his gut was telling him these days, but he had little choice but to trust it once again.

"If that's the case, then perhaps I should tell you your men need a little more practice. Or perhaps a little more... motivation."

The man behind the desk frowned. "What do you mean?"

Draven held up his hands, palm out, to show his peaceful intent. Then he lifted one foot to his other knee and pulled out his knife and set it on the edge of the desk. *El mercader* swore, loudly.

But when Draven switched feet and pulled out the small, .38 revolver, the man leapt to his feet. Draven's Spanish was better than adequate, but even he couldn't follow the string of furious words that followed. After another moment *el mercader* sat back down. Draven didn't envy the two men who were going to bear the brunt of their boss's wrath.

But the action had done what he hoped, removed the man's last doubts about his sincerity at this moment. After a moment spent calming down, the man returned to the matter at hand. He continued as if nothing had happened. So he could, Draven noted, compartmentalize, even when angry. A good sign for what he was here to propose.

"I have no interest in your little airstrip," *el mercader* said. "I do no business here."

"So I've heard."

"It is a smart man who keeps his home clean."

"And it is a smart man in your business whose real name is still unknown."

A small smile returned at the acknowledgment, or perhaps at the admission that Draven had tried and failed to learn who he was.

"My secret is satisfaction," *el mercader* said. "I am happy where I am, with my little corner. I protect what I have, but I don't need to expand. I don't trespass on anyone else's turf."

"A smart man," Draven repeated, continuing to play to the man's obviously strong ego. He'd do what he had to to put an end to this. "Smart enough to see a good deal when it's offered."

The man looked startled, then amused, and finally interested. "What kind of deal would Redstone possibly want to make with me? I find it hard to believe they are interested in my business."

"Not yet," Draven said.

One brow shot upward. "I see."

Draven suspected that he did. He himself knew that eventually, when Redstone began operations, he'd have to take the man down. Cleaning up such problems was another side benefit of having Redstone come to your part of the world. They only got involved if it impacted Redstone directly, but if they did, the problem was inevitably solved.

Draven leaned back in his own chair, rested his elbows on the plush arms and steepled his fingers in front of him. "How has life been lately?"

That twist of the lips again. "Annoying," *el mercader* said. "The esteemed Sergeant Espinoza harassing my people, Mayor Remington writing editorials accusing me, myself being followed whenever I leave the grounds."

"Very annoying," Draven agreed.

"I am tired of taking the blame for your troubles. There is enough I am guilty of, without taking the rap for things I haven't done."

Draven nodded. He'd been hoping for just that mindset.

"Then I will tell you that your immediate future can be improved."

The man looked thoughtful. Draven doubted he'd missed the implication that his long-term future was another matter, but he'd obviously decided that was to be dealt with when the time came.

"You know the locals. Do you have any suspicions on who might be involved?" Draven asked.

"I have some ideas, yes. You have a plan?"

"Yes."

The man behind the desk studied him intently once more. Draven stayed silent, knowing it was now in his court.

"Talk," *el mercader* finally said.

Draven talked.

Grace finally stopped pacing, only because the bruises were beginning to make themselves felt. When she started to limp because her hip was aching where the beam had come down on her, she finally sat down.

"Are you all right?"

Marly's voice was more concerned than Grace could recall in recent memory. When Nick had come to the motor home to check on Grace, he had inadvertently let out more details of the explosion than Grace would have told her daughter, especially about how close she had come to being killed. The girl had been a bit clingy ever since.

It was the opposite of how she'd been after the earthquake, when she'd seemed to pull away and to want little to do with her mother or even acknowledge what had happened. Grace wondered what had caused the change, but welcomed it. She hoped it wasn't just a temporary mood, as Marly's so often seemed to be these days.

"Just a little stiff," she answered.

"Can I get you anything?"

That offer was so uncharacteristic of the girl of late that Grace couldn't help staring at her. Marly flushed, as if she knew exactly what her mother was thinking.

"No," Grace said, "but, thank you. Very much."

She hoped the girl realized she meant for more than the simple offer. She thought perhaps she did when Marly looked up and gave her a small smile.

Later, when Marly and Kieren were involved in a video game as if they were both of an age, Grace found herself doing exactly what she'd sworn not to: sitting by the window waiting for Draven to return. And no amount of chiding herself for being an idiotic, moonstruck female helped.

But then, the average idiotic, moonstruck female wasn't waiting for a man who might not make it back alive.

After another hour, when Marly and Kieren had given up on the video game, Grace stood up. She winced once more as her body protested.

"Mom?"

Grace made a quick decision. "Would you go in the bathroom and find the aspirin for me?"

"Sure."

The girl hurried off to the bathroom. Grace turned to Kieren. "Where did he go?"

The young man gave her a startled look. She realized she'd used the tone she used to give orders on a job. But at this point she didn't care, she just wanted an answer.

"I don't know," Kieren said. Grace stared him down. "I mean it," he said after a moment. "All he told me was that this was going to end, now, and not to let either one of you out of my sight."

"And to call Redstone if he didn't come back?"

"Well, yeah, of course, but—"

He broke off as she turned away and headed for the door.

"Ms. O'Conner," he said, leaping to his feet.

She kept going. Reached for the door handle. Before she could grasp it, Kieren was there, slipping between her and the door.

"I can't let you go out," he said. "Mr. Draven's orders."

"I'm going," she said. "Your job is to keep my daughter safe."

"Both of you," he said.

"I'm releasing you from that."

"I'm very sorry Ms. O'Conner, but you can't do that. I answer to Mr. Draven."

"But he's not here."

"Doesn't matter. He'll expect me to carry his orders out, no matter what. I'm supposed to keep both of you here."

"Then you've got a problem."

Kieren said gently, "No, Ms. O'Conner, I'm afraid you do."

"You'll have to physically stop me."

Kieren sighed and said, "Then that's what I'll do. Reluctantly, but I will do it."

"I'm sure Mr. Draven wouldn't like it if you hurt the person you're guarding."

"No, he wouldn't. That's why he makes sure we're trained so well nobody gets hurt. But I'd be a lot happier if I didn't have to worry about it," he said.

"Mom?" Marly's voice came, somewhat muffled, from the bathroom. "I can't find the aspirin."

Grace, who had known perfectly well they weren't in there but had needed Marly out of the room for a moment, called back to her, "Try the bedroom, then. I think it may be in a drawer. Thanks, honey."

Grace, who had never taken her eyes off Kieren, continued to study him for a long silent moment. He returned her gaze levelly, never dodging, never blinking. A solid, steadfast core became evident, and in that moment she revised her earlier opinion. Suddenly she could picture him transforming as Draven had, into something powerful and dangerous.

"And if I asked you if you'd really fight a woman, and a disabled one at that?"

It was his turn to study her. And then, softly, he said, "I'd wonder if you were really the woman Mr. Draven told me about. She would never trade on her physical condition."

Kieren Buckley, it seemed, was indeed dangerous, and in more ways than one.

"I believe we have an impasse," she said.

"No, ma'am. I believe I've won."

"Presumptuous of you."

"No, Ms. O'Conner. It's just that Draven is never wrong about people. And there's no way you'd do something that would get me fired."

She gave him a sideways look, and despite her emotional state, he looked so innocently solemn she couldn't help but smile.

"You are good, aren't you?" she said. "Does Redstone have a class in Manipulation 101?"

"Yes, ma'am," he said with a grin. "Although it's got a much fancier name."

"I'm sure it does. Does your boss teach it?"

Kieren laughed. "No. He brought in a psychologist, a guy who served with him in the rangers."

The memory of what Draven had told her about Josh's brother flashed through her mind, and she wondered if Draven had seen that psychologist afterward. Her image of how he must have been back then didn't really fit with that idea. She'd always thought men like army rangers, whose motto, she'd learned, was "Rangers lead the way" because they were the first into any dangerous situation, would think themselves too macho for that kind of help. But perhaps even the army had seen the necessity. Or perhaps she'd just had the wrong idea all along.

"Got it!" Marly said as she came back into the room, carrying the small bottle. "It was in the top dresser drawer, with your leg powder."

She stopped, looking at the two of them, still standing beside the door. Suspicion crossed her face.

"Thanks," Grace said again, hoping to divert her.

"Yeah. What's going on?"

So much for that idea, Grace thought. "We were just talking," she said, giving Kieren a warning glance.

"About Redstone Security training," the young man put in.

Marly looked from one to the other, clearly doubtful.

"I'm thinking of sending you," Grace said in an effort at a diverting joke.

Marly's eyes widened. "Wow, that would be cool!"

Not the response she was expecting, Grace thought ruefully. But as a distraction it had worked. She would probably regret the joke, but—

The door swung open. All three occupants of the motor home spun around.

Draven was back.

Grace couldn't stop herself from looking him up and down. At first she was looking for any sign of injury. But when it was clear he was fine, she found herself staring at this dangerous-looking man and marveling at the fact that just a few hours ago he had been naked in her arms, in her bed...in her.

Draven's eyes locked with hers. His expression didn't change, but the green of his eyes seemed to go hot, as if he'd read her thoughts.

And as if those thoughts had the same effect on him as they'd had on her.

"It's going to be over soon," he said, still looking at her, and his voice oddly soft.

"It went well?" Kieren asked.

Draven never took his eyes off of her. "Well enough," he said.

"What went well?" Marly asked. "What did you do?"

At last he shifted his gaze, and Grace could breathe again.

"Started a ball rolling," he said.

Marly frowned. "What does that mean?"

"If it works, I'll tell you. If it doesn't, I'll keep my mouth shut and save my pride."

Marly gave him a sideways look. "Yeah, right. Like anything you do doesn't work."

Draven lifted a brow at her. She grinned.

"I've been listening to Kieren."

It was the young man's turn to look uncomfortable. "Come on, Marly," he said. "Let's get out of here for a while. Been cooped up long enough."

The girl approved his suggestion quickly, ran to get her sandals, and they headed outside.

Draven walked over to the sofa, reached down beside it and pulled up the black duffel bag. He then reversed the process she'd seen before, removing the ankle holster and the small gun it contained, then the knife in his boot. The items out of the jacket came next, and then the jacket itself came off.

He placed it all in the duffel, including the jacket, and zipped it shut. It had to have been warm with even that lightweight jacket, but he showed no sign of sweating. Nor of discomfort. That is, until he tugged his T-shirt out of his waistband as if it were too hot. The movement gave her a glimpse of the flat, hard belly she'd rested her head on this afternoon, and she was flooded with heat all over again.

Flustered, she repeated Marly's question. "What did you do?"

"I told you I was going to put an end to this."

"Yes, you did. But how? What did you mean about starting a ball rolling? What ball?"

"One that should end up at our saboteur."

Grace stifled a sigh of annoyance at his vagary. "Exactly what did you do today?"

"Feeling the need to keep track of me now?" he asked, with a lifted brow that sent a stab of hurt through her. She knew what he meant, that she was presuming on the change in their relationship. The hurt changed swiftly to anger.

"I feel," she said stiffly, "the need to know what's going on with the project I'm responsible for. As project manager, I'm asking to be kept in the loop."

"Grace," he began.

"What," she said again, "did you do today?"

He let out a compressed breath. "Made a deal with the devil."

Chapter 20

He'd really ticked her off, Draven thought. Not that he could blame her. He hadn't meant to say that, about her keeping track of him; it was simply that he wasn't used to having to account to anyone. And—somewhat to his surprise—he didn't even mind that. His question had been mostly curious. But she had obviously taken it as an accusation. And now, he had no idea what to say to alleviate the situation. But he knew he had to try. He wasn't exactly sure why, but he knew it.

"If you'd said yes, Grace, it would have been all right." *I would have liked it,* he added silently, unable yet to go that far aloud. It was hard enough to admit to himself that he liked the idea of this woman wanting to keep track of him.

"Gee, thanks," she said, her tone telling him he was still not forgiven. "A simple answer to my question, please? Without veiled references no one but you can understand?"

He was going to have to tell her, he realized. She did have

a right to know, as the project manager. And he realized with a little shock that he'd been trying to protect her by withholding the information. Not that protecting someone, especially one of Redstone's own, was unusual for him. It was just unusual for him to do it for personal reasons. And he didn't think he could deny any longer that that was what had happened with Grace.

And he had a suspicion it had been going on long before now, when he'd finally realized it.

So, he was going to have to tell her the truth. She had the right to know, and also the need to know, so she didn't inadvertently get caught up in the long row of dominoes he'd started falling today. Besides, she was going to have to be involved, if only in name as the manager of the project. He had to tell her, and he guessed she wasn't going to like that, either.

Might as well get it over with, he thought.

"I convinced *el mercader* it was in his best interest to help me stop our saboteur."

She stared at him as if he'd spoken in some strange language she'd never heard before. He felt the urge to respond to the look, to explain himself, and in rueful silence he chalked up yet another change.

"I thought he *was* our saboteur."

"I don't think so."

"Why?"

He didn't think "Too obvious" was going to fly with her. Nor would "He told me he wasn't." Yet all he had beyond that was an instinct from a gut that he didn't completely trust anymore, and he suspected that would be even less acceptable to her.

"It's my job to make those decisions."

Her gaze narrowed, as if she sensed he didn't have a concrete reason to give her. But she let it drop and went on to what obviously bothered her more.

"So you made the decision and then made a deal with a drug trafficker?"

"Made a deal with someone who's got the men and the motivation to do the job."

"A drug dealer."

"He's the tool at hand."

"The ends justify the means?"

"In this case."

She stared at him. "I can't believe this. You're cooperating with a drug dealer?"

"It's a matter of priorities."

"Priorities? That's what you call it?"

"Safety of Redstone personnel is the first priority," he quoted from the most basic philosophy Redstone was founded on.

"And dealing with some drug lord is going to guarantee that how?"

"Grace—"

"Half the reason I brought Marly out here was because a couple of her friends were getting into drugs! And now you've invited someone who deals in that evil right into our midst?"

"I didn't invite him to dinner," Draven pointed out.

That it was the wrong thing to say took only a split second to realize. And the outraged look she gave him told him this was a losing battle. And he'd already fought it longer than he ever would have with anyone but her.

"You don't have to approve, Grace."

"I just have to go along? Well, I don't think so. I'm in charge of this project, and you can just call off whatever sleazy deal you've made right now."

With a sigh, he turned to the last resort. "Do you know who has the final word on what gets done at Redstone?"

She frowned. "Josh."

He shook his head. "I do. If I tell him no, it doesn't happen."

Her mouth twisted as if she thought he was exaggerating. "You just call Josh and everything comes to a halt?"

"Yes." He saw her realize he wasn't kidding.

"I suppose you give Josh orders, too?"

"When it comes to safety, I'm his boss, yes." He looked at her steadily. "And right now, I'm your boss."

She went very still. "So you're ordering me to go along with this?"

"If I have to."

"Oh, you'll have to," Grace said, and he heard the spark of anger in her tone.

"Consider it done. Here's what's going to happen."

Grace couldn't remember when she'd been so angry. She knew a large part of it was that she felt betrayed, by the man she'd trusted enough to take to her bed.

And that man had turned back into the stoic, laconic, grim-faced man he'd been when he'd first arrived. It wasn't until now that she realized just how much he'd relaxed since then.

She told herself she didn't care, not when he'd truly made that devil's bargain. Doing anything in cooperation with the kind of slime who had nearly gotten their hooks into her daughter just went against everything she believed in. It did indeed feel like a betrayal.

She didn't even look at him as they made their way to the airstrip site, where the paving work had restarted. She didn't know if she could ever really look at him again. Didn't know if she wanted to. And now when she thought about that afternoon they'd spent together, she felt only a chilling sense of loss.

That will teach you, she thought, although she wasn't

sure what exactly the lesson was supposed to be. She told herself to look upon it as a momentary aberration and get on with business.

One of the crew approached her as soon as she got over to the trucks. "Ms. O'Conner?" one of them said. "Is it true? About Chuck dying?"

Grace still didn't look at Draven. She drew in a deep breath. She'd known this was going to be hard, hated having to do it, but she had no choice.

"I'm afraid so," she said. "Word came in this morning."

"Damn," the man said.

"Yes," she agreed.

He turned and walked back to the rest of the crew, and she could almost see the confirmation spread. Apprehension on faces turned to shock and sorrow, and Grace hated every second of it.

When, at Draven's direction, she drove them into town for the mail, she found the news had already traveled. Yvette in the post office window greeted her with condolences, then asked, "Is it true that your company has sent in their own police force, and they'll be here tomorrow?"

Grace blinked. "Well, I wouldn't call it a police force," she began.

"No," Draven agreed, the first time he'd spoken since they'd left the site. "They don't have to obey the rules the police do. They don't have to be nice, call you a lawyer or account for any injuries you might sustain. So they're more effective."

The woman's eyes widened. Grace barely kept hers from doing the same at the way he was exaggerating. At least, she thought he was exaggerating. Perhaps, all things considered, she was being too generous.

She tried to fight down the bitterness that threatened to well up inside her. Throughout everything she'd managed for the most part not to become bitter, and wasn't sure why it was so close now. Perhaps because this time it was her own bad judgment that had brought her to this.

"Is it true they will be here to avenge this death?" Yvette asked, her eyes still wide.

"We are a family," Draven said with a shrug, as if that answered the question.

Grace couldn't think of a thing to say to him as they left the small grocery and headed down the street. When they made a stop in the general store, Mr. Ayuso also offered his condolences on Chuck's death.

"And that girl of yours," he added to Grace, "she's all right. Apologized for what she did, and paid me back. She can come back in, if she wants."

It was all Grace could do not to look at Draven, the architect of that particular transformation. She didn't want to look at him, or even think about it, how a man who could do that, who could care enough to think of a way to wake up a child on the edge of trouble, could turn around and make a pact with a drug dealer.

After a few more stops it became clear that the news of Chuck's death was a hot topic. As, it appeared, was the imminent arrival of a full force of Redstone security, which seemed in most islanders' minds to be tantamount to an invading army bound by no rules.

They were back in the truck, Draven behind the wheel—like so many other things in the past few hours, he'd given her no option about that—when his cell phone rang. He flipped it open and spoke into the receiver.

"Draven." A pause while he listened. "Is that the only movement?" Another pause. "Anyone with him?" And then, finally, "I'll take it. Have your guy stand by."

He disconnected and closed the phone, tossing it on the seat beside him. "We think we've got him."

She knew it should have been that news that had the most impact, but instead it was that "we."

"That was him? *El mercader?*"

Draven eyed her warily for a moment before nodding. She suppressed a shiver.

"Go back in the store. I'll call Buckley. He can pick you up there."

She was already very tired of taking his orders. "Why?"

"Grace, I've got to go."

"Before he gets away?" She knew she was right when she saw the split-second flicker in his gaze. "Then go."

"Not with you."

She tried not to be insulted, knowing he was simply trying to protect her. That had never stopped, despite her fury with him. She also didn't relish the idea of being anywhere near *el mercader* or his men. But neither did she relish the idea of sitting and waiting like a good little girl to see if Draven came back alive.

Not, she admitted ruefully, that she wouldn't like to murder him right now. But she wanted to reserve that pleasure for herself.

Besides, if the man behind all this had really been found, she wanted to know who he was. And she wanted to look him in the eye and make him see he hadn't won.

"You can sit here and argue with me some more and miss your chance," she said cheerfully. "Or you can try to force me out of the truck, which while I won't deny you'll be able to do it, I promise it will take long enough for you to miss your chance. Or you can shut up and drive."

She expected him to yell, to swear, to do anything but what he did.

"Touché," he said softly.

And then he put the truck in gear and they started to move. Before she was over her surprise at that, he shocked

her again, reaching beneath the driver's seat and pulling out
the small handgun she'd seen him strap to his ankle before
and handing it to her.

"I hope you've kept up," he said.

She stared at the gun in her hand, felt the compact, heavy
weight of it. As per Josh's orders, any of his people who went
to some of the less civilized or peaceful parts of the world
knew how to defend themselves, so she had been through the
standard firearms course Redstone provided. She'd done
better with rifles than pistols, but she'd passed.

Of course, that had been years ago. She told herself that
didn't matter; she wasn't going to have to put every round
in the ten ring as the instructor had wanted then.

"It's a revolver," she said, remembering what the Redstone instructor, a former SWAT cop, had told her all that
time ago. "Point and shoot."

"Pretty much," Draven agreed.

She gave him a sideways glance. For some reason the day
she'd first arrived in Turkey came to mind. She remembered
meeting Redstone point man Noah Rider there. Rider had
been classically chiseled. Draven was scarred and rugged.
Rider had been open and amusing. Draven was taciturn and
solemn.

Yet it was Draven who stirred her pulse, while Rider had
left her aesthetically appreciative, but unmoved.

So is that lousy taste, or just lousy judgment? she wondered to herself.

Or perhaps it was simply that Rider radiated contentment, especially when the subject of his wife, Paige, arose.

Draven started issuing orders as he drove. "You stay in
the truck. In the driver's seat. You shoot only to protect yourself. If anything goes wrong, or you hear shots, you get the
hell out. Get back to the site and to Buckley. Got it?"

"Yes, sir," she said.

He shot her a sharp glance, but she had kept her voice carefully neutral and didn't look at him now. She didn't dare look at him, not after the image he'd called up in her mind of her sitting here wondering which end of those shots he'd been on.

"I mean it, Grace."

"I never thought you didn't."

He went silent again. They went north through the rest of the small town, then, to her surprise, past the clinic that was on the outskirts. They made a turn just beyond that and started up the slight hill that rose above the village. It was thick with acacia trees and hibiscus run wild as undergrowth, and would make for a great hiding place if you needed one.

He stopped short of the top, where the gravel road ended. Quickly and efficiently, even on the narrow road, he turned the truck around so it was facing downhill and out. For her, she realized with a sinking feeling, in case she had to run.

"If you hear a car coming down," he said, "get out and take cover off the road. Don't wait to think about it."

Her brows furrowed, but she nodded. When he got out of the truck, she slid over behind the wheel. He nodded, then turned to head toward the junglelike hillside.

Then he turned back.

"Grace?"

She looked up.

"It had to stop. This was the quickest way."

She took in a deep breath. She sensed that this was an exception for him. That John Draven didn't waste breath explaining himself. And she wondered why he'd felt compelled to do it now. It wasn't an apology, yet that was the undertone in his voice.

And then he was gone, so quickly she couldn't quite believe it. Almost instantly he was out of sight in the brush, and she couldn't even see a leaf moving to mark his passage.

She looked around, something tickling the edges of her memory. She thought she might have been up here before, but she couldn't be sure. The road and the surroundings looked familiar, but her memory was telling her it had been different.

It had been dark, she suddenly realized. That's why she hadn't been sure if this had been the same road. But she was almost positive now, and—

The sound of a vehicle approaching from farther up the hill cut off her thoughts. For a brief moment she simply sat there, listening, making sure she was really hearing it. And then Draven's order played through her head.

Get out. Don't think, get out.

She scrambled across the seat to the passenger door, yanked it open and slid to the ground. The engine sound was closer, as if it were rounding the curve just beyond the truck.

And it was coming fast.

She felt a little foolish—what if it was just some resident or tourist—but the fierceness of Draven's warning echoed in her ears, and she dove for the shelter of the huge, orange-flowered hibiscus that was the closest to the side of the road.

She crouched down, peering back through the glossy leaves, looking up toward the curve where anything coming down the road would come around the hill. She caught a glimpse of something long and white and shiny moving fast. Far too fast for the road.

It slammed into the parked truck.

The wrenching, nerve-shattering noise of the impact made her cry out instinctively. She smothered the sound, although she doubted anyone could have heard anything over the noise of the crash. The big white car hit with such force the pickup skewed sideways, and she flinched back as it seemed to be coming right at her.

The echoes of the crash finally seemed to stop, and the

only thing she heard was the slight tinkle of shattered glass falling, and the drip of something liquid. Certain someone had to have been hurt, she stood up. As she did she caught sight of the side of the truck. The driver's door, where she had been sitting, was demolished. The entire truck had buckled on that side, and she was reasonably sure if she had stayed there she would have been badly hurt or even killed.

She heard somebody swearing, and what sounded like a woman crying. The presence of the female decided her, and she scrambled back to the road and ran toward the wreck. She got there just as the driver managed to force open his door, obviously also buckled by the impact.

Her relief that the man was moving, and apparently all right, was quickly overtaken by shock.

It was Mayor Remington.

She wasn't surprised, since she'd just realized this was the road they'd driven the night he had thrown the party at his house to welcome Redstone to the island. His luxurious home was the last one at the top of the hill.

Oh, boy, Redstone's not going to like this, she thought. *We've destroyed the mayor's fancy car.*

The woman she'd heard wasn't getting out. Seeing that the mayor, who apparently hadn't seen her yet, was up and moving, she instead ran to the other side of the car. In the passenger seat was the source of the weeping she'd heard, not a woman but a girl, who looked even younger than Marly. Grace didn't see any immediate signs of injury, but since she hadn't gotten out of the car she had to think something was wrong.

Then the girl seemed to realize she was there. She looked up at Grace, her dark eyes wide and full of tears, and something else, some wilder thing Grace couldn't put a name to.

"Please," the girl gulped out.

"Ms. O'Conner?"

The mayor's voice made her straighten and look over at him. "Are you all right?" she asked him.

"I think so," he said, watching her in an oddly intent way. "What are you doing here?"

This wasn't the time to explain, especially since she didn't really have the answer.

"I think your passenger may be hurt," she said, bending back down to look at the girl. "We'd better call for help."

"I don't think so."

There was something different about his voice, very different than the jovial man who had welcomed her here.

"But she may need—"

Grace's words stopped abruptly. She'd just seen the reason the girl hadn't gotten out of the wrecked car.

She was tied to the seat.

Grace looked across the car roof at Mayor Remington in shock. And got an even bigger shock.

He was pointing a gun at her.

Chapter 21

Grace.

Draven had never felt anything like the jolt of horror that stabbed through him like a sizzling poker when he heard the crash.

He had just put his cell phone back in his pocket after *el mercader* had called again, saying their man was on the move. Mere seconds later he'd heard the vehicle on the road.

He'd known immediately it was traveling too fast. It either wouldn't make the curve, or if it did it would be because the driver likely stayed so tight to the edge he couldn't help but hit the truck.

Even as he thought it, the sound of the impact ripped through the tropical air.

Instantly he spun around and reversed his course. He couldn't be sure this was their ultimate quarry, but he didn't care. There was only one vehicle that whoever it was could have hit, and that was all that mattered.

For the first time in his life his work fell completely off the radar. Nothing was in his mind but getting back to Grace. Thoughts of silence, caution, strategy and reconnaissance vanished as he fought his way back to the road where he'd left the truck.

And the woman he suddenly and belatedly realized he didn't want to leave behind. Ever.

Only when he got within earshot did he slow enough to approach silently. When he reached the edge of the brush he saw a scene out of his worst nightmare. The mangled remains of the truck and the mayor's car sat half off the road, obviously pushed by the force of the collision. His gaze zeroed in on the driver's seat where he'd left Grace; if she'd been there, she was surely dead.

And then, after a moment when he couldn't breathe, his focus widened. He took in the entire scene. Including Grace, alive and out of the truck. He could breathe again.

She was on the far side of the wrecked car. The mayor was on the near side. And he was holding a chrome revolver pointed across the crumpled roof at Grace.

Draven had only a split second to assess. Grace was looking at something inside the car, possibly a passenger. Given what he'd just learned, Draven thought he had an idea who that passenger might be. But Grace wasn't bent down far enough to be out of any line of fire, his or Remington's. Draven's mind raced, looking for the answer.

"Stop it, bitch!" Remington yelled across the car at her, obviously unaware of Draven's presence.

Grace ignored him, and ignored the weapon trained on her. She continued to work on something inside the car, from here Draven couldn't tell what.

But Remington was starting to lose it. The gun waved wildly, and Draven thought he was just crazy enough to fire it by accident. He dodged behind the remains of the truck.

Headed for the front. Rounded it, which put him on a straight line with his target.

At the last second, he slammed his fist down on the bent hood of the truck. The hollow, metallic thud made Grace's head snap upward.

More important, it startled Remington. And he turned.

The instant the weapon was no longer trained on Grace, Draven launched himself.

He hit the man at the waist. The impetus sent him sprawling backward. They hit the ground together. Draven made sure his shoulder dug deep, heard the grunt and whoosh of air escaping Remington's lungs. At the same time he assessed. Calculated with the swiftness of long experience what he was dealing with.

The man was soft.

But it didn't take strength to fire the pistol. And Grace was still vulnerable. A wild shot could be disastrous.

The gun was the goal.

Remington realized that, too. He twisted, trying to bring the gun to bear. Draven shifted, trying to get leverage. Remington grunted, twisted.

The gun went off.

Draven felt the familiar sharp burn and sting of a bullet leaving a gouge on his right arm. Swiftly he calculated. Angle, trajectory. Decided Grace should have been safe. Rolled, until he had the man pinned. He clamped a hand over Remington's. Tightened his fingers. The man swore. Draven slid a finger and his thumb forward, gripping the cylinder so it couldn't rotate.

Remington began to flail, striking out wildly with his free left hand. He landed some glancing blows, nothing Draven couldn't ignore. At least, until he managed to squarely hit the spot where the bullet had grazed Draven's arm.

Draven winced, his jaw tightening. He turned the concentration he'd developed early in his life onto one thing: keeping his hold on the gun. He poured every bit of strength he could into his grip. He envisioned pushing Remington's fingers through the gunmetal. The man pulled desperately, trying to break free of the relentless squeeze.

In his gyrations Remington finally twisted so that Draven could see his eyes. He fixed his gaze, concentrating. Never wavering. He saw the fear dawn, then spread across Remington's face. He'd never been certain what it was about him that did it, only that it happened.

In the moment when Remington gave up, Draven became aware that someone was beside him. He flicked a glance upward.

Grace. The small weapon he'd given her in her hands, aimed and ready to fire.

He had to force himself to keep his mind on the job at hand, and even when he looked back at Remington, it was the image of Grace on guard at his side that was uppermost in his mind.

As Draven wrested the gun away from the now exhausted Remington Grace lowered her arms, thankful she hadn't had to shoot. Her gaze fastened on Draven's right arm, just below the shoulder.

"You're bleeding," she said.

"I imagine so."

"We need to get you to the clinic."

"I'm fine."

Grace grimaced. "Be stubborn, then. But there's a girl in the car, and I think she's hurt, too."

"Probably more than you know," Draven said grimly. "We'll get her to the clinic, and then we can have the pleasure of turning the former mayor here over to Sergeant Espinoza."

Remington muttered something under his breath. Grace

looked at him, then at Draven. "What do you mean, more than I know?"

Draven looked at Remington, who at the moment was looking like the cockroach he was. "He was probably going to deliver her. To a buyer."

Grace's brow furrowed. "What?"

"Seems the mayor had a lucrative little sideline going. Little girls for men with sick tastes. He's running because he heard the rumor *el mercader* started that he himself was bailing out because Redstone was sending an army for revenge."

"Little girls?" Grace gasped, her eyes widening.

"That's why he didn't want the airstrip built, or Redstone here. He thought it would interfere with his sex trade."

She glanced back at the car, where the girl still sat. The girl who was not much older than her own precious child. Then she looked back at Remington.

"Is this true?"

He called her a name in Spanish. She didn't recognize it, but with his tone that was hardly necessary. And Draven's reaction—placing his foot atop the man's throat and telling him if he spoke once more he would never speak again—just made it clearer.

"My God," Grace whispered, staring at the man on the ground.

She tried to wrap her mind around the idea, but she just couldn't. At least, not yet, while the shock was fresh. She willingly held her small gun on the man she'd thought of as, if not a friend, at least a decent person, while Draven checked the vehicles. Her aim was rock steady as she looked at him.

Remington looked up at her assessingly. It didn't take Draven's training or experience to guess what he was thinking.

"If you think I'd hesitate to rid the world of you, you're

very mistaken," she said softly. The look faded from eyes that now held only fear.

Draven paused and looked back, and his eyes met hers. The slight nod and even slighter smile he gave her felt as if he'd saluted. In a way she supposed he had.

He checked the truck first, but that didn't take long. She hadn't thought it would move on its own, not with the engine twisted sideways as it was. Then he went to the white sedan. He spent more time there, and it took her a few glances—all she would risk while guarding this subhuman—to realize he was searching it. Then he popped the trunk open—one of the few unbent areas on the car—looked inside, then walked back toward them.

"Neither one is drivable," he said.

"Now what?" Grace asked. "That poor child needs to be checked, and her parents contacted. She's terrified."

Draven didn't take long to think about it. "Are you all right with Marly staying with Nick until you get back?"

"Fine," she said, only realizing then that it was actually over.

He pulled out his cell, called Buckley and told him to leave Marly with Nick and meet them here ASAP. Then he called Sergeant Espinoza, told him where they were and to come and take custody of Remington. Then he walked over to the man and yanked him up on his feet. He propelled him toward the back of the car, and to Grace's surprise pushed him into the trunk.

Remington started to scream.

"I suggest you save some of that wind to let Sergeant Espinoza know you're in there when he gets here," Draven suggested mildly.

"Or not," Grace said.

Draven looked at her. "Feeling a bit bloodthirsty?"

"Yes," she said simply.

One corner of his mouth shot upward in a lopsided grin that made her pulse jam into overdrive. She hated that she couldn't control her response to him, even when she was so angry about what he'd done.

And now that the reason he'd come here was past, she didn't know what was going to happen.

He slammed the trunk closed.

"Now we can go tell Chuck he's alive again," Draven said.

The plan she had helped carry out had worked.

Grace sat in a chair in the small waiting area of the clinic, looking shell-shocked and a little green. The doctor had confirmed their worst fears: the twelve-year-old girl they had rescued had already been molested. She had no permanent physical injuries, but Draven doubted she would ever be completely normal again. St. John had managed to track down her family over on mainland Belize, and a Redstone escort would have them here before the end of the day.

He wasn't sure he'd be welcome, but he found he couldn't simply stand here and watch her shiver. He went over and crouched beside her chair.

"Grace," he began.

She looked up. "I went to his house. I took *Marly* to his house. I thought he was nice, for spending so much time with her, talking to her."

"You had no way of knowing."

"How did you know?"

"I suspected him because he was so insistent it had to be *el mercader*. Wouldn't listen to any other possibility."

She looked thoughtful and then, as if remembering, she nodded slowly. *"El mercader,"* she muttered, avoiding his eyes, and he knew he was still in trouble.

"He's the one who found out about the girls. He'd known

Remington was up to something, but wasn't sure what. He—" Draven stopped as the clinic door opened and a man walked in. "He's here," he ended with a sigh, thinking there was no way this could be good for him.

Grace's head snapped up, and she stared at the tall, graceful man who walked toward them. He came to a halt beside Draven, nodded, and then looked at Grace.

"Ms. O'Conner," he said, inclining his head.

She stood up, and faced *el mercader* straight on. "I'm afraid I'm not comfortable talking to people who hide behind nicknames."

Draven blinked as she said almost exactly what he had. *El mercader's* glance flicked from her to Draven and back, apparent amusement gleaming in his eyes.

"Oh?"

"You did the right thing on this," she admitted, "and for that I'm thankful."

"But on everything else I'm out in the cold," *el mercader* said.

"Your choice," she said, her voice stiff and formal.

"Not really," he said, an unmistakable tone of irony in his voice. He looked at Draven. "The girl?"

"She'll be all right. Physically."

"Are you certain you don't want me to take care of our illustrious mayor?"

Draven grimaced. "No," he said honestly. "But it's Redstone policy to turn criminals over to authorities."

"Too bad," *el mercader* said. He glanced at Grace again. "A pleasure, Ms. O'Conner. For one of us, anyway."

He turned as if to go.

"Don't forget our agreement," Draven said.

El mercader turned back. "I'm not likely to. I've done some investigating, and I'm fully aware of your reputation."

Draven nodded, and *el mercader* started for the door. His hand on the handle, he looked back over his shoulder.

"Ms. O'Conner?"

She looked at him.

"Quinn Pedragon," he said.

She blinked in surprise at the soft pronouncement of the name. Draven was a little surprised himself.

"If you take the opportunity to go straight," he said, "contact me."

The man at the door looked startled, then he chuckled. "If that should happen, I will."

And then he was gone.

Slowly she turned to look at Draven. He braced himself inwardly, wondering how he'd let himself get to the point that this woman had such power that she could make him bleed just by disapproving.

"What agreement?"

It was pointless to dissemble, he thought. She couldn't get any angrier with him than she already was.

"That by the time Redstone finishes building the resort, he and his operation will be gone."

"Oh." She glanced at the door again. "Do you think he will keep his word?"

"I do now, yes."

She looked back at him. "Why now?"

"Because now I know his name. And he knows it."

"You don't think it was an alias."

"No."

Not the way he looked at you, he added silently, trying to quash the way that had made him feel. At first he hadn't recognized the feeling that had flashed up in him at *el mercader's*—Quinn Pedragon's—frank appreciation. When he did realize it was jealousy, he had to admit for the first time just how much trouble he was in. And hearing her speak to him in that cool, detached tone was somehow worse than any physical pain he'd ever felt.

There was only one thing he could think of to do. And all the way back to the site he tried to wrap his mind around the fact that that one thing was to run.

Chapter 22

Grace found it nearly impossible to let go of her daughter, and did so only when the girl finally protested that she couldn't breathe.

It had taken Grace a while to think beyond the horror that innocent child, the child they'd returned to weeping, grateful parents yesterday, had gone through. To think beyond that victim to others. The only thing that had made it bearable was the knowledge of those that had been saved, those children Remington would never get his hands on.

Then she had finally had to face the grim reality that Marly could have been one of them.

And it was then that she belatedly understood Draven's talk of priorities. The thought of her daughter as a target of such a sick, twisted mind made her shiver with a combination of fear and outrage and fury that had her shaking every time she thought of it. And she knew that she would have done far worse than deal with a man like Quinn Pedragon to get her back.

She owed Draven an apology. A long and sincere one. She stood up, and slipped on the one shoe she'd shed for coolness when she'd gotten back to the motor home.

"Where are you going?" Marly asked, in a tone that nearly echoed Grace's own concerned one. Marly had been more upset than she'd let on about the explosion, and seemed to have finally realized how close she had come to being motherless.

"I need to find…Mr. Draven," Grace said. *John. Johnny,* she thought. "I have to tell him something."

Marly drew back, her brows furrowed. "But he's gone."

"What?"

"He left. This morning, early. One of the Nunez brothers picked him up."

"He left?" Grace was stunned. "Without even saying goodbye?"

"He said goodbye to me," Marly said, watching her mother so closely Grace wondered what had been said during that goodbye.

"I see." Despite her efforts, the hurt she was feeling seeped into her voice.

"Mom," Marly said, sounding for all the world like a parent pointing out something obvious to a child, "what did you expect? You were so mad at him we could all see it. Why would he hang around?"

Grace stared at her child, wondering at the vivid flash of adult perception.

"Face it, Mom," Marly said. "You blew it."

Grace blinked. "Blew…what?"

"Come on," Marly said with teenaged disgust. "Do you think I'm stupid? I know you were hot for each other." Grace gaped at the girl, who rolled her eyes. "Puh-leeze," she said. "Even Kieren noticed."

Recovering slightly, Grace swallowed and asked, "And if that was true, how would you feel about it?"

"You mean if you like, got married or something?" She shrugged one shoulder in an almost eerie imitation of Draven's habit. "It'd be cool, I think. We could get along, mostly. I could tell my friends I've got a real tough guy for a stepdad."

"You'd like it?" Grace was so stunned she couldn't quite take in what she was hearing.

Marly shrugged again, and then lowered her eyes. With a visible amount of embarrassment she said, "I know I messed things up for you. I heard him tell you he couldn't…deal with me. But I changed, didn't I? I paid back old Mr. Ayuso, and I worked hard, and—"

"Yes, you did." Grace was even more shocked to hear that this was at least part of the reason for Marly's turnaround. For a moment she just sat there, trying to process everything. But there was just too much, between these revelations, what had happened, and on top of it all the realization that she had let go the first man she'd really felt anything for in years.

Felt anything? Face it, you love him. You love him, and you drove him away.

Her first instinct was to go after him. She could call, say he'd forgotten something and ask where he'd gone. Or she could—

A knock on the door sent her heart hammering again. He'd come back!

When she yanked open the door to see Nick standing there, it was a great effort not to let her disappointment show in her face.

"Sorry," Nick said, "but there's a problem. The roller we rented broke down, and the rental outfit says they can't get here for two days."

"I'll handle it," she said automatically.

"And there's some environmental guy here, wants to know when we're going to get the native plants back in place."

Grace sighed. There was just too much to do right now, she couldn't afford to leave. She wouldn't do that to Josh, or to Redstone.

"I'll see him."

Wearily she pulled on her shoe and went back to work.

Grace knew she was probably exhausted, but she was too numb to feel it. In a final, hard push they'd finished the airstrip two days ago. Shortly after she filed that report, Redstone headquarters sent word to expect Josh himself to take a look.

She put the crew to work finishing the terminal, now obviously behind schedule because of the explosion. She'd gotten a copy of the Redstone report on the incident, that explained about bomb materials found in the garage of Remington's home, and that he'd paid a local who'd been making a delivery to the site to plant it, just as he had with the other incidents.

She also saw the report that the late-night prowler that had tripped the alarm was in fact one of Pedragon's men, starting his own investigation because of the increasing heat suspicion was casting on them.

The fact that all the reports were signed "John Draven," in a bold, compact hand, was something she tried to ignore. Unsuccessfully, as a sick feeling rose in her, bringing her near to desperation.

She was sitting in the shade of the motor home's awning, trying futilely to think about something else, anything else, when the sound of a jet engine from above dragged her out of her wallow of misery. She looked up and saw the familiar colors of red and slate gray. Josh Redstone had obviously arrived.

Grateful for the distraction, Grace got up as the sleek little jet banked on approach. She wondered if Tess Machado was at the controls; she hadn't seen Tess in a while, and she always enjoyed talking to her.

She realized suddenly she was still wearing the grubby clothes she'd had on when she'd done her final inspection of the charred debris that had been cleared from the explosion site. Josh didn't expect anybody to dress up for him, but she thought the least she could do was be clean. Josh would likely stop to talk to the crew anyway, that was his way. So she had a few minutes.

She dashed inside and washed her face and hands, changed into clean khakis and a light blue shirt, put on clean socks and her cleanest sneakers, and ran a brush through her wind-tousled hair. Then she started toward the airfield.

When she arrived she was startled to see Josh in apparently deep conversation, not with the crew but with Marly. Josh saw her coming, smiled and waved. But Marly reacted very strangely, almost guiltily jumping back and avoiding looking at her mother.

Josh enveloped Grace in a hug, his usual greeting for the people who'd been with him any length of time.

"Looks great," he said.

She smiled up at the lean, gray-eyed man. "Well, except for the terminal."

He waved a hand as if the delay meant nothing. "You'll have more help here in another day or so. It'll get done."

She hadn't asked for help, but she wasn't about to turn it down. She had a record of bringing projects in on time, and she didn't want to blow it on this first one after the earthquake.

"The strip is as smooth as a quarter horse's coat in the summertime." Josh's drawl was exaggerated, like it usually was when he tossed out one of those down-home homilies. She wondered how many people had been lured into thinking he was stupid or slow because of that drawl.

And then left in shock when they found out just how quick and sharp the mind behind that lazy drawl was, Grace thought with pride.

"Should I go pack?" Marly asked.

"Good idea," Josh said.

Grace frowned. "Pack? For what?"

"We're going home," Marly said, sounding excited.

Grace thought in that moment that if she got hit with one more jolt she was going to crawl into a hole.

"Just for a visit," Marly said. "We'll be back in a week, but I'll get to see my friends."

So that's what they were plotting, Grace thought.

She had thought the girl had gotten to liking it here—especially after Kieren's arrival—but apparently she was still missing home. Grace didn't like the thought that Marly might have manipulated her boss into offering this ride, but she was so excited Grace couldn't bring herself to deny her. Besides, she doubted anyone successfully manipulated Josh Redstone into anything he wasn't already willing to do.

She didn't want to be gone from the project, but she could hardly let Marly go alone. She supposed she could call Aunt Charlotte, but she'd been ill, and it was a bit much to—

"It's all right, Grace," Josh said. "Nick can keep things going for a week."

She smiled ruefully. "Am I that transparent?"

"'Fraid so," Josh said with a grin. "Go pack some things. I want to take off ASAP."

Grace knew an order when she heard one. After returning to the motor home and putting some things in a bag, Grace walked back to the strip with Marly at her heels.

"You didn't come all the way here just for this, did you?" she asked Josh.

"Nah. I wanted some hours at the controls," he said, indicating the sleek plane on the strip, his own Hawk IV.

"It's cool looking," Marly said.

Josh looked at the girl. "I need a copilot. Interested?"

Marly's eyes got bigger than Grace had ever seen them. "I don't know how to fly!"

"Then it's time you learned," Josh said.

Marly turned stunned but excited eyes on Grace. "Mom?"

"No one better to learn from," she said.

"Wow!"

The girl darted up the steps into the plane. "Right seat!" Josh called out after her. Bare seconds later Grace saw her daughter through the cockpit window.

Josh took her bag for her, and she started up the steps. Josh walked up behind her, and when they stepped into the plane he turned and hit the button that brought up the steps and closed the door. Once the brilliant tropical sun was blocked, Grace could see the inside of the Redstone jet. She'd been flown here on a Hawk III, and had thought it incredible. This was even more so, with polished woods, gleaming fixtures and the rich upholstery on the seating, more like a living room than a plane.

That was all she saw. Because at the far end of the passenger compartment, sitting at a polished, light burl wood table beside a window, was a man.

Draven.

"Work it out," Josh ordered before turning to vanish into the cockpit.

For a long, strained moment Grace simply looked at him. Then she heard the jets fire as Josh started them.

"You'd better sit down and strap in," Draven said.

He nodded at the seat across from him. For a moment she considered taking a seat at the opposite end of the cabin, but realized it would be childish. So she sucked in a breath and sat down opposite him.

"I—"

"I—"

They started simultaneously, then both stopped. Draven gestured her to go ahead.

"I'm sorry," she said. "I didn't understand. But the minute I thought about Marly in that pervert's hands, I knew what you meant about priorities. I was wrong. You were right. You did what was necessary."

She thought she saw surprise flicker across his face. "What? No one's ever apologized to you before?"

"Most often," he said mildly, "no one has the nerve to do anything that would bring on the need to apologize to me."

It wasn't said with arrogance, but was a simple statement of fact. And she supposed it was true.

"Haven't dealt with a lot of mothers?"

His mouth quirked. "Only my own. And I was usually the one apologizing to her."

He didn't seem angry. In fact, he seemed almost amused. Which surprised her. And encouraged her. Unless of course he'd simply decided she was only worth laughing at for her naiveté.

Nervous at that idea, her fingers began to trace circles on the glossy tabletop.

"You deal in ugliness so often," she said softly. "How do you stay sane?"

And suddenly the amusement was gone. He leaned forward. Reached out. Put his hand over hers, stopping her fingers. And her breath. She stared at the table as if her life depended on memorizing the rich grain of the wood. And then she felt his other hand gently lift her chin, making her look at him. And there was an intensity in his green eyes she'd never seen before.

"Because," he said, just as softly, "sometimes, if I'm lucky, there's also beauty. And goodness. And courage."

The sweet gentleness of those words from this tough,

fierce man rocked her to the core. She couldn't think at all, no words, no response came to her. So she simply stared at him, drinking in the expression on his face, in his eyes, before she even had a name for what was there.

"I'm no prize, Grace. I've got a lot of rough edges." He took in an audible breath. "I never thought there could be a woman tough enough to handle what I do and the life it demands."

"I've never let difficulties stop me," she said, aware of the breathy tone of her voice, but unable to stop it.

"I know." He hesitated, then went on. "I talked to Marly. She's okay with it. With…us. And she promised not to be such a…pain, if we promised to listen to her."

Us. We.

Grace thought she'd never heard anything so wonderful as those simple two-letter words.

Draven swallowed as if his throat were tight. And Grace realized with a little shock that he, too, was nervous.

"I've never done this. I don't… I can't… This romantic thing…"

The thought of Draven nervous, and about this, somehow gave her the last bit of courage she needed.

"Do you want to know what's romantic to me?" she asked. "It's a man who does things to make your life easier. It's a man who fixes things so you don't have to. A man who doesn't need to be waited on, who doesn't expect me to be something I'm not. Or not be what I am. *That's* romantic."

His expression changed as she spoke, the nervous edge disappearing from his voice. And slowly, he began to smile.

"I can do that," he said when she stopped.

"I know," she said.

It wasn't until much later, after they'd worked out the details, that he groaned out load as some unexpected thought obviously hit him.

"What?" Grace asked, still a little stunned at how much thought he'd put into a future for them. The three of them.

"I just realized," he said as if the thought were a painful one. "We're going to be stuck with a Redstone wedding."

She blinked. "Redstone weddings are...different?"

"Redstone weddings," he intoned gloomily, "are overwhelming."

Grace laughed. She couldn't help herself. "I'll protect you," she joked.

Draven went very still, and the look that came over his face then was one of wonder. "And you know something?" he said softly. "I'll let you."

And Grace knew then that the legendary John Draven, the man she would soon tie herself to forever, had just done the most heroic thing of his life.

* * * * *

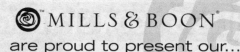

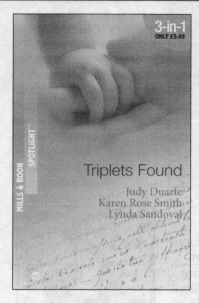

0110/010/MB253

These wealthy bachelors are ready to wed. Could three virgin brides be about to take their breath away?

**Available
18th December 2009**

These red-hot tycoons can seduce any woman they desire. Could three rebellious mistresses be about to change these rich men's lives forever?

**Available
1st January 2010**

www.millsandboon.co.uk

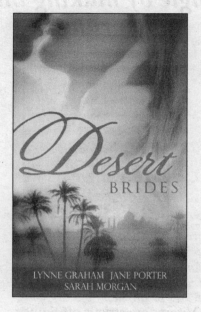

Sexy bachelors stay single by making their own rules...

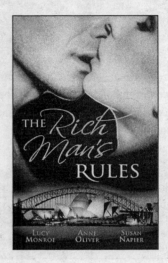

1. Virgins are strictly off-limits

2. One-night stands are for passion and pleasure, not forever

3. No strings, no commitment – and certainly no babies

But some rules are just made to be broken!

Available 1st January 2010

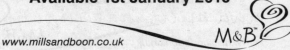

www.millsandboon.co.uk

millsandboon.co.uk Community

Join Us!

The Community is the perfect place to meet and chat to kindred spirits who love books and reading as much as you do, but it's also the place to:

- Get the inside scoop from authors about their latest books
- Learn how to write a romance book with advice from our editors
- Help us to continue publishing the best in women's fiction
- Share your thoughts on the books we publish
- Befriend other users

Forums: Interact with each other as well as authors, editors and a whole host of other users worldwide.

Blogs: Every registered community member has their own blog to tell the world what they're up to and what's on their mind.

Book Challenge: We're aiming to read 5,000 books and have joined forces with The Reading Agency in our inaugural Book Challenge.

Profile Page: Showcase yourself and keep a record of your recent community activity.

Social Networking: We've added buttons at the end of every post to share via digg, Facebook, Google, Yahoo, technorati and de.licio.us.

www.millsandboon.co.uk

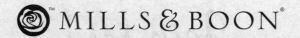